NOT YOUR AVERAGE MONSTER

A BESTIARY OF HORRORS

EDITED BY
PETE KAHLE

NOT YOUR AVERAGE MONSTER

ISBN-13: 978-0692567937
ISBN-10: 0692567933

BLOODSHOT BOOKS

READ UNTIL YOU BLEED!

A BESTIARY OF HORRORS

CONTENTS

EDITOR'S NOTE

October 28, 2015

Here we are. As unlikely as it may be.

Six months after getting the admittedly crazy idea to start a small press, our first book – the anthology you hold in your sticky little hands – is in print, and I still can't believe how fast everything came together.

I posted my idea in a few authors groups on Facebook back in April and within a month, I had a website, a name for my company *(my first idea – Primordial Press – was already taken by a company buried in the depths of the internet that had only put out two books in the last decade, but frankly, I like the name Bloodshot Books better)*, a professional logo *(created by the endlessly talented Tom Martin – check out his stuff at http://www.undeadwizard .com/)*, and submissions for this book were pouring into my inbox every day.

Initially, I expected to receive 50-60 submissions, of which I would perhaps find 12-15 worthy of publication, but my estimates were ridiculously low. The concept for this anthology seemed to have found the "sweet spot" *(to use a term from another obsession of mine – baseball. Let's Go, Mets!)* with the theme and I ultimately received over 350 short stories and novellas in 2.5 months. I guess I wasn't the only one who wanted to read about monsters other than vampires, zombies and lycanthropes.

Another way that I underestimated the response to this project was the amazing quality of stories that I received. Easily half of them were worthy of publication. Choosing which ones would grace these pages was one of the most difficult tasks I have ever undertaken, so much so that I ultimately decided to publish a second volume a few months from now, and based on upon the response I have gotten, I wouldn't be surprised if we keep rolling these out once or twice a year until the well runs dry.

When I finally read through all of the submissions, I ended up choosing 42 stories *(21 in each volume)* - 250,000 words of truly stupendous horror. The creatures within them run the gamut. I wanted variety and that is exactly what we got. We have stories from such accomplished authors as Billie Sue Mosiman, Adrian Cole, Richard Dansky and Jeff Carlson, along with tales from newer voices like Mark Carroll, Beau Johnson, Kya Aliana, Joshua Rex and Rob Lammle. There are tales that will make you chuckle, others that may make you wince, some that may ruin your dinner *(I especially apologize for my story which is admittedly a no-holds-barred gross-out. You have been warned)*, and a couple of stories that will blindside you with the emotions they stir up.

I can't tell you how proud I am of this book and I am grateful to every one of the authors who took a chance on a fledgling company. With Bloodshot Books I aim to provide a venue for authors who love the genre of horror, be they beginning their careers or veterans with dozens of tales under their belts.

Right now, this company is a one-man operation *(I hope that it's not too obvious)* starting off with a couple of anthologies, but ideally I want to eventually publish novels as well. 2015 has been great for me and I have a feeling that 2016 will exceed my expectations.

Read until you bleed,

-Pete Kahle

Owner/Editor/Chief Bottlewasher
Bloodshot Books

p.s. - You may notice that some stories use the US spelling of certain words while others use the UK spelling. That was my intent, so I could preserve how each story was written. Rather than choose one over the other, I felt this was the best way to honor the integrity of the stories. If you have some sort of obsessive compulsive aversion to one spelling convention over another, please accept my sincere apology ☺

NOT YOUR AVERAGE MONSTER

BLOODSHOT BOOKS

IT MUST FEED
BY MEGAN NEUMANN

IRIS shook her arm and watched the small bulge of flesh sway back and forth. "See that?" she said. She shook her arm again, this time faster. "I told you I'm getting fat." She tugged on the skin so that it hung down a half inch more.

"No," Abby said without hesitating. Her sister was a little rounder today than the last time they were together but that didn't matter. The response was obligatory, something you said without thinking, without looking if the fat was there or not. "You look great." Abby smiled and hoped the smile was genuine.

Iris dropped her arm and sighed. "You're lying. I can see it on your face." She stood and cleaned the remains of their dinner from the kitchen table.

Abby knew she should help. The last thing she wanted was Iris accusing her of not pulling her weight around the house. This was, after all, Abby's home now too.

As though reading Abby's mind, Iris said, "Don't worry about helping. Just relax. You've had a long day."

That morning Abby had moved her possessions from her one bedroom apartment downtown to the spare bedroom of her sister's ranch-style home. It had taken three trips and twenty-three boxes, but in six hours, Abby's independent life vanished. Now she relied on the charity of her family to get her through what her friends so kindly called a "rough patch." Abby hated the term. Only her father had been honest with her, saying, "You just need to get your shit together."

So here she was getting her shit together while her sister housed and fed her. Abby had three job interviews scheduled over the next two days. None of them sounded promising, but Abby needed to say she was trying. She owed that much to Iris.

"I don't care what you say," Iris said, standing over the sink, scrubbing bits of a pork chop from a skillet. "The scale doesn't lie. I've been gaining weight, and I don't know why."

Abby opened her mouth to protest again, but her sister held up a hand.

"I know that's what everyone says. But seriously, I run every day. I've cut out carbs. I count my calories, so what the hell?"

She turned to Abby, but once again, Abby could only fall onto that default response. "You don't need to lose weight," she said. "You're perfect the way you are." This brought a smile to Iris's face.

They spent their first night as roomies like a pair of ten-year-olds at a sleepover. Iris loaded the DVD player with three films from their past: *The Lost Boys* (they were both fiends for Corey Haim), *The Breakfast Club*, and

The Princess Bride.

They spread blankets and pillows across the floor and lay in their pajamas, snacking on junk food. Iris ate only popcorn without butter, claiming she couldn't have any more calories for the day.

Abby fell asleep sometime during *The Princess Bride*. She faded in and out of consciousness during the movie, seeing Cary Elwes's face behind the black mask. Beside her, Iris's head rested on a pillow, her mouth hanging open. Abby didn't want to wake her sister, so she closed her eyes and let sleep take her once more.

It was the knocking in the kitchen that woke her. The television played the movie's menu. Iris was no longer beside her, and Abby's first thought was that Iris had gone to the kitchen for something. Abby's eyes grew heavy again. She dozed for what may have been seconds or minutes.

The knocking was louder when she awoke the second time.

"Iris," she called out. The knocking continued, rhythmic like the ticking of a clock. Abby wondered if this was a sound the house made at night. *Houses make strange sounds sometimes*, she thought. *Maybe it's the pipes. But it was so damned loud. How did Iris sleep with that banging?*

Abby stood and walked through the dark hallway. A swinging door separated the hall from the kitchen. Abby pushed it open. The room was dark except for the green and orange lights of electronics. On the microwave, the time glowed 3:13, a temperature indicator on the refrigerator showed 34 degrees, and the coffee maker blinked 12:00.

The banging was very close now, though Abby could not see the source. She moved her hand against the wall, feeling for a light switch. She found it and flicked. What she saw made her gasp. Then she laughed.

"Iris?" she said.

Iris sat at the kitchen table, a plate in front of her, spoon in hand, her face void of expression. With the spoon clutched tightly in her fist, Iris repeatedly slammed it against the plate and brought it to her face. A beige liquid had pooled on the plate.

"Eating ice cream at night, huh?" Abby said, but her sister did not respond.

Abby walked to Iris and leaned over to whisper in Iris's ear, hoping to wake her gently. As she neared, however, Iris turned and growled.

Abby stepped back. She let out a stream of nervous laughter. *Why should I be afraid? This was Iris having a dream*. She found it difficult to move forward again. She recalled a television show that recounted tales of murdering sleepwalkers. Those were embellished stories for TV, Abby reminded herself. And Iris was her sister. Iris would never hurt her.

"Iris," Abby said firmly, but she did not move closer. The banging on the plate continued. "You need to wake up." Her sister's eyes closed and opened again, but the banging went on and on.

"Iris!"

The hand holding the spoon fell heavily onto the table. Iris's head followed with a clatter against the plate. Abby worried the plate was cracked and possibly Iris's head too.

Abby rushed forward and lifted her sister's head. Iris squinted and blinked. Melted ice cream coated one side of her face and ran down in viscous streams onto her shoulders.

"What are you doing?" Iris said. She touched the sticky side of her face and pulled the hand away quickly. A look of revulsion came over her. "What did you do to me?"

"What am I doing?" Abby said. "What did I do?" Abby scoffed. "You're the one sleepwalking and eating ice cream at three in the morning! Talking about not knowing why you're getting fat. Well, I think I know why!"

"What?" Iris touched her face again. "I've been eating? Sleepwalking?"

Abby told Iris what she found in the kitchen—her own sister eating from an empty plate and growling.

"I don't believe you," Iris said. She folded her arms across her chest, tilted her head, and appeared to lose herself in thought. "Well, that does explain a lot."

"What do you mean?" Abby asked, noticing the bruising on her sister's arms for the first time. They were small and obviously varying in age. Some were the dark purple and black of fresh bruises; others were the pale greens and browns of bruises nearly healed. They trailed up Iris's arms. *She wore long sleeves earlier,* Abby thought. *That's why I hadn't noticed.*

"I guess there have been some odd things in the kitchen lately," Iris said, still lost in her thoughts, her eyes glazed over.

"Odd things?" Abby repeated.

"Yeah, but it hasn't been a big deal." Iris shook her head. She waved her hands dismissively and rose from the table. "I'm going to bed. I have work tomorrow."

Iris left Abby alone in the dark hallway. The sounds of the fork banging against the plate still echoed in Abby's ears. She wondered what odd things Iris had recalled, and for an instant, she felt chills run up her spine. In the back of her mind, a strange thought occurred to her: Something else is here. As she had woken her sister, she felt the presence of another. But this was a silly thought, and Abby realized it.

She found her pillow on the floor in front of the television. She gathered it along with a blanket and went to her own room, which was once Iris's guest room. When she closed the door, she reached back and locked it, unsure why, but feeling safer.

A BESTIARY OF HORRORS

Abby spent the next several days at job interviews. Whenever questions of Abby's past employment came up, Abby felt her face flush. She would mumble some fluff about needing a new challenge, a new opportunity. She'd see the look on the eyes of her interviewer. They changed from understanding to skeptical the more Abby went on.

The truth was, at her last job, Abby had never shown up to work on time. She couldn't tell an interviewer that, though. She couldn't tell them that she'd had some problems with her antidepressants, that she wasn't sleeping regularly, or that most mornings she couldn't force herself out of bed. She also couldn't say that she was getting better. She had a new doctor, had been off medication for two weeks, was working out again, and felt like a real person. Her sister's support had made that happen.

At the end of an interview, the interviewer would smile and nod and shake her hand, saying something along the lines of, "they would be in touch."

Abby's only comfort was Iris. "I'm sure you wowed them," she said after the first interview. "How could they not love you?" after the second. And, "They would regret not hiring you," after the third. She'd squeeze Abby's shoulders and give that encouraging smile that broke Abby's heart.

After three weeks, Abby took a job as a waitress. She wasn't using her degree, but at least she wasn't at home eating cereal by herself. Whenever she complained, Iris assured her something would come up. Something always came up.

Iris continued to gain weight. Usually any mention of the weight gain was followed by Abby bringing up that first night when she had found her sleepwalking sister eating melted ice cream. Iris would reply by saying she couldn't blame the night eating because the night eating was a one-time thing.

"It must have been because we were sleeping on the floor," Iris said during dinner after Abby had brought up the subject again. "Doing something like that can really disrupt your sleep." That was her excuse for the first night. She had no excuses for the nights that followed.

The restaurant booked Abby to work a private party. She hated doing private parties. The hours were long and the partygoers were somehow ruder, more self-important than normal restaurant patrons. But she needed the extra money. She was saving for her own place, after all.

Around 3:00 am, she entered the house on tiptoes. She put her bag and shoes by the door and walked slowly through the living room. The lights were out, and Abby found her way through the darkness with her arms splayed in front of her.

She walked past the entrance to the kitchen and to the hall toward the bedrooms. She would have made it all the way, if it hadn't been for the crunching. She turned and walked to the kitchen doorway.

It was the sound of teeth gnashing. Abby's first thought was not of her sister, but something far more ridiculous—an animal must have broken into the house and into the cabinets with the cereal. She felt for the light switch, preparing herself for the horde of raccoons. She hoped she could scare the animals away quietly, so she wouldn't disturb her sister.

She switched on the light and found Iris cross-legged on the floor. She wore only a t-shirt and underwear. A pile of garbage and food remnants lay strewn about the kitchen. She was gorging herself on popcorn kernels. Each hand shoveled another pile into her mouth. Her teeth chewed violently. Blood covered Iris's lips and gums where the kernels had been too rough and hard.

"Iris! Wake up!" she screamed rushing to her sister. She knocked the canister of corn kernels over. They spilled across the floor, rolling in every direction.

Iris screamed too. She lurched across the floor, pausing every few inches to shovel more corn into her mouth, groaning as she swallowed the half chewed corn.

"Iris!" Abby yanked on her sister's shoulder, hoping to lift her off the floor. "Stop this right now." Iris pulled away. She arched her body forward and flailed her arms, the tips of her fingers grabbing at rolling pieces of corn. When she realized she could not reach it, Iris stood straight. For a moment, Abby thought her sister had awoken.

Then Iris turned, and behind her eyes Abby saw nothing. No consciousness. No life. Abby wanted to back away, but she moved too slowly. Iris pushed Abby against the wall, growling low and guttural sounds. Her mouth opened wide, and Abby saw her blood drenched teeth. Then Iris's head moved toward Abby's neck.

Abby screamed and slapped Iris's face. She had been expecting Iris to sink her bloody teeth into her neck, but there was nothing.

"What's happening?" Iris said. "Where did this mess come from?"

Abby tried to explain what had happened, but Iris wouldn't hear it. It wasn't until she saw her teeth that Iris realized the extent of her sleepwalking.

"I'm scared," she said. "What if I've been doing this all the time, and we just haven't noticed?"

"That would make sense considering how much weight you've gained."

"Hey! You said I looked good."

Abby shrugged. It was too late for niceties. "We could set up cameras," Abby suggested. "Then we would know how often it happens."

Iris let out a tired sigh. "I'd hate to have cameras in my house. It makes me sound so desperate and insane."

"We could put locks on the kitchen cabinets. On the refrigerator too. Then even if you sleepwalk, you wouldn't be able to eat anything."

"Even that makes me sad. It sounds so crazy. As if I don't have enough control over myself to not do—" Iris paused. "I don't know what I was going to say. I guess not do something as insane as this." She motioned at the mess on the kitchen floor.

The kernels had rolled into the living room. Abby suspected she and Iris would find them for months, maybe years. Each time they found one beneath the couch or behind an end table, they would remember this night, the night Iris had cut her lips and gums without waking. Abby wondered how long it would have gone on if she hadn't been there.

They decided to do both of Abby's suggestions. They set up cameras in the house—one in front of Iris's bedroom door, another in the corner of the kitchen, at an angle where the doorway, cabinets, and refrigerator were visible.

The locks and chains had been for Iris's bicycles. She locked the bikes in the garage and wrapped a chain around the refrigerator. All the dry food went into the pantry where the door was secured tightly with another bike lock.

"This should keep me out!" Iris said proudly, but Abby detected sadness in Iris's voice.

"You should go to a doctor too," Abby said. "Maybe you just need some kind of sleep aid."

"I'm not going to get doped up," Iris said. "This is fine." She motioned at her work—the cameras, the locks. Abby wondered what nighttime Iris would do when she found the food locked away. Would she simply go back to bed?

Abby slept through the first night, not hearing Iris rise from her own sleep and walk throughout the house. When they watched the video the next day, they saw Iris leaving her bedroom, taking long, labored steps. They saw her enter the kitchen, but not eating anything. She was only wandering, occasionally running into things like the corners of the countertops and the dining room table.

She did this for about an hour and then returned to her bed, moving in that same labored manner, as though each step was a great effort. Her head lulled back as she walked, her arms hung at her sides, and her shoulders slumped forward, as though too heavy to lift.

"You look like a zombie," Abby said.

"That's not reassuring," Iris said. Then she laughed. "I really do look like I'm in *Dawn of the Dead* or something. I wish these cameras had sound.

Maybe I'm making zombie noises too."

"I think I would wake up for that," Abby said. "I've been wondering where those bruises on your arm come from, and I guess I know where now. Weren't you suspicious?"

Iris looked down at her arms. There were a few fresh bruises present. "I just thought I was clumsy. At least I didn't eat anything."

The next night, while Abby slept, Iris wandered from her room again. This time she awoke a little later, around 4:13 in the morning.

Abby awoke a little after that from the noise.

They watched the video later to confirm what Abby had seen. She hadn't believed it at first. But no, the video on Iris's computer couldn't lie. Abby watched it over and over, replaying the last forty-five seconds.

This is what happened: Iris left her bedroom, walking in the same hulking, undead stagger. It seemed she had little control over her body. Her torso jutted forward and the rest of her hung limply, as though a force had wrapped itself around her midsection and pulled her forward.

Abby had not seen this until she watched the video. When Abby came in, she found her sister in the kitchen. A narrow strip of light shone on the floor. Abby heard the groaning first. Then she heard the slamming.

The door to the refrigerator was opened only a few itches. The locks they had used to seal the door shut allowed only so much of an opening. This did not stop Iris. She had somehow wedged one arm into the refrigerator, but was struggling to pull her arm back out. She groaned loudly and—to Abby's horror—shoveled food into her mouth despite being stuck. Each time Iris pulled, the refrigerator lifted and then slammed into the wall behind it.

"Stop it!" Abby screamed. Grabbing her sister by the waist, Abby pulled hard. Iris's head flailed wildly, slinging slop from her open mouth. A chunk of something soft and wet hit Abby's cheek. She guessed it was chewed turkey breast.

Abby thought she felt something bite her, but her eyes were squeezed shut. When she opened them, she thought she saw Iris's head turned too far to one side. Then it righted itself. It happened so quickly, Abby didn't know if she had imagined it or not.

The arm wedged inside the refrigerator loosened and the two women fell backward in a heap. Abby had time enough to see that her sister's arm didn't fit quite correctly at the shoulder. Then Iris's screams filled the kitchen.

"What's happened to me?" Iris yelled between sobs. "I think my arm is broken. And cut."

The struggle had rubbed the skin on Iris's arm raw.

"We have to go to the hospital now!" Abby said.

Iris shook her head and whimpered. Then she said, "What if there's something really wrong with me?" She looked at Abby, her eyes wide with fear. "I don't want to know."

Abby couldn't force Iris to admit what was happening, but eventually, she convinced Iris to go to the hospital. Her shoulder was only dislocated. They wrapped it and put it in a sling quickly enough, but the bruises and scrapes did not go unnoticed.

"Is there something we need to talk about?" a nurse asked Iris quietly when the doctor left.

"No," Iris said, looking into Abby's eyes as she said it.

"Nothing unusual?" the nurse asked.

"No. Everything's normal."

Iris went to work with her arm in a sling the next day, and Abby went to visit their dad.

Their father was the only person who knew them both and the only person Abby thought she could talk to about it. He was family after all.

"Night eating?" he asked.

He was in his late sixties and healthy with a full head of hair. When Abby showed up on his doorstep, he pulled her into an enormous hug and kissed her check. Now they sat at his table drinking coffee. Abby had started at the beginning, telling her father about her first night in Iris's apartment up to the previous night.

"My god," he said, putting his cup down. He gazed out their kitchen window, looking out at his manicured backyard. He kept an impressive vegetable garden. As children, Iris and Abby watered the tomatoes and zucchini in the summer. Those were good years for Abby.

"She won't get help?" he asked.

"I asked her again this morning, and she said she made an appointment with her doctor a week from now. She said it was the soonest they could see her, but I think she's putting it off. I doubt she'll show up. In fact, she's terrified of what's happening, but hoping it'll go away on its own."

"She takes after your mother," he said, "but I guess she couldn't take after me."

Abby looked up at this. Their dad rarely mentioned the fact that he was not actually Iris's birth father. She had been born before their parents met, and Iris's real father was someone their mom said was "not worth mentioning."

But their father loved Iris as his own. Abby had never doubted that.

He leaned back in his chair now. He made a small "hmmph" sound accompanied by a furrowed brow.

"What is it?" Abby asked.

"It's nothing," he said. He shook his head. "I was just thinking of your mom. When she died, she said some strange things to me."

"What kind of things?" Abby rarely spoke of her mother's death.

She had died two years earlier of breast cancer. Abby hadn't been in the country. She was off on one of her last adventures in Europe with her friends. This was a fact she regretted even now.

Their mother died quietly in a hospital bed. Iris slept beside her when it happened. Their dad stood at her side, holding her frail hand.

"It's nothing," he said. "Your mom, I'm sorry to say, was on a lot of medication. She said things that didn't make sense. I had to filter most of it to find meaning in any of what she was saying." He seemed to have stumbled upon a memory and a faint smile appeared on his lips. Then he chuckled. "It's really nothing at all."

"Even so," Abby said. "You should tell me. I'd like to know. Has this happened before? Did Iris sleep walk when we were younger? Maybe there's a trigger to it. Maybe there's something Mom did before to stop this."

"No," he said. He reached out and took Abby's hand. "If it had been something like that I would remember. Iris was only one when I met your mother." He paused, and his face grew somber. "You must promise never to tell Iris what I tell you now. It'll haunt her if you do. Do you promise?"

Abby nodded. "Of course."

"Your mother said some things she did not mean. One of them was that Iris was not her baby."

"What?" Abby dropped her coffee cup on the table. "Then who's Iris's mom?"

"I asked her that very question, though I doubted her ability to answer me coherently. She was mostly gone by then, staying conscious for only a few moments at a time. When she finally did answer me, she said Iris didn't have a mother." Then he laughed. "I told you it was just the drugs talking."

He stood. "You don't need to hear such sad things." He kissed her on the cheek, and Abby took it as a sign to leave.

When Abby arrived home, she found Iris sitting at the kitchen table staring into space. Something was wrong with her, Abby could tell. The skin on her face hung too loosely and seemed grayer than the fleshy pink it normally was. Her hair appeared to have more gray in it too. That was impossible, Abby reminded herself. How could someone's hair become gray in one day?

"Iris?"

Iris glanced up and seemed startled, as though she hadn't noticed Abby entering the room. "Oh. Hi."

"Rough day?"

Iris shook her head. "Not really. Rough night." She tried to smile, but it was weak and not genuine.

"I'm feeling really sick," Iris said.

"What hurts?"

Iris shrugged. "Tired," she said. "Nauseous."

"You just need rest."

Iris's eyes grew wide. "I don't think I want to rest yet."

Abby understood Iris's hesitation.

"What if I sit by you? I won't let you get up," Abby said.

"Would you?"

Abby nodded. "It's my turn to take care of you. I owe you that much."

Iris fell asleep almost immediately. While she slept, Abby examined her sister's face for signs of change. Something was different about Iris. Lines appeared where there were no lines a few weeks ago. When Abby had first moved in, Iris's face was plump, pleasantly round. Now it seemed as though she had lost too much weight and too rapidly. The skin on her face resembled an empty sack covering bones.

"You really need to go to the doctor," Abby whispered and decided she would take Iris in the morning despite any protests.

To stay awake, Abby drank cup after cup of coffee. By her sixth cup of coffee, Abby doubted she would ever fall asleep again.

That's good, she thought. I'll stay awake for Iris.

The last thing she remembered before waking to see Iris's empty bed was the clock displaying 3:13. When she awoke, it was 3:42, and Iris was already in the kitchen.

Abby rushed up, intent on stopping her sister before any damaged could be done.

"Iris," she shouted, moving from the bedroom, down the hall, and into the kitchen. "Wake up!"

She hadn't seen her sister yet, but she heard the scraping noises from the kitchen. Abby dreaded turning on the lights.

Iris was on the floor beside the pantry. They had tightened the locks during the day, so nighttime Iris couldn't wedge an arm between the crack of the door. Instead, Iris was leaning over, her mouth on the corner of the cabinet, chewing and snarling on the wood of the pantry.

What startled Abby most about this was how wide her sister's mouth had become. It was as though Iris's lower jaw no longer connected to the top of her skull, and yet, she chewed—up and down, over and over.

"Stop it!" Abby pushed Iris away from the cabinet and instantly regretted it.

Iris stood and moved toward Abby with her jaw hanging six inches from her head. The skin on her face was completely gray now. Her eyes had rolled up, showing only veined whites.

Abby did not recognize this thing as her sister, though in her mind, she knew it was. "Please, Iris, wake up," she said.

The thing that was Iris moved forward onto Abby. As she had in the videos, Iris's midsection moved forward first as though an invisible rope led her.

"What's happened to you?" Abby cried as the weight of her sister fell on her. She felt unusually heavy. Abby tried pushing free off with her knees, but the weight was too much. The thing on top of her tilted its head backward, but only the top of its mouth went back. The jaw still hung down over her neck. Abby cried out as she saw the gaping hole leading into Iris's throat. Then Abby she saw three small fingers reach out of darkness.

Abby screamed again, and, using her arms and her knees, she kicked Iris backwards. The thing stumbled across the room and landed on the table. Abby had backed herself into a corner, unsure of what to do. In the back of her mind, a voice was telling her, run away. But she couldn't do that. This was her sister. She had promised to stay with Iris. To take care of her.

The thing pulled itself off the table. The top of its head flopped forward and now it resembled something closer to a human.

It took a step, making a strange whining sound. Then the skin over its body pulsed. The whining grew louder. Abby screamed at this but did not move.

Then it fell on the floor.

It lay still for several seconds, and Abby cautiously moved forward. She edged closer to the body of her sister.

"Iris," she whispered. She put her hands on the shoulders of thing lying on the floor. Its skin felt cold. Abby gasped as it began to shiver and then convulsed. A ripping sound came from within Iris's body. The noise was like the ripping of heavy cloth. There was movement beneath the head, and then the head fell backwards again. Abby saw small, bloody hands clawing their way out of Iris's throat.

She watched in silence as a fleshy creature made its way out of Iris's body and onto the floor of the kitchen. The thing was about eighteen inches long and had a small patch of dark hair on its head. As it moved, it wheezed and sniffled. A ropey umbilical cord trailed behind it to Iris's body.

At that moment, Abby felt the full impact of what she had seen. She screamed until her throat was raw. She pulled what was left of Iris's body toward her and wept, calling her sister's name.

The thing in the center of the kitchen floor seemed to have no interest in her and continued its trek, pulling itself along with its arms like a toddler learning to crawl. When it reached the end of the umbilical cord, it turned and used its small, sharp teeth to chew through its last connection to Iris's body.

Abby must have passed out clutching her sister's corpse. When she awoke, a baby cried somewhere in the house.

Iris's body lay across her. Abby moved it off her lap, whimpering as she did. She didn't want to turn the body. The broken face of her sister would drive her to madness.

Abby followed the sounds of the baby's cries to the living room. The thing that had crawled out of her sister was lying in a makeshift bed. It must have pulled a few throw blankets from the couch and wrapped itself in them. Now it cried, looking up at Abby with normal blue baby eyes. With its tiny hands— hands that had only a few hours before reached from Iris's throat—it reached toward Abby as though beckoning.

"What are you?" Abby asked as the thing cooed.

Abby called her father, not knowing what else to do.

"Dad," she said.

"Abby?" he sounded alarmed. He must have heard the distress in Abby's voice. "What's wrong?"

"Iris is dead."

"What?"

"In the night--" Abby began to sob. She cleared her throat and said, "In the night, something came out of her and she died."

"What?"

"It's like a baby, but not a normal baby."

"Was she pregnant?"

"No," Abby said, and she heard herself laughing, thinking if only it were just that. "No. It came out of her throat. It crawled out of her and shed her like a cicada molting."

"My god," he said. There was a long silence. "That's what she meant."

"What?"

"Stay where you are. I'm coming over."

When Abby and Iris's father arrived, he rushed into the house and looked at the baby resting on the couch, swaddled in Iris's throw blankets.

He picked it up and held it to him. He smiled at it.

"What are you doing?" Abby asked, horrified. "That thing's a monster."

"It's not a monster," he said. "It's Iris."

"What?"

"Your mom told me that Iris had no mother. Then she told me this story.

It was insane, and I thought she had lost it. But hearing what has happened I believe her. I should have believed her all along. Sit down. I'll tell you."

Abby had not wanted to sit down, but her father forced her to sit and forced her to listen to the story her dying mother had told.

"Iris is special," he said. "That's what your mother told me. She was reborn from another woman. Your mother's friend from when she was younger. Her best friend. They had grown up together and lived together when they were in college. When your mother was in her early twenties, her best friend died and was reborn as a baby. As Iris. Our Iris."

"I don't understand," Abby said.

"Iris is special," he said again. "Don't you see? She's not a normal human. Your mom, she kept the secret until she couldn't keep it any longer because it would die with her. She wasn't even sure if it would happen again, but it has. Her last words to me were that to live on, Iris must feed. She must feed at night. And she has. Here is our little Iris. She looks exactly as she did when she was a baby."

Abby breathed quickly. This was too much, and she didn't know how to deal with it.

"So Iris is gone?" she asked.

"No, we get to live with her again. She's a beautiful baby girl again."

"No!" Abby said. "It's not Iris. It's a monster."

"You're talking about your sister! If your mother wasn't there to love her, she would have died. Are you going to let her die now?"

He held the child out to Abby, and Abby looked at it. Now that the blood and fluid had been wiped from its body, it did look like a normal baby. Abby had to admit, she could see her sister in this baby's face. She picked it up and held it to her body. The baby gurgled and cooed again and reached its tiny fingers into Abby's hair. Abby felt herself smiling. Holding the child felt right. She had made the promise to Iris to always be there for her.

Abby said, "I'll be the one to take care of you from now on. I owe you that much."

Megan Neumann is a speculative fiction writer living in Little Rock, Arkansas with her husband, two dogs, and one bossy cat. Her stories have appeared in Crossed Genres, Daily Science Fiction, and Luna Station Quarterly. She is particularly appreciative of the Central Arkansas Speculative Fiction Writers' Group for their loving support and scathing critiques.

THE NEW GOVERNESS

BY JOSHUA REX

THEY'D succeeded in getting Miss Sims sacked the same way they had Miss Hilary- by being naughty to the point of evil. While the children of other fine estates played hop-frog and hide-and-go-seek, Harold and Lucy's game was to see who could shred the nerves of the governess the quickest. No one was exempt from their devious schemes, and along with their teacher, the maids and footmen passed them in the hall as they would a buzzing hornet's nest.

Miss Sims had been Harold's victim. After five weeks of torture, it had been the huge rat he'd caught in the pantry and snuck under her sheets as she slept that had finally done her in. The thing bit her three times as she struggled to untangle herself from the bedclothes, screeching like she were on fire and waking the whole house in the process while Harold and Lucy hid in a closet down the hall, laughing. She'd left the morning after, without notice and without collecting her final pay. When confronted by their parents - the Lord and Lady Ashton- the children feigned ignorance, claiming Miss Sims to be uneven in temperament and a bit barmy. They said they'd seen her licking the condensation off the windows of their lesson room (which wasn't true) and writing endless letters to a certain deceased gentleman (which was) instead of tutoring them in Greek and piano.

The next week was rainy, dismal and boring without Miss Sims to harass, so when their mother informed them that one Mrs. Gertrude Peals would be interviewing for the position of governess the following day, Harold and Lucy were ecstatic.

The next morning, the children were having breakfast with their mother and father in the house's lavish dining room when the butler announced Mrs. Peals' arrival.

"Show her into the drawing room, Mr. Caster. Tell her I will be with her shortly," said Lady Ashton.

After they'd eaten, Harold and Lucy crouched outside the closed drawing room doors, excitedly pushing one another out of the way to get a glimpse through the keyhole. A plant partially obscured where the woman sat, but they could still see the ends of a grey skirt, wrinkly purple veined ankles and old fashioned wooden shoes.

"She's an old woman!" said Harold. "You got an easy one, Lucy. You should have her running from the house in a week."

Lady Ashton entered the room, introduced herself and sat down opposite the prospective governess. A maid brought tea and served them as their mother droned on and on about the history of the house and the family while Mrs. Peals patiently listened. At length, they arrived at the interview portion-the part Harold and Lucy were most eager for.

"You come to us with little in the way of references, Mrs. Peals. However I understand that you were briefly tutor to the Maisten children."

Harold and Lucy looked at each other. Neither was smiling now.

"I was, my lady," said Mrs. Peals. Her voice was low and grainy, with an odd wheeze as if there were a hole in one of her lungs. "Before the tragedy."

"Yes, of course. Given our proximity to Arlington Park - or what's left of it - we were acquaintances of the Maistens. I've heard the ruins are still smoldering. Utterly tragic." Lady Ashton took a sip of tea and then looked at Mrs. Peals in earnest. "Where you present at the time of the fire?"

"I was away, unfortunately. In the city."

"Actually I'd say you *quite* fortunate," said Lady Ashton, without taking her eyes off her.

"I must disagree, my lady. The last few months have been decidedly dreadful. Many nights since I've lain sleepless. The tender faces of those children still haunt my dreams..."

"And what of your family, Mrs. Peals?"

"I am widowed. My husband's been gone these twenty years now."

"And no children of your own?"

"No," said Mrs. Peals. "I wasn't able."

"I see."

"Might I ask how old the children are?"

"Harold is twelve and Lucy is nine. They can be quite... unruly at times. We've had three governesses in the last six months - all of them young ladies - and to be frank, Mrs. Peals, Lord Ashton and I have reached our wits' ends. The children need stern guidance and firm reassurance, someone committed to them, yet unyielding to their waywardness. I believe an older, more mature woman of your experience is better suited to demand obedience while nurturing their intellectual development. Is this a charge you a willing and able to assume?"

"It is, my lady."

"Then it is settled." Lady Ashton picked up a gilded bell, rang it thrice, and then folded her hands imperially in her lap. "Mr. Caster?" she called. "Will you show the children in?"

Harold and Lucy felt a shadow move over them and looked up. Caster was a big man, thick but not fat, with a dark cragged face and a full head of impeccably groomed red hair. Harold and Lucy hated him, as he was the only servant they'd failed to intimidate. He was far too clever for their tricks, and he also held a trump card - he'd been employed at Langston House twenty-two years, had worked up through the ranks from footman to butler and their father's valet long before Harold and Lucy were born.

"Shall I open the door, or would you prefer to continue spying on her through the keyhole?"

Harold rose and emphatically brushed off his pants. "I would *prefer* it if you performed your duties without insolence."

"Yes, mind your own business, Caster," said Lucy.

The butler glared down at them. "Perhaps we might begin afresh with Mrs. Peals, and find other ways in which to amuse ourselves," he said as he turned the doorknob. Harold and Lucy gave him a parting scowl and entered the room.

When they saw her they stopped short, as if they'd just walked into a den where something dangerous lived. Mrs. Peals sat at an angle from their mother, stick straight in her chair, her wooden heels crossed primly, her knobby knuckled hands folded in her lap. She wore a drab, billowy blouse and a long grey woolen skirt - both of which were at least thirty years out of date and gave off a faint mustiness. Her silver hair, streaked with white, was pulled back into a tight bun off her forehead.

"Ah! Here are the children. Harold, Lucy - I'd like you to meet Mrs. Peals."

The old woman slowly swiveled her head in their direction, revealing her oddest feature yet: rectangular glasses with mirrored lenses. She smiled at them, her teeth yellow-brown. "How do you do, children?"

"Why do you wear those glasses? Are you blind?" said Harold.

"Harold! How incredibly rude," said their mother.

"It's quite alright, my lady. It is an obvious peculiarity about which I am often asked. You see, my eyes are extremely sensitive to light. The mirrors reflect the majority, permitting only that in my peripheral to penetrate."

"But your vision is otherwise sharp?" said Lady Ashton, looking suddenly concerned.

Mrs. Peals looked back at the children, grinning. "Perfect."

Mrs. Peals moved in the following week. She brought with her only a pair of black trunks - one small and old, one large and new. Harold and Lucy watched from a distance as she carried the smaller of the two trunks herself, followed by a pair of footmen who struggled up the stairs with the longer narrower one. They stopped halfway up, breathing heavily and loosening the starched collars of their formal service wear. Mrs. Peals barked at them to continue and, looking rather frightened, they picked it up again and carried up the rest of the way to the governess' garret on the fourth floor.

Later, Harold and Lucy were outside in a shallowly wooded area of young trees flanking a creek that ran through the estate's property. They liked to go there to discuss matters of the house, away from the snooping servants and, of course, Caster. Lucy sat on a large bowed vine threaded between two trees watching Harold as he poked through the brush and decaying leaves with a large pointed stick, looking for something to hurt.

"So, what do you have planned for the unlucky Mrs. Peals?"

The question caught Lucy off guard. "I haven't decided."

Harold frowned. "Why not? Lessons begin tomorrow. You know that the first day is always the most crucial, especially since this one will be more difficult than the rest."

"I thought you said she was 'just an old woman', that she'd be '*easy*'?"

Harold paused and stared at the ground. "This one's not like Miss Sims - she's done this before. She'll be harder to break."

Lucy kicked her feet off the ground and began rocking back and forth on the vine. "She's very strange looking. Do you think she's a witch?"

Harold laughed. "No. Just an ugly old woman."

"What do you make of those spectacles?" said Lucy.

"You heard her. She can't see in the daylight."

"That's not what she said."

"Well, it's all the same."

Harold overturned a rotted log and a toad sprung out. Suddenly exposed, it leapt in the direction of the water and safety, but Harold deftly pinned it down with the stick and held it there, grinning as he watched it struggle under the point, which he began slowly pressing into its soft belly. The toad's movements became frantic, its arms and legs jerking and spasming. Finally with a *pop*, Harold impaled the creature and held it up for Lucy to see.

"It's dancing!" Lucy laughed.

They watched it die, then Harold flung it against a tree and went back to searching along banks.

"What if she started the Maisten fire? You don't think she could have, do you Harold?"

"No."

"What if she's lying?"

"Why would someone burn down the very place they are employed? Some clumsy maid knocked over an oil lamp, that's what I think happened."

"Yes, you're probably right."

Lucy gathered a handful of stones and began skipping them in the creek. On a low branch to her left, she spotted a bird's nest filled with hatchlings. It instantly became her new target. Harold picked up some rocks as well and joined in. He succeeded in knocking it out of the tree- sending the squawking chicks into the water. The mother bird flew in suddenly, cawing and screeching above her babies. Lucy brought her arm back and winged her last stone, striking her in the head. The bird froze midair, then plummeted in a spiral of loose feathers into the creek.

"Well done!" cried Harold.

Lucy beamed back at him.

Lucy lay in bed for hours that night, going over a mental list of tricks: salt in her tea, a spider down her shirt, a nasty rumor about something illicit between her and Caster...

She's done this before - she'll be harder to break.

The words appeared in her mind as if a light had shined on them - and suddenly the idea came to her.

She slipped out of bed, crept down the hall to the butler's pantry and took a small bottle of lock oil off a shelf. Lucy pulled the stopper while picturing herself pouring a line under behind the governess' desk.

She's old...the fall might kill her...

She stood there a moment, considering this. Then she re-corked the bottle and started back to her room, grinning.

Oh, then how proud Harold would be!

"So what do you have in store for her? Something *wicked* I hope." Harold was sitting with his fork in his fist, tines up like a rebellious peasant, waiting for his food.

"Oh, it is wicked indeed," said Lucy.

"So, what is it?"

Lucy told him.

"Brilliant!" he said, with a mischievous grin. "If we eat quickly, we might get there before she does, that way we can set the trap early."

The servants set down their plates. Harold dug into his eggs while Lucy chewed on a toast point. She was too excited to eat anything more. They finished quickly, then hurried down the hall to the lesson room, Lucy fingering the phial of oil in her pocket as they approached door. But when they opened it, their cheerful expressions faded.

Mrs. Peals was already there. She stood like a statue with her back to the blackboard in the well-lit room. The mirrored glasses reflecting the early morning light like coins over a dead man's eyes. She wore the same outdated outfit, but with an added cameo at her throat and she held a thin white baton like a wand which she pointed at a pair of small desks and stated, emphatically, "Sit."

Harold and Lucy glanced at one another, then moved toward the little desks and sat down.

"We will begin today with a lesson in the science of anatomy," said Mrs. Peals stepping away from the blackboard. Pinned on it was stunningly lifelike

illustration of a flayed man. His chest was butterflied and all his organs were neatly labeled. He was nude and completely shaved except for his beard and the hair on his head, and all of his intimate details were on display- the penis cross sectioned, the scrotum cut open to reveal the design of his testicles. Lucy blushed and looked away. Harold frowned and cocked his head as he looked at the chart.

"This is a rendering of a deceased male, aged thirty-one," Mrs. Peals began.

"This is *ghastly*," said Harold.

"Children are not to speak out of turn, Mr. Ashton," snapped Mrs. Peals.

Harold's nostrils flared. "*You* are to address me as *Master* Ashton."

Mrs. Peals came toward him, her wooden heels like gavel blows on the floor, and stopped at the edge of his desk. She peered down at him, an image of wide-eyed Harold in each mirrored lens, and Lucy noticed that the image in her cameo was a human skull.

"You are a child, Mr. Ashton. Children are masters of nothing, save error. As your elder and superior in this classroom I will be accorded that respect at all times, is that clear?"

Harold stared back at her, mouth open, his face a conflicted mask of affront and fear.

"*Is that clear,* Mr. Ashton?"

"Yes, Mrs. Peals," he said finally, in a boyish little voice.

Lucy watched this exchange speechless. Miss Chambers had been the last who'd attempted to chastise him. Harold responded by hitting himself in the eye with a doorknob and claiming that she'd struck him. Miss Chambers was gone before dinner bell that same day.

Mrs. Peals returned to the blackboard and smacked the chart with the baton. It made a sound like a bone snapping.

"Continuing then... this drawing details the remains of a man killed in the prime of his life, in peak health when - *yes*, Mr. Ashton?"

"I'm sorry to interrupt, Mrs. Peals. I was only wondering how the man died?"

"He drowned. Note the slightly swollen larynx and the burst capillaries along the walls of the lungs..."

Harold squinted at the rendering, rapt, his eyes following the baton as she circled the areas on the dead man's throat and chest.

"Why are you *showing* us this, Mrs. Peals?" Lucy blurted out.

"So that you may gain a better understanding of the workings of the human body, Miss Ashton."

"But we are not medical students, and that man is, well, *exposed*," Lucy said, "indecently displayed. It is scandalous! Father would have us whipped for merely speaking of it!"

"There is no indecency in science," said Mrs. Peals. "It is a man-made idea which exists solely to establish behavioral boundaries in society. In truth, we are no more than animals going about in slacks and sashes, and *your* meat is no different than *their* meat. A pound of flesh weighs the same, no matter its origin."

"But-"

"What is that yellow thing near the man's stomach?" Harold cut in.

"That is the pancreas, an endocrine gland which produces important enzymes which aid in digestion," said Mrs. Peals.

Lucy scowled at her brother and crossed her arms over her chest, refusing to participate as he and Mrs. Peals spent the next two hours going over the man's entire anatomical makeup. By then it was time for lunch, but Lucy felt even less hungry than at breakfast.

The anatomy lessons continued the next day and the day after that, without a single Greek letter nor a note from a minuet making an appearance alongside the Latin names for organs and tissue and the 206 bones in the human body. The charts grew more grotesque as well. On Monday of the following week, Mrs. Peals produced one of a murdered woman. The body was scored with slashes and chops- each wound labeled according to its severity- with two in the throat and one in the abdomen marked FATAL.

And every day at the end of the lessons, Harold became irritable and sometimes violent. In the great hall, he would meticulously set up his thousand-strong army of toy soldiers in epic battle maps, only to kick them over in a fury or crush them in his fist like some merciless god come to claim them. Lucy tried to get him join her in terrorizing the maids, but Harold had little enthusiasm for anything now except their macabre hours spent with Mrs. Peals. Along with Harold's bad temper grew Lucy's anxiousness. It wasn't so much the drawings of human cross-section and dissection that distressed her, but rather the way Mrs. Peals grinned that yellow grin when Harold got the answers right.

One day when they went down to lessons, they found Mrs. Peals standing behind a table on which the small black trunk stood, lid open.

"Thus far I've relied on diagrams to illustrate the lecture material. Today we will be examining some actual specimens."

Lucy's heart began to gallop as Mrs. Peals reached in and brought out a jar in which something dead floated and set it on the table.

"Do either of you know what this is?"

Harold raised his hand. "It's a shark!"

Lucy squinted at the thing through the murky fluid. It was indeed a shark.

The pewter grey dorsal fin was small but distinct, as were the rows of arrow shaped teeth just visible through the A-shaped mouth on its ivory underside. Its eyes were opaque and gelled with a faint dash of cold blue at the center and its angular tail, designed for pulsing thrusts through the sea, was curled and still in the stagnant water of the jar.

"Correct, Mr. Ashton. It is an infant Great White, caught before it was able to be on its own. A tiny predator, unaware of its lethal capabilities."

She went back to the trunk and took out another jar- this one much larger- and set it next to the shark. At first glance it appeared to be full of hair; a knotted black clot in the fluid, but then as she turned it they saw a face- eyes half closed, with a mournful expression. It was too hairy, its features too pronounced to be human. Lucy had only seen photographs, but she recognized the oversized lips, large square shaped teeth and the brown wrinkled skin stretched over the prominent cheekbones. Jagged vertebra entwined with a few ugly veins stuck out from its severed neck, propping the head up off the bottom of the jar so that its right cheek rested against the glass.

"It's an ape," said Lucy, gravely.

"Very good, Miss Ashton. A chimpanzee, to be specific."

"Did you kill it, Mrs. Peals?" said Harold.

The old woman laughed, a sound like a saw cutting through wood. "No, Mr. Ashton. I did not."

"Well, whoever did made crude work of it," said Harold, half rising out of his chair to get a closer look. Lucy looked at him and frowned.

"Indeed," said Mrs. Peals. "An early attempt... practice, shall we say."

She took out a third jar. This one contained a baby's head. It was completely white and the top of its skull was removed so that the brain was visible. At the sight of it, Lucy's stomach lurched dangerously. She stumbled away from her desk and ran from the room and into the hall where her breakfast came up all over the glossy marble floor- and her father- who happened to be passing through. He looked down at his vomit spattered shoes and glared at her.

"Father, forgive me," Lucy sobbed. "It was Mrs. Peals' fault! She showed us something *awful!*"

Lord Ashton said nothing. His eyes narrowed on the lesson room door, and then he started toward it. Lucy followed on his heels like a scolded dog. But as they entered, she found a very different scene. The jars were gone, the trunk lid shut. Now there was only a chart detailing a dissected cat pinned to the board. Harold, scribbling notes, stood when he saw his father. Lord Ashton looked at the picture, then the black trunk, then Mrs. Peals, his stony expression never changing.

"What subject is this, madam?"

"The science of anatomy, my lord."

"For what purpose?"

"So that they may obtain a clear picture of physiology," said Mrs. Peals.

Lord Ashton paused, eyeing the pen and ink rendering of the innards.

"Well, perhaps you might utilize examples less visceral? Those which will not render my daughter physically ill?"

"Certainly, my lord. I shall make the adjustments."

He turned and left the room without another word, summoning Caster for a clean pair of shoes. Lucy watched him go, reluctantly, before turning back in her seat. Harold was staring at her.

"I'm disappointed in you, Lucy," he said. "I thought you had a stronger stomach."

Mrs. Peal was staring at her too, as were the empty eyeholes of the skull in her cameo.

The following week, the Lord and Lady were summoned by special request on the occasion of the prince's engagement gala and Mrs. Peals took sick, leaving the children to amuse themselves. It was overcast and dreary, with periods of intermittent rain so they stayed inside most of the time. Lucy played with her dolls until she couldn't stand them anymore and decided to go looking for Harold. He'd been cold to her since the incident with their father, but she wanted to talk to him about Mrs. Peals while she had the chance without the old woman lurking about.

She found him on a window seat in the library, staring out at the black clouds rumbling above estate's bright green lawn. He didn't acknowledge her when she sat down across from him.

"Harold?"

"What is it, Lucy?"

"What if mother and father find out?"

"About what?"

"Mrs. Peals - about what she's *really* teaching us."

Harold looked up at her and blinked in a slow deliberate way. "Why would they find out?" said Harold. There was a threatening edge in his tone which made her pause, and choose her next words carefully.

"What if Caster's been listening in?"

"Ha! Caster," Harold scoffed, leaning back into the nook and threading his fingers behind his head. "The only place he's been snooping is the wine cellar. You know, I caught him tapping father's Madeira last week. I've got him in my pocket now. One word of it and he'd be banished from this house forever."

"But doesn't she frighten you?"

"No," he said flatly, looking out the window. The clouds grumbled and cracked.

"Well I *am* frightened. I think I'm going to tell mother what been going..."

Harold shot up and grabbed her braids. Lucy squealed and cried out, but he only pulled harder the more she struggled.

"You won't, Lucy! You *won't,* do you hear me?" Harold hissed.

"*Harold!* My *hair*! You're *pulling* it -"

He pinned her down with his knee on the dark red window seat cushion. His teeth were bared and there was a touch of madness in his eyes. The rain began, striking the library windows like a volley of arrows.

"You won't say anything to mother *or* father, will you Lucy? *Will you*?"

"No! No! I *promise!* Just let me go, Harold- *please!*"

He released her and settled back into the cushions with his hands behind his head as if nothing had happened. Lucy whimpered, ashamedly wiping the tears off her chubby cheeks. He hadn't bullied her that way in years, and she'd come to think of them as equals, associates in their evil games. But in a flash he had reasserted himself as *Big Brother*- a figure to be *Feared* and *Obeyed* - and Lucy was far more hurt by this sibling demotion than the hair pulling. She composed herself and began fixing her braids as the rain lessened to a steady patter on the leaded glass.

"What do you find so fascinating about her?"

Harold thought a moment. "She doesn't think me wicked."

"Neither do I," said Lucy, her voice thick with hurt.

"Yes," Harold sighed. "But *you're* just a child."

Lucy felt the tears return. She ran sobbing from the room and into the hall, where she saw Mrs. Peals hunched and limping across the dim corridor toward the staircase. Her gait was odd, disjointed, as if she couldn't make her legs do what she wanted them to. She had a small glass bottle in one hand, and a candle holder looped around one crooked finger in her other. The dripping stub of taper stuck on the iron spike illuminated her sagging, mottled face and the long dead looking hair that hung on either side like shredded curtains. *She looks ill indeed... like death*, Lucy thought. *Why is she downstairs?*

To spy, she realized, on her and Harold. A sudden rage filled her, and she marched down the hall, calling out with all the haughty, aristocratic authority her nine year old voice could muster.

"Mrs. Peals, what *are* you doing down here? Were you not instructed to remain in your room when you are not giving us lessons?"

The old woman stowed the bottle in her robes as Lucy approached. There was a cloying floral scent doing battle with something rank beneath, mixing into a nauseating cloud that hung around her like a physical presence. She wasn't wearing the cameo, her collar was unbuttoned, and there was a black thread sticking up through the gap. Lucy eyed it curiously, then looked back her, doing her best imitation of the stern and disappointed expression she'd seen her mother give the servants countless times.

"What is that you have? Something you've stolen?"

There was a long pause where Mrs. Peals only stared back. Then, slowly, she leaned in close, her body creaking and groaning as if lowered by ropes and pulleys, and lifted Lucy's chin so that she was looking directly at her own frightened face reflected in the glasses. The sensation of those ragged nails on her flesh gave Lucy instant, spidery chills.

"I know what troubles you," said Mrs. Peals, her words thick and choked as if her throat were a clogged drain. "You think that I'm trying to drive a wedge between you and your brother. That *I* am the reason for his recent distance towards you. But you see, Lucy, learning is as much intuition as instruction. It is recognizing and then coming to terms with one's own nature. Harold understands this - he knows the true color of his heart. But not you... you struggle with what you are, like one kicking at the walls of her own house."

Lucy took a step back. "No, it's *you*. You're corrupting him. Ever since you came, he's been different."

"But don't you see? I am only a catalyst, giving water to the weeds of thought so that they might flourish."

"You and your *lessons* are macabre and uncouth, and I am going to tell my mother and father straight away when they return," said Lucy, moving around her and starting up the stairs.

"And what would big brother think of you then?" Mrs. Peals called up after her. "How will he react when he learns *you* were the one that tattled?"

Lucy stopped, turned back. The old woman was grinning at her, her teeth the color of infected phlegm in the taper light.

"I've said all, Mrs. Peals. The next time you see either of us will be from the window of the carriage after your dismissal."

Lucy steadily mounted the stairs. The moment she was out of sight, she ran the rest of the way down the hall to her room, and for the first time in her brief life, she locked the door. She'd never been so scared.

The next day Caster went missing.

A servant girl had gone to his room after he'd failed to show up for the breakfast service and, after much knocking and calling to him, found the door unlocked and entered. Everything was immaculate - bed made, his things there, but he was nowhere to be found. The contention was that he'd unexpectedly gone into town on some sudden errand. But as morning turned to afternoon and finally evening, concern became dread. The house was searched- from the servants' quarters to the cellars- and finally the outbuildings and the grounds and lastly the shallow woods. But neither Caster nor any sign of him turned up.

During all the commotion, Lucy was looking for Harold. He'd been at breakfast, but then had gone off somewhere and she hadn't seen him for the rest of the day. Their mother and father wouldn't return until the following evening, and as night fell, moonless and rainy, Lucy began to feel lonely and very frightened. It occurred to her she hadn't seen Mrs. Peals since their encounter the previous night. Since she was unwell, no one had disturbed her in the search for Caster. With dread enveloping her like a cloak, Lucy climbed the stairs in the semi-darkness.

A door opened and closed above her as she gained the third floor landing. Lucy hid in a gap between the wall and a grandfather clock, holding her breath as a figure slowly came down the stairs. It was Harold. He was walking slowly, trance-like, his face blank and his skin so pale it glowed in the gloom like a ghost. Lucy's eyes widened when she saw there was dried blood on his clothes. She peeked around the clock, making sure Mrs. Peals wasn't following, and whispered: "Harold... *Harold?*"

Harold didn't respond, or even look up. He kept walking like a catatonic down the stairs and disappeared into the blackness below. A few moments later she heard his bedroom door open and close.

A sound above distracted her - a loud thud. Harnessing her fear, Lucy went up to the last flight of stairs, creeping along the wall in the darkness and stopped outside the governess' door. She could hear the tinkling of glass and the sandpaper scratch of lids being unscrewed. Lucy swallowed hard, knelt in front of the door and looked through the keyhole.

Centered in her line of vision was a long wooden table. The small black trunk stood atop it with its lid raised. Beside the trunk was a white wash basin full of steaming water, a line of empty glass jars without lids, a spoon with a long handle and a spool of thick black thread stuck with a needle. Mrs. Peals was bent over, getting something out of the large trunk on the floor. She rose, turned around and set it on the table. Somehow, Lucy managed to keep in the sharp little girl scream that wanted out.

She could only see the back of it, but immediately Lucy recognized that flame of red hair, now damp and tousled and sticking up like the feathers of a shot bird. She'd never seen a hair on his head out of place; the sight of it was strangely worse than seeing his head no longer attached to his body. Mrs. Peals had her arms out, searching for something - a short wooden chair which she pulled up to the table and sat. Lucy could see her full on now; her whole face drooped like melted wax, her teeth crooked in her gums like old weathered headstones. The mirrored glasses reflected the orange flames blazing in the fireplace. She brought the head closer, turning it so that it literally faced her and gave it a pat as if it were an animal she wanted to stay put. Then she brought her hands up slowly and took off the glasses.

Lucy gasped- Mrs. Peals was staring back at her through the keyhole. But something was wrong with the eyes. The whites were grayish and the pupils, dark and misshapen, were coated in a thick opaque glaze. When she looked down at the head, only the right eye went in that direction. The other slid left, then rolled toward the ceiling. Mrs. Peals blinked several times, then stuck her fingers into her left socket and pulled out the roaming eye. It made a sick squelching sound as it came away in her hand. She plopped it on the table where it lay like a scoop of half-melted ice cream, then picked up the long handled spoon and, digging her nails into scalp to steady the head, scooped out the left eye. After severing the stringy muscles that trailed it, she popped it into her empty eyehole, then did the same with the right eye and closed her eye lids. When she opened them again, it was all whites at first, but then slowly Caster's olive irises rolled into view.

Mrs. Peals tossed the head in the fire and went to the small trunk. The sound of clinking glass jingled in the room like lively piano music as she pulled out several jars, filled with assorted organs, along with one beaker of blood. She set them on the table beside the empty ones and unscrewed the lids. Then she rose, unbuttoned her blouse and pulled it back off her shoulders so that it remained tucked into her skirt but hung like a tattered apron around her waist.

Lucy cringed. The body beneath was emaciated. Her skin was blotchy, the color of boiled chicken, and her breasts hung to the sides like two pieces of dried leather. There was a long black zigzag down the center of her chest where the skin was sewn together, ending in that thread Lucy had glimpsed earlier, jutting like a worm out of her throat. The old woman pinched it with her fingers and pulled. The opening began to gape; then a smell like the breath of Death wafted through the keyhole, forcing Lucy to cover her nose and mouth with her skirts. Mrs. Peals coiled the grimy string on the table, put her fingers inside the slit up to the knuckles, and pulled. The ribcage swung open like a pair of well-oiled doors. It looked like a fire had raged through her insides. The organs were shriveled shadow masses and the lungs flapped and rattled with her breathing like popped balloons. She started with the lungs, then the liver, kidneys, and continued on to other viscera, alternately dropping the used up ones in the clean jars, rinsing her hands in the white basin, then inserting the fresh organs. When the transfers were complete, she picked up the large jar of blood, feebly brought it to her lips and took a few slow sips, grimacing, but then drinking in earnest, hungrily draining the beaker of every drop before setting it back on the table.

Now all was left was the heart, tiny and black, like a beating chunk of coal.

Mrs. Peals sat again, stuck her hand into the fetid cavity and grasped it. The heart struggled like a tiny animal in a trap, beating quicker and quicker but then sagging and almost liquefying as it came away in her hand. She dropped it in one of the empty jars, a black smear streaking the side of the clear glass, and rinsed her hand in the steaming basin. Then she plucked the fresh one from the jar and inserted it in the former's place. But the new heart didn't beat, it just hung from the arteries like an over ripe fruit, and the old woman slumped sideways in the chair and went still.

Suddenly the heart twitched, began to beat irregularly, shuddering at first, then becoming stronger until it was throbbing steadily in a perfect cadence of beats. Things began to change. The snake-like blood vessels swayed as the blood flowed, turning everything grey-black but pulsing and vibrant, a dark forest coming alive with a terrible magic. Mrs. Peals' outer appearance was changing as well, her drooping jowls lifting, the crooked teeth settling back into the gums, the black splotches on her skin fading and then altogether disappearing. She snapped awake, drew a long gurgling breath and closed the ribcage. Then she took up the black spool and sewed the skin back together, the needle finding the old holes without any trouble. Afterwards, she dressed and pulled her hair back, silver and lustrous again with an oily sheen in the firelight, and began the task of disposing of the dead organs, tossing them in the flames and rinsing the jars in the basin before replacing the lids and returning them to the small trunk. The smell of the rotten meat burning made Lucy wretch, and the tiniest involuntary cry escaped her. Mrs. Peals looked at the door like a cat about to strike. She put the glasses back on and stealthily slid around the table, her movements now eerily smooth and fluid.

Lucy ran, her footsteps reverberating through the hall like a drum. She turned around only once as she rounding the corner. Mrs. Peals was standing in the doorway, watching her with a malignant grin.

Lucy went straight to Harold's room and pounded on the door until he let her in. His eyes were puffy from crying and Lucy noticed he'd changed his shirt.

"What do you want, Lucy?"

"Let me in. *Quick*!"

Harold frowned hard and his eyes drifted down the hall. He moved aside just enough for her to enter the room before shutting the door and locking it.

"What did she make you do, Harold?"

Harold looked at her, his eyes widening slightly, but he didn't answer.

"I saw you in the hall. I saw the blood."

A long pause. "It doesn't matter. He was already dead."

"How do you know that? Is that what she told you?"

"He had a heart attack, Lucy," said Harold. "He died in his bed."

"Maybe he did, or maybe *she* killed him. Either way, she made you cut him up!"

"Since when were you so fond of Caster?" said Harold. He'd tried to put some edge to his words but his voice cracked.

"Harold, she's a *monster*!"

"What are you talking about?"

In a low voice, Lucy told him what she'd seen.

'You're mad," Harold whispered, looking away.

"I am not! I saw her do it with my own eyes and -"

Lucy broke off, not wanting to say it, not wanting to admit she'd been caught. Harold angled his head slightly and frowned.

"What?"

"She saw me."

Harold swallowed.

"We have to leave," said Lucy. "Even if just for the night. We'll come back when mother and father return tomorrow evening."

"And where will we go, Lucy? The woods? The village? Where would we stay?"

"There's a cave on the other side of the creek - remember the one we found last summer? We can sneak out the back in the morning before the servants rise."

"How will we know when mother and father have returned?"

"There's a good view of the northern road from that spot of the woods."

Lucy got up and started toward the door. Harold grabbed her arm. He looked terrified. "Where are you going?"

"To gather food. We'll need something to eat if we're to be gone all day."

"I'll come with you," he offered weakly.

"No, you stay here. I'll only be gone a minute or two - just to the pantry and then to my room for a cloak. I think we should sleep in the same room tonight."

"Yes," said Harold, exhaling with relief. "I was thinking that as well."

As she went to leave again, Harold called out after her.

"I'm sorry I pulled your hair," he said.

"It's alright. I know you didn't mean it."

Harold gave her an awkward smile. Lucy smiled back, then slipped out of the room and silently hurried down the back steps toward the pantry. There, she filled a wicker basket with bread and jam and fruit and a pair of mince meat pies along with some linens and a bread knife and then went back upstairs and gathered her cloak and boots before returning to Harold's room. Harold propped a chair under the door and then the two of them got under the covers. They didn't put out the candle.

◉   ◉   ◉

Lucy woke just as the windows were beginning to grey with the first hint of dawn. Rolling over, she stared at the empty pillow beside her for a second or two before she realized.

Harold was gone.

Lucy shot up in bed and scanned the room, her heart beating an allegro. The chair was cast aside, the door ajar. She got up and cautiously peeked into the hall, an acute terror seizing her as she stared into the blackness.

She's snatched him.

Lucy took the bread knife from the basket and crept up the stairs to the fourth floor. The door to the governess' room was opened slightly, and a soft light penetrated the otherwise black hall. She listened for a full minute before continuing, inching along the wall. When she reached the door she paused again and listened, this time longer, and then peeked through the gap.

The room was neat and silent, without a trace of Mrs. Peals, save the pair of trunks; the small one on the table and longer one on the floor. A newly lit taper stood on the candle holder in the center of the table like an eerie sentinel. She pushed the door open and a little further and took a couple steps inside. A smell hit her at once - a fuel scent like lamp oil or kerosene. Harold wasn't there. A desperate feeling took her over as she stood in the center of the room, the knife shaking in her hand.

"Harold?" she whispered.

"Lucy!"

The sound of her own name spoken in the empty room made her jump as if a ghost had said it.

"Harold! Where are you?"

"I'm in the trunk!"

Lucy set the knife on the table and went to the trunk. The key was still in the lid. She turned it and Harold popped up like a Jack-in-the-Box. Lucy threw her arms around him.

"What happened? Why did you let her in?"

"She made her voice sound like mother's. When I opened the door she held a cloth with ether to my face. I woke up here."

"Where is she? Where did she go?"

"Who cares? Let's just get -"

A sound in the corridor - wooden clogs coming down the hall. Lucy looked around in utter panic. It was too late to run.

"Quick, Lucy, get in!"

Lucy climbed in and Harold brought the lid down just as she came around the corner. They heard the footsteps enter the room and stop. The bread knife was picked up and set down, and then the footsteps started again, heavy and deliberate, toward the trunk. The key turned in the lock, followed by a wild, piercing laugh that gave Lucy a cold sensation in her chest. There was a small *tick*, followed by a *whoosh*, and then the sound of the jars jingling, first in the room and then down the hall accompanied by more feral laughter.

Lucy understood the smell of kerosene now. Harold was shouting, slamming at the lid. Lucy began shouting too, for help, for the servants, for their parents, for anyone. But no one came. And as the flames rose around them, Harold and Lucy held each other and cried.

Joshua Rex writes scary stories. His work can also be found in Fresh Meat: 2015 from Sinister Grin Press.
He lives in an old house in Cleveland, Ohio with his girlfriend, the poet Mary Robles

TUNNEL VISION
BY JEREMY HEPLER

TEN minutes before sunset. One minute before the wreck. Austin, Texas. Two days ago.

Traffic on the Missouri-Pacific Highway (MoPac) was bumper to bumper as usual, moving at a steady fifty miles per hour pace. Driving the northwest library's bookmobile van, I entered the two lane tunnel Austinites call The Pac-Man in the right lane, seven cars behind the now infamous solid white armored truck. My girlfriend Kim and our five year old son Chase were five cars behind me in her Taurus. We were on our way to look at a three bedroom house I'd put a down payment on the day before, but I'd led them to believe they were following me to a new Chinese restaurant on the south side of town for a buffet dinner.

We'd lived in a small apartment for five years struggling to make ends meet, Kim and I working two jobs each at times, but unbeknownst to her I'd been saving the little chunks of money I'd made from selling my paintings online. After three years, I'd saved enough for the down payment, a new bike for Chase, and a nice ring for Kim. The red and blue bike was parked on the back porch. The ring was sitting next to Chinese takeout on the kitchen counter, hidden under the proposal poem I'd written.

Normally, when Kim and I ventured to the south side of town, we traveled via I-35 rather than MoPac to avoid going through the Pac-Man. The tunnel's nickname originated in the mid 80's not only because of its curved roof and bright yellow underbelly, brightened even more by fluorescent lights, but more notably because of its seemingly insatiable desire to chomp through cars and lives much like the little round arcade hero did to pellets and ghosts. It had been named one of the most dangerous stretches of highway in Texas for three consecutive years and is now scheduled for redesign in 2015. But excitement had gotten the better of me that day. I couldn't wait to reveal my surprise, which was located two exits south of the Pac-Man.

I was about halfway through the mile-long tunnel when I heard a loud pop. I looked up, and the next ten seconds—at least in recollection—passed in slow motion.

Bits of rubber flew from the front right tire of an RV about ten cars ahead of me in the left lane. It seesawed back and forth, scraped off of the cement wall to its left, and then crashed onto its side. Sparks flew as it skidded toward the tunnel exit and stopped with a violent jerk, blocking off the entire left lane and most of the right. The two vehicles behind the RV crashed into it, and then two more—one a motorcycle—ran into those, creating a lumpy tangle of metal that looked like some abstract sculpture.

The armored truck ramped up the motorcycle, skipped off the fender of an Escort with its front left tire, and was about to slam into the right side of the tunnel when my van hit the back of a Geo Storm and I lost consciousness. (The bookmobile only has a lap belt; my face and head whipped forward and kissed the large steering wheel, hard.)

I don't know how long I was out, but it couldn't have been more than a couple of seconds. When I came to, the chain reaction running through the tunnel like a pencil across a simple connect-the-dots hadn't ended. In the distance, I could hear blaring horns and the screeches of skidding tires and the hollow bang of metal crimping metal as I struggled to unbuckle my seat belt and stumbled out of the van.

My entire head was throbbing. My lower stomach burned where the seatbelt had dug into it. The skin on my left cheek had unzipped from chin to ear in a long arc, and I could feel warm blood dribbling down my neck. Dazed, I leaned against the side of the van and looked toward the tunnel exit.

The armored truck was angled up against the tunnel wall at about fifteen degrees. Its right side was dented in and its back doors ajar. Five other vehicles–some on all four tires, some not–had joined the huge mass of hissing metal. The heap blocked all but the top quarter of the exit where the setting sun streamed in. I saw a few people writhing inside their cars just before the row of fluorescent yellow lights lining the ceiling flickered a few times, flared, and popped out.

I'd seen news clips and pictures of more than a dozen major pile-ups in the Pac-Man over the years, and had been on the tail end of one when I was eighteen, but I hadn't seen anything like this. As the reality and the magnitude of what had happened sunk in, dreadful thoughts about Kim and Chase kick-started my legs and I took off running.

With intersecting headlight beams lighting my way, I passed an overturned Scout, climbed over the hood of a Mustang, and then weaved around five or six other vehicles before I saw Kim's Taurus. The driver's side was wedged up against a suburban. The interior light was on, and I could see Kim's black ponytail whipping around in the front seat. I ran around to the back passenger door, crawled in next to Chase and unbuckled his seat belt.

"Are you all right?" I asked Kim.

"My left leg is stuck," she answered in a strained voice. "Is *he* okay?"

I sat Chase on my lap and scanned his body. His giant brown eyes were dazed, but he wasn't crying. "Does anything hurt?" I asked him.

He shook his head.

"He seems fine," I said, "Just dazed."

I held Chase for a moment, then placed him back in his booster seat. "Sit right here for a minute, Bud. I need to help Mommy."

Kim had raised her right leg up onto the seat for leverage, twisted her body, and was trying to free her left leg with violent jerks. Pain was etched across her small, clenched face.

"Hold on," I told her. "Let me check it out."

I leaned over the seat and felt her leg. It was slick with blood and obviously broken below the knee, pinned between the caved-in door and the seat.

"It's not trapped too bad," I said, "but I don't think we should move it."

She snapped her head toward me, her canted eyes desperate for help. "I have to get out of here. I can't stay in here like this. You know I'm claustrophobic."

"But I don't think —"

"Aaron! Please!"

"Okay. If you turn back around, I think we can slip it out."

She twisted back around, facing the steering wheel. Lying down in the back floorboard, I wiggled my arm into position and placed my hand on the back of her calf.

"Now when I push, you pull up and then forward, okay?"

"Okay."

"On three. Ready? One...two...three."

I gave her calf a firm shove, and with a grunt, she jerked her leg free.

She immediately climbed into the back seat. I wrapped my arms around her, slid her out onto the road, and sat her up against the cement wall. The interior light fell across the left side of her body. A deep gash had ripped open from her calf to her mid-thigh along the outside of her left leg. Chase crawled out and she gave him a quick once-over, spinning him around and running her fingers through his thick black hair.

"Are you all right?" she asked, looking up at me.

"My head hurts a little, but I'm fine." I knelt down to examine her leg. "We have to do something about this cut. It goes all the way down to the bone around the knee."

I reached into the back seat and grabbed Kim's Whole Foods apron and one of Chase's spare T-shirts off of the floorboard. I lay the T-shirt across her open wound and tied the apron tight around her upper thigh.

"That should slow the bleeding," I said. "But you need to keep pressure on it."

Kim took in a deep breath, closed her eyes, and pushed down on the T-shirt with both hands.

"The front of the tunnel is blocked, and I don't how long it'll be until they can get paramedics in here," I said. "I'm going to run to my van and get the first aid kit. It'll only take a few minutes. I'll be right back."

I dug through the van for what seemed like hours. The books I toted around to various orphanages (on Tuesdays and Thursdays) and retirement homes (on Mondays, Wednesdays, and Fridays) were scattered all across the back of the van, and the first aid kit had fallen off its hook on the back door and was hiding somewhere within the mess. I finally found the white tin underneath a large-print copy of *Huckleberry Finn*, but when I lifted it, it felt light—too light. Inside I found only three Band-Aids, a few packets of Tylenol, and two cotton swabs. I pocketed those and crawled out of the back of the van.

On my way back to Kim's car I glanced down at the overturned scout (the headlights of another car spotlighted into it), and in the back window, next to a shimmering machete, I noticed a bold red cross on the center of a bright white box.

I stopped and ducked into the open passenger side window. An elderly man hung upside down in the driver's seat, held afloat by his seatbelt. His arms dangled like two limp noodles, his knees were angled up under the wheel. His mouth hung slightly open. His eyes stared straight ahead, as if gazing at something magical in the darkness ahead of him.

"Sir? Sir? Are you all right?" I called out, but there was no response.

Knowing that Kim's leg needed immediate attention and thinking that this man, who was wearing a wedding ring, would surely understand, I squirmed through the passenger side window on my belly, reached into the back and snatched the kit.

I was standing up when a horrific scream echoed down the tunnel. It carried a contagious fear with it that prodded me to dive back into the scout and grab the machete before I ran.

I found Kim and Chase in the same position as when I'd left. One of Kim's arms was looped tightly around Chase's shoulders, and her wide, paranoid eyes were darting left to right, left to right, scanning the road and wreckage. They relaxed when she saw me approaching.

"Did you hear that woman scream?" she asked.

I nodded.

"It sounded like..." Kim glanced down at the machete. "Where'd you get that?"

"I'll explain later." I dropped to my knees and opened the first aid kit.

This one had everything I needed: two rolls of gauze, anti-bacterial cream, iodine, tape, scissors, Band-Aids, three butterfly bandages, and along with individual packets of Tylenol, a half-full bottle of Vicodin prescribed for Paul Harris.

Moving over to Kim's leg, I found Chase's T-shirt already soaked with blood and dripping onto the road. She grabbed my wrist and groaned when I peeled it off.

"Sorry. I'll make this quick."

I handed Kim the bottle of Vicodin, poured iodine onto the gaping wound, smeared anti-bacterial cream over that (which elicited a few jerks from her as she dry-swallowed the Vicodin), pulled the wound partially closed with butterfly bandages, wrapped it with gauze, and taped it up. Then I retied the apron around her upper thigh.

When I finished, she reached for the anti-bacterial cream. She wiped the blood off my face with her hand and lathered my cut with the cream. After crossing three Band-Aids over it, she kissed my cheek and hugged me.

"I love you," she whispered into my ear.

As I rubbed her sweaty back with one hand and tousled Chase's hair with the other, I heard fast footfalls thudding on the pavement behind me. I grabbed the machete, jumped up, and spun around.

A tall man in black coveralls jogged by, repeatedly glancing back behind him. Fear sparkled in the blue eyes hovering above his blood-smeared cheeks as he passed through a set of headlight beams.

"What's going on?" I asked, stepping toward him.

He never looked at me, but I could hear him whispering, "It's out... it's out... it's out..."

After he drifted out of earshot, another horrid wail soared through the tunnel.

"We have to get out of here,' I said. "Something's not right." I took Chase's arm and pulled him upright. "We have to help Mommy get up so we can walk that way. Be a big boy and help Daddy, all right?"

He nodded.

"I don't think I can walk," Kim said.

"When I lift you up, throw your arm over my shoulder, and I'll help you hop on your good foot. Chase, grab Mommy's hand and hold it tight."

"What did that man say?" Kim asked as I helped her up and we headed deeper into the tunnel.

"He said, 'it's out, it's out, it's out.' And he looked terrified."

"What's out?"

"I don't know, and I don't want to find out."

◉   ◉   ◉

The wreckage became easier to maneuver through the farther we went. Most of the people had exited their vehicles. A few people were headed the same direction we were, others just stood around, stunned. Injured people littered the tunnel. Some leaned on bumpers, others sat on their hoods, others in the road.

We passed a giant graffiti Pac-Man someone had spray-painted on the wall about a third of the way into the tunnel a couple of years back. About ten yards ahead of that, nine or ten people were standing around a Saturn. Three of them stood in the headlight beams arguing. A jack-knifed, swivel-head Penske truck and a mini-van blocked all but a small gap of the road behind them.

All of their heads snapped toward us when Kim blurted out: "I need to rest for a minute."

A fat man in a pinstriped suit standing in the headlights aimed his gun at us and we froze. He stood motionless for a moment, then lowered the gun and turned back around. The man in black coveralls was standing directly in front of him. Another guy, a college student I guessed from his Radiohead T-shirt and baggy jeans, stood next to Pinstripe, smoking a cigarette.

I helped Kim sit down and lean back against an Explorer's tire about twenty feet to the left of the Saturn. Chase sat down beside her and snuggled close. She threw her arm around him, kissed his head, and then let out a long, shaky breath.

"It'll be all right," I told her, kneeling down and taking her hand. "When that Vicodin kicks in, it should take some of the edge off." I gave her hand a firm squeeze, and we held eye contact for a moment. "I'm going to go see what's going on over there real quick."

I kissed her hand and walked over to the Saturn and stood at the back of the group, angled where I could keep an eye on her and Chase. I noticed that the cigarette in the young guy's hand was actually a clove. Definitely a college student, I thought. He was questioning the man in black.

"What was in your truck then?"

"I don't know," the man said, keeping his eyes on Pinstripe's gun. "I already told you, I'm just a driver."

"Bullshit! If it was in your truck you have to know something."

"No, I don't. I'm just a driver."

"Who do you work for?" the kid asked as he stomped out his clove. "The government?"

"I don't —"

"Yes you do." Pinstripe interjected, raising his gun and tapping it on the man's chest.

"They didn't tell me. I swear."

"He's lying," the kid said.

"You *know* what was in that truck," Pinstripe added.

"No, I don't. And I don't think we should stand here talking about it either."

Pinstripe pointed the gun at the man's face. "You came over here looking scared shitless saying '*it's* out, *it's* out.' Now why would you say it like that if you don't even know what the hell *it* is?"

"Because I heard it breathing... or hissing... or something," Sweat drizzled down the man's face. "And then it grabbed a woman crawling out of her car back there and... and...."

"He knows more than that," the kid insisted.

"I agree," Pinstripe said. He moved the gun closer to the man's face. "Well?"

The man's lower lip quivered, and he squeezed his eyes tight. A second or two later they sprang open. "The trackers who loaded it into my truck were talking about a cave with carvings in South America... or South Africa... or South something. That's all I heard though. I swear. I told you, I'm just –"

A woman's piercing scream cut the man off. She sounded close. My fingers tightened around the machete handle. When her screams stopped, a loud, eerie, I heard a rhythmic rustling that sounded like millions of leaves spiraling around in a tight formation on a blustery fall afternoon.

After a brief pause, everyone around the Saturn bolted toward the Penske truck and the mini-van in a panic. Some of them squeezed through the gap, some climbed over the vehicles, and others crawled underneath them.

Holding Chase, Kim was trying to stand. Chase gazed at me over her shoulder as I ran toward them. He looked confused and scared. I took him from Kim, and we rushed toward the small gap.

As Chase sidled between the two vehicles, a deafening gunshot rang out up ahead of us. I jerked him back and held him against my leg for a moment, but when the ringing in my ears subsided and the rustling became audible behind us again, I quickly nudged him onward.

I held the machete high and stood guard while Kim slowly worked her way through the gap, and after I squeezed through, I ducked under her arm, Chase grabbed her hand, and we hurried off.

There was less wreckage in the last section of the tunnel, but the road had a slight incline making it difficult for us nonetheless. Other than a young couple who stood arguing in front of a Corvette, and two people who ran around us, we didn't see anyone as we trudged uphill, trying to outrun the rustle.

After a couple of grueling minutes, the mouth of the tunnel came into view. The night sky was out, the moon visible just above the horizon.

"Look," I said, pointing with the machete. "There's the –"

I broke off when Kim moaned and fell limp, forcing all her one hundred and twenty-five pounds onto me. I squatted her to the ground. She looked pale. The gauze-wrap on her leg was dripping with blood, the apron on her thigh loose.

I quickly stooped over to retighten the apron, and as I finished, another gut-wrenching scream sailed down the tunnel. A few seconds later, the man who'd been arguing with a woman in front of the Corvette sprinted by us.

"We have to go," I said. "It's not much farther."

"I don't think I can..." Kim whispered, her eyes nearly closed.

I turned toward Chase. "I'm going to pick up Mommy and carry her the rest of the way. I want you to stay right next to me and hold on to my pants, okay?"

He didn't respond but grabbed my left pant leg.

I pulled Kim up, lay her belly-down over my left shoulder (I'm only two inches taller and thirty pounds heavier than she is), and we continued on. I struggled to hold her in place using only my left hand and held the machete in my right.

When we were about twenty yards away from the mouth of the tunnel I saw a fire truck and an ambulance approaching on the center median. The first four paramedics on the scene were tending to people on the pavement. Pinstripe and the clove-smoking college kid were standing with a large cluster of people around one of the three police cruisers.

I exited the tunnel, trotted another twenty yards, and lay Kim down. One of the paramedics ran over to us and knelt beside her. I turned around to pick up Chase, but he wasn't there. He was standing just outside the mouth of the tunnel, facing me, starry-eyed, and two large black hands with uneven, jagged fingers were emerging from the darkness behind him.

"No!" I screamed, rushing toward him.

I jerked him up by his shirt and tossed him aside. As I cocked the machete and backed up, an awkward, hunched creature stepped out into the moonlight. It took three slow steps forward and stopped about five feet to my left. It was solid black, dull black, uniform black, and crude—as if some mad mechanic with no eye for detail had used a stash of dirty oil to sculpt the foulest beast his weak imagination could conjure and then jolted it to life with a car battery and jumper cables. Its gnarled hands were attached to long, unnaturally thin arms, and the feet, attached to similarly thin, slightly bent legs, mirrored the hands. When it turned its oblong head my direction, it didn't have any obvious eyes, or a hole for a mouth, or an exact nose, or ears, though it had vague divots and protrusions that slightly resembled those things. But the one thing that was glaringly obvious was that its skin was rippling, and that the ripples increased in size as the rustling sound, which seemed to be coming out of its entire body rather than a mouth, intensified.

Driven by a primal instinct to destroy anything that threatened my offspring, I lunged at the monster and slashed at its neck. Looking back, I think now that this may have been exactly what it wanted because it didn't react. Its head sloughed off without resistance and slapped onto the ground with a splat, like a large brick of warm butter. The body briefly tottered, then fell on top of the head. There were no bones or tendons inside the neck or base of the head to hint at structure. It was black and gooey, nothing more.

I was slowly back-pedaling with the machete cocked, watching the ripples slow, listening to the rustle fade, when one of the feet twitched and I lunged forward and began chopping at the decapitated body, screaming. I must have sliced through it twenty or thirty good times before I dropped the machete and went down to a knee with my back to the mutilated creature.

I took a few deep breaths, knuckled my eyes, blotted the sweat from my face, and was just getting back to my feet when the rustling started up behind me again. I sprinted forward a ways and spun around. The individual pieces of gelatinous flesh that I'd chopped the body into had morphed into rippling spheres and were rolling away from one another. And growing. I watched in disbelief as each blob became a slender torso and sprouted thin arms and legs, large, crooked hands and feet, and oblong, indistinct heads.

They stumbled around like newborn deer for a second or two before coalescing in a mass at the edge of the tunnel. Their collective rustle escalated for what seemed like hours, but it couldn't have been more than a minute before they rushed toward us, fanning out, galloping on all fours. Terrified screams shot across the humid night air.

I turned around and saw Chase walking toward Kim, about fifteen feet behind me. I darted toward him with outstretched arms, yelling his name, but one of the creatures slammed into my back and knocked me over. I jumped up quick but didn't see Chase anywhere in the chaos—people were running, the creatures chasing. The rustle was deafening, disorienting. Gunshots rang out. I was spinning in frantic circles searching for Chase when the rustle suddenly cut off and the all creatures stopped moving. A few seconds later, they stood up on their hind legs and dashed off, each clutching at least one victim in their hands. As they disappeared into the dark hills on the west side of MoPac, I sprinted to the edge of the pavement yelling Chase's name over and over, louder and louder, hoping he'd come running back and dive into my arms. But he didn't. He was gone.

Trembling, I looked back and saw Kim lying alone on the road, her head slightly angled up. I ran over to her, knelt down, and clasped her arm.

"Chase?" she whispered, her eyes begging for the right answer.

"He's... he's...gone," I stammered. "They took him... they... I couldn't... I... I'm sorry... I... I... couldn't..." She slowly shook her head and tears started streaming down her cheeks, but she never said another word.

It's been two days now, and she still hasn't spoken. She won't eat or drink, either. I'm staying with her at a psychiatric facility on the south side of town where she's under evaluation. I bathe her and read to her and brush her hair ...and try not to cry in front of her.

She'll probably never know about the three bedroom house I put the down payment on. I don't think I'll ever go back there, anyway. Not even to get the ring. It's not worth it. Seeing the bike would hurt too much.

We haven't gotten any answers about Chase or what was in the tunnel yet. I've heard rumors that the police and military officials found nine bodies inside the Pac-Man. Supposedly, they were shriveled and black and unidentifiable. Supposedly, around fifty more unidentifiable bodies have been found over the past day and a half in a wooded area north and northwest of Lake Travis. But nothing has been confirmed or denied on the news.

Some Austinites think the government's responsible, that the creatures are aliens or genetically spliced humans or something. Others, citing old Mayan and Aztec stories, claim the original creature was the guardian of the entrance to the underworld. Others are in denial; they think the whole story's absurd, inaccurate, and misconstrued, that the creatures don't exist, can't exist. I personally don't know who's to blame, if anyone, but I do know that the story you're reading is accurate and the creatures most definitely exist. I also know that wherever they're from, whatever they are, they're spreading, fast (some people are saying a soft rustle was heard outside of San Antonio last night) and everything we're doing to defend ourselves and protect our families—like my hack job for example, and like what a farmer did with a shotgun in San Marcos yesterday—is helping them multiply.

Right now, as I type this with Kim silently staring out the window next to me, I can hear an ominous rustling outside, and it sounds louder than it did last night. If you close your eyes at night and listen well, I'm certain that in the near future you'll hear it too, no matter where you are.

NOT YOUR AVERAGE MONSTER

Jeremy Hepler is a stay-at-home dad who lives the Texas Panhandle with his wife and son. In the past six years he's had twenty-three short stories published in periodicals, anthologies, and online. Most recently, he placed second in the Panhandle Professional Writer's Short Story Competition and is shopping his first novel, The Boulevard Monster.

Contact or follow him via Twitter: @JeremyHepler where you will find links to his blog and Facebook author page.

ONLY A MATTER OF TIME

BY ROSE BLACKTHORN

BLOOD; there was so much blood. Splashed on the walls, splattered across the ceiling, and the floor—the floor was awash with blood. It filled the room, almost an inch deep. Missy sat in a corner, not moving, barely breathing. The seat of her pants was soaked with blood, her shoes saturated and squishy with blood. She closed her eyes; the coppery meaty *raw* smell filled her nostrils. She wouldn't breathe through her mouth, because she could taste the rich scent on her tongue.

From somewhere beyond the room, there was a growling grunting sound, and she didn't move because she didn't want to draw any attention to herself. The door to the hall was open about a foot, the only light in the room a narrow slice of glare from that opening. She had shifted once, planning to get to her feet, and had seen the shallow ripples travel across the pool of blood. If something was out in the hall, and saw ripples moving across the floor, it would know she was in here. It would come inside to find her.

So she sat still, listening to the vicious, hungry sounds coming from somewhere else in the school. This was like one of Gram's horror vids, she thought. The genre was dead; the powers that be had determined horror and violence and scripted fear were not good for the mass psyche, and so all the old movies and books had been destroyed. No one these days would even admit to ever having seen one of those old shows, or read those old books. They were still available on the black market, but were a major taboo. Missy only knew about them because of Gram.

Gram had grown up before the government took complete control, deciding what was good for people, and banning what was bad for them. She had loved the old movies; creature features, slasher flicks, demonic possession and ghost stories. She'd seen them all, so she said—Freddy Krueger and Jason, Aliens and Poltergeist, Dracula and the Wolfman and zombies galore. During the day, out in public, she was the perfect picture of propriety. A grandmother who had taken in her orphaned grandchildren, hair pulled back into an elegant twist and bleached-white teeth belying the black market cigarettes she smoked on the sly. But at night, safe in her own home, she regaled Missy and her brother Billy and their younger siblings with stories of mummies, swamp creatures, and in-bred hillbillies searching for young nubile breeding stock.

Missy thought about her Gram's stories while she stayed perfectly still in her hiding place behind the teacher's desk. Her arms were locked around her knees, hugging them to her chest to stop her shaking. The guttural noises continued unabated outside of this small classroom. The windows were dark, no security lights brightening the panes. The room was shadowed, and she was glad; she didn't want to look at her dead classmates anymore. They were ripped and slashed, disemboweled and beheaded, a gore-fest that surely would have delighted Gram. It would have brought back so many fond memories of her childhood.

Another thing that Gram had told her grandkids about was the heroes of those old forbidden movies. There was always one person, sometimes even someone as young as Missy herself, who was brave enough and smart enough to survive the attack of whatever kind of monster was ravening through the plot. That one person would sometimes be able to kill the monster, and sometimes just escape with their life. After all, that's where the sequels came from. Missy wondered if maybe she was meant to be the hero of this nightmare. She had no intention of trying to hunt down and kill the monster that had massacred everyone except her in this classroom, and possibly the rest of the school. All she wanted was to be smart enough and brave enough to survive. If nothing else, if she could make her way to the safety of her home, surely Gram would have enough forbidden knowledge to know how to fight it.

Slowly, breathing shallowly so she wouldn't miss any warning sound, Missy braced her back against the wall and her feet on the blood-washed floor, and carefully pushed herself up to a standing position. Out in the hallway, or maybe in the room across the hall, the ripping and meaty chewing sounds continued. Cautiously and as quietly as she could, Missy crept toward the door. She stayed close to the wall, partly to stay out of the thin slice of light coming through the doorway, and partly to use the wall for support. Her feet were cold in her blood soaked sneakers, and the blood had begun to congeal in the treads, making the floor even more slippery.

When she finally reached the door, she took a long slow breath to calm herself and cautiously looked around the edge. For a moment she could see nothing; the brighter light in the hallway struck her dilated eyes like a knife edge, and tears welled as she forced herself to focus.

There was blood in the hallway as well, though it hadn't pooled on the floor as it had in her classroom. It was splashed in garish swipes along the boring taupe-colored walls, and even up to the white foam drop-ceiling tiles. The monster that had savaged the students was not in the hallway, but there were two bodies crumpled against the wall; one missing its head, the other disemboweled and with ropey lengths of gut strung along the hallway.

Missy pressed the back of her hand to her mouth, waiting for nausea to reveal her presence to the monster, but she didn't become sick. She could hear wet tearing sounds down the hall to her left, toward the administrative offices. All the rest of the building was now silent. If there were any other survivors, they were as mute as the dead. As quietly as she was able, she slipped through the doorway without opening it any further, and stepped into the hallway, turning right.

A disembodied head lay against the wall just past the door, its neck ragged and wet, its expression more surprised than afraid. Missy recognized the face. Mr. Jenkins had been her English teacher, a man who had seemed lost since so much of the curriculum had been deemed unfit for the student body. He'd been left with spelling, grammar and punctuation, no longer allowed to teach poetry or classic literature.

Missy gingerly stepped around the head and continued down the hall. In about a hundred feet there was an intersecting hall, and if she turned right she would be to an exit door in another hundred. She gave a moment's thought to heading for the gym, where her older brother Billy would have been when the carnage started. But all she wanted was to get out of this abattoir and back to Gram's house. Once there they could call the police. Once there, she would be safe.

She had made it almost to the intersecting hallway when a shadow loomed from the left. She bit her bottom lip, glancing quickly around; her only choice was to enter one of the rooms either right or left just behind her. But both doors were closed, and she was afraid that opening one would alert the creature to her presence. How had it gotten ahead of her?

With no time to deliberate, she quickly stepped back to the last door, reaching for the handle with one blood-covered hand. Her attention was on the shadow, waiting for the monster to come into sight. When she turned the handle and pushed on the door, her back foot slipped. She was unable to silence the squeak that came from her throat as she fell, hand still locked on the doorknob, and then a cry of pain as her shoulder nearly dislocated.

The monster came around the corner into the hallway, less than twenty feet from her. Missy scrambled, trying to scoot back into the classroom, her hand still clutching the doorknob, tears of pain stinging her eyes.

It was tall, standing on two strangely bent legs and hunched over to keep from striking its head on the ceiling. Long arms dangled from wide shoulders, ending in viciously clawed hands covered liberally in gore. It had long dark hair hanging down from a narrow misshapen head, and fangs glistened in its open maw. It grunted, long tongue snaking out as it licked its upper lip, and it started toward her.

Missy crabbed backwards into the room, startling a cry from herself when she backed into another dead body. A quick glance revealed Mrs. Roberts. The science teacher had been clawed open from throat to crotch, her organs spread around her as though on display. Missy bit her lip hard and crawled away from the body, seeing without really understanding that ten-penny nails had been used like dissecting pins to hold the teacher's chest and abdominal cavity open.

Another yowling grunt brought her attention back to the monster that was maneuvering its way through the doorway to follow her. She hurried to the window, her blood-soaked shoes slipping on the floor. The window was locked, and with shaking fingers she tried to release the latch.

Behind her the monster approached, a low throaty grunting coming from it that Missy guessed was laughter. Her heart was pounding, her fingers slipping again and again from the lock, and she knew suddenly that she wasn't the hero of this horror story. She was just another one of the victims.

A high-pitched shriek came from the hallway, and both Missy and the monster wheeled toward the sound. Outside the open door was a second thing, bent and contorted like an old gnarled tree. Blood and viscera covered its face, chest and belly. Like the first one it had long stringy hair, talon-tipped fingers and sharp fangs filling its mouth. But this second one was larger, wrinkled as well as horrifyingly misshapen, and made no effort to hide the drooping breasts that revealed it was female.

Missy screamed, beating her clenched fists on the stubborn window.

The monster in the hallway snarled at the one in the room, and the smaller creature slumped and turned its head away. There was a moment when it seemed the larger monster was berating the smaller.

The window wouldn't open, and the glass wouldn't break. Missy felt dizzy, light-headed from fear and dehydration and the overpowering stench of dying people. She fell back into the corner, curling up into a ball, "Like a pill-bug," she thought to herself. She tucked her head down, wrapping her arms around it, hoping only that when they came to kill her they would do it quickly. She didn't want to scream and scream as so many of her classmates and teachers had done.

The growling had stopped, but Missy heard movement. She didn't lift her head or open her eyes, just scrunching in upon herself as much as she could, wanting to become the *size* of a pill-bug. There were scraping, scratching sounds and the harsh stuttering screech of a chair being shoved across the linoleum floor. Missy flinched and shuddered, biting the inside of her cheek to keep from screaming.

For a long moment it was quiet, just the muffled thunder of her heart pounding in her chest, and the thin high whistle of breath being forced through her constricted throat. Then, far off in the distance, the shrill warble of a siren. Across the room, perhaps from the doorway, there was a heavy sigh.

Missy didn't want to look, but suddenly had to know. Was one of them crouched over her, just waiting for her to peek? She couldn't simply cower in the corner and pretend they weren't real. She turned her head a fraction of an inch, lifting her arm just enough to steal a glimpse.

Mrs. Roberts still lay motionless on the floor, ripped skin pulled wide and nailed to the floor on either side, her organs placed artistically around her—except where Missy had scrambled through the viscera to reach the window. Blood was pooled beneath the dead teacher, smeared and splattered messily around her. The creature that had followed Missy into the room was gone, long bloody footprints showing its return back to the hallway. Standing in the open doorframe was the female monster, staring back at her.

Missy froze, holding her breath, unable to take her eye away from the thing that gazed at her. As though it knew she was watching, it tipped its head to one side and bared its teeth. The siren was getting closer, maybe more than one, and Missy wondered who had gotten away and called for help.

The monster turned its head, seeming to consider the approaching sirens. Then with teeth still bared, it wiggled its claws at her, a parody of waving goodbye. Without a sound, moving as lightly as a nightmare, it disappeared from view.

Missy stayed in the corner, pretending to be a pill-bug, until the police officer shone his light into the room. He exclaimed at the sight of the teacher, and swore when he caught a glimpse of Missy.

"Get a medic, Charlie! There's a live one in here!" he called over his shoulder, then picked his way around the displayed entrails to crouch near her. "It's okay sweetheart. You're safe now."

"Are they gone?" she whispered, squeezing her eyes shut. "Are the monsters gone?"

Paramedics loaded her onto a gurney and carted her outside, taking the route she'd been trying to make on her own. Flashing lights in bright blue and red strobed the front of the school. Someone had finally gotten the security lights on, and white spots reflected from darkened windows. Left unattended, Missy got off the gurney and huddled just inside the open door at the back of the ambulance. She clutched a faded blue blanket someone had draped over her around her shoulders, trying to stop shaking. Men and women in uniform went in and out of the school, all of them pale and grim-faced in the stark lighting.

One of the policemen had asked Missy's name and home number so they could call Gram. She didn't know what she would say to the old woman who had taken her in along with her four siblings after their parents died. She didn't know what had happened to Billy, and didn't know how to explain her survival if he was dead like so many others. At least the three younger ones hadn't been here.

By the time Gram arrived, there were two rows of covered bodies on the grass before the school. Parents had shown up in long lines of cars, some screaming and crying while others prayed silently, waiting to find out if their children were alive or dead. When Gram strode to the ambulance where Missy still rested, straight-backed and thin as a heron with her long gray hair hanging loose rather than pulled back in its usual twist, the paramedics were bringing out another live one.

"That one's mine as well," Gram called, a haughty tone to her voice as though she were issuing orders to the rescue personnel. "Stand up straight, Billy."

Missy's older brother stood straighter with a grimace, and the paramedics on either side of him exchanged an aggravated glance. Billy was liberally covered with blood, and was walking with a pronounced limp. With so much blood, it was hard to tell where he was injured.

"There's no need to baby them," Gram went on, as imperious as a queen, and she flashed a bleached-white smile. "I'll take them home now. They'll be fine."

"Ms. Megara, they need to go to the hospital," one of the paramedics said with forced patience. "They have to be checked for injuries, and everything documented for evidence."

Gram snorted, "Don't be silly. They need to get cleaned up and rest. They can do that best at home." She reached into the ambulance and took Missy's wrist in a gentle grip. "Come now, Missy. Let's get you home."

"Ms. Megara, really I must insist..." the other paramedic said, but Gram just ignored him.

"It's alright, my girl," Gram said, her tone gentle for her eldest granddaughter. "This time tomorrow you'll feel back to your old self."

Missy stepped down, pausing to lay the borrowed blanket on the gurney. When she turned back, she noticed something odd. Gram was wearing sandals, the ones she could just slip on in a hurry. And there was blood on her toes.

"Come on, *baby*," Billy said soft enough that the paramedics couldn't hear him. "Cowering in a corner. Thought you were tougher than that," he added, limping along beside her.

"That's enough," Gram said sharp and low, giving him a pointed look. "Keep it up, and no more scary stories for you."

Billy hunched his shoulders, turning his head away at the chastisement, reminding Missy of something she'd seen earlier.

Gram led them to her old car and helped Missy into the front passenger seat. Billy slid into the back at another hard look from Gram. Before the old woman could get in the driver's seat, one of the police officers caught up to them.

Missy could hear him arguing with Gram, but she just kept cutting him off.

"Ms. Megara, the kids have to –"

"Officer Neeley, I am taking them home. I'm not arguing with you about it."

"There are procedures that must —"

"It's going to be a madhouse at the hospital, and it'll be more than the ER can handle, Officer. My kids are okay, they're just in shock. I'm taking them home."

"We have to document —"

"Not another word. You have plenty to take care of here. I'm going to take care of my own."

"But —"

He was still standing on the curb with his mouth hanging open when Gram got into the car and pulled away.

The house was quiet and dark when they got there. It was set back from the road in a stand of old trees and wasn't even visible until the car's headlights struck the screened-in front porch. Gram parked and removed the key from the ignition. She looked at Billy in the rear-view mirror, and simply nodded once.

Then she turned to Missy. "Come on now, my girl. Let's get you cleaned up."

Missy accepted Gram's steady hand for support going up the stairs, noting without commenting that Billy's pronounced limp was now missing. "Where's Ginny and Pete and Randy?" she asked softly as Billy opened the front door and flipped on the lights.

"They stayed at a friend's house tonight," Gram answered.

"That's good," Missy whispered, and let Gram lead her to the big downstairs bathroom and pull shut the door.

"I'll start a bath for you," Gram said, leaning over to turn the hot water on. "Are you hurt anywhere?"

Missy kicked off her blood-soaked sneakers, now tacky and hard to slide off. "My shoulder," she answered, sliding her blood-stiffened jeans down her legs to lie crumpled in their slaughterhouse stench. Her t-shirt was next, then panties and bra. "I wrenched it when I fell."

Gram nodded, checking the temperature of the water, then turned to look at Missy with a circumspect gaze. "Get in then, child. The hot water will help."

Missy stepped into the deep claw-foot tub and cautiously sat down. Immediately the water turned pink.

"I know this seems a mighty tragedy," Gram said, leaning over to pick up Missy's soiled clothing. "Death is always hard on the survivors. You already know that. But people die every day, my dear. Even if no one talks about it anymore."

"Can I ask you something?" Missy asked, her voice barely above a whisper. The water gushing from the faucet almost drowned her out.

"Of course," Gram replied, with Missy's bloody clothing draped over her arm.

"How did you get blood on your feet?"

Gram looked down thoughtfully, wiggling her toes as she studied the rusty red stains.

"How did you know me and Billy weren't hurt?" Missy went on, guessing the answer but still afraid to hear it. "How did he know I hid in the corner like a baby?"

Gram sighed. It was a heavy sigh, reminiscent of something Missy had heard earlier. Like the sigh from the monster in the hallway. The one that had smiled at her, and waved.

Gram looked up and met her gaze directly, not so much as if to stare her down, but as if she were deciding. Then she tipped her head and smiled, revealing dazzling white teeth. "Why do you think I've been sharing all my old horror stories with you, Missy? In this day and age, when you're protected from everything that the higher-ups think might damage you, you still have to learn about your heritage."

"And Billy?" Missy asked. Hearing the truth wasn't as bad as she'd thought it would be. In some ways, it explained a lot of things.

Gram's smile faded, and that stern expression came back into her eyes. "He was out of control, and there'll be a reckoning for that. Going after his own sister!" and she *tsk*ed as though utterly disgusted. "You finish your bath, my dear. Take as long as you like. When you're done, I expect you'll have more questions."

"Mom and Dad?"

Gram nodded once, her expression grim. "Yes, them too." Then she left with Missy's ruined clothes and closed the bathroom door behind her.

Missy soaked in the tub until the water cooled and her skin pruned. Search as she might, she was unable to find sign of a claw, fang or any unexpected new joints that would make her limbs bend the wrong way. But she suspected it was only a matter of time.

Rose Blackthorn lives in the high mountain desert with her boyfriend and two dogs, Boo and Shadow. She spends her free time writing, reading, being crafty, and photographing the surrounding wilderness.

She is a member of the HWA and her short fiction and poetry has appeared online and in print with a varied list of anthologies and magazines. Her first poetry collection Thorns, Hearts and Thistles was published in February 2015, and is available through Amazon.

More information can be found at the following links:

- ➤ *Twitter - https://twitter.com/rose_blackthorn*
- ➤ *Blog - http://roseblackthorn.wordpress.com/*
- ➤ *Facebook - http://www.facebook.com/RoseBlackthorn. Author*
- ➤ *Amazon - http://amazon.com/author/roseblackthorn*
- ➤ *Goodreads - https://www.goodreads.com/author/show /5758684. Rose_Blackthorn*

THE GOLDBUG
BY JASON PARENT

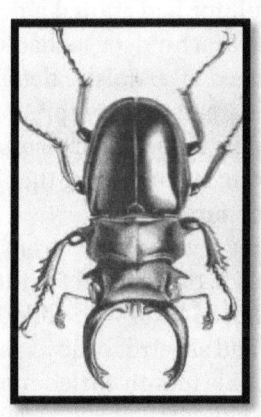

NOT YOUR AVERAGE MONSTER

IT called to him. Karl spotted the figurine as soon as he entered the novelty shop. He whizzed by pewter trinkets, costume jewelry, antiquated rocking horses, creepy looking monkeys mindlessly banging cymbals together and an army of waving porcelain kitties. None compared to the object of his desire.

He had never seen anything like it. Coleoptera? No. Ixodida? Whatever class it belonged to didn't matter. It was something new, unique. Karl was certain of it. Even if it was only a cheap replica, he sensed power in it, something radiant and alive. He reached for it, but stopped short, afraid he might damage it.

He leaned in close. What amazing craftsmanship. The figurine might have been a brooch of some sort, or perhaps a tie clasp or an over-sized cufflink missing its mate. From afar, he'd guessed it was a model of an unknown insect, but the eight legs he now counted told him otherwise. This arachnid, segmented like an ant but with short, multi-jointed legs and an abdomen as fat as a blood-gorged tick's, was unlike any specimen he'd ever examined.

Either the statuette's sculptor had crafted a fictional creature that blurred the lines between insect and arachnid, or he had captured through art an unclassified species. Entranced by exquisite detail—the striations in the exoskeleton, the crisscrossing patterns comprising its two strainer-like fly eyes, and the sharp edges of its inch-long incisors, Karl had the strange conviction that he was looking at something that had once existed or might yet exist. He had to know for sure.

"She's a beauty, isn't she?" a voice called from behind him. Karl jumped, startled out of his thoughts. He turned and for the first time noticed a short, dark-skinned man with a shaved head who glided toward him from the other side of the room. The man had shrewd, beady eyes, buried behind thick-rimmed glasses. One side of his mouth curled into a thin smile, while the other side was pressed into a flat line. Pockmarks marred his cheeks. He wore a white-button down three sizes too big for him that hung like a dress over black slacks and sandaled feet.

He slipped behind the display counter, his half-smile unwavering. "It's twenty-four carat gold."

"I doubt that." Karl downplayed his interest, though he already knew he'd be buying the little masterpiece.

The salesman raised his right hand. "It's pure gold, scout's honor." He made a "V" with his index and middle fingers.

Karl had never been a Boy Scout, but he'd been in enough back alley antiquity shops to know that their salespeople generally lacked honor. He shook his head. The insect-arachnid statuette didn't look cheaply constructed, but he was sure it was made out of lead or a more malleable metal, aluminum maybe, then dipped in gold paint. He saw no chipping to lend credence to his theory, but only an idiot would place a gold nugget the size of his palm on a shelf where anyone could steal it. The salesman, who Karl assumed owned the place, was probably shady, but he didn't look stupid.

"What do you call it?" Karl asked.

"Ah, that's a rarity indeed! We call it the goldbug, because—"

"Let me guess: because of the Edgar Allen Poe story."

"No, because it's gold, and it's a bug."

"Very original." Karl sighed. "It's actually not a bug. It's an arachnid. You can tell by its eight—"

"Arachnids are bugs."

"No they aren't. Insects are bugs. Arachnids are arachnids."

"What makes you the expert?"

Karl smiled. "I'm an entomologist."

The shopkeeper's forehead crinkled. "A what now?"

"An entomol... a bug expert."

"That must really help with the ladies."

Karl rolled his eyes and released a breath. He tired of the conversation. He just wanted to buy the damn thing and bring it home so that he could study it closely without interruption.

"So, how much?"

"I was selling it for one fifty, but since you're a big-time entomologist, one seventy-five."

"What? You're crazy! This thing's worth five bucks tops."

"Okay, okay. Maybe it's not pure gold, but it's gold plated. Pick it up. See for yourself."

Karl's eyes widened. He couldn't resist. As his fingers moved toward the statuette, the store owner grabbed his arm.

"Careful. Those pincer things are sharp. They've pricked me more than a few times."

With his thumb and forefinger, Karl gripped the goldbug by its midsection and lifted it from the shelf. It was heavier than he'd anticipated. Afraid it might slip from his grasp, he rested it gently upside-down on his other hand and ran his fingertips down its underside.

"Remarkable," he said aloud, forgetting to disguise his admiration. "So detailed..." The goldbug's entire exoskeleton was covered with an intricate mesh of tiny hexagons. The pattern made it look almost granular. Like sand? Camouflage? Karl was more convinced than ever that the figurine replicated a real creature that once existed—maybe still existed—somewhere in the world.

"Where did this goldbug come from?"

"Africa."

"Could you be more specific?"

"The desert."

Karl rubbed his forehead. Desert insects and spiders could be large and strange, so the source was plausible, but it was maddeningly nonspecific. Did the man really know that little about his merchandise?

"The Sahara Desert?" Karl clenched his jaw. "Or the Kalahari desert?"

"Don't know. People who live there don't have return addresses."

The Bedouins and the San didn't do this kind of art work, either. "So how did you get it?"

"Mail."

Karl's frustration mounted. "So how did you pay...? Oh, forget it!" *I'll figure out this creature's origins myself.*

"I'll give you fifty bucks for it," he said.

"It's worth eight times that."

"You just said you normally price it at one fifty."

"Did I? One fifty then."

"Fifty."

"A hundred."

"Seventy-five?"

"Deal."

The shop owner extended his hand. Karl didn't take it. Carrying the goldbug as if it were a Fabergé egg, he followed the man to the counter. Reluctantly, he set his treasure down and pulled out his wallet. The shopkeeper packaged the statuette in bubble wrap, placed it in a small cardboard box and dropped it into a bag. Karl gave the shopkeeper eighty dollars, received his change and headed out the door with his purchase. On his way out, he passed several No Returns signs posted conspicuously everywhere his gaze moved. He'd been so entranced by the goldbug he hadn't seen them on his way in, but it didn't matter.

He cradled the package close to his body. "Don't worry," he whispered. "I have no intention of returning you."

He jumped into his car and placed the bag on the seat beside him. After turning the key in the ignition, his hand instinctively went to adjust the heat. He hadn't realized until then how cold the store had been, almost as chilly as the outdoors.

Is he too cheap to put on the heat? Karl shrugged, rubbed his palms together and drove off.

He headed straight home, eager to learn what he could about the mysterious creature the figurine portrayed. If it had been an actual specimen, it would have been an extraordinary scientific find. His gut told him that the scientific community was not aware of the creature's existence, had somehow passed it over in surveys of African desert arthropods and entomofauna. He imagined the laurels that would come his way if he could he present his peers with a newly discovered species.

But a species of what? Its leg count suggested arachnid, its segmentation insect. It was closest in appearance to a large stag beetle. The goldbug's protruding mandibles, curved like scimitars, resembled those found on the males of several of the 1,200 Lucanidae species, save for their unusual size and sharpness. Karl wondered if the statuette's creator might have been frightened of the creature and played up its more monstrous features in his rendition.

As he drove, he studied it in his mind. *Maybe it's some kind of crustacean.* He rubbed his forehead. *I'll have to classify it correctly, or I'll look like a fool.* He recalled its feet. They did look like little lobster legs, bi-segmented but much sharper, like needle-nose pliers with honed edges and actual needle points. *Maybe it was some relative of a crawfish that had evolved to survive where water had long since dried out.* Karl wouldn't rule out the possibility. He knew what this discovery could mean for him. He laughed. *I'll certainly give it a better name than "goldbug."* Something that incorporated a Latinized version of his own name, he presumed. For now, though, goldbug suited it just fine.

He pulled into his driveway and hustled into his home, a small cottage forty miles outside the city, which he shared with his house cat, a black longhair named Beetle Bailey. Bailey was the best friend Karl could ask for: largely self-sufficient and rarely in the way.

Karl headed into the kitchen and placed the box on the counter. Bailey was perched on his cat-shelf in the window, waiting for him. Karl bent over to pet him and the cat nudged his forehead against Karl's cheek. As Karl stroked him behind the ear, Bailey purred, offering his caregiver a few more gentle headbutts. The house was cold, so Karl adjusted the thermostat. After feeding his pet, he grabbed his laptop and sat with it at his dining room table. While the computer powered on, he got up to brew a pot of coffee, then retrieved the box containing his prized purchase and carried it over to the table. When he opened it and looked inside, his breath caught in his throat. The goldbug was gone.

Calm down. It's not as if it could walk off. He examined the box. At one of its bottom edges where interlocking tabs overlapped one another, he found a space that was large enough for a small object to escape. It looked as if it had been sliced open. Karl immediately imagined the worst -- that its sharp edges had penetrated the packing materials and it had fallen in the street.

He glanced at the counter and released a loud sigh of relief. The goldbug sat next to where the box had been. That was lucky.

Delicately, he carried the goldbug to the table and placed it beside his computer. Although he treated it as if it were fragile, he guessed that he could have whipped it against the wall without so much as scratching it. "What are you?" he asked it in a reverent whisper.

He spent the next half hour panning through his files and those of the university where he taught. During that time, Bailey crunched away on his cat food. When he finished, he leapt onto the table for some human affection. But when he saw the goldbug, his attitude changed.

The cat emitted a low, guttural growl. His back arched and his tail stood erect. He slowly backed away from the figurine, hissing and swatting at it.

"What's gotten into you?" Karl asked. He couldn't recall a time when Bailey had been so upset. He tried to pet him, but Bailey kept swatting. His claws connected with the back of Karl's hand, breaking the skin.

"Ouch! What the hell, Bailey?" Karl lunged at his cat, wrapping one arm around his chest and another beneath his belly. Bailey squirmed, growling as Karl carried him to the bedroom. He tossed Bailey onto the bed. The cat jumped off and headed for the door, but Karl was quicker. He backed out of the room, shutting the door as he did. Bailey scratched at the wood, begging for his freedom.

"I'll let you out when you learn to behave," Karl said, his hand still stinging.

He returned to the kitchen and pulled back his chair, ready to resume his research when his heart skipped a beat. Where is it? That goddamn cat must have swatted it off the table. If he broke it, I swear I'll—

The noise was faint. It sounded like scissors opening and closing. *Schikt-schikt. Schikt-schikt.*

What was that? Karl couldn't determine where the sound had come from. He scanned the table, looked underneath it, then checked the kitchen counter and the tile floor. The goldbug was nowhere to be seen. He scratched his head and tugged at his graying hair. Where could the bug possibly have gone?

"Ah!" A sudden pain shot through his ankle. He looked down. Blood was soaking through his white sock. He rolled it down, exposing an inch-long gash just above the ankle bone. It wasn't deep, but it hurt.

He glanced at his bedroom door. It was ajar. I must not have pulled it closed all the way.

"Damn it, Bailey!" he shouted. "What the hell is your problem today?"

His shoulders heaving, Karl stormed into the bathroom. He opened his medicine cabinet and pulled out a bandage. After sopping up the blood with a tissue, he covered the cut and went back to the table, hoping to find the goldbug and resume his work.

The first part was far easier than expected. "How did I miss you there?" he asked the goldbug, which sat on the table exactly where he had placed it. "Maybe I should get my eyes checked." He shrugged and sat down at his computer. The clock in its bottom right corner read "7:15 p.m."

A familiar low growl followed by hissing startled him from a daydream. He looked at the clock: 7:27 p.m. Karl slapped his palms against his thighs and stood. The screeching grew louder. He loved his cat, but Bailey was trying his patience.

Walking toward his bedroom, Karl grumbled, "What now, Bailey?"

A howl so ghastly it sent shivers through his bones came from the behind the door. "Bailey?" he stuttered, his lips quivering. His cat had never made a sound like that before—not when he was sick, not when he was hurt, not even that time when the door slammed shut on his tail. Karl's stomach turned. Bailey was in agony.

Fear seized Karl as he raced to his companion. Oh God, Bailey! What have you done?

He pushed open the door. Bailey lay on the floor just inside the room. The cat had gone silent. He wasn't moving.

"Bailey!" Karl shouted, crouching beside his feline. He shook him gently. "What's wrong, buddy?"

The cat's fur felt oily. Karl placed his hand flat against the animal's side. It was wet. He pulled back his hand. Blood covered his palm.

Karl's eyes began to water. Bailey didn't make a sound, but his belly rose and fell faintly. He was still alive.

Karl stroked Bailey gently, feeling for the wound. His hands ran through matted fur. As he went against the grain, he saw the cause of Bailey's distress: a golf ball-sized tunnel behind his front legs. From it, a small river flowed. Something had excavated a hole straight through him.

What could have done such a thing? The question crossed his mind, but Karl had no time to dwell on it. Saving his cat was his first priority.

Leaving Bailey where he lay, Karl ran into the kitchen. He grabbed his wallet and keys off the counter and shoved them into his pockets. Then he hurried into the bathroom for a towel to wrap Bailey. The emergency veterinary clinic was only fifteen miles away. He hoped Bailey could hang on a little longer.

But as he hustled through the dining room, he saw something out of the corner of his eye that stopped him dead in his tracks. The goldbug sat on the table where he'd left it. But it wasn't gold anymore. It was dark red. Blood red.

"What the..." His words trailed off as he turned to face the goldbug. Other than its color change, the figurine looked the same as it had when he'd purchased it. A wave of nausea came over him. Those mesh-like eyes seemed alive, black and white speckled like television snow, here and there a dot of red.

Schikt-schikt. Karl's mouth dropped open. He was sure that goldbug had just moved, its pincers crossing over like knives sharpening against each other. It was still again. A soft buzzing followed. Was it coming from the figurine?

Karl took a step back. His eyes never left the goldbug.

The buzzing amplified. Four thin membranes peeled from the goldbug's back. They rose and vibrated. The goldbug rose with them.

Karl bit down on his knuckle. Wings? This thing's alive? He took another step backward. The goldbug hovered in place.

Schikt-schikt. It shot itself at Karl.

He screamed. The goldbug hit him hard against his chest and latched itself to his sweatshirt. Its pincers snipped feverishly, shredding the cotton beneath them.

Karl batted at his shirt, but the goldbug held firm. Afraid to grab it, he instead tore off his shirt, pulling it quickly over his head. He threw it against the kitchen floor where it slid into the wall in a crumpled heap.

Karl froze. He watched the pile intently.

The sweatshirt moved. The goldbug crawled beneath it. Enraged, Karl stomped his loafer repeatedly into the pile, remembering Bailey, knowing this thing was somehow responsible. By the time he stopped, he'd broken into a sweat. The goldbug had ceased moving. He must have squished it. After all, as vicious as it was, it was only a bug. An arachnid, he thought, laughing uneasily.

With his eyes fixed on the shirt, he began to calm. It still hadn't moved. *I'm okay*, he told himself, his hands shaking. He examined his chest. A few red lines streaked across it, nothing more than scratches. He took a deep breath. *I'm okay. I can get Bailey now—*

The sweatshirt moved. First pincers then antennae emerged from beneath it. The rest of the goldbug followed. It paused on the floor, its wire-mesh eyes staring right at Karl. Its wings expanded and began to flutter. Karl turned to run.

His hand was turning the doorknob, almost outside, when he felt the thud against his back. The goldbug clung to him. It began to dig.

A shriek arose from somewhere deep inside Karl. His back seared with red hot pain. The fucker was tunneling into him.

His panicked screams grew weaker as he struggled to breathe, tears coursing down his face. The goldbug stripped away skin then muscle, burrowing deeper and deeper until its head and thorax writhed under his flesh. Beneath the tissue, it continued to cut and tear.

Karl reached behind him. His arm bent at an awkward angle, swiping and groping for the creature. Its bulbous abdomen wiggled, driving the head in deeper, each time his fingers made contact. His efforts to remove the bug only exacerbated his anguish. Pain, centralized around the bug's entry point, spiraled out through his nervous system.

His thumb and index finger finally latched around the goldbug's abdomen, halting its progress. "Got you!" he shouted, laughing hysterically. Karl pulled and twisted in spite of the pain, but he couldn't wrench his tormentor free. For a moment, they had reached a stalemate.

I'll call 9-1-1, he thought. *If I can just hold it where it is until help arrives...*

His grip began to slip. "No, no, no, no!" he stammered. "Why is this happening?" He had the bug firmly within his grip, but suddenly, holding it was like squeezing wet soap. Agony shot through him with renewed intensity. The goldbug was free, and it was tunneling.

Karl glanced at his hand just long enough to notice some kind of yellow secretion covering his fingers. The goldbug pushed itself inside him, now entirely under his flesh. It burrowed along his ribcage from the center of his back outward. Without Karl impeding it, the goldbug soon made its way to his side.

"Where are you going?" he cried. "Get the fuck out of me!"

Karl's pain was nearly debilitating. Still, he clung to hope. It took all his strength to remain on his feet. The light seemed to flicker. His hearing dulled. *No!* He shouted inside his head. *Fight it!*

Shaking off the dizziness, Karl clawed at his side. The goldbug mounded his skin. He cupped his hands around the lump, trying to stop it, but it was no use. The creature only burrowed deeper.

He stumbled into the kitchen and grabbed a knife, the longest, sharpest one in the rack. The pain he'd have to inflict couldn't be worse than what he already felt. With only a second's hesitation, he took aim and plunged the knife into his side.

Clink.

It barely broke his skin. The goldbug's armor-like exoskeleton repelled it. Karl's hope faded. I'll have to cut it out.

Without giving himself a chance to change his mind, Karl stabbed again, this time a quarter-inch in front of the bug. He shrieked. The cut had been deeper than he had intended. Still, it had blocked the creature's path. It stopped moving.

The knife jiggled in Karl's hand. Every minute movement brought with it a surge of pain. The knife fell away from his body. The point of the blade was missing, lost somewhere inside him.

"You have got to be kidding me!" he shouted. He was furious with the goldbug—furious that it had defiled him, furious that it yet tormented him, enraged by the fact that no matter what he tried, he couldn't beat it.

Karl paused to collect his wits. He would defy it at whatever the cost. Whatever the cost.

As if mocking him, the goldbug squirmed forward. It lodged itself behind his pectoral muscle. Was it going for his heart?

Desperate, terror blanking out logic, he grabbed his butcher's knife. Its stainless steel blade gleamed under the light above him. He hoped it would cut him as cleanly as it did meat.

With a howl as wild as his thoughts, Karl hacked at his chest. The blade cut deep, severing the muscle from his frame. The knife fell bloody from his weak hand. The amputated tissue, with the goldbug embedded inside, fell to the ground beside it. So did Karl.

He looked down at his chest. Blood poured from the wound. He tried to stand, to reach his phone and call for help, but he lacked the strength and collapsed against the stove. He prayed a neighbor had heard his struggles, maybe had called the police. The sinewy mass that was once part of him lay flat against the floor like a raw steak. Karl laughed, pain and desperation blending into mania. The bug had exacted a pound of flesh. The flesh twitched.

Schickt-schikt.

"No," Karl mouthed, his fear paralyzing him. "Leave me alone!"

The goldbug crawled out from beneath the meat and lifted its wings. They beat at the air, the rhythmic buzz drumming into Karl's ears. The creature rose, hovering higher and higher until it and Karl were face-to-face.

With the remaining power in his lungs, Karl screamed. The goldbug struck.

The shopkeeper heard a knock at his door.

"We're closed," he said. "Can't you read the sign?"

The knock came again, this time louder, more urgent. He rubbed his eyes and headed toward the door, muttering curses the whole way.

"What do you want?" His breath turned to frost in the night air as he swung open the door. He stared into an empty alley.

A broad smile wormed its way across his face as he looked down at his feet. "Back so soon? I take it your new home was not to your liking?"

The shopkeeper crouched. He placed his hand flat against the pavement, palm up. "Well, don't just stand there. Come in! Come in!"

The goldbug walked onto his hand.

He stroked its shell-like exoskeleton as he carried it back to its shelf. "Don't you worry, my little friend. We'll find you a new home soon enough."

In his head, Jason Parent lives in many places, but in the real world, he calls New England his home. The region offers an abundance of settings for his writing and many wonderful places in which to write them. He currently resides in Southeastern Massachusetts with his cuddly corgi named Calypso.

Please visit the author on Facebook at https://www.facebook.com/AuthorJasonParent?ref=hl, on Twitter at https://twitter.com/AuthorJasParent, or at his website, http://authorjasonparent.com/, for information regarding upcoming events or releases, or if you have any questions or comments for him.

BLOODSHOT BOOKS

WAR WITHOUT AN ENEMY, ENEMY WITHOUT A WAR

BY ADRIAN CHAMBERLIN

NOT YOUR AVERAGE MONSTER

That great God who is the searcher of my heart knows with what a sad sense I go upon this service, and with what a perfect hatred I detest this war without an enemy; but I look upon it as sent from God...
- **General Sir William Waller, 1643**

WITH the trickling of blood through his fingers, jubilation turned to guilt. His pride, his sense of victory in capturing the Royalist colours vanished into the twilight, just as he himself was swallowed by the mist that followed him from the soggy battlefield like the ghosts of the slain.

Matthew Collier halted, then stared at the crimson fluid that coated his knuckles – knuckles that had tightened on the flagpole, tore it from the ensign's grasp and not loosened since. He whimpered, and felt a chill finger poke his empty stomach through the thick hide of his buff coat.

He was just a boy, the same age as myself. Did I have to kill him? He lowered the pole and felt the blood-soaked flag wrap itself around his legs, coiling like the hangman's rope.

Yes, I did. He was but a junior company officer, his role as ensign was to protect the enemy regiment's colours with his life. He failed to do so.

That was what he told himself. But Matthew couldn't prevent the guilt take a full hold of him. *In God's name, the ensign had been just a boy! Seventeen summers, my age!*

Battle frenzy. His first kill, and it sickened him. Yes, it was a great personal victory, one that would surely see him rise within the ranks. From apprentice blacksmith to infantry recruit in the London Trained Bands serving Parliament, now a fully blooded soldier. Cavalry or ordnance next, and then, when he had proven himself with horse and cannon, maybe a commission to officer and the chance to serve directly under Fairfax - or even Cromwell...

That was what he had wanted. What he had *believed* he wanted. But the barely human cry of pain as the ensign's guts slipped to the ground, trampled underfoot by Matthew's spurred boots, still rang in his ears and dispersed any sense of glory. The bulging, terror-stricken eyes that pleaded with Matthew to stop; the hands raised in futile defence against the mortuary-hilted rapier that slashed again and again into the ensign's body; the blood that splattered the flamboyant clothing...

It was the ensign's dying plea for his mother to make the pain go away that finally parted the veil of red mist that had blinded Matthew Collier.

This was no enemy, no ravaging Papist hound of hell. This was just a boy, and closer inspection of the tiny burn marks and scars on what remained of his hands told Matthew that this ensign had been a blacksmith's apprentice as well.

In truth, what difference is there between us?

"Well done, Master Collier!"

The beaming face of Colonel Lewis swam through Matthew's red mist, the snorting plumes from his mare rising with the steam from the ensign's innards. The hearty slap on his back that followed, one of congratulation, froze at the sight of the slaughter. Matthew thought for a moment that Lewis whitened, as if he himself had not witnessed such brutality. Self-control was reasserted almost immediately, a mask of congratulation over the look of horror and disgust.

"The battle is almost won. Now, take up that piss-stained rag and return to Haverton. Post haste, Master Collier! Post haste!"

The guilt was momentarily assuaged by the sense of victory and purpose he felt when he lifted the enemy colours. The six-foot square flag was emerald green, of pure silk and taffeta, a contrast to the dour grey canvas of his own regiment's. The flag of Lord Meekins, leader of the Royalist army that Lewis's more disciplined force had engaged.

Matthew grinned, felt power surge through him as he brandished the Royalist colours. A power that was far greater than that obtained from wielding a firelock musket or a sword, far greater than carrying a pike or halberd.

This was the enemy's colours! Taken by force, a great dishonour and a destroyer of Royalist morale! As he raced past the ranks of battling infantry, pike blocks fighting at point, mounted Royalist officers aimed flintlock pistols and fired at him, their whitened faces disappearing in a fog of smoke.

He laughed, full of joy and life as the musket balls flew wild and the flag billowed in his wake, a taunt to the supporters of King Charles. He thrilled to the thunder of hooves behind him, the cries of pursuit and fury. He ran into the autumn sunset, delighted in the golden rays that painted his face and dried the sweat, ran until his lungs felt fit to burst, his body as hot as the forge the War had taken him from, his legs pounding like the smithy's hammer he used to wield.

The sun sank below the cliffs of the rocky headland, turning the sea beyond a dark crimson. Only when he was certain the battlefield was far behind him did he allow himself to pause. Panting with exhaustion, he looked behind, into the darkened expanse of moorland that gave rise to October mist.

Neither sight nor sound of Royalist pursuer. He turned again and headed for the woods that bordered the road to the garrison hamlet of Haverton.

He must have been more tired than he first realised; it took a monumental effort to climb the rise. The sodden grass sucked at his heels, the ground beneath as marshy as the bloodstained battlefield he had fled.

His breath came in ragged, uneven bursts. Sweat poured down his face and back, the shirt beneath the buff coat a sticky, uncomfortable second skin. The sweat soon chilled on his body as the day gave way to night.

He thrust the pole into the marshy ground with trembling fingers; whether through the adrenaline coursing through his body or fear brought upon by the sudden cold he didn't know.

Only then did he feel the blood dribble around his bruised knuckles, the pole coated in a slippery fluid that he had taken for sweat. Only then did the full horror of what he had seen – what he had done – return to him. He sank to his knees and wept.

That was not battle frenzy, surely. It was the action of a demon.

His tears of self-hatred ran dry, and exhaustion took him. His eyes closed, and his dreams filled with the sounds of hammering, screaming, and dying.

Rain roused him. He sniffled and looked up, wondering if God was mocking him for his actions. Only then did he become aware of his surroundings, and the shifting things he had taken for boughs creaking in the breeze.

They were not tree branches. And the fluid that fell down and splattered his upturned face was not rain.

"I will have none of it. The standard has been lost by your own stupidity, and I'll not risk further loss of life to salve your tarnished honour. *My lord.*"

The last two words were sneered, an insult to the corpulent man who stood with pudgy hands on hips, his jowls wobbling in astonishment at this open defiance from the seasoned soldier whose cold, grey-eyed glare never wavered from the watery blue of his commanding officer's. Around the two men, the tattered remnants of the Royalist regiment stood, silent and motionless. For the moment, weariness and despair were forgotten. So too were the dead and dying.

The blood of the butchered ensign had ceased to flow, but the flies clustered around the gash in his dismembered torso furthered the illusion of movement.

"You disobey me, sir?" Lord George Meekings spoke in a high pitched, tremulous voice. "You dare to disobey His Majesty - "

"I disobey *you*, my lord." Captain William Lambert forced himself to speak calmly. Losing his temper would not help him. *But by God's truth, dealing with this fat, self-important buffoon does severely test me!*

The young Parliamentarian trooper's ferocity had shocked them all – even Lambert, who saw shades of his own youthful, adventuring side in the lad who had hacked the ensign to pieces.

Small wonder that Meekings wanted him caught and made an example of. But it was futile. The young trooper was long gone, doubtless back with his comrades.

A new hero will be made tonight. But at what cost to his young soul? Will he remember the berserk he succumbed to? Will it sicken him, fill him with remorse and guilt? Or will he relish it, tap into it again...as I once did?

Lambert had resisted ever since: now approaching his fortieth year and his second decade on earth as a professional soldier, he had not succumbed to that spirit of rage and ferocity.

The young ensign was barely seventeen summers old. A boy. And yet all His Lordship had been concerned about was the loss of his precious colours. *And now this. To be ordered to race after it when men are dying...*

"It is pointless to retrieve your colours. The battle is lost."

The battlefield was a smoking ruin. White smoke from musket and cannon remained in the air, cooled by the approaching night into a thick fog that obscured the few moving figures. Wounded infantrymen writhed on the sloping ground before being despatched by swords wielded by victorious Royalist cavalry. Their horses whinnied at the fresh flow of blood, as though they too gloried in the slaughter of these traitors to King Charles.

The last of the sunlight faded, the tired orb slinking away between a gap in the woods beyond as if it, too, was sickened by the day's slaughter. With the failing light, the shining – *and untouched*, Lambert sourly noted – breastplate and crimson sash of the commander of the Royalist forces began to lose their lustre. Meekings had already discarded his *zischarge* helmet, the piece of armour thrown to Lambert's feet. The articulated metal plates, designed to protect the neck, reminded the captain of the scales of a dragon.

Or a lizard, he thought. *Truly, this "gentleman" belongs under a stone!* He kicked the helmet away and forced himself not to betray any signs of pain.

"Your tactics, my lord, have ensured our defeat. You ordered your horse to charge at full gallop into the rebel infantry!"

Even now, Lambert could not believe what he had seen. Meekings had thought artillery would be enough to break the Parliamentarian lines, despite Lambert's protestations that the range was not sufficient. And then to compound his mistake by ordering the entire main horse into the enemy lines – without even waiting for the white smoke to clear – was unforgivable.

That was when Captain Lambert had been proved correct. The lines of infantry were untouched, their pikes standing firm despite the terrible noise of ordnance and the ubiquitous smoke.

Meekings' eyes shifted guiltily, glancing at the nearest trooper who held a sodden piece of cloth to his comrade's chest wound. Lambert caught the exchange between the men, saw the hatred and accusation from the soldier attending the dying sergeant.

Another victim of his Lordship's incompetence! He snorted. The main horse would have been safe had the Parliamentarian infantry not pounded metal-tipped stakes into the ground. The fog of war blinded the Royalist horse, and the wickedly sharp "swine feathers" did their lethal work, to both trooper and mount.

Granted, the terror of charging cavalry could have a fearsome effect on men unused to such sights – especially fresh soldiers who had not been trained to stand firm. But horse could only break resolute infantry by attacking the rear or the flanks of tired men already engaged in fighting other infantry.

The opposing army was too well-disciplined, too battle-hardened, to fall to Meekings. Colonel Lewis had trained under Cromwell, and his regiment was just as effective as Cromwell's Ironsides. *And professional,* Lambert thought sadly. *Discipline before rank and privilege.*

If Meekings' desire to reclaim his colours was born from a sense of vengeance, a desire to ensure the young ensign's death was avenged, Lambert could have understood. But his Lordship's first reaction upon hearing the news was to kick the mutilated torso of the ensign and spit in his smashed skull pan.

Weakling! Losing my colours to a mere strip of a Crophead bastard! You are naught but a peasant boy, undeserving of the honour to bear my standard!

Lambert had felt the rage return. A burning, liquid sensation that rose from the pit of his stomach, one that flooded his body, demanded he succumb, surrender to the darkness within. To hate. To rage...

No!

"Captain Lambert. I am ordering you, *for the last time*, to give chase and retrieve my colours!"

Lambert stared at the shadowy figures on the darkening battleground. The harsh cry of ravens filled his ears. Carrion crows had circled since the grey dawn, knowing there would be rich pickings at the day's end. It would not be long before the human ghouls came, pillaging the dead for their meagre coin and valuables.

It was ever thus, he thought. It did not disturb him, it was merely a fact of life; a gruesome but thankfully predictable epilogue to the business of soldiery.

A business. Not an upper class adventure as this fool takes it for. Lambert looked again at the ensign's corpse, heard the last gasp of life from the sergeant, and made his decision. He spat at Meekings' feet.

"Prepare yourself for surrender, my lord. Be an honourable prisoner. I am done with you."

Lord Meekings' cheeks were as scarlet as his sash. He took a step

 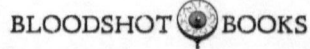

forwards, but halted when the captain placed a hand on his flintlock.

"You have no respect for His Majesty's forces, Captain! Mayhap you would prefer to fight for Parliament!"

"Mayhap I would," Lambert sneered. "Cromwell and Fairfax understand what it is to be the *professional* soldier. Their coin is as good as the King's."

The blow seemed to come from nowhere. Lord Meeking's fist whirled with lightning speed and connected with the captain's lacerated cheek.

"Nothing but a mercenary!" Meekings spat. "Just like those others who fought on the Continent! You have no *honour*, sir!"

The blow did not hurt, but the shock was so great Captain Lambert was thrown into instinctive action.

No honour? Before he knew what he was doing, he had the fallen ensign's rapier in his hand. The red mist descended, anger and hatred for this idiot of a commander who had dared to strike one of his own officers, who had no shred of decency, honour or humility.

Not even in Germany, where he had fought against the ranks of the Swedish rebels and witnessed atrocities beyond imagining, had he been assaulted by one from his own side.

The twilight was replaced by the same red mist that descended over the Parliamentarian soldier who had butchered the ensign. Once again, a mortuary hilted blade wielded by an Englishman hacked into the body of a fellow Englishman.

The red mist became corporeal, a liquid presence that filled Lambert's nostrils and throat with the scent and taste of death, blinded his eyes with splattered life fluid.

"In God's holy name! *Stop!*"

The sole trooper's voice filtered through the red mist. Captain Thomas Lambert wiped his eyes and stared in bewilderment at the butchered remains of the Royalist officer. A piece of meat that had once been part of the lord's limbless torso twitched and shivered, before expelling steaming ordure.

Lambert's breathing was harsh and rapid, misting in the cool evening air like the gases from Meekings' belly. His arm and shoulders ached with the exertion of the butchery, and he realised he had expended more energy on slaughtering his commanding officer than fighting the Parliamentarians. The slaughter was not a novel sight to him – but the lack of restraint, the sheer fury that had powered it, was not his own doing.

In God's name, what caused this? Was I possessed?

He saw Meekings' surviving retinue advance, their movements wary and cautious, but emboldened now they saw the confusion in his eyes and how spent his energy was.

Aye, possessed. Just as that young trooper was...

He glanced around him, saw the few returning harquebusiers turn curious eyes in his direction. The coming of night and the dip in the field had obscured the murder from all but the sharpest eyes.

Few eyes were as sharp as Lambert's. He noticed the orange colour of the sashes, and knew instantly which side these men were on.

He saw his chance. He broke the hold of Meekings' men and ran to the cantering Parliamentarians.

Surrender first, then offer my services. Even if they refuse, mayhap I can talk sense into that young lad, ensure he does not follow my path....

He ran without looking back. To do so would be death. The battlefield was treacherous with holes gouged from the soil by hoof and artillery ready to ensnare and break a wrongly-placed ankle, but that was the least of his worries.

"Halt, traitor!" Behind him, Lambert heard the striking of matchlocks, the hiss of powder flaring in the pans and the thunder of musket balls. He fell to the ground, twisted his body into a roll that spared him the musket volley but planted his head firmly in the corpse of an infantryman. Lambert felt the skin burst beneath him, and the cold, gelatinous innards reached up to smother him.

Matthew Collier stared in horror at the forest of poles. It was far better to keep his terror-filled gaze on the ash shafts and their coating of black blood and intestinal juices than lay his eyes once more upon the things that crowned them.

Pike shafts. They would have been each sixteen feet tall at one point, unless some of the pikemen had opted to cut a few feet off for ease of mobility. Now they thrust a mere eight feet into the night air, the points of the shafts deeply buried in the soil to ensure they held the impaled bodies of the Parliamentarian garrison upright.

Upright, and squirming. Still alive. They could not cry out with their suffering because the pike points had come up through their sternums before piercing their lower jaws.

Moonlight turned parts of the leaf-shaped points that were not coated in blood a cold silver, and illuminated the whites of the dying men's eyes. Blood bubbled from the thinner, younger infantrymen, their light weight ensuring they took longer to slide down the pole. They took longer to die.

A forest of pikes...an entire troop, put to death with their own weaponry! What could do such a thing?

Now he looked up, tried to follow a path through the impaled pikemen to the garrison hamlet of Haverton. He clapped his hands over his ears to block the sounds of the ash poles creaking in the ground, the bubbling of blood on

lips and the trickling of life fluid down wood, and the muffled croaks of men breathing their last.

One pole was lower than the others, and the clothes of the soldier were more flamboyant, more expensive than those of the soldiers surrounding him. The pole was lower because it was shorter. A partisan, a pole-arm wielded only by the senior officers.

Colonel Lewis!

Matthew Collier froze as the pole supporting the colonel shifted. There was a wet, rending sound, and the blade of the partisan pressed further upwards and parted the lips wider. Was it only a few hours ago that those lips had parted in a wide smile, a friendly laugh as he called out: *Well done, Master Collier...now, take up that piss-stained rag and return to Haverton. Post haste, Master Collier! Post haste!*

Matthew's trembling hands clutched the flagpole. The flag was soaked in marsh mud and blood, and felt heavier than before. Either his strength was failing or the fluids had made the silk heavier. Was there any point taking it further? What use was it to his regiment now?

He stared through the final poles: to the gateway of the churchyard. Where this troop of the regiment was billeted.

Will there be any survivors? Will there be sanctuary in God's house?

He lifted the flagpole with a great effort and hoisted it over his shoulder. The movement reminded him of the last time he had lifted it: brandishing it at the defeated enemy, a taunt. Now it taunted none but himself and his dead comrades.

He broke into a run, but the tip of the pole caught the unsteady shaft of Colonel Lewis's partisan. Matthew stumbled, caught his heels on the sodden flag that wrapped around his ankles and thighs like a winding sheet. He crashed to the ground, gasping in pain. His vision blurred and his head swam. The stars spun on invisible cartwheels and the forest of impaled pikemen with their fruiting corpses reared above him like the spars of a foundering ship.

One of the spars crashed to the deck, unfurling a shroud. The expensive cloth and finery of a gentleman officer gave way to the exploded innards of a dying man. The steel edge of the partisan blade missed Matthew's head by inches, but he was unaware of this small mercy. The moist, rubbery insides of his commanding officer smothered him and sent his mind screaming to a darker place.

By the time Lambert regained consciousness, one of the three harquebusiers had pulled him from the exploded corpse and sat him upright next to a shattered gun carriage. He blinked, coughed and spat blood and intestinal juice. It had the familiar tang of gunpowder. He spat again and looked up at his rescuer, was about to speak when the scream of a man behind him made him freeze.

The screams of the dying held no discomfort for him, but this was different. It was the searing cry of a man being violated as he died, accompanied by the moist, meaty sound of a wooden pole penetrating damp earth. The scream rose as the man was hoisted into the air.

The ground trembled behind Lambert as the pole sank deeper into its securing hole. The sound of steel slowly penetrating flesh and organs was only just audible over the rapid panting and barely human screeching of the impaled man.

Not since he had seen his first battle over twenty years ago on the Continent had Captain William Lambert felt such terror that rooted him to the spot. He could not move, dared not look behind him. He only raised his head to face the dismounted trooper when the point of a sabre pressed under his chin and jabbed upwards.

Moonlight silvered the *pott* helmet and breast plate of the harquebusier. The three vertical face protectors of the helmet looked like the desiccated ribs of some strange animal. The face was hidden by the shadow of the helm; nothing but blackness greeted Captain Lambert.

Now his terror mounted. He cast his eyes downwards, wished he could blot out the sounds of sadistic murder behind him.

The orange-tawny sash around the trooper's waist that Lambert took to be a mark of Parliamentary forces was strangely stiff and unyielding to the night breeze. It had more of the texture of tanned hide, or...

A cry escaped Lambert's lips. He knew what that material was.

Skin. Flayed, human skin.

The scudding clouds allowed the moonlight to give the impression the hide still moved, still had life. That the face of the child it had been taken from was animated by an agony from beyond death.

The trooper leaned closer, but the moonlight still did not reveal his face. Instead, it showed the contents of the helmet.

The blackness was thick, a physical entity that had a life of its own. A darkness that had corporeal presence, a force that had no right to walk the land. Lambert felt the rage that emanated from it; hatred and wrath that could not be human. A force that was not alone. Over the keening of the impaled men behind him, Lambert heard the soft footfall of spurred boots. Horseman's boots.

He remembered there had been three of these harquebusiers on the field. The other two had finished their duty and were now coming for him.

"Are you for the King or for the Parliament?" His words were flat and toneless in the night, until the giggle escaped him. Madness stroked the edges of his consciousness, and he was grateful to succumb.

There was no reply to his words. Gauntleted hands fell upon his shoulders, lifting him to a standing position. The gloved fingers imparted a chill that cut into him like knife blades. He could barely remain upright, his legs trembled so much.

"Neither. We war for all."

The words soughed around him, whispers on the breeze that could have been the parting breaths of dying men.

The innards of Colonel Lewis slipped from Matthew's face. He felt the weight of his dead commanding officer lift from his body, and warm, soft hands upon his sweating brow.

Still he would not open his eyes. *I cannot witness anymore!*

"Be still, child. You are safe... from me, at least."

A woman's voice. One that was familiar, and despite the hint of a foreign accent, oddly comforting. Now he opened his eyes.

Moonlight to the left cast shadows of writhing, dying men on their execution poles against the pale stone walls of the church; a shadow play of agony and inhumanity. It also illuminated the face of his companion. Through a bonnet of blood-spattered crinoline, startlingly green eyes stared back at him with motherly concern.

Those eyes glanced at the forest of corpses behind him without so much as a shudder. Instead, there was a flicker of hatred.

He gratefully took her hands and allowed her to help him to his feet. She pulled him up with a strength that belied her diminutive frame, then regarded him with a faint, weary smile.

"Master Matthew, is it not? Matthew... Collier?"

That accent again. Where does she hail from? And those marks on her face...

"D'you not recognise me, child? I'm Máire."

He nodded dumbly. Máire. One of the 'Leaguer Ladies', whores who attached themselves to the baggage train and attended the soldiers when their blood was up and could not be satisfied by alcohol, battle or plunder.

The prostitutes were generally well-treated, but Máire was the exception. The mottled bruises on her cheeks and forehead, the odd cast of her nose where it had not been set properly after being broken, and the simmering fury in her eyes were all enhanced by the cold moonlight.

Coming from Ireland, it was small wonder she had been so ill used, particularly by those soldiers who remembered all too well the atrocities of the Irish Uprising and the massacre of English Protestant settlers at

Portadown. He had wondered why she had never returned to her country: why continue to service the needs of men who hated her countrymen so?

"You're cold, child. Come in to the warmth."

Framed by the lych-gate, he saw small fires in the glassless windows of the ruined church. A sense of guilt overcame him as he followed her: most of the glass had been intact when his troop had been billeted here, as had been the carved likenesses of saints. Peppering the stained glass with musket fire, and destroying the statues with sword and cannon: target practice after nights of drink-fuelled revelry.

It mattered not at the time. Even Colonel Lewis had not protested too much when the chaplain had complained. *Far better Popish images than able soldiers, chaplain!*

Matthew sighed and picked up the flagpole. It felt even heavier, the silk sticking to the ground, as if a force within was unwilling to allow its entry to hallowed ground.

The booty of a murderer! his inner voice screamed. *It has no place in God's house, and neither do you!*

He ducked his head in guilt as he went through the lych-gate, relieved to be putting space between the soldiers who would not be destroying anything ever again. Máire hunched forwards as they made their way to the shattered nave, her breath misting in the air.

It no longer appeared like the inside of a church. The altar railings had long been stripped for their precious metals. The pews were smashed, rendered to so much firewood. Small fires lit the entrance to the nave, the sacristy and the chancel. Indeed, each doorway that led into the building was marked by a fierce fire. Yet the light did little to dispel the shadows in the far reaches of the building, and little warmth was imparted by these fires. If anything, it seemed colder here than outside.

"Are you alone, Máire?"

She waited until they had passed the headless carving of some unknown saint before she turned to answer. "As are you, Master Matthew. The Lord surely watched over you when your comrades succumbed." Her eyes fell to the flagpole. Even the firelight could not impart any life to the mud-splattered mess.

He remembered his butchery of the ensign, the demonic rage that powered his sword, and wondered what sort of God would watch over him while allowing him to perform such evil. He swallowed, tasted bile and prayed it was his own.

"What... what happened, Máire? When I did leave the field of battle, we had routed the King's men. What unholy reserve army did they have waiting for us?"

"'Tis not the work of men, Master Matthew." Máire's green eyes blazed in the firelight. "What killed your comrades did take those on the baggage train as well. The wives who could not bear to be left behind... and the children..."

"Children?"

"Only three o' the poor little mites... oh, dear God, how they suffered..."

The fire did not warm him. He wondered if he would ever feel warm again. "What did this?"

She removed her bonnet and ran a withered hand through her hair. What remained of it was a coppery gold colour, unwashed and thick with grease and blood from the scalp where locks had been torn away.

"In the Old Country, we called them the Wrathful Ones. An enemy without a war, always seeking man's hatred and rage to feed their power. My husband, may he rest in peace, did see them on the Continent when he fought against Gustavus Adolphus... and right richly did they feed upon man's inhumanity there."

Matthew stared, wide-eyed. Spirits? And yet... he had heard of the atrocities in Ireland, and in the Low Countries where the Wars of Religion incited brutality beyond belief. Now the stories he had heard from the veterans were no longer the tall tales he had dismissed so casually.

"I never did think to see them, not in my lifetime, and not on an English battlefield." She glanced at him with that curious mixture of sympathy and distaste she had given the impaled infantry. "Because I never did believe anyone would be so cruel, so evil, to perform the rite that brings them to battle. 'Tis a terrible thing, Master Matthew, to think that your own countrymen, who so despised my people for their actions in the rebellion – indeed, soldiers on your own *side* - could flay a child alive."

"We war for all," the words soughed again, and then Captain Lambert realised.

The flayed child's skin, the impenetrable darkness behind the helmet, the incorporeal presence that inflicted such barbaric punishment upon the living.

In the Low Countries, where children had been crucified in the name of God, he had heard whisperings, mutterings from the superstitious ones who believed only demons could inflict such barbarity upon a human being. A professional soldier scorned such fancy, knew only too well what a man – and indeed, a woman - was capable of.

This war between the King and the Parliament has been comparatively free from atrocity. That would change now.

There was no denying the unholy butchery that he heard behind him. Impalement, a technique that had reached its infamy in the Wallachian states under Prince Vlad over two hundred years ago. Since then, a favoured means of execution amongst these spirits of war, spirits that stripped every semblance of humanity from those engaged in battle.

There was no denying what faced him. The trooper stood still, motionless save for the writhing of the baby's skin-sash.

"The Wrathful Ones," he said in a hoarse whisper. "So, you *do* exist."

"You know of us."

He swallowed, felt fresh sweat break on his brow and chill in the cold mist that caressed his skin. He heard the sounds of a hole chopped out of the ground behind him. It would not be long before he took his own place amongst the impaled ones.

"How did you come?" The words came to him unbidden, a soldier's fast reflexes powering speech in an attempt to prolong his life. "What brought you here?"

Its gauntlet indicated the sash and the screaming face of the child. *"Your enemy made the offering."*

"Impossible!" Lambert took a sharp breath. "None would perform such an abomination! They are English soldiers, they fight with honour! You lie, demon."

The soughing became a laugh. *"You do underestimate your enemy, Captain! Not all fight with pike and musket... not all differentiate between regiment and rank. King or Parliament, Catholic or Protestant... the cause, the standard under which the battle is fought... it matters not to us. To she who summoned us, maybe. But not to us."*

"She?"

Unseen hands pulled him to the ground and held him, pinned by wrists and knees to the cold mud. Staring up at the moonlit clouds, Lambert saw the bodies of his former comrades, writhing upon their pikes. He felt the sting of a blade cut into his breeches.

"She summoned us... but it is human wrath that keeps us with you. We have waited long for this war. We will turn the fields and towns of your country into the same Hell we turned the Low Countries."

The pain ceased. He held his breath, each second an eternity as he waited for the agonising incision that would precede impalement. He finally opened his eyes.

The three harquebusiers stood before him. The farthest one held in his formless hands the wobbling hunk of meat that had been Meekings' torso. Its companion held aloft the butchered remnants of the ensign. Apart from the fat of the former, the two torsos were remarkably alike in the ferocity that had been visited upon them. Now they were held side by side, and Lambert saw the injuries were identical. The limbs had been severed at exactly the same junctures, the ribcages crushed and piercing the flesh.

The empty, faceless helmets with their impenetrable darkness inclined towards Lambert, regarding him. The only movement of the Wrathful Ones was the shifting of their hide-sashes in the breeze, the sobbing and keening of the impaled soldiers the only sound upon the battlefield. Even the carrion crows had fled.

"You did this?"

"Aye. What of it?"

"You butchered within your own ranks? You succumbed to the rage?"

Dread settled in Lambert's gut as the Wrathful One brandished the torso of Meekings. Clotted blood fell in lumps through the mist. *By God's hooks,* he thought with self-hatred. *Aye, I did succumb to the rage.* He suspected what was to follow, and knew it would be worse than impalement

The empty helmets turned inwards. Silent conferring.

Then hands reached for him. Pulled him to his feet.

"You will come with us."

"You lie, woman! No-one would do such a thing to a man, let alone a child. There - "

Her head shot round and her eyes blazed. "You know *nothing* of battle, Master Matthew! How little you know of your own comrades, and what they are capable of!"

This does not feel right, he thought, regarding her with a cold – yet fearful – appraisal. *Her loathing of my comrades seems… false. In truth, what is she really?*

Wood crackled in the fires by each of the doors. An occasional flame reared higher than the others and licked the stones of the nave, but no gusts of wind caused this. Now he had begun to recover from the horrific sights outside, he was more aware of his surroundings.

Yes, we did smash all the pews. But to make cots from, to sleep upon. Where are they now? I see naught but firewood.

The "Leaguer Ladies" had come here nightly, to offer their services to the men. He had partaken – who had not? – and this very morning there had been signs of their habitation. Indeed, some of them had still been abed when their clients rose and readied for battle.

Now, nothing. A log slipped from a cluster of smaller sticks on the nearest fire. His nostrils wrinkled with the smell of burning fat and skin, and…

'Tis no log! He stared at the charred stick that had fallen, no longer held to the blackened ribcage now the tendons had burned away. He looked back to the Leaguer Lady. She smiled.

"When you fight a war you have many enemies, Master Matthew. Enemies you do not always see… enemies you do not realise you had made." Her smile hardened. "Your comrades paid the price for what they did to my people in Ireland. For what they did to me here."

Revulsion filled him more than fear. He saw the size of the bones in the fire, how small they were. "For your people? Or for *yourself?* And what price did you pay for your vengeance, Máire? The children, the wives you offered to these... these *things*. What did they do to deserve being dragged into your war?"

"'Deserve' has naught to do with it." She moved forwards to kick the child's femur back into the fire. It roared at the disturbance, before settling down quietly to feed. Her emerald eyes gleamed in the firelight as she turned back to Matthew. "But why did they spare you? You were a'slumber when they did hoist your comrades into the sky. Mayhap they have a fate far worse in store for you..."

The fire roared once more, but Máire's smile was frozen. This time, air fed the flames. Air from the doorway of the nave, carried by the four new arrivals and their burdens.

Matthew Collier stared in horror. The man in the centre of the group looked familiar, an infantry captain on the Royalist side. His facial scars and cold grey eyes spoke of an experienced – and disillusioned -soldier.

The captain lifted his head and stared at Matthew. Recognition flared in his eyes – and Matthew knew it was not just the memory of witnessing his slaughter of the Royalist ensign.

'Tis almost as though he recognises a kindred spirit. Am I as he once was? He had seen grizzled soldiers like this one before on his own side, and until today had wanted to become like them. Professionals, experienced killers, fighting for a just cause.

He had not paid much attention to the cold, detached gaze they bore, nor the lack of delight they took in killing. But there was more than detachment and weariness in this man's eyes. There was despair, a sense of helplessness. Resignation to a hideous fate.

He was clearly the prisoner of his comrades.

The three harquebusiers who surrounded the Captain brought a fresh chill to the church. The firelight flared in greeting, but did nothing to dispel the shifting, liquid blackness that churned and roiled within their *pott* helmets like dark pools of blackened blood.

Two disembodied torsos were thrown into the doorway. Matthew's face flushed with the realisation that one belonged to the ensign. He felt the unearthly scrutiny of the three troopers upon him.

Are these devils? Am I to be judged? He glanced nervously at Máire, but there was no comfort to be found in her presence.

She began to shudder, her wasted bosom heaving and pulsating in the cold. Her face was pale, her eyes bulging with fright; this time, they did not flash like emeralds in the sun. Her voice was a tremor that scarcely raised an echo from the vaulted ceiling of the nave.

"Your task is complete, Wrathful Ones! In the name of the Dark One, I abjure you! *Go!*"

"You summoned us, woman. But you have not the right to make us depart."

Matthew was chilled further by the thing's words. They did not emanate from the faceless helmet; rather, they came from the cracks in the stone walls that allowed the cold night air access. They came from the spitting fat of the fire's contents. They came from the groans of the dying, impaled men outside. The words spoken were from the voice of cold, of fire. Of hatred and death.

He stared once more at the cracked remnants of the baby's bones in the fire. Fear turned to hatred as he considered what this woman had done... but she was oblivious to his hate-filled glare. She now had fear of her own.

"What? I have paid with the flesh of babes, as tradition dictates. You destroyed the regiment that murdered my people, as I ordered! Now, you are ordered to - "

"We will not be banished. We have found this war needs our... direction. These two soldiers have shown the way. They succumbed to the wrath that fuels hatred. They fight their own people, and now commit murder within their own ranks. Truly, this is a war without an enemy. Our favoured meat and drink. Brother against brother, father against son, young against old...

"Just as in Germany and the Low Countries, just as in Ireland, we will ensure that war will tear the land apart."

Now the Royalist captain and the Parliamentarian trooper stared at each other. A pained look passed the captain's face.

"No. A moment's madness, nothing more. 'Twill not happen again."

His voice was as gravel, but Matthew could tell there was no mistaking the determination and the self-reproach in his words. *The wrath that fuels hatred...*

"Captain... did you commit slaughter as I did?"

"Aye, lad. I gave into... wrath. Hatred. Hence, there was no restraint in what I did." He gave a sad smile. "I had not done so since... since I was your age. I... gloried in it."

"And it did set you on the road to a full time career in killing?" Matthew's mouth was dry. For now, the Wrathful Ones were forgotten.

"Aye... but I swore to learn restraint. To kill only when necessary – not to allow hatred and anger to cloud my judgement. And I did keep my oath. Until today."

Now anger rose in the captain. "And all for what?" His gravel voice struck sparks; flints of fury. "For what cause do we butcher? We fight our own people... and kill within our own ranks! Under what standard do we declare this war?"

Standard... it felt like years had passed since the recruiting sergeant had come to his town. Then flocking to the banner, pride in bearing the colours...

A hiss from the three harquebusiers echoed along the porch of the nave. A hiss of fear. Matthew Collier broke his gaze and stared at the Wrathful Ones.

There was agitation in their movements, a fidgeting, restless twitch of limbs – the restlessness he had experienced and witnessed among his own troop before battle.

'Tis a human reaction! To what? His mention of 'standard'...

Then he knew. The object that had inspired such bloodlust in him – the colours of Lord Meekings.

The regimental flag. The banner to rally the troops – the cause of his demonic bloodshed.

The Royalist captain's eyes follow his to where the flag lay, in the blood and soil it had collected from the battlefield. A weary smile played on the scarred lips of the captain as their eyes met once more and understanding passed between them.

"My commanding officer did order me to retrieve those colours – and to kill you in the process."

"To do to me what I had done to his ensign," Matthew said with a grim smile. "An order you disobeyed, sir." He moved towards the flag, bent down and held it to the fire. The flames allowed light to pass through the heavy material, revealing the full glory of the insignia and colours.

The hissing from the creatures Máire referred to as the Wrathful Ones became louder, more piercing. She had started to mutter words he could not understand: perhaps a reversal of the incantation she had used to summon them.

"Your rage has been harnessed by us. You are ours to command."

The harquebusier lifted a gauntlet above the fire and pointed towards Matthew. A wall of heat slammed into him.

An unnatural heat, a fire that burned yet did not displace the cold that froze his very core of being. A fire that brought a thin veil of red across his eyes, a scarlet mist.

A red mist of rage. A desire to kill, to butcher.

NO!

The mist dissipated, just long enough for him to see the Royalist captain's eyes burn with hatred, his sword drawn, before it came down upon his vision once more.

To kill, to slaughter... but that is what THEY desire, not myself!

His thoughts were drowned by an internal screaming, a howl of rage, fury and hatred that was not human. A last-resisting part of him finally recognised the howling as his own.

He was aware of a presence before him, one that danced in time with the fires, matched his sword strikes blow for blow; experience and rage more than a match for his youth and wrath.

The colours!

He still had the flagpole in his left hand. He knew now what to do.

He fell to the floor, felt the captain's blade carve the hot air above his head, and twisted. His sabre cut deep into the Royalist's left boot and the flagpole swept around, into the fire that the captain, bleeding and disorientated from the wound to his ankle, fell into.

The colours of Lord Meekings erupted into flame, imparted a fearsome heat that was more scarlet than the crimson mist of his vision. The flag was a sheet of fire that enveloped himself and the captain, who still hacked away at him with his sword, regardless of the super-heated metal that fused the mortuary hilt to his knuckles.

Pain swept through Matthew, a purifying, human pain that diminished his fury. The howling of his inner demon of rage was replaced by the vanquished screeching of the three Wrathful Ones.

He heard howling from the woman who had brought this unholy visitation upon them; a scream of pain and physical agony, accompanied by the wet, meaty sounds of tearing flesh and muscle. Blood sizzled as it dripped from the vaulted ceiling into the fire that consumed himself and his opposite.

He knew then that the Wrathful Ones were articulating their frustration and fury at being denied their two champions who would have heralded unprecedented rage and atrocity on this land.

Through the agony, through the fire, the young Roundhead trooper thought he saw his opponent – an officer and a Royalist – smile in approval at his actions. The Wrathful Ones would return, they both knew that; and next time they would probably not need a crazed witch's incantations to bring them to life. Man's hatred and brutality alone would suffice.

But that is for future wars, he thought as he looked to the man who should have been his enemy. *That is for other generations of warriors to deal with. Pray God they do not give vent to rage and hatred in war and abandon their humanity as we once had.*

As his young life slipped away, Matthew saw the sadness in the captain's eyes before they bubbled and melted into the fire. It was a look that intimated his prayer would not be heard.

NOT YOUR AVERAGE MONSTER

Adrian Chamberlin is a British writer of dark fiction and lives in the small south Oxfordshire town of Wallingford that serves as a backdrop to the UK television series *Midsomer Murders*, not far from where Agatha Christie lies buried, dreaming in darkness. He is the author of the critically acclaimed supernatural thriller *The Caretakers* as well as numerous short stories in a variety of anthologies, mostly historical or futuristic based supernatural horror. He co-edited *Read the End First*, an apocalyptic anthology with Suzanne Robb (author of the acclaimed thriller *Z-Boat*) and has many other projects in the pipeline.

His next release will be "This Envious Siege", a Lovecraftian account of the Battle of Trafalgar, in Exaggerated Press's *Darker Battlefields*, a collection of supernatural warfare novellas scheduled for October 2015.

He is aware of the concept of "spare time" but swears it's just a myth.

Further information can be found on his website, archivesofpain.com.

BLOODSHOT ● BOOKS

MONSTERS

BY JEFF CARLSON

HIS name doesn't matter. He had a job in which he invested forty-odd hours of his life each week, a car that was only two years old, and a small apartment with a view from the kitchen window of an undeveloped hillside where the sun came up. Because of this, he usually breakfasted standing at the kitchen sink, whereas he ate most of his dinners in front of his girlfriend's TV. His days passed with little adventure or romance -- a speeding ticket here, oral sex on the hall carpet there; hardly the stuff of legends -- and he was content.

As he pushed through the theater's heavy door with his shoulder, protecting an armload of popcorn and soda, some kid in the front rows yelped like a puppy. He barely noticed. His girlfriend jammed a finger into his ribs as she brushed past, even though it was her snacks that he'd drop, and he said, "The whole thing's designed for us to sit dead-center. The picture, the sound system..."

She flashed her wild smile and shook her head. "Some tall dork always plunks down in front of me."

"No one's even here." He didn't much care what his vantage point would be for this "sweeping Victorian epic," yet by appearing to give in now he was more likely to win a later dispute. He'd already racked up big points just by agreeing to see a movie completely lacking gunfire or killer asteroids.

In front, the kid who'd yelped was on her feet, rubbing her butt and talking in a squeal. The woman beside her said two short syllables in an embarrassed tone. The kid shook her head. The woman growled something that sounded like okay fine and they moved over a couple seats. That was all.

On the far left side of the theater, he sat down next to his girlfriend. Something hard and very thin lanced into his thigh and he stumbled up, careful not to spill his Coke. "Ow. Man!"

"What?"

He thought she'd jabbed him, payback for his earlier sermon on the top ten most boring aspects of chick flicks, but his wound really hurt. Her idea of fun was to pinch his nostrils shut when he overslept or to deflate bowling scores. And her puzzled grin became a frown when she saw his expression.

"Look," he said. The tiny steel shaft was almost the same color as the maroon upholstery, but specks of bright metal showed through a dry sticky coating of red-black.

His stomach lurched as he realized the crust was blood, some instinctual need to purge himself. He would remember that feeling later on restless nights, in muted hospital rooms, during slow dead hopeless hours. There were other moments that he could resurrect in his mind, heartbeats in which his body reacted before he could think. Most came playing roller hockey: saves, scores, falls that should have resulted in broken bones but because of a last second lunge or judo-like roll had cost him only bruises. Others were more alien, random; a sense of knowing a strange woman that went beyond physical attraction; shadows of fear; an aggressive predatory urge when bumped on a crowded sidewalk. Instinct, primal emotion, seemed in many ways quicker and more powerful than the intellect.

"Man. Oh, man." He rubbed at his flank exactly as the kid in the front row had done. The dim lights went out. Previews started as he investigated his seat. In the dark blue flickering glow of an ocean storm, he found a note taped to the underside.

It was only three letters long. HIV.

In the brown gloom of a courtroom scene, he shouted at the crowd. Three people hollered back at him to shut up. He tried again, panicking, but his girlfriend tugged on his sleeve. She didn't care about them.

He went straight to the emergency room. Two hours passed before the insurance papers were complete and a doctor was available. The desk nurse suggested that he leave and visit his primary care physician the next day. Sweating, certain that he could feel it scratching in his veins, he pleaded that money didn't matter, he wanted to see someone now, right now, please.

His girlfriend sat as close as the hard plastic chairs would allow, holding his hand, while a parade of strangers kept them waiting -- a guy his own age whose shattered forearm seemed to have an extra wrist; two children with dog bites -- none of whom honestly seemed in more danger than himself.

"It was a prank," his girlfriend said. They stared at the tile floor. Later she whispered, "They can kill it with drugs on the first day, I think."

He lifted his head to kiss her in a sudden delirium of fear and need. She leaned back, avoiding him. Later he'd understand her reaction as an important lesson -- that he was ultimately alone in this no matter how many times his parents and friends promised to be there for him. The thick dirty flood of hate passed quickly, but for a moment he trembled with energy. He almost stood up and shouted. He almost hit her. Then he slumped back in his seat, already defeated, already dead, pushing her hand away and crossing both arms across his chest.

Her eyes were horrified. "I'm sorry," she said.

"You can't get it kissing somebody.

"I'm sorry."

When the ER doctor told him that HIV infections cannot be detected for six months, disbelief clogged his head. For most of a week he managed to hope, numbly, that nothing had happened. Then police technicians announced that the needles did indeed carry a virulent strain. Every professional he visited put the odds at ninety-plus percent that he was blood positive, because his puncture wound was rough and deep.

He'd become a different man with what felt like someone else's future. It lay in wait for him ghoulishly.

Great strides had been made in minimizing and controlling the effects of the disease, but there was no cure and might never be. In fact, most researchers had given up on overcoming the virus. The current focus was on creating a vaccine to prevent infection in the first place. Protease inhibitors could drop HIV to below detectable levels, and with care and some luck he might live most of his normal life-span -- yet how normal would it be?

Each day he lived out sixty years in his mind, breathing in claustrophobic phantom mobs of might-have-beens and cruel visions of himself as a bed-ridden husk. The effort was exhausting, lethal, and he tried to shut down his mind. There were more danger zones than safe areas now. He needed to be smaller.

He kept busy. Another new lesson was that action of any sort was better than waiting, worrying.

"Stay positive," a therapist told him, not understanding the irony of her word choice. "You've got a long time ahead of you, son," a specialist promised.

There were no fingerprints on the needles or the notes. Interviews with theater employees and the small number of movie-goers who'd come forward generated not one lead.

If there had been any point, any profit, it could have been the perfect crime, but it was only perfect madness.

A ninth victim discovered more needles in the coin return slots of three payphones down the block, but again there were no clues or witnesses. Short of receiving a confession, the police might never be able to explain who had done it or why.

He'd become a statistic. For what? He dwelled on lunacy, though greater minds than his had offered only more questions or cures that helped few at best. Monsters in all their many forms were a perverse cancer that would have been abolished by now if evil was not inherently part of the human being. Shooting sprees, arson, child molestation -- the insanity had become so constant that most people tried to ignore it.

Others sought out chaos and pain, some to feast, some to heal. In the days after the theater incident, he was harassed by both types. And half a year later, when tests proved that eight of them were blood positive, the circus

started again.

He'd become a celebrity in the national media, especially the tabloids. There were plenty of other crazies and their deeds to celebrate (Golf Club Killer Bludgeons Neighbors; Sabotage Kills 4 In Subway), but he and the other infected victims were walking dead and this insidious aspect played well -- as did the fact that their only mistake had been to sit down. Everyone sits down. On buses, in restaurants, at ball games. Everyone.

His notoriety wasn't anything that a man could properly capitalize on, of course. Women would never clamor for space in his bed, employers wouldn't compete for him. His buddies started picking up the tabs for beer and food, but very soon he was seeing less and less of them. Some of this distancing was his own fault, partly because he ran to see every specialist his insurance would cover, mostly because he couldn't stand rehashing what had happened or getting maudlin about the good ol' days.

Much of the gradual separation was their doing, however, and he quickly learned who was a friend and who had been a mere acquaintance. Losing his girlfriend was the hardest.

Her pity hurt. Her revulsion hurt. Memories hurt. Hope and regret and wishes hurt. She was experiencing her own myriad of anguishes, but he didn't care. He couldn't afford to.

He'd stopped answering his phone during the blitz of calls from media, friends and family (and from oblivious telemarketers who made him smile bitterly). The plaintive voice on the machine no longer sounded familiar. He erased all her messages.

A lawyer approached him with the news that six of the other victims were filing a liability suit against the theater, a national chain which was at least sure to settle out of court. "I'm in," he said. What had happened could hardly be considered the theater's fault, but protracted phone calls and paperwork and meetings with representatives of his insurance company had him frightened. Money meant more doctors, more treatments.

He visited the lawyer's office twice briefly but continued to avoid the other victims, despite his therapist's suggestions to join group sessions. He didn't want to know those people. In a sense, he wished he no longer knew himself.

He hoped work would be an escape. All he wanted was to be ignored. Instead, he was avoided, a different thing altogether, which he deeply resented. His first life had been full of casual contact -- handshakes, the brush of fingers when exchanging files -- but now he walked in a ghost world, isolated and damned, unclean. Once he even caught a woman emptying out the coffee pot in the break room after he'd poured himself a cup.

"You need an outlet for your anger," the therapist told him. "Paint. Play music. Let it out."

He blasted ten thousand spaceships on his PlayStation and smashed baseballs at the batting cages until his hands and wrists throbbed. He went skating but ached deep in his soul when confronted with rollergirls whose firm-bodied health had always been the stuff of fantasy.

There were dating services that linked HIV-positive singles, even heterosexual drug-free singles. He'd never have oral sex again or experience intercourse without the sensation-killing barrier of prophylactics (mixing viral strains at random would only hasten his decay), but the possibility of intimacy did exist, no matter how sad and unappealing. Nonsmoker, professional, likes movies...

The note left in his cubicle read: Faggots rot in hell!

He should have laughed at this ignorant cowering bluster. His therapist would have been proud. Yet it was a full minute before he stopped shaking and unballed his fist from around the crumpled paper. He showed it to his boss, establishing a record, then did his best to provoke his suspects, visiting their cubicles often, volunteering exaggerated reports of his treatments and future symptoms. With luck, they'd strike again. Another lawsuit meant more money. And he enjoyed his plotting with fierce joy. It was wonderful to be the aggressor again.

The skinny old woman in the free clinic that only charged fifty bucks had trouble finding his antecubital vein. The inside of his elbow might as well have been a dartboard.

"Here," he said, with all the patience he could muster.

Flying out to California had not been a great idea -- mom made him chicken soup thirteen times in two and half weeks, and dad no longer seemed capable of looking him in the eye -- but he couldn't afford a real vacation. The liability suit had yet to be resolved, and he'd missed too much work during the past year.

There was solace in resignation. Even a bad game of golf with his dad was better than rotting alone. Iced tea tasted as good as ever. Fresh-cut grass still smelled amazing. But the yuppie foursome that had played ahead of them ripped his heart. The breeze had been full of the men's advice and cheerfully crude propositions, the women's laughter. He should have been one of them. Let go, let God, was his mother's mantra, and he tried to believe it. He practiced meditation now, energy-channeling, and color therapy. These were acts of desperation rather than faith, unfortunately.

Anger flared in him like a migraine when the old bitch missed his vein for the third time. Familiar, powerful anger.

He'd hoped to get through the summer without subjecting himself to more blood work, but his doctor wanted to try a new anti-viral and needed a fresh count. His insurance, which had begun clamping down, declared this an elective process, so instead of visiting real professionals he'd come here, exposing himself to a lobby full of sicknesses borne by others who couldn't afford better care.

Even worse was the humiliation of revealing his secret to new people. The dark-eyed receptionist had been polite but he knew what she was thinking. He wished she wasn't so pretty. He wished no one was that pretty.

The skinny old bitch forgot to apply pressure after she withdrew the hypo. He grabbed a cotton ball from her supplies and jammed it down on the puncture himself, so that he wouldn't bruise. He almost said something caustic, but in his new life he'd encountered plenty of workers who were ill-trained, indifferent, condescending, too busy.

It did not surprise him that trust was a mistake.

"There's no need for alarm," said the man on the phone. "We just want you to come down for retesting, just to be safe."

Rather than disposing of disposable needles, the silly bitch had washed them with hot water and soap, thinking she was doing good, being thrifty. Her training had consisted of two four-hour classes and she would have continued to mix and match blood-borne diseases in unsuspecting people except that a more experienced co-worker happened to observe her at the sink.

Of the more than five hundred people this woman treated, only eleven were infected. Various officials declared victory.

Six of those eleven had passed through the clinic immediately after him. Ironically, all were healthy twenty-or-thirty-somethings, for the most part sexually active, in their prime. Exactly like he had been, not so long ago. All six had chosen to be tested merely for peace of mind after seeing too many community service commercials.

Now they had his strain of HIV as well as the Hepatitis B that he'd picked up from another man.

He remembered a few faces and articles of clothing from the waiting room, a strident voice, nothing more. What had happened wasn't his fault -- it had never been his fault -- but he felt a connection that had never existed between himself and the other victims of the movie theater incident. Perhaps he was weaker now, after months of constant isolation and loss.

He tried to seek them out but confidentiality rules made this difficult, as did a circle-the-wagons mentality on the part of the clinic, which was already under threat of several lawsuits. Neither of the two women he managed to track down wanted anything to do with him. One was hysterical. Both seethed with blame. He understood, yet it might have helped to create a special tribe. People to die with.

Hepatitis would ravage his compromised immune system.

When he woke the next morning, the sun was strong and promising and two fat scrub jays screeched energetically in the flowering shrubs. He watched them without expression.

He'd finally achieved the narrow thoughtlessness that had eluded him for so long. He understood why now, knew what dark instinct had driven the nameless monster who'd killed him, as random and insane as it must seem to the healthy, the secure, the happy.

He had been infected in that theater in more than one sense.

After breakfast, he stabbed himself with a dozen needles and went out to booby-trap some park benches.

Jeff Carlson is the international bestselling author of PLAGUE YEAR and THE FROZEN SKY. To date, his work has been translated into sixteen languages worldwide. His new novel is FROZEN SKY 2: BETRAYED.

Readers can find free fiction, videos, contests, and more on his web site at jverse. om

REBORN

BY THE BEHRG

NOT YOUR AVERAGE MONSTER

"I used to believe in God, then I believed in the Devil. Now I laugh at both and only believe in Evil."

- Diary of Darius Maggiolini, Archbishop, spoken on his deathbed

IN 1974, the Catholic Church sent out a declaration to every bishop, presbyter, and deacon who resided within a sanctioned diocese. This formal document, which you will find (though partially torn) at the end of my tale, has since been repudiated, as have all official communications regarding the *Sancto Saepes Motu Proprio*. Ask any secretariat of the Church about the rumored incursion and you will receive only shaking heads or grudged denials. You will however find that the mandates held within this clandestine document are stringently, if quietly, upheld to this day.

The following is taken directly from the declaration:

From this day... forward... no infant child abandoned on or before [a Church-affiliated domicile] shall be admitted within said domicile by a member of the clergy. This sanctioned decree is to be upheld without exception.

My tale, and those unfortunate souls who experienced similar trespasses, will provide more than enough evidence as to why.

It was an April evening in 1971, a day that had been muddled with a constant downpour. It is important to note that this was a time when I still believed in a Higher Power. At twenty-three I was young to have been chosen as chaplain of the Sacred Heart Basilica of the Immaculate Conception. So young, in fact, that I still believed I was doing God's work.

Evenings in Bridgeport, Connecticut were quite dull, and with the hellacious storm our evening services amounted to a dress rehearsal, only vacant pews and the occasional scurrying mouse in attendance – the rain always drove them inside. Sister Bedford, a motherly nun in every sense of the word, had taken to mopping the nave, humming an amalgamation of hymns that no choir would recognize. She was deaf in one ear and tone deaf in the other, but her jovial cheeks and maternal charm warmed the soul (not to mention her chocolate chip cookies which were absolutely divine!). I hurriedly gathered the hymnals pew by pew, ready to call it an early night.

There was a chill in the high-ceilinged halls and Father Maggiolini, an old-world coot and the attending Bishop, had gone off to check the pilot of the furnace which was always blowing out. If I recall correctly I believe that rainy season we had a leak in the basement. The water pooling against the outer walls of the church seeped through the porous stones rotted with age. It made for an eerie walk through those long corridors below ground, as if the very walls were weeping.

As we mindlessly went about our evening duties thinking only of the warm wool comforters awaiting our shivering bodies – or at least such were my thoughts – a shocking boom resounded from the outer cloister doors. Sister Bedford dropped her mop, her hands going to her ample, yet covered, bosom. The teetering, towering pile of hymnals which I had collected were sent scattered across the hard marbled floor, pages bristling and book bindings breaking. Who would be out at this hour in such conditions? And why a single knock and nothing more?

My heart seemed to answer the resounding thud with a steady knocking of its own. Please remember, I was but twenty-three, at an age where imagination could still conjure demons from shadows and redemption from a statue of a man on a cross.

Footsteps echoed from the west wing, Sister Nettles appearing, a small candle cradled in her hands. "You're not going to open it?"

Her British accent tugged at the strings of my heart which was no good, considering she had already tied them into a jumbled knot. She was adorable, Sister Nettles – a tiny thing at only five foot two. A small crook for a nose, long neck and bony chin and eyes which were much too large for her face, but the disjointedness came together like a tightly woven collage creating something far more magnificent than the sum of the individual parts on their own. While I would not have admitted so back then, I see no harm in doing so now; I was taken by her, and despite my vows there were many nights when she visited me in the lucid realms of sleep.

Before I had a chance to gather my thoughts, Nettles swept past both Sister Bedford and me, cupping her hand around the flame so as not to let it die.

"Allow me!" I shouted, hurrying after her.

She, of course, did.

The ornate iron doors, crested with scenes from the bible so analogous each square could represent your pick of stories, were set in the floor with heavy pins that dropped down latching them closed. The pins, each a good eighteen inches in length, required an inordinate amount of effort to free from their catch not only due to their weight but the levers within the flooring that had to be turned just so. Once I wriggled the damnable pin free, I pulled the door open, sliding the pin beneath as a doorstop, as we commonly did at the time.

Heavy rivulets poured down just beyond the alcove of the porch, the night black beyond the stoop. I swallowed hard, noting that no one was there – no gust of wind could have come at the doors with that much alarm, and then

Sister Nettles was crouching down, her little bottom pursed out towards me. With reddened cheeks almost as rosy as Nettles', I quickly glanced away. The sound of that sweet Sister cooing brought my attention back, her soft voice answered by a piercing wail.

A baby.

Someone had dropped it at our porch. Like a bag of groceries or an advert for the local theater. And whatever depraved soul left it, had failed to turn it from the stuck position of *ff* - FORTISSIMO.

Nettles motioned for my assistance, gathering up her skirt and glancing out at the darkness. I noticed that despite the lack of a breeze, the candle's flame had blown out. I took in the woven reed basket and infant swimming within a sea of churning pink cloth. Her face was the color of a plum and I marveled at how much anger something so small and innocent could manifest. Oh, if we had only known.

After carrying the bundle inside, I placed it on a raised bench. Sister Bedford crowded in beside me. Her heavy jowls curved her lips downward in a permanent frown though it was apparent she was beaming inside.

"Oh, she's such a sweetheart!" Not surprising – I did mention she was partially deaf.

While Nettles still hovered out on the stoop, Sister Bedford reached down taking the screaming infant, blankets and all, and brought her up to bounce against her ... well, bouncy chest. "Shh, shh, shh, you are a sweet thing, aren't you?"

"You should wait for the Olfac," Nettles said.

"Huh?"

I knew the name by which Maggiolini was called by the attending nuns, Olfac or Factory, in reference to the persistent body odor which always accompanied the man, redolent of a wet and hirsute dog. It was said that the Archbishop Alcote had once nearly fainted in Maggiolini's presence and, while he had attributed it to his fasting, we all knew the true offender. '*If thy right eye offend thee, pluck it out, and cast it from thee.*' Not so simple with the pungent musk of one's own pores.

Knowing that Sister Bedford was just as habituated with the name, I presumed she just hadn't heard. "She said you should wait for Father Maggiolini," I said.

"Nonsense. We used to see this sort of thing all the time at the Rectory on Forty-Second – young girls knocked up by married men who should exchange their wedding rings for chains, if you ask me. And besides, a man – even a Father, Sister Nettles – lacks the proper equipment. Now close that door! It's drafty as a turnip field in Poland in here."

"I'll get it." My enthusiasm this time wasn't for aiding Nettles but rather born of sheer desperation to escape the gales of the child's cries.

"Here, here, you sweet thing. Now when they haven't a teat to suckle you can slip them a finger and most times they'll pacify themselves to sleep."

"That's disgusting," Nettles crooned.

"That, my dear Sister, is biology."

I always wondered what Sister Bedford heard next. Whether, for instance, the rending of flesh and snapping of bone and cartilage, melded with the sickeningly frantic slurps and bellicose sucking noises, came to her as something other than what it was. I'm quite certain, however, that she heard her own screaming.

The baby dropped from her arms as Sister Bedford backed away, a smear of gristly red coating its small chin. Somewhere along its descent I realized, it was no longer crying. A stream of blood flowed from Sister Bedford's finger like the curved spray of a drinking fountain. Hysterical and dazed, she tumbled against the back pew, falling onto her considerably padded behind with a loud harrumph.

I braced myself for the thud of the child connecting with the marbled floor but watched with fascination as it adroitly righted itself in the air, landing delicately on outstretched fingers and toes. With the blankets torn off, you could see the rippled muscles in its tiny arms and legs as it held itself in a pushup position. Shoulder blades extended, triceps and deltoids flexed – it was like watching some freak carnival showing off a grown man the size of a baby.

Until I saw its tail.

It slithered out the top of the cloth wrapped around its waist, the appendage ending not in a point but a four tendon knob. The digits gripped the cloth diaper at its posterior and tore it free, twirling it once before casting it aside. Then the tail dropped to the ground, its four tendons spread out like talons, the fleshy knob raised slightly above.

The tail started vibrating. Then the creature was launched into the air.

Sister Bedford, who at this moment was mid-scream, grappled for anything nearby with which to ward off her attacker. Unfortunately we were in a church, not a junkyard or garage or office where miscellaneous items could be quickly requisitioned and repurposed. The hymnals, while scattered on the ground, were several rows up, and all of the wall hangings and architectural ornamentation had been anchored to walls and pillars long ago.

The creature landed between the crux of Sister Bedford's outstretched legs, the skirt of her dress bowing inward and drawing up with its weight. Beyond the tethered muscles which rippled beneath its pale flesh, and of course, the tail, it was difficult not to see a helpless infant propped awkwardly between the nun's quite hairy legs.

"MotherofMercysendthisdemonbacktoitsprisonandblessuswithyourholylight." The words came out in a single gasp and must have struck the infant beast like a psychic blow. It began wailing a piercing and heartrending cry.

"BytheFatherandtheSonandtheHolyGhostIcommandtheetoleavethisholypl aceatonce!"

The creature let out a burp. A chunk of what must have been flesh or maybe a nail dislodged from its mouth, skipping with a wet slap along the floor. The crying immediately stopped. It hadn't been Sister Bedford's words that had caused its panic; just an upset stomach.

The beast's tail shot forward, puncturing a slit in Sister Bedford's dress through which it promptly disappeared. A moment passed in which only our breathing was heard, then Sister's Bedford's eyes tripled in size and she cried out with renewed vigor.

"Get it ... out of me!" Her legs kicked wildly and she doubled over, a strained consternation coming over her face. "Get it out!"

Whatever paralysis had held Nettles and I bound was lifted, incredulity replaced with a need to act, to save. Though we were accustomed to believing in that which could not be seen, we had little experience with doubting that which was directly before our eyes.

I slid to the floor on my knees, reaching through the slit in the fallen nun's gown, the fabric tearing further beneath my weight. The baby was not on the ground between the Sister's legs as I had hoped. No, the atrocity before me was so unimaginable, so damning to both spirit and body, that I quaked at the sight. As a virgin, this was the first time I had ever seen the workings of a woman. But what should have been a curious fascination was vilified by the sight of two extended feet slithering upward into the cavity of Sister Bedford's vagina, the pronged tail sticking out, pressed deep into the flesh of her inner thigh, leveraging its ascent.

This was not the rebirth I had read of in the Holy Bible.

Sister Bedford's screams by now filled the entire chapel and let me tell you, no choir had ever sung so loud within our humble halls.

Nettles fell against me, frantically clawing at Sister Bedford's dress. "Where is it?"

"It went... up," I said, "where a baby comes out."

Elocution had failed me.

I stood, unable to watch as Nettles plunged her arm in after the creature. I don't remember consciously going back to the open door; perhaps I had wanted to leave, to escape the insanity that had stumbled onto the doorstep of our lives, but instead I shoved that heavy door closed, gripping the metal pin in my hand. The feeling that came over me next was what some might consider, revelatory. I felt like a vampire slayer, divinely called to rid the world of evil, armed with only righteousness and a holy wooden cross – or in this case, an eighteen inch bar of ribbed steel.

"No, no, no, no, no!"

Nettles' arm and neck were slathered in blood. She now knelt atop Sister Bedford, pressing both arms against the older woman's torso where a pronounced mound beneath the skin continued climbing northward. The off key screaming had subsided, a milky substance bubbling from Sister Bedford's mouth. I moved back toward the two women, the pin gripped like a miniature baseball bat. A firm calm and determination had settled over me; I knew what had to be done.

Before I crossed the threshold, Sister Bedford's neck bulged, her jaw dislocating with two distinct mercurial pops. And then, from within her gaping lips and saggy cheeks, the top of a head began to crown. Like a bubble blown from chewing gum, the pink head expanded until, with a sickening suction sound, the creature's full head popped free of Sister Bedford's mouth. The rest of its tiny and slime covered body wriggled out, slipping down her face to the marbled floor.

The creature leapt off the ground just as I swung the metal pin toward it, my calculated strike instead slashing open the side of Sister Bedford's face from lip to jaw. Another misplaced swing sent fleshy pulp splattering upward, disfiguring the poor motherly Sister even further, though by this point she was quite dead. When the infant scrambled over Sister Bedford's body toward Nettles I acted only as any gallant knight might, but the creature avoided each assault with an uncanny dexterity. Its tail suddenly plunged down against a thick bony knee, vibrating ferociously, then it launched itself at the thin nun weeping over Sister Bedford's body.

Footsteps echoed from the hall, Father Maggiolini's raspy voice lost behind the blood thrumming in my ears. The creature was in Nettles' arms, tangling itself in the tassels of her white smock, trying to scale her. I brought the pin back, leaping forward with my thrust. The chiseled tip of the pin sunk through the creatures flesh as if I had been wielding a sword. It shrieked a piercing cry cut short as the metal rod slid through its small body, puncturing both organs and life.

I exhaled a deep breath, an inner peace coming over me. I had exterminated this foul monster, this infernal beast that had risen from the seventh circle of hell. Then I heard the clatter of a small box of tools dropping to the ground behind me.

"My God, what have you done?"

Father Maggiolini stood at the end of the arched hallway, his eyes giant saucers within murky ponds of wrinkles. His jaw hung open, a puppet no longer in use.

I turned back to Nettles, pulling the pin free from the vile creature in her arms. It slid out with much more difficulty than it had going in, ruptured organs and stringy tissue clinging to the inanimate object. I looked for confirmation on Nettles' face, the corroboration of my innocence, of the true culprit of the massacre we had just witnessed.

Without a word, the child slipped from her hands. It smacked the marbled floor with the heart-wrenching thud I had anticipated earlier, when it had caught itself on fingers and toes. While I could still see the hint of wiry muscles beneath, its taloned appendage had withdrawn, tail somehow retracting into smooth, if wrinkly, skin. The blood leaked from its two gaping wounds in its torso like an overturned jar of ink.

And where the baby once had been, Nettles held a pool of crimson blood cupped within her hands. Dangling from the hole in her gown was the creature's tail. It had speared right through her stomach, ripping into her intestinal track. Liquid feces, mixed with blood, spilled from the puncture wound.

Her legs gave out just as I turned back to Father Maggiolini.

"Look – its tail!"

I never heard him coming. He struck me with the end of a candelabra and I followed my Nettles down.

I was convicted of triple homicide. Life, with no chance of parole. Thanks to our corrupt legal system, and untraceable bribes from the Vatican, a plea of insanity landed me, thankfully, in a more hospitable residence than a federal detention facility. They claimed, of course, that the tail was merely mangled flesh, a part of Nettles' intestines. That I suffered a psychotic relapse, remembering my own abandonment as a child, and was caught up in a schizophrenic hallucination. And the creature – well, dead, it looked as innocent as a newborn. With no biological family to press for an autopsy, it was quietly swept under a very thick Italian rug. What's one cover-up in the history of a Church that is riddled with them?

But I know the truth because I'm not alone. There are others just like me. A nun in Tampa, Florida, who set an infant child on fire; a priest in Tacoma, Washington, who threw a baby from the top of a bell tower; a groundskeeper in Southern Utah, who buried a trowel through an infant's skull. They've seen what I've seen. They know.

And they're not the only ones.

There's a reason that *Motu Proprio* was sent out to every church and domicile under the authority of the Pope. And if you don't believe me, ask around. You'll see – they'll all say they don't know why or when the practice of bringing abandoned infants into the church was abolished. But if you look closely while they're giving their answers, you'll notice a bead of sweat trickle down a forehead. Nostrils flaring, when their sinuses were fine before. They will quickly excuse themselves to other matters while apologizing that they couldn't give you more of their time. And then you too will know.

Evil walks amongst us. Or crawls. Cries. Screams.

And we are the ones who must stop it.

 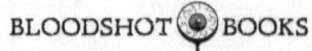

Sancto Saepes Motu Proprio:

The Second Vatican Council, in adherence to the infallible truths set forth by the Magisterium, has ascertained the need to set forth, in divine promulgation, the ensuing statute, requiring the immediate and universal assent, both in faith and by works, of all magistrates whose ministries extend to any sacred domiciliary station including, but not limited to, cathedrals, churches, convents, oratories, monasteries, rectories, or any other place of worship or sanctioned tutelage:

From this day, the 22nd of May in the year of our Lord 1974, forward, and ever looking backward, for God is the same today, yesterday, and tomorrow, no infant child abandoned on or before the holy grounds of an aforementioned domiciliary station, or any analogous edifice, shall be admitted within said domicile by a member of the clergy. This sanctioned decree upheld without exception.

In the event that such a circumstance should arise it is advisable in the establis

which said domicile should subscribe, namely in relation to the governin contact the local authorities. Such an outreach should be made w wherein the presiding council will convene to determine th file, in the Church archives, both the discovering p with accordance to the doctrines of the eve and His Holy Word in which all m

Further council should recording names without th apol

The Behrg is the author of dark literary works ranging from screenplays to 'to-do' lists. His debut novel, Housebroken, was a First-Round Kindle Scout Selection, and semi-finalist in the 2015 Kindle Book Awards. His latest novel, The Creation, is the first in a dark supernatural trilogy about a 'god-like' being starting the seven days of the Creation over again. Books two and three are due out in 2016. The Behrg's 'to-do' list should be completed by 2017... (though his wife is hoping for a little sooner).

A former child actor turned wanna-be rockstar, The Behrg lives in Southern California with his four children, pet Shih-Tzu, and the many voices in his head.

Discover why he writes as "The Behrg" at his website: TheBehrg.com

SOFT-WALKER

BY CHRISTINE MORGAN

NOT YOUR AVERAGE MONSTER

WE ARE THE CORN-PEOPLE
WE ARE THE BLOOD-PEOPLE
WE ARE THE GOD-PEOPLE
MADE FROM BLOOD AND CORN

TUAPECMAL imbued his voice with all the confidence he could muster as he led the morning's chant.

But the listless villagers only mumbled their responses. Most did not even bother to look at him, keeping their gazes downcast rather than lift them to the sun rising behind the altar-stone.

A haze hung already in the sky. Not a breath of breeze stirred. The surrounding jungles fumed a green and sweaty steam. Any relief the cooler shade beneath the trees might promise was made a lie by the steady, droning, teeming hum of biting flies, *chinche* beetles and *mosquito*.

The men leaned heavily upon their digging-sticks, as if at the end of a long work-day rather than the beginning. In the *milpas* where they grew their crops, the earth lay parched and dusty. The women all looked weary, when they had not yet begun their ceaseless treks to and from the deep *cenote*. Empty buckets carried down rough steps hewn from cavern limestone, full buckets brought back up. Fretful younger children tugged at their sisters or grandmothers.

Tuapecmal raised the offering-bowl of *atole*, the drink brewed from honey-sweetened cornmeal. It was very weak, very watery. The gods might not be pleased, but what else was there to do? He did not know. He was no priest. He was no prince.

They had tried the ritual bloodletting, piercing the flesh of every person in the village with spines of dried and sharpened corn-stalk, dripping it onto scraps of corn-husk paper and burning it to waft as smoke. The hunters had trapped a live tapir, which had been adorned with flowers and thrown into the dark sinkhole that led to Xiabalba.

Finally, in desperation, Great Ixlat their leader ordered his own son taken to the altar-stone. Ixatalan was the best of them, a fine youth, strong and handsome, a hunter and a skilled player of the ball game, loved by all. He went bravely to his fate, with his last words imploring the gods to have mercy and bring favor upon the People. Then the obsidian knife, wielded by his father's hand, had cut the beating heart from his breast.

Such a noble sacrifice, the People believed, *must* appease the gods!

It was therefore a terrible surprise to them when, a few days later, they woke to find the Great House empty. Ixlat, his queen, and the high priest were gone, along with most of the household and many treasures of gold, jade, and *quetzal*-feathers as could be carried.

Their leader-king had abandoned them.

Abandoned them to suffer, to wither under the heat of the worst dry season they had ever known.

Had the gods abandoned them as well?

No one wanted to believe it. Were they not the Corn-People, the Blood-People, the God-People made from blood and corn? Were they not the favored ones? The chosen of all creation?

So it was, so had it always been, so had they been told. How Sky-Heart, in loneliness, made the world, filling it with plants and animals... but when those could not sing his praises, the other gods suggested he give life to creatures that could think and speak.

First, Sky-Heart had formed the People-of-Mud, but they sat and did nothing, and he let them melt away in the rain. Next, Sky-Heart fashioned the People-of-Wood, who walked and talked but were empty in the head, so he destroyed them with flood and fire.

Then, at last, Green-Maize-Woman brought Sky-Heart the ripe corn, and showed him how to grind the grain upon the flat *metate*, and wet it with his own god-blood, and from the resulting clay-paste he shaped the first true People. They honored him with sacrifices, sang his praises, and were faithful and good.

Each day, they reaffirmed this in their chant to the rising sun. As they had done this morning. As they did every morning.

Yet, now ...

Could Sky-Heart have turned his back? Did the god no longer watch over his creations? Would he not protect them from injury and sickness? Had they failed to please him? Had he not been entertained by the ceremonial ball-games? By the offerings?

Why did he leave them to the cruel predations of Black Macaw, Bringer-Of-Thunder-Without-Rain, who had countless hungry, greedy offspring?

Or did Sky-Heart test the People? Test their loyalty with hardship, so that if they won through, they would be rewarded?

Tuapecmal had no answers for these many questions. He had no answer for why it was that the villagers looked to him. All he had been, before, was Ixatalan's closest friend, the prince's inseparable companion since boyhood.

Now, Ixatalan was dead, the life bled from him on the altar-stone.

And all, it seemed, for nothing. The three eldest of Black Macaw's brood –

called Drought, and Blight, and Swarm – continued to plague the People. Their myriad younger siblings swept down in feathered numbers to peck the corn-grain from the new stalks or the fresh-planted *milpa* rows. They tipped over baskets, raided any grinding *metate* left unattended, and the bolder ones might snatch pieces of corn-dough from a child's hand.

They were relentless in their thievery. Relentless.

The village women had tied cloths on lines in hopes their wind-stirred waving might scare the birds away. But with no wind to stir them, the cloths hung limp, fading in the sun's glare, gathering field-dust.

When chased off or struck at, the birds returned at once. Barking dogs did not deter them. Nor did boys throwing rocks. The flap and flutter of their wings was mocking laughter. Each caw and chirp was taunting insult. Trick-likenesses of men, made from cornstalks, sticks, and rags, only provided places for them to perch. There, they preened and chattered.

The sun climbed higher. The day warmed further. The offering of *atole* that Tuapecmal had poured upon the altar-stone dried to a smear, explored by buzzing flies. He returned the bowl to the Great House, then stood there in its vacant, unaccustomed silence.

He closed his eyes, though not with any foolish hopes that, when he again opened them, he would see it as it used to be.

Tears stung behind his eyelids. A lump felt lodged within his throat. Tightness gripped his chest, as if his heart – the heart he would have gladly given up, taking Ixatalan's place on the altar-stone beneath the obsidian blade – was caught in a god-fist. His breath shuddered.

"Tuapecmal," whispered a voice.

A familiar voice. A voice he knew. A voice he loved. A voice he never thought he'd hear again.

A voice that, although known and loved and familiar, sounded different somehow. Cool and dark, damp, with a hollow echo that made him think of the deep *cenote*.

His eyes opened. While he still did not see the Great House as it used to be, neither did he see it as he knew it was. It, too, was cool and dark. Shadows rippled on the floor like the surfaces of pools.

And, like an upright reflection on the rippling surface of such a pool, the vague image of his friend appeared before him.

"Ixatalan," he said, or tried to. His mouth mutely shaped the name.

"Tuapecmal."

It was Ixatalan, it *was*. Not as Tuapecmal had last seen him – back arched, head back, arms splayed, awaiting the cold, sharp touch of the sacrificial knife – but as Tuapecmal remembered him best. Smiling. White teeth shining. Leaning, almost lounging, at his ease. His gaze welcoming and warm.

A breechclout swathed his lean hips, its ends beadwork-decorated. Around his shoulders, he wore a strip of jaguar-skin knotted at the chest. Jaguar claws hung from it, pale curves against his unmarked, muscular flesh. Another such strip of jaguar-skin bound his black hair back from his high brow.

Yes, it *was* Ixatalan.

The tears he had withheld threatened to return. A single one succeeded, trickling down Tuapecmal's cheek. He slowly extended a trembling hand. Ixatalan's folded around his, fingers insubstantial as smoke. The sensation of that spirit-touch sent a chill through him.

"You must help the People," Ixatalan said in his cool and hollow voice. "They look to you now."

"Me?" Tuapecmal shook his head, uttering a ragged laugh. "Why me?"

"They know you were dear to me, dearer than any friend or brother."

Another god-fist seemed to clutch at Tuapecmal's heart, to crush it with grief.

"But, Ixatalan, what can *I* do?"

"If Black Macaw's hungry children are not driven away, the People will starve."

"We've tried. There are too many. As soon as we plant more grain, they peck it from the earth. They devour the corn faster than it will grow!"

"Then find another way."

"How? They are bolder than ever. Nothing frightens them."

"Nothing?"

Tuapecmal paused. He again felt a chill course through him. He could not speak.

"Nothing?" Ixatalan said again. His familiar smile changed, the white teeth still shining, but shining in narrow, elongated points. His warm and welcoming gaze changed as well, becoming less welcoming and far warmer, a warmth like the smoldering glow of an ember. "In all the old stories, what does Black Macaw most fear? Who is Black Macaw's dreaded, hated foe?"

"In the stories?"

"When Seven Deaths sent Black Macaw to kidnap Green-Maize-Woman's daughter. Surely you remember. Black Macaw carried the girl high into the Great *Kapok* tree, where she could not get down. And Green-Maize-Woman asked the creatures of the jungle for their help."

"Ah yes." Tuapecmal said, recalling how they had listened raptly to the tales when they were boys. "Root-Sniffer, the wild pig, was willing but could not climb. Loud-Howler, the monkey, was the best climber but too noisy. Only Soft-Walker, the jaguar, could do both."

He understood then the change in aspect that had come over Ixatalan's features, the long teeth, the ember-glowing yellow eyes, the spotted fur that seemed to sweep along his chest and limbs, as if the jaguar-skin he wore grew to cover his body.

"And Soft-Walker," Ixatalan said, his whisper almost a growl, "climbed the Great *Kapok* tree, frightened away all the birds that Black Macaw had left to guard Green-Maize-Woman's daughter, and rescued her before Seven Deaths could come to claim her. Since that day, Black Macaw and Soft-Walker were sworn enemies. You know what you must do."

Tuapecmal nodded. "But what about you, Ixatalan?"

"Soft-Walker the jaguar goes between the worlds," he said, not quite in answer. "Soft-Walker goes by day and night, by land and water, by earth and tree, and between underworld and heavens."

As he spoke, his image began to fade and his voice to turn more ghostly. Tuapecmal sought to cling to his friend's hand, but there had been nothing of substance for him to grasp in the first place, and his fingers curled in on emptiness until they touched his own palm.

"Stay," he begged.

Then a dark sleep fell over him, and when he roused he found himself sprawled on the Great House's floor. Ixatalan, if he had ever been there, was gone. The vision, if vision it was, had ended.

He made a new likeness out of corn-stalks, sticks and rags. This one did not have the shape of a man, but was half again the size. It stood long and low upon four legs, with a thick tail of strung-together corn-cobs and a round-eared head carved from a lump of wood.

Into the hollows for its eyes, Tuapecmal set disks of polished jade. Into its gaping jaw went sharp white teeth, and into its cloth-padded paws went hooked slivers of honed obsidian.

Last of all, he wrapped the likeness in a spotted jaguar-skin, which Ixatalan had given him as a gift. He hefted it onto his shoulder and carried it through the village.

The People stared at him as he passed with his awkward burden. It was a crude, clumsy, shabby thing. They must have thought that he'd gone mad. No one spoke to him, though they murmured to each other behind his back.

He did not care. He did not speak to them, either, or acknowledge their astonished looks.

In the *milpas*, birds flitted and hopped from row to row, scratching at the dirt, pecking for planted grain. They perched on posts, flapping their wings, fanning their tails. They puffed their chests. They strutted. They chirped, cawed, called, and chittered. Their droppings splattered white and greenish-black.

Men swung at them with their digging-sticks, cursing. Boys, armed with nets and stones and branches, chased them off again and again. Dogs ran around, barking, yipping wildly. When disturbed, the birds rose scattering in a bright flurry of colored feathers, but no sooner had the disturbance moved on than they went back to what they had been doing.

Thieving. Feasting. Gorging themselves on the corn.

Some even flew at the men and boys and dogs, darting at their heads, battering with rapid-beating wings, jabbing with beaks and talons, drawing thin lines of blood. It even seemed the birds licked at the redness, lapping it up with thirsty greed.

The Corn-People... the Blood-People... Tuapecmal thought as he approached.

A flock descended on a girl who had been bringing the laborers a midday meal. Her basket tumbled into the field, spilling thin rolls of corn-dough stuffed with a cold mash of boiled beans and squash. She shouted furiously at the birds, slapping with both hands, until a scarlet-banded one gouged a deep wound in her cheek. Then she fled, wailing and sobbing, with her arms crossed over her face.

The largest of the birds was a brilliant blue macaw with jagged yellow markings and an insolent plumed crest. It screeched, shifting from claw to claw, atop the tattered remnants of one of the man-shaped likenesses.

That one – Blue-Lightning-Crest, Tuapecmal decided he would call it – must have been their leader, a favored child of Black Macaw. Its cries seemed both mocking and triumphant as it watched its brethren tear apart the spilled bounty of squash and beans and corn-dough until not a scrap was left.

Blue-Lightning-Crest broke off its screeches as Tuapecmal brought his burden into the dusty rows. The plumed head tipped to one side. Black eyes glittered, fixed on him. The other birds also ceased their noise. The sudden hush made Tuapecmal shiver despite the sun's heat glaring through the haze.

Men with digging-sticks and women with buckets also stopped to watch, heads tilted in much the same inquiring manner. A dog yapped, took a step, then sat on its bony haunches with its tongue lolling.

He felt foolish. The skin-wrapped likeness was not fearsome. It was absurd. It more resembled an oversized child's toy made from twigs than it did a jaguar. He set it on the ground and it promptly fell over.

A single harsh and jeering caw from Blue-Lightning-Crest was the only sound. Tuapecmal's face burned with shame. He righted the likeness, balancing it on its four padded cloth paws. The disks of polished jade shined blankly. Its jaw gaped at nothing. Its corn-husk tail drooped in the dirt.

Tuapecmal sighed. He crouched beside his ridiculous construction, elbows braced on his knees and his head hanging. His shadow puddled beneath him.

What had he been thinking? He must have dozed off in the Great House, had a dream, and mistaken it for a vision or spirit-visit. He sighed again. The ground upon which he crouched had been recently turned, for all the good it did. Already, the ravenous birds had pecked up most of what had been planted. Glimpsing one that they'd missed, he pinched up a tiny, dry, wrinkled piece of corn-grain. He rolled it between his thumb and forefinger, sighing a third and heavy time.

"I am a fool," he said to the jaguar-likeness. "If Ixatalan could see this, he would laugh until he split. What kind of Soft-Walker could someone like me create?"

He stuck the grain of corn into its mouth as if feeding it, and only further proved his foolishness by pricking his finger on the point of a sharp tooth. He winced at the quick stab of pain, got up, and turned to trudge away with shoulders slumped and head still hanging.

A streak of blue and yellow glided past him. He looked back with dull and useless anger, already knowing what he'd see. Blue-Lightning-Crest alit on the stick and corn-stalk spine of the likeness, claws plucking at the spotted skin. The bird's wings ruffled proudly. It waggled its tail-feathers and shifted its stance, as if debating where first to void its splatter.

The dog that had been sitting with tongue lolling gave a startled yelp and lurched backward, kicking puffs of dust. A bare heartbeat later, the corn-stalk jaguar whipped about with all the sinuous strength and speed of a living jungle-cat. Its jaws snapped shut on Blue-Lightning-Crest's neck. The teeth sank deep. The bird flapped and shrieked in pain. The jaguar shook it in a furious, violent motion. Blood splashed the earth. Blue and yellow feathers flew. Hollow bird-bones cracked.

Then every other bird gathered around the *milpas* took in terror to the air. The sky darkened from the masses of wings and bodies. The air splintered with a thousand panicked cries.

Tuapecmal ducked, raising his arms to shield his face. A couple of birds smacked into him and fell dazed into the rows. One pecked at his ankle and he stamped it flat under his sandal.

When it seemed safe to do so, he lowered his arms and looked. He saw others doing the same, digging-sticks let fall, buckets of *cenote*-water overturned. The dogs had dashed from the fields. Villagers called out alarmed questions.

And the birds...

The birds, except for those few feathered corpses such as the one he'd crushed, were gone.

The corn-stalk likeness of a jaguar stood just as he had placed it. Unmoving and unmoved, jade-disk eyes gazing blankly at nothing. But thick red wetness, and flecks of blue and yellow, stuck to its wooden jaws. Shredded tufts and entrails, and a lone stiffened claw, were all that appeared to remain of Blue-Lightning-Crest.

"Soft-Walker," Tuapecmal said, without realizing he intended to. He glanced at his finger. He thought of the piece of grain he'd been putting into its mouth when the sharp tooth pricked his flesh.

The Corn-People... the Blood-People...

They gathered, the People. They stared at him again. This time, the stares were of a very different nature. None suggested he might be mad... unless they all were, because enough of them had seen it too. The jaguar, that swift strength and lithe grace. The large blue macaw ripped to tatters. The *milpas*, deserted of the countless birds.

No one spoke.

Perhaps no one could. Perhaps no one had to.

The first to move was an older woman, not a grandmother but not far from it, with scrawny but tough brown arms and legs and a grubby *huipil* with faded embroidery at collar and hem. She retrieved the buckets she'd been using to bring water from the *cenote*, peered into them, tutted, poured the dregs, and swept the rest of the villagers with an impatient look.

They resumed their labors.

All the rest of that day, and the next, and the next day after, the People worked in the *milpas*. The men turned the earth, dug the rows, planted what they still had saved to plant. The women carried water, bucket after cool bucket from the deep cenote.

And the birds did not return. Not in their previous numbers, coming nowhere near the village or the fields. Some might be seen in the jungle, quick flashes of color against the green as they darted from tree to tree. Their calls and cries could still be heard, but distant.

Soft-Walker remained in place. Tuapecmal cleaned the bloodied feathers from the jaguar's muzzle. The girl who'd been taking the men their meal that day, the girl with the wound upon her cheek, collected the other blue and yellow feathers to fashion into an ornament for Tuapecmal to wear.

More days passed.

The green corn grew in abundance. The hunters had good luck, killing wild pigs and deer. The guava bushes fruited. A boy, searching the storerooms, found a jar of old cacao beans that had been overlooked when Great Ixlat and his household left the village.

It soon became the custom to, following the morning chant, take small gifts and offerings to Soft-Walker. The best cuts of pig-meat, the sweetest and ripest guava, garlands of jungle-flowers, strings of beads, other trinkets.

Then, though, came a day when the sky was thick and yellow-tinged. The air hung heavy, hot and oppressive, not damp but dry and somehow brittle. Everyone woke thirsty, lips chapped, skin cracked, throats rasping, tongues parched in their mouths. They could not void their bladders. The nursing mothers found their milk would not pull. The crying babies shed no tears. The women who went to the cenote found that the constant water level was constant no more, but had sunk low until their buckets had to scrape the limestone bottom to come away even half full.

The People gathered worriedly in the shadow of the Great House. Their anxious gazes turned to Tuapecmal for answers. When he went out to the place where the jaguar-likeness stood, amid the rows of sprouting corn, the People followed.

A shrill caw fractured the heavy air. A shape flew from the jungle, a bird-shape, thin and ungainly, a vulture-turkey long of neck and scraggly of feathers. Where the shadow of its ragged wings passed over dense growth, the leaves and foliage withered and turned brown.

Its face, they saw as it flapped closer, was that of a hideous old woman, pinched and sneering, a hooked beak where a nose might have been. Shriveled teats dangled against her scraggle-feathered breast.

Drought had come.

Drought, one of the three eldest and strongest of Black Macaw's thieving brood.

"Do not let her get near the corn!" cried Tuapecmal.

The villagers rushed to comply, the men with bows and arrows, the boys with sticks and stones, even the girls and women seizing whatever was at hand. Shouting, they hurled their weapons at the ugly, flapping creature.

She cawed again. Several corn-stalks dried up, husks curling and flaking, the tender young and budding ears seeming to sizzle. A dog jumped at Drought, biting off a mouthful of tail-feathers, and dropped instantly dead with its hide shrunken to its bones as if it had been buried in hot sand for many years.

Tuapecmal ran into the field. "Soft-Walker, help us!" Remembering what had happened before, he pushed his hand into the tooth-studded muzzle, slicing his flesh and letting fall some grains of corn.

A sudden force drove him flat into the earth. The jaguar-likeness vaulted over him. Its stick and corn-stalk body, wrapped in the spotted hide, sprang up out of the growing corn, and brought down the vulture-turkey in a frenzy of jaws and claws.

The hideous bird-woman shrieked. Soft-Walker snarled. Blood, dust, shredded corn-husks, tattered feathers and stringy meat flew.

In moments, it was over.

The jaguar-likeness once again stood motionless. Drought was a bony, shrunken carcass at its feet. By the time the People composed themselves, by the time Tuapecmal had their best hunters pick up the scrawny body to burn it to ashes, a thick cool band of clouds had formed.

An unseasonable, gentle rain fell all the rest of that day, and for many days thereafter. The corn grew higher and healthier than any in the village had ever seen. The *cenote* filled to brimming. Creeks ran swift in creekbeds, leaping with silvery fish.

Then the sky one morning dawned an infectious greenish-grey. The People

 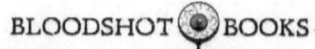

were stricken miserable with running sores and wet, itching blisters. Blotches speckled the jungle leaves. The guava fruits sagged, soft and rotten. The creeks turned a sickly color skimmed with foam, and in them the fish floated with their dead eyes bulging.

Blight came.

Blight, another of Black Macaw's three fearsome eldest children, shed filth from beneath his tail and his moist corpse-grey wings. He was as fat and bloated as Drought had been thin. He stank of rancidness. His cries gurgled with phlegm. Pus oozed, dribbling, from the nostril-slits in his scabrous beak. Instead of birdlike talons, he had pale fingers with peeling nails and more pus oozing from beneath them.

On the corn, which had been nearing ripeness, dank spots began to flower. The corn-flax went dark and slimy. The husks sloughed off like boiled skin.

Again, as the People rushed out with their weapons, Tuapecmal went straight to the jaguar-likeness. He cut his palm on a sharp tooth and made another offering of corn and blood, asking for Soft-Walker's help.

And, again, Soft-Walker gave it.

With a powerful bound, the likeness launched itself from the field. A swipe of its obsidian-bladed paw gashed open Blight's drooping underbelly. Guts dumped out in a putrid pile. The sound as Blight struck the ground and burst was something that threatened to haunt Tuapecmal's dreams for the rest of his life.

Once Blight was dead, the People stopped itching. Their sores and blisters healed. The green jungle leaves lost their blotchy speckles. The rotting guavas dissolved to foamy mush and firm, new ones fruited. The creeks ran clear again. The fish no longer floated dead against their banks.

As for the corn ... the dark, dank spots upon the corn ... these did not vanish but blossomed into the rich and pungent *huitlacoche*, a savory delicacy richer than any mushroom.

But, their troubles, the People realized, were not yet over. Some days after Soft-Walker killed Blight – that body, also, was burned – they woke to a sky tinged the murky orange-brown of smoke from a thousand fires.

At first, they noticed nothing else out of the ordinary. Then they became aware of a low, pervasive, constant hum. It swelled into a buzzing drone. The sky dimmed further as an immense mass roiled into a whirring, advancing cloud.

Swarm, the last and angriest of Black Macaw's eldest children, led the way with wings spread wide. His torso was that of a warrior, painted with battle-stripes in yellow and black. Atop his head streamed a crested headdress redder than fresh blood. Instead of a feathered tail, he had a venomous stinger like a spear, and where a bird's beak would have been, serrated pincers glistened.

This time, the People did not attempt to make a stand. They fled and hid in terror from the teeming cloud of insects – biting flies, wasps, *mosquito*, ravenous far-leapers. They fled also from the tide that seethed along the ground – fire-ants, scorpions, worms of a hundred legs, shiny-shelled *chinche*-beetles.

Fleeing and hiding did little good. Through the tiniest of cracks, the insects streamed in determined lines. They bit and stung. They descended on the *milpas*, settling onto the corn-stalks, nibbling and gnawing and devouring.

Tuapecmal ran through them, half-blinded, swiping insects from his face and eyes, spitting them from his mouth, choking. They crept up his nose and into his ears. They crunched beneath his sandals. They burrowed in his hair. When he stumbled, his knees came down hard upon them. He crawled past rows of corn. A legged worm longer than his forearm scuttled over the back of his hand.

His head collided with something wooden and hard. Not able by then to see at all, he groped for it. His fingers found the familiar carved contours, the rounded ears, the smooth disks of polished jade set for eyes.

Sucking what thin breaths he could through gritted, insect-filled teeth, he thrust a fistful of corn-grains into the jaguar's mouth. Sharp points raked his knuckles, drawing blood, cutting him to the bone.

He gagged and spat. His words emerged in a garbled croak.

Yet, it was enough.

Soft-Walker heard, and answered.

Tuapecmal felt the jaguar-likeness shoulder past, knocking him off-balance. He threw himself flat, pressing his face into the soil, everything inside of him an endless silent scream as the horde engulfed his body.

His last thought, as his senses left him, was one of relief.

His next thought, an untold time later, was one of confusion. He had not expected to ever wake again.

Yet, wake he did, and soon saw that Soft-Walker once again had saved them. The seething insects were gone, having barely had a chance to more than begin their crop-rending feast. Of Swarm himself, the only signs remaining were the red feathers of his war-crest, and the spear-length of his disembodied stinger.

The jaguar-likeness stood motionless, in the same place, though the spotted skin wrapped around its body of sticks and corn-stalks was partially torn. Many of the People had been stung and bitten, but the welts and bumps were already melting away.

In the days that followed, the corn flourished like never before. It promised a harvest of untold wealth and prosperity. So much early-ripened that they almost could not pick it fast enough. The baskets in the storerooms overflowed with grain. The stone *metates* were busy grinding from dawn until dusk. The women made thick cakes of corn-dough filled with pork and guava. They baked in a corn-meal coating fish stuffed with the savory *huitlacoche*. The *atole*-drink was sweeter than they had ever tasted.

Tuapecmal saw to it with diligence that the best portions were saved aside and offered to Soft-Walker. The likeness went on being regularly cleaned, adorned in flower garlands, beads, and ornaments.

Men skilled with chisels carved scenes of Soft-Walker's victories upon limestone *stelae*, setting these up one to either side. Cloths decorated with intricate embroidery and featherwork hung between the *stelae* to serve as shades.

All was well, until the morning that the sun did not appear. It rose, but could not be seen through turbulent dark clouds. From every direction rolled the ominous rumble of thunder-without-rain, and high behind those same dark clouds flashed flat sheets of deadly light.

"Black Macaw is coming," Tuapecmal said.

They had little time to prepare. The women and the children, the aged and the infirm, and all the more vulnerable among the People, took shelter within the Great House. The remaining men – hunters and warriors – gathered by the *milpas*, near the jaguar-likeness.

Tuapecmal poured a pouch of the best new corn into his palm. It heaped there, ripe, full, smooth and golden. As the storm closed in, thunder growling with rage and intensity, he slashed his other palm against a pointed jaguar's tooth. He hissed at the pain, the red blood welling, then cupped his hands together.

"We are the Corn-People," he said to the staring disks of polished jade as he dropped the red-soaked grains into the wooden mouth. "We are the Blood-People. We are the God-People, made from Blood and Corn."

Above them, a darker shape unfurled from the clouds. Vast black wings spread across the sky. Terrible thunderous winds whipped from them, lashing at the jungle treetops. Where talons might have been, clawed yellow forks of lightning sparked and crackled. More lightning made up the beak, which clacked a shattering thunderclap, and outlined the white-yellow blazing eyes.

The corn-stalks bent like rippling reeds, bowing away as Black Macaw swooped down. The lightning-talons clutched the tops of the carved limestone *stelae* to either side of Soft-Walker. The decorated cloths that had been hung as shades ignited into flaring smolders. The stone *stelae* themselves split with jagged lines.

Men cried out in fear, averting their faces. Tuapecmal alone met the thunderbird's deadly, baleful gaze.

Then, with a sharp, snapping pop and flash, Black Macaw transformed, diminishing in size but not in presence, standing with one foot braced atop each of the *stelae*. Only the blazing eyes remained the same, white-yellow and almost too bright to look upon.

Black Macaw's shape now was that of a goddess-queen, robed in blackest feathers, adorned in gold, with a high feathered headdress and living lightning-bolts gripped in either hand.

"You *dare*," she said, and her voice was thunder. "Wretched clumsy dolls of dough, you dare?! You dare to call yourself the People, the God-People, the chosen? All the seeds and grains and fruits of growing things upon the world should belong to *my* children! Sky-Heart and Green-Maize-Woman had no *right* to --"

Soft-Walker moved with sleek and silent speed. In that moment, the likeness was no humble, crude construction wrapped in a tattered skin, but flowed into a huge shadow-jaguar with shimmering jade-green eyes and teeth like daggers.

The suddenness of its pounce caught Black Macaw by surprise. She made a wild and ungainly leap, screeching in fright. Her black feather-cloak billowed. She stabbed with her lightning-bolts and only struck scorched craters in the ground. Attempting to land again upon the *stelae*, she lost her footing and tumbled into the corn.

The jaguar hunkered, fangs gleaming, long tail swishing with anticipation. As Black Macaw lurched awkwardly upright, indignant and outraged, Soft-Walker swung a paw in a playful, batting gesture. A playful, batting gesture filled with obsidian-sharp claws.

She screeched again and turned to run. The jaguar gave chase. It sprang and swatted, sending Black Macaw spinning in a storm of shed feathers. Soft-Walker stalked and chased her all the way to the edge of the village.

Seizing at the flapping edges of her torn cloak, Black Macaw flung wide her arms. They blurred into long wings, beating madly at the air. Sputtering tendrils of lightning snaked out, crackling around her fleeing, changing shape.

"Go, and do not come back!" roared the jaguar... or Ixatalan through the jaguar's throat. "You and your greedy children will leave these People in peace!"

As the bird flew frantically skyward, the dark storm clouds swirled in a spiraling maw like a gaping mouth. Black Macaw vanished into it. The clouds were sucked in after her. With a final earth-shaking blast of thunder, the day was abruptly calm and clear.

The jaguar-likeness had returned to its normal state, between the cracked stone *stelae*. The scraps of burnt cloth, the scorched craters, and the shredded feathers strewn throughout the corn-field told the men they had not imagined what they'd seen.

From then on, the village was untroubled by Black Macaw or her hungry brood. The only birds that came near were of the ordinary sort.

The corn grew better than ever, healthy and lush. The harvest was more prosperous than any in living memory or legend. The People had more fruit and fish and meat than they knew what to do with. No sicknesses or injuries befell them. They discovered a new grove of cacao trees. A woman gave birth to twins.

Word of their wealth traveled. They made the Great House into a temple, and brought the ragged and weather-beaten likeness of Soft-Walker there. They asked Tuapecmal to rule over them, but Tuapecmal refused.

Then, their former leader-king, Great Ixlat, returned to the village. News of their prosperity had reached him; he was eager to be home again among them, his People, so favored by the gods. He returned with his wife-queen and high priest, and household, and the many treasures and valuables that had so mysteriously vanished with them.

"Show me this jaguar I've heard tell of," Great Ixlat commanded. "This protector, this guardian of yours."

Tuapecmal obliged. But Great Ixlat was not pleased to see that the likeness had an honored place in what had been his Great House, was not pleased with the humbleness of it, and was very much not pleased with the way the People looked now to Tuapecmal.

"I will not have this here," Ixlat said. "It has served its purpose. Take it away."

In an eyeblink, Soft-Walker leaped upon Great Ixlat. It knocked him to the floor and pinned him there as everyone, stunned, looked on.

"Murderer," it said, in Ixatalan's voice. "Son-killer."

"Ixatalan?" cried Great Ixlat, sweat beading on his brow. "Ixatalan, my beloved son? Is it your spirit that speaks to me?"

"My spirit, from the underworld, where I was shown the truth. You made no sacrifice, but rid yourself of what you thought was a rival. Beloved son? You hated me. You'd gone old and fat and weak, Father, and you hated me."

A swift paw swiped, obsidian claws splitting the skin of Ixlat's chest from collarbone to quivering belly. The leader-king screamed as flesh parted to expose the pale cage of bone. Blood ran like flooding water.

"You feared the People would come to love me better," said the jaguar. "So, you killed me, and called it sacrifice, and abandoned them to their fate."

With that, as Ixlat continued to scream and plead and gibber, Soft-Walker's carved wooden jaws bit into his ribs. Bone cracked and gristle crackled. The jaguar's muzzle burrowed deeper. Its teeth closed around the frantic pulsing knot of meat that was Great Ixlat's heart, then tore it free in a single triumphant motion.

The heart twitched for a moment like a landed fish, then shuddered and went still. The blood that had been spurting from its trailing severed veins slowed to a dribble. Ixlat lay dead, eyes wide and blank with horror.

The likeness of the jaguar took a single step and fell in upon itself, nothing but a bundle of sticks and corn-stalks draped in a shabby spotted hide. It trembled. It stirred. Stirred, then moved and heaved.

From beneath the jaguar-skin, emerged a hand ... an arm ... a body, young and strong and handsome ... whole and alive.

Tuapecmal, sobbing with joy, stepped forward to help Ixatalan to rise. They regarded one another for a moment, Great Ixlat's body at their feet. Then, as the People began to cheer, they laughed together and embraced.

Christine Morgan works the overnight shift in a psychiatric facility, which plays havoc with her sleep schedule but allows her a lot of writing time. A lifelong reader, she also reviews, beta-reads, occasionally edits and dabbles in self-publishing. Her other interests include gaming, history, superheroes, crafts, cheesy disaster movies and training to be a crazy cat lady.

She can be found online at https://www.facebook.com/christinemorganauthor and https://christinemariemorgan.wordpress.com/

CEMETERY OF THE SKY

BY D. MORGAN BALLMER

SLYFIELD gestures to the photographs spread out Tarot-style upon the splintered, ale-stained table. The images bear the hallmarks of an amateur photographer; incongruous framing, sickly color temperature, and a blurry depth-of-field resulting from an over-reliance on the camera's auto-focus. In the dim lighting of the Grand Oak Tavern one could easily mistake these crime scene photos for a student art project. Slyfield is not oblivious to the bush league caliber of the pictures. He tugs absently at the sleeves of his suit as the Native American man slowly looks them over.

"Obviously Ansel Adams had the day off. This is all we have from the scene of the... disappearance," Slyfield says. "You can see the cell tower site, number 3276 here. Seems to be a remote stretch of wilderness, yet the public demands their cell coverage, eh?"

Tall Elk studies each photograph, his stoic expression impenetrable to the investigator. Slyfield watches with particular interest when the native man's eyes fall upon the image of the engraved boulder. The antediluvian wedge of granite is overgrown with moss. A rubella rash of lichen spreads across its surface, bridging the network of cracks left by the passing of ancient glaciers long ago. Visible in spite of this damage are the petroglyphs. A chiseled umbrella-like shape floats beneath a crescent moon; it is tethered to the body of a man-shaped symbol by a thin line. The rock cuttings appear too advanced for stone-age tools. It is unlike any other Native American artwork Slyfield has seen.

"That is the place," says Tall Elk.

He maintains a stony expression rivalling the heads of Easter Island. Slyfield is unable to determine if he is naturally dispassionate or under the influence of medication. He knows from the police report that Tall Elk is missing a fair portion of his left leg. Everything from the knee down was torn free when they found him dangling from his tether like a bloody puppet near the base of the cell tower. The second contractor, Andy Gilmore, was never found.

The fact that the native man did not bleed out was heralded by responding paramedics as a miracle. Slyfield has little faith in miracles that severely maim one man and completely vanish another. Add the possibility of a generous life insurance payout into the mix and his faith in miracles approaches zero.

"Can I get you a drink?"

Tall Elk waves his hand dismissively. The investigator smiles, then summons the lone waitress working the floor. He taps his glass and awaits his second whiskey sour while quietly observing the network of veins that climb

Tall Elk's nose like latticework. Clearly the native has enjoyed alcohol in the past, his decision to forego it now strikes Slyfield as noteworthy.

"All right. So tell me, did you or someone you know carve that rock? Is this some kind of cult thing? Was Andy Gilmore a part of it?"

Tall Elk coolly regards the investigator. Slyfield's sharp gaze and slicked-back hair lend him an air of intensity, but his perpetual and reflexive drinking undermines his razor-sharp facade. His well-fitted suit is wrinkled at the shoulders and elbows as happens when such garments are slept in overnight.

"You are not the police, I owe you nothing," Tall Elk says, "You have wasted my time."

Slyfield drops his hand inside his vest then flings a metallic container across the table. The object bounces twice before slowing to a stationary spin before Tall Elk. It is a whiskey flask, battered and tarnished to the point that light reflects as a milky glow upon its surface. Beneath the grime the elegant curves of an inscription are faintly visible.

"I promised I had something that would interest you, there it is. Pick it up and take a good look before you decide you don't want to talk to me," Slyfield says.

The native lifts the object level to his eyes hoping to overcome the limitations that dim lighting and age have wreaked upon his vision. He turns the flask until the engraving is clear. It reads: *A. Gilmore*

"What should this mean to me?" Elk asks.

Slyfield retrieves the flask with a sudden lunge. His left hand removes a transparent bag from the pocket of his vest. He shakes the bag crisply before dropping the flask within and sealing it.

"It means that I have something that the police overlooked. Something of interest to numerous parties, the flask of the missing man which now bears your fingerprints. In turn, you have something I want, something I am willing to trade for," Slyfield says.

This is not the investigator's first underhanded negotiation with an unwilling participant. He is a master of the hard sell, which is why his investigative services command top dollar. It is also why he packs fifteen million volts of stun gun in his left pocket. Negotiations sometimes go awry. As he watches flashes of rage cycle through Tall Elk's features he hopes things won't come down to a physical confrontation. The flask is, after all, a fake. Slyfield ordered it online, beat it with a ball peen hammer, and buried it in his yard for two weeks. There's no way for his victim to know this, which is why the tactic works, and has worked in various incarnations countless times before. It is one of the many paradoxes of life he has come to accept, that learning the truth often requires acts of deception.

"I will tell the authorities what you've done," Tall Elk says.

"That seems a bold gamble to me. The cops might believe you, eventually.

After multiple interviews, subpoenas, and lawyer fees. Then there is your insurer. Your disability was awarded in spite of the lab contaminating your fluid samples from the night of the accident. Those who work under the influence aren't eligible for worker's comp, as you know. Fingerprints on a liquor flask look bad. Of course, you might win that battle too. Still, the time and money you'll have to invest to set the record straight..."

"And if I answer your questions you will give me the flask?"

"You have my word," Slyfield says.

Tall Elk studies the investigator, noting the thin sheen of alcohol sweat that covers his face like a translucent mask. He mentally counts to himself in his native tongue knowing that hasty responses bring regrettable consequences. Once he shares what he knows it cannot be taken back. Knowledge changes the path of the enlightened, forbidden knowledge even more so. This is why his people have long hid their secrets from others. Yet this investigator is as relentless as he is ruthless. He is a salmon constantly pushing upstream, unaware that his journey ends in the jaws of a grizzly bear. Yet what man can change the destiny of a salmon?

"The cycle is neither cruel nor compassionate," Tall Elk sys, "It simply is. An ancient dance that the stars began and we are merely witness to."

A bemused smile pulls at the edges of Slyfield's mouth.

"You ask to understand parts of an eternal performance that was never meant for you. Perhaps never meant for man at all. Those who glimpsed these truths lived more primal lives, they were more attuned to the cycle."

Tall Elk lays an earth-toned finger upon the photograph of the petroglyph depicting the man connected to the umbrella form beneath the moon.

"This is not graffiti. Your eyes tell you as much. See where the rock cracks cross over the symbols? The edges where they meet are flawless. These carvings existed when the glaciers split the stone. This is an ancient message reminding us that men stand not only beneath the heavens, but beneath those who drift below the heavens. These truths are what killed Andy Gilmore. Why sacrifice your own life for answers that will bring you nothing?"

His words pass over Slyfield with a refreshing coolness. It is a pleasant change from the vulgar rants Slyfield usually receives after putting the screws to someone.

"Well that's where you're wrong. There's quite a bit of money hanging in the balance. My share of the pie depends on what you tell me about the disappearance of Andy. You say he's dead? I really hope that's not the case, but if it is take me to the body."

Money.

Of course that is what brought the investigator here. Tall Elk cannot remember a point in his forty-seven year span when an outsider approached him over matters concerning anything else. The cycle is neither cruel nor compassionate, but his slice of eternity is filled with those whom have no love but for profit. The human complexities of former eras are reduced to the tracking of a single number, a bottom line, a profit margin, a bank account balance.

"You will not find his body any more than you will find my leg. They are buried in the cemetery of the sky. Leave the flask and go home, your search is over. There are no bones to present to your master."

Slyfield feels the combustible mixture of fatigue and anger percolating within his breast. He finishes his whiskey, bringing the glass down hard on the table. The few sickly patrons slouched over the bar do not bother turning to look. Only the disheveled waitress reacts, raising an irritated brow at him from across the room. Slyfield taps his glass in response, hoping the drink arrives before his temper overpowers his good judgment.

"If there are no bones then how do you know he's dead?" Slyfield says.

"I saw him die."

"Do tell."

Tall Elk closes his eyes and places his palms flat on sticky surface of the scarred table. He breathes in deeply, seeking tranquility but instead inhaling the loathsome scents of stale beer accented with a hint of urinal mint. Slyfield waits patiently.

"To understand the Uhridanawa, you must first understand something about the spirit world. For over a decade I climbed the cell towers for any contract company that was paying. My body grew strong. It had to. My biceps became like stone, my legs pillars of marble. But my spirit was sick. Cold nights, long hours, and seeing too many friends plummet to their deaths or lose limbs only to be replaced as easily as one might replace old shoes..." He pauses, his chest moving with an uneven rhythm. When he opens his eyes they are moist at the edges. Though his penetrating stare is directed toward Slyfield it seems focused on a point far past him. "It was difficult. I handled it as many men do, with drink, smoke, and painkillers. I climbed great heights every day yet my view of the world never changed. My body became powerful like a bear but in my heart I was a worm, burrowing into chemical bliss as if it were the dampened earth. I sought the comfort of a living grave."

Slyfield quietly sips his whiskey. He wonders if his patience will result in a payoff. Andy Gilmore's widow has spent six years begging the courts to declare her husband dead. The slow wheels of justice have begun to turn in her favor, an event that displeases Slyfield's employers. If Andy is dead, Safeguard Life Insurance will have to honor the three million dollar policy he took out on himself. For that kind of money Slyfield can afford to entertain the deranged ramblings of the sole witness to Andy's disappearance.

"You know some animals can tell when a person is near death? Dogs can smell cancer on their owner's breath. Cats in retirement homes sometimes visit the next patron to die, guided by unknown abilities. Likewise there are similar creatures of the spirit. Primal things that hover above the earth, things which watched ancient men gather themselves tightly within the circle of the first campfire light. As animals can smell the fatal sickness building within a body so too can the Uhridanawa smell a spirit that are sickened unto death."

"I assume there's some connection between this story and the disappearance of Andy Gilmore," Slyfield says.

Tall Elk points again to the photo of the petroglyph laying a calloused fingertip on the umbrella shaped symbol beneath the crescent moon.

"This is the Uhridanawa. That is the name my people gave it, though the rock was carved long before our ancestors ever beheld it. It hovers beneath the moon. This line connecting it to the man shows how it follows humanity from its unseen place in the heavens. I knew when I first set eyes upon the petroglyph that Andy and I were in its territory. Yet I paid no heed, because the prophecies of my people have brought us nothing but tears in modern times. I treated this warning of the ancients with the same skepticism you show on your face right now."

Slyfield shrugs. Whiskey has somewhat alleviated the oppressive atmosphere of the tavern. Hard, dark edges turn fuzzy, the oppressive air of hopelessness is buoyed by his heady buzz. He's slowly coming to accept that this one-legged Indian really thinks he will be bluffed by some cock-and-bull story about sky spirits and boogeymen. As if he can return to his employers with nothing but a fake flask and an empty report to drop on their desk.

"I'm listening," Slyfield says.

"We were replacing a main antenna that night, a two man job. The air was heavy with frost, so we warmed ourselves with drink and spoke of the ways we would waste our overtime pay. That is how it was in those days. The climb was nothing special. I held the antenna in place while Andy worked to connect it. From that height a man can see a great distance. Yet my spirit, poisoned with alcohol and frivolous desires, took no joy in the view. I did not bother looking toward the stars until a number of them began to shift and ripple as if underwater." Tall Elk lifts a soiled drink coaster holding it a few inches above the table. He places his other hand beneath it, then wiggles his fingers while raising them upward. "Then it is like this. Everything falls upward, the tools, the antenna, loose bolts, us. Fortune smiled upon me and my tether held. Andy had forgotten to fasten his to the tower. I watched him fly up to the place where the stars were trembling and then vanish. I too fell toward this place but was stopped at the end of my lanyard. There I dangled upside down, confused, cold, and terrified. I screamed nonsense prayers, useless words of slurred panic, but I howled them nonetheless. Then, pop! I felt my body jarred by a swift force like an ocean wave and I fell toward the ground. I did not know my leg was gone until I awoke at the hospital."

Slyfield slaps the top of the table with enough force to nearly tip over his half-full glass, "C'mon, now! You're going to tell me the sky ate him?"

Tall Elk folds his arms across his chest, his expression never registering more than a bored disinterest. "What does the evidence tell you? Where is the body? Where is my leg? The police do not know and neither do you. Only I know, and I have kept my end of the bargain. Give me the flask. Or are you not honoring our deal?"

Slyfield stands, patting the vest pocket containing the flask with one hand while gathering the photographs with the other. "I'll hand this over when you hand me something useful. Call me at my hotel when you're ready to have a real talk, but don't wait too long."

Tall Elk rises from his chair, steadying himself with the edge of the teetering table. "Wait! Let me leave first. I can sense the presence of the Uhridanawa. Remember the cord on the petroglyph that connects it with the man. I can sense when it is nearby, ever since it took my leg. We are connected, and I tell you it is close by now. Even if you do not believe, humor me."

Slyfield snorts. "You're a regular Captain Hook of the sky crocodiles, chief. I don't think so. The fact is that Andy is still missing and you were alone with him when he vanished. I'll take my chances with the spirit world before I follow you into the dark of night. Try not to get vacuumed up yourself."

Tall Elk considers making another attempt. He considers shouting after him "My spirit is healed, I will be buried in the earth, like a man." Yet he knows any attempt to change the path of the investigator will only hasten him more quickly toward his destiny.

The cycle is neither cruel nor compassionate; the eternal dance simply moves forward.

Slyfield exits the tavern, never to be seen again.

Weeks later the police come asking questions. They talk to the barkeep, to the handful of people present on the night that Slyfield disappeared. Tall Elk answers their questions while wisely avoiding mentioning any details that may endanger his disability benefits.

The search drags on for three months before the Native American is contacted again and questioned over the only evidence that will ever be found in the case of the missing investigator: *the bizarre discovery of his dress coat hanging atop a tall pine tree about mile away from the tavern.*

NOT YOUR AVERAGE MONSTER

D. Morgan Ballmer lives in the Pacific Northwest with his wife and two daughters. Their home has only two full bathrooms. Boom, you just got a bonus horror story in the author's bio. His work has appeared in Three-Lobed Burning Eye Magazine and on the Halloween Forevermore website.

IN THE COURT OF THE PUMPKIN KING

-A NICK NIGHTMARE NOVELLA-

BY ADRIAN COLE

USUALLY when I hear some kind of commotion down in the alley outside my office, especially near the end of my working day, I'm inclined not to pay it too much heed. Drunks arguing over their last bottle, kids smashing windows in the empty warehouse opposite, cats, dogs, rats and so on, it's a laugh a minute down there. However, when you've spent a dreary October afternoon trawling through a bunch of tax returns for your accountant who insists on giving the Revenue boys something to chew on once a year, you'll take anything that'll give you a break. So I went to check things out, one of my twin Berettas leading the way: I always like to be able to get off the first shot.

At the bottom of the stairs, I slowly tugged the door open to be met with a wall of darkness – almost all of the goddamn outside lights were busted – and a mother of a storm. Wind howling, rain gusting, temperature dropping deep down into brass monkey territory. I almost shuffled back to the figure work.

I went outside, collar up and peered back. Rain was gushing from a broken gutter across the narrow alley, a small waterfall that sploshed down onto what at first looked like a big sack. Some jerk had dumped a bag of garbage in here and hightailed it. Not for the first time. The alley was empty now. I would've ignored the thing slumped up against the wall, except that I had a bad feeling about it. I went over to it and kicked it.

It was like kicking a sack of wet mud: my boot sank in. Now that was odd, because I could see that it wasn't a bag of garbage. Such things did not have arms and legs.

It was a body.

Its legs were buckled up under it like they were composed of modelling clay. Its head sank down on the chest, almost melted into it. I knelt down. The face was starting to *slide* off the head, the features already distorted beyond any proper recognition. I looked back over my shoulder. If this was a warning to me from any number of thugs I'd upset, it would have been no surprise. How many more times was my alley going to be used as a depository for a corpse? I'd seen more stiffs here than at the local morgue.

This was a weird one, though. Flesh and blood, but no bones. I knew the kind of creatures that might have done this. And they knew me, and they didn't like me. Too bad.

I went back to my doorway and tugged out my cell phone. I'm no big shot with technology – Ariadne, my occasional employer, told me to keep it on all the time. 'It's a *mobile* phone, not an immobile phone,' she told me, with that angry look that makes me nod quietly and be a good boy.

I rang Rizzie Carter, my local Police Chief, and he bawled down the phone so loud I thought it would go into meltdown in my hand.

"For Chrissakes, Nick, I hope you're not going to dump on me at this time of the day. I was just about to head for the homestead, buddy." He was speaking through a mouthful of something, a fat burger most likely, so the words were distorted.

"Sorry to screw up the party, Chief, but I have a corpse sitting outside my office. Seems to be short of a bone or several dozen. I know nothing about it, other than that it's wearing a scuffed pair of old brogues; ergo I take it to have been a man. Dressed like a tramp. A real mess. But I'll do some investigating of my own. See if I can pick up a trail before it goes cold." A trail? Who was I kidding?

"Okay," he grunted, resigned to following up. He'd be here with a bunch of his terriers in no time, while I did my own digging. I knew he'd expect me to, given that this was a weird one. He always asked me to lend a hand with the weird ones. Nick Stone was done for the day and Nick Nightmare was about to emerge.

I thought about moseying on down to the Sleaze Sisters' bar, where I could usually rely on someone to slip me a tip or two, but the truth is, Sal and I had pretty much split up after a slightly rumbustious relationship. We'd parted amicably, but she was a volatile lady and not averse to heaving furniture about when the mood took her. Right now I didn't warm to the prospect of having a loaded ice box dumped in my lap, so I re-thought my next move. I decided I'd look up Craggy MacFury in the diner he ran. He had the longest ears in town.

The rain had eased by the time I got there, but the wind was cuffing me about viciously. I had to stuff my hat inside my coat and button it up tight. The diner, an elongated torpedo-shaped metal beast, was situated in a remote part of the city, and only a select few were ever able to find it. I know MacFury has some very strange friends, more than capable of putting some kind of hex on the diner to deflect unwelcome guests.

For once, the place was packed. There was some kind of Irish festival in full bloom, so the food was in plentiful supply, as was the booze. I was greeted cheerfully enough and for once I was surprised not to be cannoned off my feet by the host's enormous wolfhound, the Hooligan. Perhaps he'd been confined to quarters because of the seething mob of celebrants. If a ruckus broke out, the Hooligan was likely to tear off a few heads, being an excitable beast.

"You'll have to excuse the hullabaloo, Nick," said MacFury, slapping me on the back with his great spade of a hand. "I've enough customers here to fill a dozen diners. Warming up for Samhain. Whether I've enough Guinness is another matter. Now – what'll you be having?"

NOT YOUR AVERAGE MONSTER

Usually even the very thought of eating in Craggy MacFury's diner is enough to set me salivating – I cannot imagine food anywhere comparing to mine host's fare, so I was powerless to refuse. After he'd brought me a potato pie, drenched in thick liver gravy, and I'd put worldly affairs aside and dived in, MacFury elbowed his way through the throngs and waved a bottle of his best wine at me.

"I dare not," I grinned. "Work restrains me."

"Ah," he said knowingly. "You'll be on a case then?"

"Yeah. You may be able to give me a lead. I've not seen Montifellini for a while and he's always good for a tip off." I was referring to another particular contact of mine, the driver of the most extraordinary bus in this or any other world, and a man whose knowledge of events outré was second to none.

"Oh yes. But he's taken that bus of his off somewhere. Not seen him either. Even missed his Friday night feed, he did. So he must be on to something unusual, Nick. I can't believe he's in trouble, but I do know that something big is brewing. And I don't mean the Festival. So what's with you?"

I told him about the corpse in my alley. He listened intently, and then nodded.

"Now if that's an ordinary boneless man, you'd be talking about any one of several night beasties that could have been responsible. But if it's a Boneless Man, with capital letters, then that's an entirely different kettle of fish."

"Whoever dumped it in my alley," I said, "meant me to find it. My guess is, it's a baited trap."

"Well, you'll not want to go blundering into it. I know the very person you need to see, that I do. The Lady of the Stones."

It was a new one on me, but MacFury's reliability was pure pedigree. "Point me in her direction, if you will."

"You'll need to enlist the help of Caliban."

Caliban? As in *The Tempest*? Really? He was kidding me. But, no, although MacFury had a sense of humour, in these situations he played it straight.

"Come with me," he said and I got up and followed him. He shouted instructions to the staff he'd got in for the night and we went outside and round to the back of the diner, into a compound where, for some reason, the wind was held at bay. "I had a feeling you were coming tonight," said MacFury. "And that we'd need Caliban. It's why I had the Hooligan confined to his quarters. Oh, don't mind him; he has a bone the size of a mammoth's thigh to keep him happy. But the truth is, he and Caliban don't get along. You'd not want to be witnessing World War Three, now would you?"

I was getting a mite clammy about meeting this Caliban character. Even more so when I saw what was in the middle of the compound. It was some kind of wooden structure, used for hanging meat, like maybe pheasants.

MacFury could get such fare, whatever the season, but that wasn't what he had in mind tonight. Instead he went to some kind of cold storeroom and emerged with two long strips of fish, which he hung up on the wooden tripod.

Then we waited. It only took a few minutes, but then the open gate opposite us, which framed a deep pool of darkness, seemed to blur like an image in water. Part of the darkness thickened and from out of it emerged the biggest cat I'd ever seen. I mean to say, domestic cat, although this was a stray, given its chipped ears, matted fur and decidedly wild look. The size of a small dog, it gazed at us with feral, yellow eyes, like it was studying an inferior breed, and then sauntered over to the hanging fish. It reached out lazily with one clawed paw and tore down the first strip, chewing it up and digesting it with worrying speed. The second piece went the same way.

"Caliban," said MacFury, watching the huge black monster as it made a cursory effort to clean any remains of the fish from its claws. "Allow me to introduce Mr. Stone. He wishes to visit your mistress."

The cat ignored him and yawned. It had more teeth than any normal cat had a right to possess.

"The Lady of the Stones is a fine lass, but I have to say a little eccentric. She's not had a happy life. Her real name is Molly Malloy, but don't be calling her that. You must address her as Scathach. And this is her familiar. She will know if the Boneless Men are active."

Caliban at last deigned to look at me. He turned away and stood in the gateway, waiting for me. I thanked MacFury and followed the cat as it slunk up the alley. It was the beginning of a curious journey, like Alice's trip down the rabbit hole. I've been to any number of bizarre rat-runs in this city, and I guess more than a few of them breach other worlds, so the labyrinth through which Caliban now took me was nothing new, despite its weirdness. It was like we were in a city that had died and fallen into a semi-ruined state. I clambered over torn fences and heaps of rubble.

I reached a small square, lit by one solitary bulb, like it was the last light in the city. The wind had died down and the rain had stopped, but it was cold in here, my breath a white cloud in front of me. For a while I'd lost the cat until a movement up on a window ledge caught my attention.

There was a small figure up there, dangling its feet over the ledge. For a second I thought a gargoyle had cut loose from a local church, but even this squat, bulbous creature was more grotesque than any gargoyle I'd seen, with his bulging eyes and wide, flapping mouth. Instinctively I knew that it was Caliban, who'd changed shape. He grinned at me, but it was not a warming expression.

"You want to see Scathach, my mistress?" He had a voice that reminded me of claws being raked across a blackboard.

"Sure," I said. "MacFury told me she might know about the Boneless

Men."

"Have you seen one?" His eyes were lidded, like a serpent's, brimming with distrust.

"I think maybe I have." I explained my dilemma.

He listened, nodding, then scampered off, still in the quasi-human form, apparently satisfied that I was not necessarily a mad assassin in search of his mistress with murder in my heart. For another half hour, deep into the night, I followed him until we came to an opening in one of the numerous alleys we'd taken. Beyond it was a wider area, which I could see at once was overgrown. Stones, rounded and sculpted, poked up from the thick grass. It was a cemetery. From the state of it, I could see it had long been abandoned. So the Lady of the Stones was, I guessed, the Lady of the Headstones.

The place was much bigger than I'd first thought and a mix of mist and darkness obscured its boundaries. After a lengthy hike through the grass, I saw a light up ahead. I could see some kind of mausoleum, partly collapsed so the front presented an opening, with a leaning stone roof. Underneath, in an impromptu cave, there was a fire glowing. No cauldron, but there was a skillet, metal legs astride the fire.

Caliban made himself comfortable on a fallen gravestone and a moment later the modern Hecate appeared. She kind of floated in, wearing a combination of silks and, well, more silks, some of which were scarves, and there were tiny bells on bangles. The most striking thing about her was her red hair, which had exploded around her so that she looked as if she'd just come from a Grateful Dead concert in their heyday. Not Hecate, then, more like Miranda, though I know that Shakespearian lady wasn't a witch.

She made some curious gestures with her arms, her fingers curling and twisting like she was pulling something magical from the air. Who was I to say things were otherwise? She ended her little performance with a gesture for me to join her at the fire and like Caliban, I dropped on to a former gravestone.

"Nick Nightmare," she said, in a cool, crystal voice. She had the greenest eyes I'd ever seen, even in this light. I put her age at anything between twenty and thirty, but heck, if she had magical powers, she could be a hundred and thirty. She had a kind of sadness about her, partly hidden under that dizzy air, which I guess could have been an affectation to hide what was really going on inside.

"Scathach," I answered.

She bowed her head, apparently pleased that I'd addressed her the right way. "Warm yourself – have some food," she said, indicating the skillet. Having already eaten at Craggy MacFury's, I was going to decline, but I guessed it might upset her, so I took the dish she gave me and used a chunk of bread to mop up the thick, meaty stew. Now, that gave even MacFury a run for his money, and it went into my bloodstream like a mainline drug.

"I have been reading the night," Scathach said, lifting a slender hand and sifting the air like she was again tugging secrets from it. "It tells me there is a cruel darkness gathering, preparing to unleash itself on this world."

She had a curious accent, not quite Irish, and for sure her style of speaking was Old World, but it sort of fitted her appearance. She'd not have looked out of place on a stage, wafting to and fro, mesmerising her audience.

"I was told that you would know about the Boneless Men," I said.

She shuddered. "Yes. They are moving at last. The Pumpkin King is cultivating an army of them, his purpose obvious. Conquest in the name of an even darker master."

"The Pumpkin King?" It was a new one on me.

"He may have been human once, but the dark powers suborned him and, like so many, his greed thrust him deeper into their ways. A terrible intelligence festers in him, which is why he has become the ruler of the Boneless Men. Addicted to power, his hunger is insatiable. His dark masters know this and use it to manipulate him to their own ends. This world offers him everything his vile appetite craves. Already he has sent forerunners here. You have seen them?"

"A guy with no bones was dumped outside my office. The cops are dealing with the corpse."

"They must burn it!" she said theatrically. "Burn it and all its seeds."

"What did it want?"

"You, Nick Nightmare. Their master fears you and what you can do. You and your allies. Already you have thwarted his plans. He wants you destroyed. The Boneless Men slip from human body to body like parasites, discarding each body once it has served their purpose. The first was a warning – there is a second abroad."

I was getting to feel even more uneasy. "Is it just me they want?" *Don't tell me they want Ariadne, too.*

She looked directly at me, her expression clouded by a sudden thought. "All of you who defy their ruler. You fear for Miss Carnadine. There will also be a Boneless Man hunting her."

I growled something crude. The idea that Ariadne Carnadine might be in the soup was like a kick in the guts. "You know where they are?"

"The first, yes. It extracted itself from that corpse you found and went back to its lair. It must be destroyed."

"I'll drink to that." I stood up. "Just point me in the right direction."

"You'll need help," she said, her expression suddenly hardening. "I know these creatures. Know them and abhor them."

"No time like the present: let's cut to the chase."

She seemed happy enough to concur and picked something up - a long, steel object, and in the fire glow I could see it was a spear, or javelin. "This is the Gae Bolg," she told me. "The spear of mortal pain, the death spear. It has been handed down my line across the generations since the first Scathach. Only I can use it. It is death to anyone else who touches it, but it will serve us well." She turned to Caliban, who'd slid down from his perch, waiting, more dog than cat, for a command. At a gesture from his mistress, the familiar scampered off into the concealing grass.

We followed in silence. I wanted to ask her more about this Pumpkin King – I got a real feeling her own past was mixed up with this monster in some tortured way - but she'd withdrawn into herself, gliding like a wraith through the overgrown cemetery. I couldn't see the stooped figure of Caliban – or the cat, if he'd changed back – but she probably had some kind of telepathic thing going with him. The mist thickened and we eventually left the cemetery by an overgrown path beside a stream and, for all I knew, we had crossed into some other realm. As long as my twin Berettas worked here, I was ready for anything, or so I told myself.

In time we got to another field, not a cemetery as far as I could tell, seeing as there were no obvious graves. More grass and weed, tangled shrubs, like somewhere long surrendered to nature. The air was very still, no storm here. Mist continued to swirl around, drifting up from the ground like steam from a sweating beast. Scathach pointed to a soft glow to our right. I could make out a couple of trees, bent over arthritically.

We approached slowly, stealthily, and I slipped out my two guns. Scathach shook her head, *don't go using them*, was the message in her eyes.

There was a small clearing under the trees, a patch of ground that incongruously appeared to have been tilled, the soil raked, the weeds cut back from it. In the centre of this area was a large growth, which I guessed at first was some kind of big mutated cabbage. From the cover of the long grass, we watched as the leaves unfurled to reveal the dirty orange of a pumpkin. Only this was no ordinary pumpkin, I can tell you.

For one thing, it had a face. Not some kid-carved Halloween face, but a contorted human face, bulging outwards, mouth open in a savage grin, more like a grimace. What made the whole thing really freaky was the fact that light shone from within the goddam thing, just like it does from a scooped out pumpkin with a candle inside it. When that bizarre head twisted from side to side, I dragged out one gun, regardless of Scathach's views.

So this was the Boneless Man who had left that sack of flesh and blood in my alley. It had returned to its earth-based pit and now was again struggling to get up from the soil that nurtured it, like a vampire rising from its grave. Roots and leaves flew this way and that as the creature broke free of the ground. Scathach waited, the spear held at the ready, giving her the look of some manic harpooner. The pumpkin horror fixed its bright-eyed stare on me and lurched forward. Nothing subtle about its tactics.

Scathach chose her moment and launched the spear. It ripped into the gut of the Boneless Man and held firm, as if a dozen barbs had opened up inside it. The thing let out a scream like steam escaping from an engine and started to writhe frantically, this way and that. Light poured from its chest and belly, like the spear was turning it molten, until, with a noise like a huge sack of wet mud hitting concrete, the creature ruptured, bursting apart so we had to duck to avoid the flying vegetable mess.

Scathach quickly reached for the spear and used its now glowing end to burn up every last vestige of the former Boneless Man she could find. When she'd finished, she turned to me, a mite breathless, like she'd found the whole disgusting business kind of enjoyable. "Bullets will kill them, Mr Nightmare, but they won't burn up the seeds."

I nodded, checking to see that none of the gloop had splattered my coat. I didn't relish the thought of being infected.

"Go to Miss Carnadine," said Scathach. "She is safe for the time being. Caliban will take you back to your streets."

I looked across to where the big cat was cleaning itself, pretending to be oblivious to its surroundings, as though his mistress and I were unimportant.

"So – when shall we three meet again?" I grunted, unable to resist the quip.

Scathach smiled patiently, like she was indulging a kid. "Well, Mr Nightmare, it won't be *after* the hurly-burly, I can assure you of that."

It was not far off dawn when I rang Rizzie Carter. I knew from his irritable tone – more so than usual – that he'd been on the case of the body in my alley. No sleep for the wicked, I told him. Never mind what he said back.

"Whatever did that to the deceased," I said, "moved on. I caught up with it and there was a shoot-out. I'd like to have brought the killer in alive, Chief, but you know how these things go."

"With you, yeah," he said. "So you blew the jerk apart? Ya been reading too many Ned Killigan yarns. He's a bad influence."

"So who was the stiff?" I grinned at my inadvertent choice of words. The corpse left outside my office had been anything but stiff. "My guess is, it was a nobody. A street bum, right?"

"You got it in one. No details. We'll never know. At least I don't have to go find his family and give them the bad news. I don't like it, though, Nick. It's no way to die, even for a nobody."

"Well, the killer's paid for it. I took care of it and had a little improvised cremation. Ashes to ashes and all that stuff. You don't want to know."

"No, I don't."

"Listen, you have to burn your corpse, too. You hear me?"

The Chief swore and for a couple of minutes he was grumbling like a bear with a whole lot more than a sore head. He knew me and my methods and he also knew the kind of nightmares I invariably got mixed up in. He'd experienced a few of them first hand.

"Do it, Chief. I'll explain when I see you."

"What the hell is it, a freakin' vampire?"

"You don't believe in vampires."

"No, we've enough monsters in New York without that. Okay, okay, I'll have the thing burned. I just hope the Mayor don't get to hear about this."

I was able to get an audience with Ariadne Carnadine that afternoon. It seemed to me she ran a business empire the size of China, and liked to keep ahead of all the moves, but it was rare that she couldn't squeeze me in whenever I rang her. As always, she chewed me out for not keeping more regular contact and demanded to know what I'd been doing and why hadn't I involved her, if it had been dangerous, and if I kept this up she'd have me horse-whipped, and romantic stuff like that.

She was slightly mollified when I gave her a brief résumé of some of the stuff I'd recently been mixed up in. She poured tea – a special ritual we had, and it was getting addictive. I like a slug or three of whisky, but that tea of Ariadne's was something else.

"So what's the problem?" she said.

I told her about the Boneless Man and about my trip to see the Lady of the Stones, and that potent magic wand of hers. "It kind of ties a lot of things together," I told her. "Something's abroad, something big and very nasty and it's not going away. It's hotting up." She and I had not long messed up the satanic plans of a smooth operator called Lucien de Sangreville, and as a result of that and certain other skirmishes with the powers of darkness, Ariadne and I were for sure down in some little black book, or more likely, a Big Black Book, right at the top of its hit list.

Reluctantly I also told her about the likelihood that the Boneless Men would be looking her up. "Scathach reckons we've become too much of a threat."

"Divide and conquer. I think you'll find that'll be their method." She set her cup down and regarded me with those cool eyes. Mentally, I could imagine her already kitted up in the black Ninja gear she favoured when we went into action, twin swords flashing. Just a little fantasy I liked to indulge in, like every five minutes.

"I know you have a bunch of bodyguards dogging your heels night and day," I said, and it was a fact, she did employ some tough characters. "But while these punks are creeping around, I'd like to keep close."

"You need an excuse to keep close?" She got up and came to sit beside me on the sofa, putting a hand on my shoulder and idly twirling my hair. "You don't think I'm capable of looking after myself?"

"Hell, I know you are, Ariadne. It's just – this whole thing bothers me."

She gave me a peck on the cheek and laughed softly. "I know it does. Listen, I need a break from work. My people can survive without me for a few days. What do you say I take you away from all this? You know I have a lodge up in the mountains. The Adirondacks are a bit cold this time of year, but in the lodge we'd be as snug as two bugs in a rug. We can decide on a plan of action."

"My mother warned me about girls like you."

"Is that a no?" she said in mock outrage.

I grinned my best idiot's grin. "Where do I sign up?"

I managed to gulp down the last of the cool mineral water and flopped back into the lush seating. I knew my face would be more than a whiter shade of pale, the sweat still beading on my brow. I do not like flying. I can barely manage to force myself into one of those aerial leviathans they call jet planes, even if my life depends on it. I have been flown by that demonic air ace, Damien Paladin, in the metal bucket he calls a De Havilland-something-or-other, with the world spinning and churning about me like the whole shebang was caught up in a cosmic whirlpool. But zooming up and down like a bumble bee on LSD in a helicopter from New York City to the mountains was about as bad as it got for me.

Ariadne, still mildly amused by my transformation from hard-boiled granite man to pasty-faced, near-puking human wreck, came over and dabbed at my face with a cold flannel. If she told me to relax one more time, I would throw up over her expensive carpet. I didn't, of course. Mercifully I was starting to ease back on the shivers.

We'd come out here to her mountain lodge without wasting any more time. One of her bodyguards flew the helicopter, and two others sat stoically with us. My guess is if we'd hit a hurricane and turned upside down, they'd have remained stoic. They had Olympic medals in stoic, those guys. Ariadne told me there would be four more who'd gone on ahead to the lodge. Once we got there, they'd all blend into the scenery like Navy SEALS, in spite of their suits. We wouldn't be disturbed.

Once I was more myself, with a couple of cups of coffee inside me, I started to feel hungry, so I knew I was okay. The lodge was cut into a sloping hillside, surrounded by forest, high up, with a view to die for, not that I had any intention of kicking any buckets. The place had every mod con, with superb furniture, carpets, *objects d'art*, as well as facilities that would have graced any of the city's top hotels. After all, the Carnadine dynasty was very, very rich.

Ariadne had spent some time in the kitchen, hell bent on cooking us a meal herself. From the smells emerging from in there, I guessed Craggy MacFury was going to have another rival.

"Seems to me, dear heart, that if we really are going to be under attack from the satanic forces that seem to be amassing, there's strength in numbers. Even for lone wolves like you. There are a few amazing people we can call on, but we can't rely on the old brigade. This situation calls for new blood. We need to put together a new fighting unit. A new Vengeance Unlimited."

She was referring to a bunch of guys who'd operated against evil since way back, but who were now getting pretty long in the tooth. She was right, of course, and I nodded. "So we need five, for the core. You and me makes two. I have an idea who we might enlist. There's one possible member –"

Ariadne gave me that look that said, I can see right down into your tiny little mind, Stone. You're not bamboozling me for one minute. "Oh, so the witch lady *did* make an impression on you, didn't she?"

"That spear of mortal pain – we could do with that when we have to face off with these Boneless critters."

Her teasing grin changed to something more serious. "I agree. I've heard of the Gae Bolg, in legends. I have a feeling it's no coincidence that you met Scathach. Craggy MacFury engineered that meeting for a reason. Would she join us?"

"I guess. The way she set about that crazy vegetable, I'd say she was more than up for a second helping. She sure turned on the venom. Maybe I missed something about her. It's a start."

Ariadne was pacing the carpet now, padding back and forth like a lioness. I watched her, me probably not like a lion, my concentration on recent events in danger of being sidetracked.

"Perhaps," she said abruptly, "we'll find out through the actions of our shady opponents. They'll be trying to destroy anyone they think could band with us. They may be one jump ahead of us. You look uncomfortable. Something you haven't told me?"

She had a way of reaching deep inside me, to places I'd kept shut away for a long time. Since Martha had died. Died in a cruel car crash, with me driving the machine. Me surviving, Martha dying. For years I'd believed it was my fault, my reckless driving that had killed the one woman I'd ever loved. Then I'd learned the truth – I'd been drugged. My nemesis, a sharp operator called

Erik van Brazen, had set me up, letting me think I was rescuing Martha from his grip and making a mad dash for freedom with her. Like a mug, I bought the whole packet and drove Martha to her death, just like the bastard planned it. I was supposed to have snuffed it too. It was the one thing van Brazen got wrong.

I'd told Ariadne some of it, reluctantly. Now, the last thing I wanted was to risk her safety on my account. It was a constant fear of mine. She knew it, of course, and harangued me for it.

"There's something about Vengeance Unlimited," I said. "The original team operated under their own rules. One of which was, no romantic involvements. It would compromise the team. Make them emotionally vulnerable, that kind of thing. You know what happened." Two of the members of the team had been secret lovers and it had led to near-disastrous complications.

Ariadne sat with me and leaned very close. "Listen, tough guy, I know you're thinking about my skin and I like that. I'd be hurt if you didn't. But I'm not a china doll, Nick. I can handle myself."

I kissed her gently. "I know." I also knew that the things we were taking on would use us against each other and against any allies we had. It was an old, old story. One other thing I knew: it was too late to go back. I was in deep and Ariadne hadn't brought me out here to play cards all night.

She got up and went to the kitchen. She knew when to push me for information and when to ease back. "Anyway, you go and have a shower and I'll get the food ready. We've got all day tomorrow to work something out."

I took a shower, luxuriating in the jets of hot water and the steam womb that was the bathroom, driving out the last unnerving residue of the helicopter flight. I changed into lighter gear and as I emerged from the sumptuous bedroom and went downstairs, my nose went into overdrive - I could smell an amazing aroma of cooking. Ariadne was right – we could worry about Vengeance Unlimited and all the connotations tomorrow.

Except that she was wrong.

She wasn't in the lounge, or the kitchen. I called her name, instinctively lowering my voice. Beads of dread already sprang out on my forehead. I'd left my coat draped over one of the sofas, with the two Berettas, so I slipped one from its holster and began searching the lodge. It was larger than I'd realised and it took me some time, padding about softly, to understand that Ariadne was not in here. If she'd gone outside for some reason, she wasn't dressed for it – her own coat was hanging up, along with her scarf, and the bag with her own special kit, the Ninja gear as well as her swords, was below it.

I checked in the bag. One of the swords was missing, but the Ninja clothing was there. I decided against slipping out of the front door – I'd be an easy target if someone was out there. There was a side door from the kitchen.

I went in there and switched off the electrics before the food started to spoil. I put my coat on and ducking low, went outside into the late afternoon, where the sun was just starting to drop into the distant forest horizon.

It was cold out here, high up in the forest. I listened, but couldn't hear much other than what I took to be forest sounds. I'm a city boy and I was conscious this was not my natural environment. Moving around the edge of the lodge, past the shrubs and lawns, all of which had been kept in immaculate condition by invisible staff, I saw the first evidence of trouble. Across one lawn, a corpse, one of the bodyguards, was kind of *strewn*, its head missing. I eased over to the mess. The head had been sliced off and there it was, further away, a smashed pumpkin, dripping orange gunk. Beside it lay Ariadne's missing sword, which had obviously been responsible for the ghoulish decapitation.

What bothered me most was that the bodyguard must have been absorbed by another of the Boneless Men. We'd come all this way, yet they'd followed us. My reluctant guess was, there must be others. So where was Ariadne?

I picked up the sword and started back across the lawn. Something shifted in the nearby forest edge and I dived for the ground, rolled over and loosed off a couple of rounds. I'd fired deliberately high, in case it was Ariadne in there, but I saw I'd flushed out another of the bodyguards. With his own gun in hand, he came for me, his first shot zinging over my head as I did another roll and this time I let him have a head shot. When people shoot at me, I shoot back and I don't aim to wing them.

I hadn't lost my touch, and the guy's head exploded like a melon being thumped with a baseball bat – well, make that a pumpkin. He'd also been infested. I had to assume that the others had suffered the same indignity. There'd been seven of them. My basic maths told me that left another five. I didn't have long to wait to find out where the next one was. He wasn't stopping for a polite conversation either. He just came out from around the side of the house, gun blazing and this time I hit him in the gut. Not a nice way to kill a guy, it's slow and very painful, as I knew well enough from past fire fights, but I needed information about Ariadne and I was in no mood to be merciful.

The guy crashed to the ground, his gun flying across the grass. On my way over to him, I picked it up – it was a Magnum, a heavy little number – and stuffed it into my belt. I reached the bodyguard and put the tip of Ariadne's sword under his chin, lifting his head up. Jeeze, but these Boneless Men were freaks. That head was not exactly a pumpkin, but it was more like one than a human head, the man's original face, which I'd last seen when he'd been piloting the helicopter, almost unrecognisable, pulled out of shape, its features engorged by the bulging head.

"Where's Miss Carnadine? We're a long way from medical help and my

 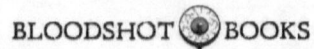

guess is it'll take you a day to cross the line to the last sleep, buddy. Tell me where she is and I'll make it easy for you." My Beretta was aimed at his shining forehead. I may as well have been talking to a tree. I wasn't going to get an answer. Exasperated, I swung Ariadne's sword in a short, effective arc, and sliced off the head. It jumped into the air and landed on the paved path beside a thick tangle of ferns, where it burst like a bladder full of blackcurrant cordial.

I studied my surroundings, wondering where the next attack would come from. Everything had gone very still and silent. Even the birds had stopped their din, maybe thinking they were next on the list. I was getting very anxious about Ariadne, but there was one ray of hope in this dark affair – the helicopter we'd arrived in was over on its grass pad, untouched since we'd landed. And its companion was likewise parked nearby.

Movement up on the roof had me diving for cover among the lush ferns. For once I was glad of them, even though they were starting to die off for the winter.

"Nice shooting, Roy Rogers," came a surly growl from above me. I couldn't see anyone, just a chimney stack. It took me a moment to recognise the voice. Not another bodyguard. What the hell, it was Scathach's familiar.

"Caliban! That you, you ugly little runt?" I called.

Sure enough, the gargoyle-like features popped out from around the stack and he glared at me. "Who you calling ugly, Mr Razorface?"

"Razorface?"

"You didn't even make the back of the queue when they were handing out the good looks," he snorted, dropping from the eaves on to the grass. He was a weird looking caricature of a man, but I can tell you, I was pleased to see the little hobgoblin.

I laughed softly. "Hey, this look is cool. The ladies like this look. Tall, dark and handsome is out this year. The Razorface look is in."

"If you say so. Now stop preening yourself and listen to me. We got big problems."

My amusement melted. "You know what's going on here?"

"I do. Your girlfriend's been abducted. Three of the Boneless Men grabbed her and dragged her off into the forest. They won't do her any harm. Maybe she'll have a few bruises, that's all. She didn't want to go quietly."

"She's okay?"

"Yeah, relax. For now, anyhow. They're takin' her to the court of the Pumpkin King. He knows you'll follow. He wants both of you, but let's not dwell on that. You need help."

I was like a coiled spring, eager to get on with this. He could see that.

"We can't stop them takin' her to him. We need to follow on very carefully. First, you got work to do." He pointed to one of the bodyguard corpses. "Burn these three and every last trace of them, seeds and all. That or the woods'll be full of 'em by morning. They breed like maggots."

Despite his telling me that there was no immediate rush to set off in pursuit of Ariadne, I was impatient as all hell.

"Listen, wise guy," he said, "the gateway to the Pumpkin King's realm opens at sunset and dawn. The three bozos you killed have done enough to hold us up so's we'll miss the twilight run. Our immediate priority is to clean up here before we leave."

I could see there was no point arguing so I got on with the job of dragging the three corpses – what was left of them and any remains I could scoop up – to one of the helicopters and I dumped them in it without ceremony. I found a spare can of fuel and sprinkled it liberally about the machine before setting light to it. I can't say I didn't enjoy my revenge on that flying beast as it exploded all to hell and beyond. The second chopper remained intact, silently waiting on its pad, like it was telling me, it would be here when I needed a lift back to civilization. Not if there's a mountain bus service, I was thinking.

I switched everything off in the lodge and picked up Ariadne's kit bag. It now contained her Ninja gear as well as both her swords. With any luck she'd get a chance to use them before this caper was over.

Darkness cloaked everything when I'd done and I was looking for a flashlight when Caliban appeared, holding some kind of lantern-thing. Straight from the faerie realm was my guess, but it was one less thing for me to worry about. He'd incinerated any last remains of the corpses and their offending seeds and pronounced himself happy with his work.

"So where we headed?" I asked him.

"Deep forest. Scathach will be waiting. We'll cross at dawn, when she can open the way."

I was glad to keep moving, trying to wrench my mind away from the fact that Ariadne must be in danger. Her abductors may have been given instructions not to harm her, but whoever this Pumpkin King was, he wasn't necessarily going to apply a soft touch, not to either of us, judging by what Scathach had told me. Caliban lit the way and for a little guy he moved swiftly through the forest terrain, obviously born to it. I just about kept up with him, but grew more and more uneasy. My night vision was okay, but the trees were so thick here that I felt crowded in, muffled in darkness. I could hear what were probably ordinary nighttime forest sounds, but they weren't what I was used to in the city, so my blood ran a little cold.

Eventually we reached a clearing, a grassed slope that led down to a stream. It was lit by another of the small lanterns, which hung from a tree. In the glow I could see Scathach, motionless as an obelisk. Caliban had reverted back to his black cat shape and sprang up easily on to a low branch.

"This must be the bank where the wild thyme grows," I quipped.

Scathach smiled, but it barely dissolved that underlying sadness. "Nick Nightmare. I am sorry that we meet again under such circumstances."

"You know where she is?"

She nodded. "Three of the Boneless Men took her through the gate and they will waste no time getting her to the court of the Pumpkin King."

"Three?"

"Yes. We have to wait until dawn before we can give chase."

"There were seven bodyguards. Three are dead. Caliban and I converted them into hot ashes. That leaves four. Three are with Ariadne. What about the fourth?" I don't like loose ends, especially when they're sneaking around with a gun.

She frowned, puzzled. "We must be wary." She sat herself cross-legged and I noticed the Gae Bolg stretched in the grass beside her. She patted the ground and invited me to sit with her. "We can only be patient."

"So how come you're in on this? I know you don't care much for these Boneless goons –"

"I have my reasons for defying the Pumpkin King and the vile creatures he serves," she said, cutting into my words, her green eyes sparkling with anger. "I would not see Ariadne Carnadine suffer as I have suffered. I will gladly side with you against those monsters."

"You want to tell me about it? If we're going to wait it out until dawn, you may as well fill me in."

She was a curious mixture of vague hippy waif and wild kind of mystic, turbulent and angry and probably very fierce. When she'd been using that spear, she would have made a good warrior woman, leading a mob of painted Brits into battle. Sassy was not the word for it.

"Not so many years ago, I lived in a scruffy old apartment in the Bronx with my lover. His name was Kulkain. He was an actor, a few months older than me and just as full of dreams as I was. He was very good, a natural talent and that's not just the love-smitten me talking." She was the gentle version again, the warrior woman submerged under the memories that ignited her as she spoke. "We shared everything and spent most of our lives studying the natural way of things. I don't know how it began, but Kulkain was wooed by the darker powers – they saw a potential in him to further their aims. We knew what they were capable of, and we avoided them. Oh, but they are cunning, deceitful. They worked on Kulkain insidiously, slowly winning him over with promises of success, the one thing he craved, perhaps even more than me." Her tears glistened in the lamplight.

"I had my own power and gifts of wild magic, things passed down through my bloodline. I warned him of the dangers, but he was given the roles he'd always craved and he was increasingly seduced by the dark. Then one day, he'd gone too far. Vaulting ambition had undone him and there was no way back. He was lost to me. The theatre, too, lost him, as he came completely under their control, almost as an addict succumbs to the drugs he depends on. The last I heard of him," she ended, "he had died. Taken across to their bleak regions, far beyond my reach."

Yeah, well that wouldn't have been the first time a guy had got too drunk on ambition. She'd referred to Macbeth and I was catching on to why she liked to quote it, although I recalled that it had been his good lady wife who'd prodded him towards the fatal path to power. Her and the witches.

"Was the Pumpkin King part of this?"

"He serves the same master. The time is fast approaching when the darkness will cast itself over the earth. Part of its preparation is to eliminate those who stand against it – those who know the truth of its rise. The apathy and cynicism of men works in favour of the enemy. Those who know the truth, such as you and your companions – those you call Vengeance Unlimited – they are recognised as a threat."

"Yeah, this isn't the first time we've come under attack. So you're with us?"

I liked her defiant glare. "I am. To the hilt. The Pumpkin King will soon be ready to launch his invasion. He will infect you and Ariadne with Boneless Men and hold you up as slaves in his army, unless we foil him. He will not be expecting me, nor the Gae Bolg. My hand will guide it into his black heart. It will rip him asunder!"

"You have a plan?"

"When we cross into his realm, you will take the path to his court and play the part of the anxious lover, eager to storm the court and rescue her."

I'm no actor, but I was thinking I could play that part pretty well.

"He will expect you to tumble into his trap. Why shouldn't he be confident of snaring you?"

"You're going to tell me why, right?"

"Caliban and I will come upon him unawares. A direct, unexpected strike to the very core of his blighted kingdom. It's dangerous, but we'll not waver. We'll screw our courage to the sticking place."

I was nodding, but I was getting a mite uneasy about Macbeth as a recurring theme here, given what happened to that particular dude.

"You must get some sleep," she told me.

"Sleep? At a time like this –" I didn't finish my protest – she simply reached out and pressed her cool fingers to my brow and the lights went out.

It was close on dawn when I came to. I felt well rested, so Scathach had worked some kind of magic, which was just as well, given my anxieties about Ariadne. Scathach brought out some cold meat, rabbit maybe, and I chewed it hungrily, washing it down with cold water from the stream. We left at once and Caliban padded along a narrow trail, set on either side by old stones that looked to me like they'd been set here by folks a whole lot older than the original Indian tribes who had probably once lived hereabouts. We reached another, slightly wider river and I didn't much fancy wading over it, not in this autumnal cold.

We didn't have to. Dawn's rays sliced through the trees and obviously the timing was right because Scathach indicated some stones under the water that were picked out by the bright light. We crossed and slipped into the reeds beyond. I knew that we were no longer in my world. Wherever the hell this was, it was alien. If I expected the sun to rise and brighten everything up, I was to be disappointed. The place was gloomy, a twilight region, the heavens padded out with layers of cloud, greys and purples, shrouding the landscape in a dour kind of gloom.

We were out of the reeds almost immediately, heading along a path that was bordered on both sides with tufts of grass and marsh, as far as the eye could see. There was enough solid ground for us to make progress, and we did so for a long time. There were no birds overhead and very little sign of life of any kind. Occasionally something would disturb the reeds, or there'd be a distant splash, like a body diving underwater, but we went on our way unmolested.

When we finally got to the far side of the marshy land, there were fields rolling up gently beyond. We were following a rough path and as we went into the fields, we could now see the rows of massed green leaves, with their pumpkin hearts. Countless thousands of them! Row upon row of pumpkins, all of them as big as a human head, all that sickly orange-brown colour I'd seen back in Scathach's field. We got to a crossroad and Scathach pointed ahead.

"Keep going until you come to a wall. The Pumpkin King's court is within its confines, up on the hill. Caliban and I will branch off here and come upon the place from another angle. We'll choose the right moment to join you. You shouldn't be impeded. His eyes will be upon you, once you reach the wall. In the meantime, if you see any of the Blind Gardeners, keep well clear of them. As their name suggests, they cannot see as we do, but they have a keen sense of smell. Keep to the path, or they'll deem you to be a threat to the plants. If they do, avoid them."

I didn't need telling twice. I watched her and the black cat take off down the right hand path and moved on with a shrug. I had my guns and I had Ariadne's bag, with her twin swords, but right now what I really needed was an armoured tank. I wasn't picky - I'd have settled for a bulldozer. Boy, did I feel exposed.

As I trudged on, the sun didn't get any brighter and the rows of pumpkins showed no sign of thinning or diminishing. I couldn't make out if these things had faces, but my skin was crawling like someone was studying me, like a kid studies an ant crossing a paving slab. I could hear a constant rustling sound, like the quasi-human plants were stirring, maybe thinking of getting up. Scathach had told me I wouldn't be attacked, given that I was an expected guest at the castle.

After several miles I caught sight of something vague and very bulky moving about on the near horizon, a huge shape with long, spindly arms, a vegetable harvester. It had no neck, its head like a huge hump on its shoulders and it was too far away to see details, but it had no eyes. A Blind Gardener, I assumed, plodding along in its daily round of tending the endless array of plants. I saw a few of these things, happily far off, and they didn't pick up my scent.

I guess it was coming up for midday (not that you'd have known by the dreary light) when I reached the wall. It stretched across the path and ran away to the left and right, bisecting the huge field. It was about eight feet high, composed of ancient bricks that had been roughly hewn what could have been a long time in the past. Vines and creepers had more or less taken the wall over, burying it in places. I could see a broken down gateway, but there were no guards. Open house, then.

I put my Berettas away and opted for Ariadne's blades. Okay, so I wasn't going to be jumped on out here, not till I got to the Pumpkin King's place at least, but I didn't buy into going in naked. I'd used the swords before and must admit it had been fun doing the Conan the Barbarian thing. I could see why Ariadne worked out with them.

Beyond the gate, I was in what could once have been stately gardens, but they were so overgrown with weeds and shrubs that had run amok, it was tough to keep sight of the path and its half buried paving stones. The grass was chest high, so I could see some way ahead to where a hill rose up into the mist. It had the look of a big burial mound, the sort of thing that would get an archaeologist's juices flowing. I thought there were movements up on the slopes, but couldn't be sure. I moved on.

There was a path leading up the hill that became a deep incision, like some crazy god had whanged his sword down into the earth. I went into its shadows and there were steps that made the climb easier. It was as cold as a tomb, my breath even cloudier in the semi-light. Also, the place had a weird smell to it, rotting vegetation and rotting something-else. Burial mound was probably right, and some of the inhabitants had been left here recently.

Emerging, I was on the flattish top of the mound, its dimensions obscured by the mist, or low cloud. I could see a ring of very tall stones – I believe they call them menhirs or sarcens in archaeology-speak. They weren't the regular shapes of the stuff at Stonehenge. These were more random, sculpted, possibly by the weather, into weird shapes, hunched and twisted, like frozen demi-gods. Just the kind of mutated shapes you'd expect to find in the court of the Pumpkin King. Speaking of mutated shapes, a whole bunch of them emerged from the mist and arranged themselves around the stones, hemming me in.

I went on to the centre of the place and there he was, in all his splendour. Well, not splendour, not by human reckoning. There was a paved area, roughly rectangular, and beyond it an expanse of mud and therein resided the huge deformity that must be the Pumpkin King. He had a body that could once have been human, but which was now an immense mini-zeppelin, with two bloated arms, the lower part of the body submerged in the mud, the way the lower half of a plant is buried in soil. And the head – now that was something else entirely. It was the biggest pumpkin-like growth I'd ever seen and would have taken the Gold Medal at every Biggest Pumpkin event imaginable, and some. It had that same sickly colour - degraded orange - but also a face that had been *stretched* over it, as if it had started normal but then been contorted by the growth of the thing.

Round, yellow eyes gazed at me like there was a fire behind them, in the hollowed-out skull, although that had to be some kind of illusion. There was a gash of a nose, but the mouth – man, this had to be a bad dream. Like a garden pumpkin where the features are chopped out with a knife, this mouth, almost as wide as the entire bloated head, had vegetable teeth, interlocking and slick with drool, as if the wriggling anaconda that was the tongue within was far too big for the mouth.

I stood in fascinated silence, though I felt like a fly in front of a chameleon, about to be zapped and swallowed.

"Mr Nick Stone. Or Nightmare, as you prefer," said the creature in a voice that completely threw me. It was strangely cultivated, not the voice of a mutated vegetable. I think the monarch was smiling, but that expression would have curdled milk.

"So nice of you to drop in on my little kingdom."

"You know why I'm here." It was meant to come out as a derisive snarl, or at least sound defiant, but it was more of a hoarse croak.

"Ah, of course. The beautiful Ariadne Carnadine. I can understand your impatience. Very well, let's not beat about the proverbial bush." He lifted one of those massive arms and made some sort of gesture. Mud sloughed off him and fell with a *plop* back into his private bath.

There was movement behind him and my heart thumped in my chest as a group of figures – among them three of the converted Boneless Men who'd been her bodyguards – dragged the writhing Ariadne out onto the stones. They had gagged her – I could imagine the stream of invective she'd have hurled at them if they hadn't – and tied her hands tightly behind her. She was wearing the simple dress and soft shoes I'd last seen her in, hardly suitable for a night out here in this wilderness. Her eyes met mine and I was relieved to see the fury in them. The goons may have trussed her up, but she was still ready to spit hell and fury given half a chance.

"I gather you two have been causing a good deal of trouble," said the Pumpkin King, that revolting tongue slopping about, flicking gobbets of drool across the slabs. "Very inconvenient for the dark power I serve. I've been commissioned to put a stop to it."

I flexed my arms gently, the twin swords gleaming in the pale light of day. It would have been a cinch to jump him and slice him up, but he knew he had me.

"Don't be foolish, Mr Nightmare. It would be a shame to kill your beautiful friend in front of you, but you'll appreciate that's exactly what I'll do if you as much as take a step towards me. You're not the only one here with weapons."

The ex-bodyguards all had their guns trained on my chest.

"Exactly what do you want from us?" I snapped.

"Well, tomorrow night is Samhain. It's a highly significant time, in this world as well as yours. We have our celebrations to attend to. And our sacrifices. You and Miss Carnadine will be our offerings to those you have frustrated. It doesn't have to be painful, but your blood, mingled on our altar, will be a very special libation. And I will allow you and Miss Carnadine to spend a little time together before we begin the ceremonies."

At another gesture from him, the Boneless Men cut Ariadne's bonds and her gag and pushed her towards me. The Pumpkin King obviously remained confident that we wouldn't rush him. I gave Ariadne a brief hug and she took one of the swords. I whispered a warning not to chance an attack to her. And I was thinking, where the heck is Scathach? Now would be a good time to gate-crash this little soiree.

Maybe the witch was psychic because I heard a commotion by the tall stones to my left and several of the Boneless Men there broke apart to reveal Scathach, clearly in Boudicca mode. Her red hair flew about her like a sheet, her hands gripped the Gae Bolg like a pike and her expression was one of boiling fury. I have to say, it was a big improvement on the dancing Ophelia version.

"Ah, you're here!" said the Pumpkin King. His face warped itself into what I took to be a beam of pleasure, though it would have sent small children and animals racing for cover.

Scathach stepped forward, the point of the Gae Bolg aimed directly at the Pumpkin King's rotund belly. She had him at her mercy. I couldn't see how he was going to hold her off. One strike and he'd be boiled alive. I started to duck, expecting a hailstorm of fleshy pumpkin parts.

She went right to the edge of his muddy pool and the Gae Bolg couldn't

have been more than a few inches from his face.

Amazingly, he just grinned. He said something to her and for a moment neither Ariadne nor I could see his face, our vision blocked by Scathach's form. She acted as if she was the one who'd been punctured by a spear, lurching back, almost falling. And, as if that didn't take the goddam biscuit, she *dropped* the Gae Bolg. I got a look at her face and it was ashen with horror, her body shaking. Hell knows what he said, but we'd gone from triumph to disaster in a few syllables.

To confirm that we were all properly in the soup, a number of large shapes loomed over the standing stones, one of them squeezing between them to tower over us, bulbous but blind eyes gazing emptily on the scene below it – a Blind Gardener. It reached out with one of those absurdly elongated arms and flicked the Gae Bolg across the slabs, out of harm's way. Ariadne eyed it as if she would make a play for it, but I whispered a warning to her not to touch it.

"What's wrong with her?" she whispered back.

The Pumpkin King laughed, a sound like someone gargling phlegm. "It seems my little trap has well and truly been sprung. Nice to have Miss Carnadine and Mr Nightmare in my clutches, but dear Scathach was the prize I most coveted. I felt sure the romantic in her would respond to the call for help from two such star-crossed lovers. That is the expression, isn't it? I know how much Scathach loves the Bard. And now I have three of you. Almost the full set."

Ariadne and I glanced briefly at one another. We knew only too well what he was getting at. I had no time to puzzle out the how.

"I've long been an admirer of dear Molly Malloy, I admit it. Even someone as physically unique as I am has emotions, you know. Quite powerful desires. And a king should have a queen, don't you think? Dear Molly, you would suit me *so* well. Your powers and mine, well, such an addition to the forces that arraign themselves against mankind. What a combination we will make."

Scathach didn't seem inclined to argue, still numbed by whatever he had said to her.

"We can make Samhain a really joyous occasion. Blood sacrifices *and* a wonderful wedding."

A new sound broke out among the Boneless Men by the stones. It was a kind of hissing, high pitched and weird and it suggested pain. Something was among them, doing something very nasty to them. Ariadne and I watched the chaos unfold as a large black shape burst out from the collapsing ranks and leapt at the exposed upper thigh of the central Blind Gardener.

"Am I going crazy, or is that a panther?" said Ariadne.

I grinned. "Yeah. I'll introduce you later. Unless I'm wide of the mark, that's Caliban. Scathach's familiar." My eyes were glued to the muscular black beast as it ripped and clawed open the vegetable flesh of the Gardner. The

Pumpkin King may have been smug about luring Scathach here, but he hadn't bargained on Caliban joining the fun in extreme mode. The Blind Gardener opened its mouth soundlessly like a fish out of water and toppled over, shouldering into one of the tall stones, which itself collapsed under the impact like it had been hit by an express train, throwing the whole darn place into further utter confusion.

At least it had dragged Scathach out of her mental cave. She sprang back and retrieved the Gae Bolg. I gave Ariadne the other sword and pulled out my Berettas. The three former bodyguards looked bemused by all the sudden noise and movement, their guns wavering. It was all I needed - I let them have it, blowing all three of their grotesquely transformed heads into a pink mist. Ariadne used the twin blades to carve up a bunch of Boneless goons who'd woken up, rushed us and tried to pin us down.

The fallen Blind Gardner was thrashing about with its long limbs, doing more damage to the bunched Boneless Men than Ariadne and me combined. We'd have gone for the Pumpkin King, but he'd seen the way the wind was blowing and had started to submerge himself in his bed of mud, double quick time. I fired off a couple of rounds at him, but the bullets just whanged off his thick hide like golf balls off a rubber wall. For some reason, Scathach would not close in and use the Gae Bolg on him. My guess was he'd used some kind of hocus-pocus on her that had frozen her will to kill him.

At least she was otherwise mobile. "We must get away," she called, pointing to the path I had climbed to get here and neither Ariadne nor I wasted any time in following her. With their King ducking for cover, the Boneless mob were about as coordinated as a bunch of chickens in a thunderstorm, getting tangled up with themselves rather than making a play to recover us. Behind us, evidently enjoying himself, Caliban ripped and tore a whole bunch of Boneless Men apart. It was no contest, like a ton of vegetables being run through the granddaddy of food processors. The whole place was a mess, but we had no time to watch it. We raced down the path and into the shadowed declivity.

"Would I be right in thinking you've got something in my bag for me? You have? Good. So, cover me for a moment," said Ariadne, grabbing the bag off me and pulling out her Ninja gear. I grinned, but looked back to see Caliban slowly coming down the path, pausing only to slice up another Boneless Man or six. We had the upper hand, but there were a lot of those guys and hell knew what would be waiting for us down in the fields. Sooner or later they'd get their act together and likely bury us under sheer numbers.

Ariadne did a quick change, complete with mask and we followed Scathach down and beyond the narrow walls of the hill, surprised to find no reception committee waiting for us. Moments later, Caliban, still in his muck-spattered black panther form, joined us. The pursuit appeared to have thrown the towel in. Yeah, right.

"I don't like it," I said. "I mean, I do like it, but I smell a whole pack of rats. Why have they cried off?"

Scathach spat, and coming from her, even in warrior mode, it looked kinda out of character. Maybe the spell that had held her was properly snapped. "He won't let us go, not without a fight. But he is afraid of the Gae Bolg."

I wanted to ask her why the heck she hadn't used the goddam thing and skewered him, but Caliban nudged me and I almost toppled over. He was urging us to follow him. Must be he knew a way out of here. I didn't think heading back through the fields of pumpkin things was a good idea, so I was happy enough to comply with Caliban. We all were, so let him lead us around the base of the hill to another overgrown path.

We followed it, listening out for sounds of pursuit, but the entire place had fallen very silent, unnaturally so. It stayed that way as we went further and further away from the hill and reached the reed-choked banks of a river. It was no more than a few yards wide and on its far side the undergrowth was so rampant that it would have been impossible to penetrate it if we'd gone across. I wondered why Caliban had brought us to what looked like a dead end.

He was way ahead of me, though. He went along the bank and stood above something in the reeds. I checked it out and grinned back at the two women. "It's a boat. Hell knows how it got here, but it's usable. No oars, but we can use our hands."

Scathach and Ariadne initially looked dubious, but I held the low craft steady and they got in it. Caliban sprang off into the undergrowth and moved along the bank in his own way. I got on board, a mite shakily, and pushed us off. Pretty soon we were drifting down the river, paddling the boat carefully. On the opposite bank, we could sense things in the tangled mass of overhanging greenery, but we went on unmolested.

"Where are we headed?" I said.

Scathach was nodding, as if reading some invisible signs. "This river runs into the bigger marsh and leads to the place where we entered this realm. We should reach it before the sun sets. Then I can open the gate back to our own world. However, we must expect the Pumpkin King to be waiting for us. He'll not let us slip through his grasp so easily. We have no more surprises for him. I was a fool to think he wasn't expecting me."

I could see to our left the rising slope of the endless fields of pumpkin plants and once more the distant shape of a slow lumbering Blind Gardener. If any of them were aware of us, they made no show of it. I still felt like a rat running along a pipe towards the rat catchers. The sky was darkening, even more moody and brooding than the landscape.

The river widened slightly. Scathach had us paddle the boat in to the shore and we found an area of more solid ground to disembark. I say solid, but it wobbled disconcertingly underneath us. Caliban emerged from a clump of reeds and led us in a zigzag towards an open expanse, beyond which we could see the river and what I took to be the place where we had first crossed it. I couldn't see the stones below the surface, but I guess we needed the sunset for that. It seemed like we had maybe about an hour to kick our heels before that happened. I didn't think we would get bored.

At first the air was pretty still, but after a while we heard a sound like the incoming waves of a tide, only this wasn't the sea. The vegetable army was on the march, and we were surrounded on three sides as the pumpkin hordes moved in on us, this time with something more like a concerted effort. Our one advantage was that they wanted us alive, so my guess was they were going to close in and smother us to the point of unconsciousness and not beyond. Something to be thankful for. We arranged ourselves in an arc, backs to the river - Scathach, Ariadne, me and Caliban.

The lines of Boneless Men – thousands of them – drew up and halted no more than thirty yards from us. I tried not to think of the Alamo, Custer, General Gordon, that kind of inspiring scenario. It struck me that if this army did invade my world and start infesting the streets of New York, things were going to get very unpleasant indeed. I stopped thinking about Custer's Last Stand and moved on to the Invasion of the Body Snatchers. I used to like that movie.

We waited, but things had gone very quiet. I could imagine what they were all waiting for. The Pumpkin King was about to make a grand entrance, although there was no sign of his coming among the massed ranks of his minions. That was because he was behind us.

Between us and the river, there was a muddy area with a narrow path running through it. The whole of it burst upwards like a small bomb had gone off underneath it, sending a rain of foul-smelling mud and twisted reed skywards. We just about ducked out of its way, turning to face whatever had caused the mess. No prizes for guessing it was the Big Pumpkin himself. His bloated body heaved itself up from the mire as though he had travelled here via some unwholesome underground system, a fat walrus emerging from a sea of mud.

He seemed even bigger than he had done on the hilltop, his gross arms steadying himself on a reed bank on either side, gently rocking like an overloaded barge. That grotesque face glared at us, lit from within by whatever weird magics sustained him.

"You left without even saying goodbye!" he called in that croaking voice, his thick tongue licking muck from his mouth.

Instinctively I aimed my two Berettas at him. I may not be able to blast him apart, but I was ready to try for an eye or two. He could go join his Blind Gardeners. Speaking of which, a few of them had added themselves to the ranks of the Boneless Men, just to even up the numbers.

Caliban snarled, claws revealed, scimitars in the fading light. I reminded myself not to call the guy ugly again. Most opponents would have shriveled up and crumpled when faced by the panther's challenge, but the Pumpkin King completely ignored the big cat, moon-like eyes fixed on Scathach. Lust rippled and bubbled in those eyes in a way that made my flesh crawl, so I couldn't imagine how she felt about it. She gripped the Gae Bolg and I was praying that this time she had a better hold of it. Maybe she'd had time to fortify her resolve. The way the King was drooling over her, she had enough incentive to do the deed. That or our bacon was cooked.

"There's no need for unpleasantness," said the Pumpkin King. "Let me suggest a compromise."

Ariadne and I exchanged glances, although we were both coming from the same place. No compromises.

He turned to us. "Give me the witch, and you others can go back, unscathed. You came here to rescue Miss Carnadine," he said to me. "So take her away in your shining armour. I'll forget about the sacrifices. I'd be more than happy to make do with a royal wedding and its conjugal rights." His eyes beamed even more brightly with lust and I could see Scathach shudder.

Okay, girl, I was thinking. You got a second bite of the cherry. Now would be a really good time to rush forward, get a firm grip on the killer lance and *drive the goddam thing into the Pumpkin King's overblown belly.*

She did take a few steps towards that palpitating mound of vegetable flesh, but, just like before, she hesitated. Ariadne also edged forward and my guess was, she would use those twin blades of hers if Scathach wasn't prepared to cut the mustard. Okay, so I'd go for the eyes. Between us we ought to do some serious damage, even if we couldn't render the Pumpkin King into mash.

It was like something – a spell, a curse, whatever – had got to Scathach. Her face twisted with mixed emotions – horror, fear, pity maybe. She drew back and I was about to open fire, thinking maybe the least I could do was break this crippling spell, but Ariadne suddenly nudged my left arm. The gun went off but the bullet tore harmlessly into the upper atmosphere. I gaped at her.

"Don't shoot him," she said under her breath.

What the hell? Was this curse getting to her as well? "Hey, he's the bad guy, right?"

"We have to let Scathach do it. I'll explain later." She said it with a sort of catch in her voice and I wondered what in blazes was going on here. It was a girl thing, obviously, and I was just the hired help. But we needed some action or Scathach was going to find herself up to her neck in not so wedded bliss.

Mind you, some girls like that kind of thing.

Maybe the sound of the gunshot got through to Scathach as she was stepping forward again, the Gae Bolg held out in front of her. The Pumpkin King was unmoved, even swelling his breast as if to welcome a thrust. The weapon rose, drew back, but it still wavered. It was all I could do not to shout out encouragement.

The glee on the face of the Pumpkin King was almost more than I could bear, but that expanded face changed, as if the monster had already been stabbed. The features writhed – it was like someone, someone huge, was pulling the flesh this way and that, clawing at it. It seemed like there were two faces there, but I couldn't make out the details because the whole body started to roll this way and that, like it was reacting to a whole series of electric shocks. It convulsed, thrashing about in the mud, which again spewed out of the bath, this way and that.

The Pumpkin King looked like he was fighting himself, clubbing at his own body, punching himself, rolling and writhing. It would have been a bundle of laughs if it hadn't been horrifying. Scathach was staring in horror. This whole ludicrous performance obviously meant a whole lot more to her than it did to me.

"Do it! Do it now!" I heard the words, a voice a few octaves higher than the Pumpkin King's, squeezed out of his mouth as his inner turmoil threatened to boil over. It was a plea to Scathach, but she was shaking her head.

Ariadne pointed across the river. The sunlight, such as it was, was starting to weaken noticeably. Sunset had crept up on us and I realised with a jolt that we didn't have a lot of time to get out of here. Ariadne shouted to Scathach, who finally responded. She seemed almost relieved to have something else to do.

"Go!" called the voice from within the Pumpkin King. "I can't hold him for much longer!"

Scathach wrenched herself away and was about to lead us to the river, when the Boneless Men abruptly burst into life, like they'd figured out we were going to make a break for it. As one, they surged in and within moments the four of us were engaged in a no-holds-barred, no rules battle, Caliban ripping and tearing into the enemy, Ariadne likewise using her swords. I was happy to blast away with the Berettas – and the spare Magnum I'd taken from one of the bodyguards I'd dispatched. I knew, though, that I only had so many bullets.

Ariadne was wise to it, too, and tossed me one of the swords. It wasn't the first time we'd stood back to back, using them to dispatch an ugly mob with murder or worse on its mind. I was glad to see that Scathach had no problems using the Gae Bolg against the Boneless Men, who came at us with no regard for their own safety, and light blazed up as she burned a path through them.

We had to fight for every last inch of ground, and as we did so, the frantic struggles in the mud pit reached some kind of crescendo, the details blotted out in a mud storm.

It was a long, bloody haul to the river bank, and as we got there the sun was about to disappear. Rays of waning light lanced across the river and picked out the underwater stones. Caliban led the way across, jumping lithely on to the other bank and slipping into the thick forest there. Ariadne pushed me over next and followed hot on my heels, with Scathach, now fully revived and handing out holy hell to the pursuing hordes, bringing up the rear. As we all reached the far bank, she bent down and plunged the Gae Bolg's point into the water.

It churned and boiled, clouds of steam rising. The Boneless Men held back on the bank we'd left, some of them stumbling into the water, immediately fried alive. I couldn't see what happened to the Pumpkin King – numerous mounds of gelatinous muck obscured everything. Maybe he sank back into his mud bath.

Once the four of us were in the forest, back on the winding path, the sudden silence closed in, like we'd slammed a great door shut. There was no indication of pursuit. If there was a gate back there, it had closed, at least for now. Sealed by the sunset, I guessed. We'd made it by the seat of our pants.

"It's good to be back," I said. "But I kind of get the feeling this isn't over. That is one very big hornet's nest we've just kicked over and man, those hornets are very pissed."

"You're on the money there, honey pie," said Ariadne.

She and Scathach and I were all exhausted, ready to slump down. Caliban had gone on ahead, swallowed by the coming night. We forced ourselves to walk for a while, but the first grove we came to we paused for a rest. Scathach sat some way apart from Ariadne and me, her head bowed, her body slumped. The battle had taken a lot more out of her. And were those tears staining her face?

I sat close to Ariadne on a fallen log and watched her as she cleaned muck off her twin blades with sheaves of grass.

"So what gives with Scathach?" I asked her softly. "She could have nailed him more than once."

"Even you, Mr. *Stone*, must have noticed the air of sadness about the girl," she said. "Hmm? A deep melancholy."

"Sure. It's like there's two sides to her. The warrior and the maiden. Like two different people. She told me about the man she lost, Kulkain. It hurt her. Deep."

"I've seen that hurt before, Nick. When you lose someone that special, you lose a lot of yourself as well," Ariadne said pointedly.

She meant Martha, I knew that. I'd pushed all that deep down inside

myself and although in the past I'd opened up a little to Ariadne, I hadn't told her the full story. It was still like a knife in my gut. Sometime soon I was going to have to tell her all about it. Maybe that would be a way to pull that knife out of me.

"What happened to him - Kulkain?" she asked.

I told her something of what Scathach had said to me. As I was talking, the coin dropped in the slot and realisation hit me. I stared across at Scathach, whose eyes were closed. My guess was, she was reliving the confrontation with the Pumpkin King.

"Hell, so that was it. She said the dark powers had won Kulkain over. Absorbed him. So, back there –"

"The Pumpkin King was fighting himself. You heard that second voice. It's why she couldn't use the Gae Bolg to destroy him."

"Kulkain was in there, part of him. Just as the Boneless Men absorb their victims, the King had absorbed Kulkain at some point. Only he still had enough humanity left in him to fight back. He saved us."

"Right," said Ariadne, her own face clouded.

It came to me then what it must have meant to Scathach. She would have been torn. I couldn't think of anything more soul-destroying than that knowledge. And how had it ended back there? What had been the outcome of that lunatic contest?

Ariadne broke into my thoughts by kissing me gently.

"That's for being noble," she said, a smile returning.

"Ma'am, I was too freaked out to be noble."

"Not at all. You could have taken the Pumpkin King up on his offer to swap you and me for Scathach. We could have walked free if you'd agreed. You would have been saving me. What could be more important to you? But of course, you were thinking of Scathach."

"Wait a minute, lady, what are you getting at?"

"Nothing. She's important to you, of course." She gave me a look of pure mischief. I felt like a mouse surrounded by a bunch of cats.

"Hell, there's no pleasing you dames."

She laughed, unable to keep up her teasing. "Ah, but there is. And you did okay."

Scathach had heard Ariadne's laughter. She got up and came to us. "It's over for now," she said. "I won't fall into that trap again."

"We were all suckered in," I told her. "Me, right from the start. But we know what we're up against now. We need to go back home and think it through."

She nodded. "I'll say goodbye for the time being." That was it. A last smile, then she was off into the darkness, following Caliban. I would have gone after her, said more, but Ariadne gently pulled me back.

"Private time," she said. "Maybe she'll talk to us later."

I bowed to her judgement and after a few minutes we went back through the forest, barely able to see the way until we reached another grove where there was a small lantern hanging in a tree. Leaning on the narrow trunk was the hunched form of Scathach's familiar, now in his gargoyle form.

Ariadne was taken aback for a moment, but I hailed the little man.

"You two want a light back to the lodge, or you planning on stumbling about in the dark until breakfast?" he grumbled.

"Yeah, we could do with some help. Lead on, MacDuff."

"That's *lay* on, bonehead."

"And cursed be he who first calls hold, enough."

"Would you two gentlemen stop bickering and get us back into the warm, please?" said Ariadne in a voice that even Caliban wasn't going to ignore.

He took down the lantern and handed it up to me. "Say, you did a good job back there. Most guys woulda took the money and ran when it was offered. I thank you for not going down that road."

"You'll have me all emotional, you ugly runt."

"It's what's inside that counts, Mr. Razorface. See you around." He nodded to the bemused Ariadne and moments later was gone.

She stared at me. "*Razorface?*"

"We like to trade insults."

"I don't know, though. It sort of suits you."

When we reached the grounds around the lodge, the whole place was cloaked in darkness, although a bright moon ducked in and out of the clouds and gave us a better view of the lawns. We reached the wide windows of one of the lounges and after a brief look around me, I set down the lantern and fumbled for the house keys, handing them to Ariadne.

"I made sure the place was locked when I left," I told her. "I didn't want the raccoons to get in and mess the place up."

I waited while she chose a key and unlocked, sliding one long window aside. She flicked on an internal light switch and was about to enter, when something snagged her attention. She turned back to me. I was several feet away from her, looking up at the roof and generally checking the place over. It was still too quiet, even for night.

"Don't move until I tell you," she whispered and the air was so static I caught every word. I knew then that there was something behind me. Something of hostile intent that made my blood slow down and almost clog.

Ariadne had slipped her swords into her belt as we came here, but now she pulled one free, softly as a shadow. Her eyes indicated that I should move to my right, and fast. I suddenly flung myself that way, crash landing almost in the shrubs, just as she drew back her arm and threw the sword like it was an oversize throwing knife. I watched it turn end over end, silvered by the moonlight, hissing through the air.

Behind me, the blade *chocked* into something solid. I rolled out of the clinging vegetation, gun in hand, just about in time to see the last of the bodyguards, the seventh, stagger backwards, his head cloven in two, squirting whatever pink liquid served for blood over its chest. Ariadne was on the creature in a flash, using her other blade to finish the grisly work. Another bonfire to attend to.

I went to her and put an arm around her. "I knew my maths wasn't wrong. Three died here and three died back in Pumpkinville. That left one. I'm getting slow. Should have remembered."

"He would have shot to kill, Nick," she said, with a shudder. "Rather than let us escape, this one was left here to kill us. As a last resort."

I retrieved the lantern, took out its weird candle and applied it to the dead Boneless Man. In moments it had become a blazing torch and we stepped back from the blast of heat. She was right. And the others I'd shot here earlier had been easy kills. They'd been here to delay us, not finish us.

We went inside and both slumped into the plush seating, too bushed to say much for a while. My guess was, she'd be able to explain the missing seven bodyguards to the police. That was, if anyone asked about them. It went with the territory.

"Do you want me to see if I can rescue anything of that meal?" she said, tugging off her mask.

I nodded. "Either that or I'll start eating the shrubbery."

"Pour us both a drink. Stiff ones."

I didn't need asking twice. "One good thing has come out of this mess," I told her, with what might have passed for a wry grin. "You've lost all your pilots. Unless you've got a wagon stashed away in the garage, we've got a long walk ahead of us."

"Not quite all," she said, with a grin that sent a shiver down my spine. "I'm quite capable of flying a helicopter myself. I'm fully licenced."

Yeah, well I should have known as much. "Is that so? No hurry, though. Let's give it a week or two. Or more."

She came over and put her arms around me. "I think we better get back to the city in the morning. This place isn't a safe haven anymore."

"Could we make that late morning?"

"Of course. As long as we're back before closing time. I've some shopping to attend to."

"*Shopping*?" I said it like it was one of the worst words in the dictionary. Let's face it, I got that right.

"Yes. I need a new kitbag for a start. Given that a certain person left mine back there in the wilderness. Not to mention the sweet little dress that was in it."

A BESTIARY OF HORRORS

I tried to grin, but failed miserably. Dames and their clothes. "Then in the evening, we can celebrate. After all, it will be Samhain."

Adrian Cole began writing at the tender age of 10, although he wasn't ready to submit professionally until he was much older – at 19. His first published work was a ghost story for IPC magazines in 1972, followed soon after by a trilogy of sword & planet novels, THE DREAM LORDS (Zebra, US) in the 1970s. Since then he has gone on to have more than 2 dozen novels published and many short stories and his work has been translated into a number of foreign editions.

He writes science fiction, heroic fantasy, sword & sorcery, horror, pulp fiction, Mythos and has had two young adult novels published, MOORSTONES and THE SLEEP OF GIANTS (Spindlewood, UK)

His best known works are the OMARAN SAGA and STAR REQUIEM quartets and these have also been published recently as ebooks under the Gollancz SF Gateway imprint and are also being released as audio books (Audible).

His most recent novel is THE SHADOW ACADEMY, sf from Edge (Canada). In October of 2015, he received the British Fantasy Society Award for Best Collection for NICK NIGHTMARE INVESTIGATES (Alchemy UK), the first arc of stories about his hard-boiled occult private eye who confronts the various minions of Lovecraft's Mythos as well as other monsters and horrors in different, bizarre locales.

He has been nominated for numerous other awards, and has appeared in Year's Best collections.

A native of Devon, UK, he lives in Bideford with his wife,

Judy, and enjoys frequent dips in the sea and an occasional bike ride up into the forests of the local area, about which the less said, the better.

For more information, visit adriancscole.com

RESTY ACRES

BY BEAU JOHNSON

IN the beginning I didn't believe him; nor would you, all told. The tip-off should have been the coffee he brought me.

In the six years I had known Emil Dimpton, he had never given up anything to anyone free of charge. In his infinite wisdom (add sarcasm here), I think he thought that buying me my morning joe should have made me more inclined to believe his tail of fancy. He'd been wrong, of course, as I have already stated, but only for a while; in the end, but perhaps more so in the middle, I came to believe as much as he. God, I say, should help us all.

My name is Walter Meade and I am seventy-six years old. I am writing this because there needs to be an account of what went on here - what is going on here. As I did not believe Emil there at the beginning, no one has believed it coming from my mouth either. Of this I am sure and why I have chosen to detail it this way instead. No matter. It needs to be noted. It needs to get out. I will write and make copies and send them by mail. It will appear as though I am sick, the conclusions drawn unavoidable; that I will seem the senile old fart, sane but for a dementia which lurks. This is the risk I take. This how scared I am. With what life I have left, I wish to remain.

As you are aware, I am crippled. My light and legs lost to me long ago, each to the same event - the one which took my wife as well as my mobility. I live in this retirement home someone - some young upstart I've no doubt - decided to call Resty Acres. Some funny, huh? That name. Resty Acres. No, not really. Kind of sad, actually, when you really sit and ponder it. It is a nice enough place, very quiet, very clean, consisting of a menu which still finds ways to surprise me.

Also, I have yet to be beaten since my eldest dropped me here some eight years ago. And just so we're clear - I don't hold it against you, Barry, for leaving me here like you did. You are the oldest, the responsibility fell to you. If it were me in your shoes I would have done the same. Not only because I had become a burden, but because you have your own to take care of now. I am old now, yes, what more could one such as me have to offer someone like you? Just because I brought you in this world, fed you and clothed you, nurtured and guided you, ensured you received your schooling and then your doctoring, what would I deserve in return? Nothing. As you've given, son - as you've given. I wish you well, boy. As I do your brothers and sisters.

Pricks. The lot of you. Am I bitter? Little bit.

Back to it then.

It was a Tuesday when Emil came to me with the free cup of joe and right from the get-go you could tell that something was off, that the man was struggling; some unseen weight seemed to be pulling at his corners, the ones which keep the majority of us in check. For an old codger awaiting his last day he was an unusually upbeat fellow is what I mean to say, but he was far from that on this particular day. No, this day Emil was scared. I would go so far as to say terrified even. His color was off as well, his face almost ashen except for these dark circles which hung beneath his eyes like two used tea bags---the round kind, not the square. He kept wiping his head too, with that damn handkerchief of his, which would have been much weirder if the old boy still had hair. Slowly, he explained what had happened as best he could. Done, he pleaded with me to believe him, that he didn't think anyone one else would. I agreed with him, as it was poppycock, what he told me, but balderdash was the word I think I used to explain it to him.

"But Walter, it took Vera! I don't want to be next."

"And you won't be," I said, more than a little patronizingly. "Emil: if what you say is true, then size will prove your friend; it makes you too big for it to take you. Besides, how do you know Vera hasn't had one of her episodes and only went wandering, as she's been known to do? You don't. Therefore until she turns up, you cannot know. Not for sure."

He looked at me then, and I could tell his confusion remained, thicker now than when he first sat down. This had not been my intent.

Around and around his handkerchief went, damn thing wiping whatever it needed to wipe. He said: "But I am losing weight every week, Walter. I am only above one hundred and twenty as of this morning. I am very close to the pattern weight I think."

"Emil, seriously; we are too old to believe in things such as these. There are no vampires, especially ones which eat entire victims. When have you ever heard of a vampire doing that? How would it be possible even? Is it not only for the jugular, the drinking of and what not?"

"Do not patronize me, Walter!" And there was real anger there, a flash of it anyway. "Three of us have gone missing in the last two years, four now with Vera. All unaccounted for. Off wandering they say, always in the middle of the night, all of it conveniently blamed on senility of course. Do you think I have not thought this through? Do you not think I have seen?"

"Emil, you yourself said it was dark when you saw and that you couldn't really see."

"But the noises I heard!"

"Yes. But hadn't those awakened you? Is it possib--

But it was too late. He was up and gone without so much a glance back towards me, that damn handkerchief searching for something, searching as always. It was only later that I realized I hadn't even popped the lid to the coffee Emil had tried to bribe me with. I'm sure if some shrink thought hard enough they would be able to form some sort of correlation between this and what was about to happen.

Yes, quite sure.

I didn't see Emil much after that morning and the times that I did he did not look much better than when he first told me about the vampire he believed was hidden amongst the elderly here at Resty Acres; his appearance seemed to be on the decline, deteriorating little by little each time I saw him in the weeks which followed. I don't know exactly when it happened, but there actually came a time when he chose to no longer dress himself. Moreover, his hygiene was beginning to suffer as well. Ultimately, he ended up wearing nothing more than underpants and that housecoat of his, the one with black stripes. He still had his handkerchief, however, that same old red one, although it seemed to be getting less and less work the more times I saw him; mostly I would see it dangling from his hand, limp as his new demeanour. It was when Emil himself went missing that things began to change for me. Or rearrange, if I am to be truthful.

When the talk Emil and I had on that Tuesday morning was given new perspective.

I am very close to the pattern weight, I think.

That is what he said, there at our table in the breakfast room. Odd, yes, but as I think back over the times I saw him wandering to and fro in that housecoat of his, it occurs to me that Emil did seem to be on the decline in weight as well. The man was becoming *less* is what I mean to say, smaller and thinner each time I took notice I suppose.

Still, thinking back, maybe I could have prevented some of this; maybe, maybe not. At least I could have put forth an effort, which is something I did not do, not then. And of this I am ashamed, just so you know, as it places my character beneath a light I am unfamiliar with.

Before all that, however, I received my new roommate. His name was Stanley Chesterfield, and if that name isn't a handle then I don't know what is. I called him Flat Stan on account of his face, which really needs no further explanation. He was a smaller man, and frail, from years of bed rest I'm sure. He was also uncommunicative. Not totally, but unable to hold a conversation concerning the here, the present and the now; poor Flat Stan had come to be my roomy while he found himself trapped within the end stages of Alzheimer's.

This prison, Alzheimer's, is a disease no one would wish upon their worst enemy. It is rampant here at Resty Acres, perhaps the disease du jour, and believe you me when I say it is as powerful as it is heart-wrenching. A fear of mine, I'll admit, but no longer my number one. No, that place is now reserved for the impossible proved possible, for the stuff I used to know as make believe.

I have looked evil in the eye, my friend. I am afraid to say it does not blink.

A meeting was called concerning Emil's disappearance, the entire residence escorted into the auditorium before lunch three days after the search had been called off. The smell was there, of course, as it always is. And don't think we are immune, because we aren't. We know it's there, hanging over and rising from us like an invisible prophet. The death smell is what I'm referring to; the yellow smell of the elderly, of chemical and approaching death. In a room such as ours, with over two hundred seniors... well... you get the drift - no pun intended.

Dr. Hamilton is the guy who runs the show here, the Big Tuna as it were, and has so since before my children decided me a member. He's a slick one, is Dr. Hamilton, him and that new-age ponytail of his. I didn't always know he was this slick, and only came to after this meeting. Oh yes. Indeed. It was when he started in on how Emil had been battling what I had previously called the disease du jour that I really began to see the situation for what it was: a railroad, as in we were being.

Emil Dimpton never had any such disease. This is true. This I know.

We were then informed that stronger security measures would be in place by week's end. This in light of the "now recurring" and "very unfortunate" theme which had found its way into the "very heart" of Resty Acres itself; that with Emil's disappearance as well as Vera's, lest we forget Hickman and Robalard, (whom he did not mention by name, just so we are clear) that the board had gathered---in the eleventh hour, I'm sure---and voted unanimously on a new mandate, one which was to be "swift" and "immediate" in its "execution" and "implementation." Ah. How nice. They care! They really, really care.

What I said was this: "Dr. Hamilton?"

"Walter, yes; you have a question?" Not Mr. Meade. Walter. There you go.

"Yes," I said and paused, momentarily wishing for the deadwood to work once more. I wanted to stand as I said my piece is all. No reason why, just did; just something which happens to me from time to time. Mostly I'm good with what my situation is, having come to terms with it moons ago, but still, as I've said... it happens... momentary lapses. "I have known Emil for six years." I continued. "In that time I have never seen any of the symptoms you associate with Alzheimer's. How could this be? Are you sure is what I'm asking?"

I half expected to see something register in Hamilton's eyes at this, a darting flash of guilt perhaps, some glaring sheen of hate. What I received instead was something quite the opposite. Squatting to his knees, the man offered me a tenderness I was up until that point unaware he possessed. He said: "Walter. He was someone you probably saw on a regular basis, was he not; your friend, maybe? This never makes us the best judges, on our best days. I am a trained physician and Alzheimer's the field I specialize in: I would know. Emil was suffering. Silently. And it was coming on fast towards the end, before he went missing. It comes to no surprise that many of you failed to notice."

And the slick bastard had me, honestly; hook, line and ponytail. It was when he threw in the wink, there at the end, that two things became very clear, very fast. One was that it had always been an inside job, just as Emil had suspected from the get go. Two was that I had just made myself a target.

Now... it is not like any overt changes occurred once Dr. Hamilton let me in on the little secret Emil had been silenced for. No long looks from across the room when I saw him in one of the lounges or many of the hallways or anything like that. Neither was there hissing or the producing of fangs, just so you know. Everything remained as it was before the latest disappearances, Resty Acres reverting back to what it has always been - a retirement home, the kind which serves Jell-O after each and every meal.

I was neither hounded nor touched is what I mean to say. Even though I now knew, and knew that Dr. Hamilton knew I knew, I remained alive. And don't get me wrong, I do not know for certain that Dr. Hamilton is the vampire Emil spoke of, only that he is part of the conspiracy residing here.

Days passed; weeks. And as most of you know I tried to get you word, calling as many of you as I could. Do you remember that, Barry? Do your brothers and sisters? How do you recall the times I called and tried to convince you of the plight I faced? What did they tell you when you called back to inquire about the state of your father's mental health? What I think they told you; what I believe they tell all who inquire about the darkness which goes on here; do they apologize and tell you it is senility setting in? Perhaps a bit of the early Alzheimer's even? We'll do some tests though, yes, yes, a batch of them, and get back to you with the results. Did it go a little something like that, Barry? I'm pretty sure it did.

Do you see how slick this makes them?

Do you?

 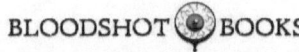

Human beings are complex individuals. This has been said before. We are also simple, and at times stupidly so. Like many of us, not much scares me anymore. Some things yes, like disease and war, but none of it gutting me as completely as it had when I was a boy.

I am an abrupt talker and always have been; loud with opinions. It tends to lead people to believe I am cantankerous by nature, and an arse-hole by choice. I am not, however, but far too old and much too tired to explain it away in the document before you. If my wife were alive she would verify the things I have just mentioned. My kids? Not so much. And that is their choice. It was always my way or the highway beneath the roof I built and placed above their heads. I was a stern parent - the need for them to know and understand respect the very top upon our list. This is all I will say about that. They know their bed and how they must lie. What I must get back to is the fear I mentioned earlier, the stuff from my childhood. It is back inside me now, a thing come home to roost. Unwilling to relent, it screams for release.

I have seen the creature at work. As Emil Dimpton believed, it does do more than drink.

I had gotten used to Flat Stan's snoring. Not that I had much choice in the matter - he slept most of the time. When he did wake we would talk about the old days, when the grass was greener and all that jazz. During these conversations I was usually somebody else, a Johnny or Duncan, sometimes a David. This didn't bother me, and poor Flat Stan never knew the difference. I think he did come close to the surface once, as there was a pause and then the question of how I ended up in the wheelchair. When I began to tell him my story, he asked me what I was talking about and if I thought mother would approve. At this I was back to being Duncan, the older of his two sons. This was how my relationship played with Flat Stan - two parts sleep, one part conversational window into his past. Realizing this forces me to acknowledge that Alzheimer's is not unlike the creature which stalks me, that both are draining forces of utter destruction, time and method the only differences I can find between them.

It was the very night I came to this realization that the vampire awakened me - overrode the snores I had adapted myself to; as I rose to consciousness I came to know the sucking sounds Emil had spoken of months ago, the ones which now replaced Flat Stan's exhalations. Poor Flat Stan - there would be no more stories concerning Johnny or Duncan and sometimes a David; I am certain the man was dead before I turned on my reading lamp. In doing so I bore witness to the thing I am writing about, to that which has been preying upon us here at Resty Acres. I can't say for sure that it is a vampire, not in the truest sense of what I know. What I can say is that it shares a lot of the same characteristics you and I have been shown in movies and TV. Not all, but some. Other things reminded me of leeches, similar to the ones I used to fish with.

Big is unable to do it justice - the thing was massive, six five from head to boot. It was wide as well, as wide as it was thick it seemed. Bent over, its mouth and chin were buried deep into the middle of Stan's chest as it drank, the throat of it bulging to the point of where I thought it might burst. You would consider me turning on the light and sitting up would have made it notice me, yes? Would think I'd be screaming my fool head off for help, no? Both of these things should have happened but neither of them did. I watched if hypnotized, stared as the vampire exsanguinated my roommate completely, listened as it sucked and sucked and sucked. It was only when the draining was complete that it turned to me, then and not a moment before. I remained silent as it regarded me, lost within the caverns of the eyes before me; they were black like oil, those eyes, black like death; nothing of white at all. It moved towards me, touched me: a finger to my paunch. "Too much meat," it said, and the words were wet - still coated, swimming in the blood which used to run Stan. This was when my bladder let go, or when I believe it let go; I can't say for sure, not then, not now. After this it turned from me, its attention back to Stan - of what remained of Stan. Standing over him it opened and closed its mouth, a tocking sound accompanying this. At the time I did not know it was flexing. Now, however, I do. It was readying itself, you see; ensuring the route was able.

Slowly at first, then faster, its mouth began to expand, widening to receive another set of fangs, ones which erupted first from the upper part of its jaw and then from the lower. As was the creature, so were the teeth that came: massive; large and long and sling blade sharp.

You realize, of course, that the drinking was done?

Okay. To the hole then, back into it; as this is where it went. Slowly it leaned down and re-entered the open cavity of Stan's chest. I watched as it latched on and I watched as I heard it create a seal between its mouth and Stan's wound. After this there came another sound, this one louder than the first, the one it had been making with its jaw. It was deeper too, coming from the breast bone it was making its way through. Once it did this, once it broke through - this is when I truly understood what Emil was trying to convince me of that morning in the breakfast room, the day in which I patronized him more than a little bit.

I am very close to the pattern weight I think.

I am only above one hundred twenty as of this morning.

I think it can only consume around that much each time, roughly a hundred pounds a pull; its maximum, give or take. Amazing, no? A vampire who does it all! No fuss, no muss, no mess, no body. This is why it chooses the elderly, I think. Not only because we are probably the easiest of prey but because of the practicality we represent; that most of us are already the size it might require, each of us the lightest of light snacks.

The organs were next, all of them, and then the bones, followed, of course, by skin. All of it going, gone, and into as it continued to feed. Stan's body receding or deflating as it was depleted, everything being pulled up and into the supernatural vacuum it was attached to. Its throat was so engorged with the pressure it was creating that again I had the sense its neck was close to bursting. And I don't know how... but I must have missed something, even though I witnessed it all; it did not chew is what I mean to tell you. Not once. I do not know if it expelled some sort of compound as they were linked - if this is what helped to liquefy what remained of Stan, because, as I've said: there was not an ounce of chewing that went on that night, none, and humans bones, last time I checked, were still as hard as they ever were. It seems a logical assumption, no? That it might produce and secrete a toxin to help with what it devours? I know, I know: Where is the logic in any of this? Quite a quandary I've found myself, yes? Yes. Yes, it is. I am more worried about what it said to me as it left, however, when it turned back from the door to my room once it was ready to leave. *Soon* was what it said to me; one word, nothing more. It was later that I noticed Stan's bed sheets; that even they did not remain. Taken or ingested I cannot say for sure.

That was four months ago. In the time between then and as I write this many things occurred. The police were called for one, and more than once at that. After the third time I was dismissed with prejudice, informed I would be charged if another instance arose. I told this officer to shove it where the sun didn't shine and that if he felt so inclined then he should go ahead and do it, my pension would hold. Upon reflection, I realize this was wrong and ill-advised at best. I was doing exactly what I am trying to warn you about: that no one will believe and the more that I protest the more I seem unstable. Unstable leads to other words here at Resty Acres, words which begin with capitals. I have none of these impairments, however, and of that you can be sure; my faculties intact, in tune without a touch. But this is protesting, is it not? Fine. About it I will say no more. Instead I will tell you that I'm scared, that the fear remains.

Too much meat.

That is what it said to me; there in the room I shared with Stan. I know now it was referring to my weight, of the extra amount I had there. When you are suddenly paralyzed it is hard to maintain your previous body weight. Let no one tell you different. It seems you are only eating for half a body, and effectively you are, but the amount you had been used to, that doesn't go away - never has for me, anyway.

What I am trying to get across is that everything I ate seemed to fall and hold to the centre of my being once my spine had been severed, the distribution lines breaking down somewhere along the way - the same line my spine had run upon, perhaps.

Bottom line: I had a paunch, the creature touched it. At the time it did this, I was roughly one hundred ninety pounds. It is not this I worry about, not anymore.

That I have dipped below one hundred and twenty as of this morning is what does - Emil-weight if you remember - on the day he brought me coffee.

This is what terrifies me.

Because I am unable to stop what is happening, that I have been stripped of a basic control. The creature did something to me. It must have. Dr. Hamilton would disagree, I'm told, and has expressed as much. He thinks that what I'm doing is to be commended, that it can do nothing but prolong what he already sees as a long, full life. To his credit, he kept a straight face. Have I informed you of how slick this man is? Yes, I think I have. He is not the vampire, though, as I think I have also mentioned. He is only a facilitator. Perhaps a disciple even, Resty Acres being the place he chooses to worship. I don't know; will probably never know. Can only hope I will not die as the others have died, that I will remain uneaten. Tomorrow I will try again, after I have made copies and secured them to the mail. I will need a key, however, and that is where you come in. Can you secure it? Moreover: will you? All the guards have one - it hangs from their shirts. They are new, these keys, no longer metal but instead made from plastic, each of them a rectangle in shape.

New security measures: that is what they said.

Too much meat.

Immediate and swift in implementation and execution: that is what they did.

I am very close to the pattern weight I think.

I can see now what they've done: can you? They have locked us in here with it, isolating its prey. We are boxed in, all of us, the lid done closed and the sides taped shut. Better yet, you could even say we are now its Jell-O, the menu always red. It drinks us and then eats us and no one lifts a finger, not even with me screaming for any who would hear. As I have said before - this is how slick they are, how cunning and keen; running it all out in front there, just below our noses.

For the record: I hope I am loud when it comes. If I know anything about myself, I imagine I will prove to be. That is all one can ask for in this type of

 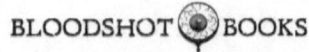

situation, I suppose; that in my dying I might (as Emil did for me) wake and enlighten another as to what is really going on here. Perhaps in doing so, he or she will then take up the fight as I took up the fight.

Unlike me, perhaps even he or she might prevail.

Beau Johnson has been published before, usually on the darker side of town. Such fine establishments might include Out of the Gutter Online, Shotgun Honey, Spelk Fiction and/or the Molotov Cocktail. He also managed to somehow marry above his pay grade. On top of this he received three boys he can tolerate and love. Go figure.

BLOODSHOT BOOKS

MEEMAW'S FROGS

BY RICHARD DANSKY

MEEMAW bought Luther a couple of frogs for his birthday, and Luther's Pa didn't like it one bit.

"Why you got to go and buy him frogs?" Pa asked. He tapped the side of the plastic cube the frogs swam in with one meaty finger, and the frogs kicked and jerked in response. "Boy his age, you should be buying him a football or something. Gonna buy him a pet, whyn't you buy him a dog?"

Meemaw, who was Pa's mother and thus used to him spouting off, just shrugged and kept up working on her cross-stitch. "Luther don't want a football none," she said. "Luther don't play no sports at all. Boy just stays home and reads, is what he does."

Pa stared at the frogs for a minute. They were tiny little things, maybe an inch and a half long, all green and brown spots with bug eyes damn near popping out of their skulls. They'd come in this plastic cube mostly full of sand and water, with an ugly-ass plant in the middle of it and a little space for air up top. The cube was sealed, with just a hole a quarter-inch across to drop food pellets into. "Damn things creep me out. How come the box is filled with water?"

"Girl at the store said they breathe water, Pa," Meemaw said patiently. "She said they didn't need nothing but food once-twice a week, and that they lived mebbe a year or so."

Pa squinted suspiciously. "Don't need to change the water?"

Meemaw kept cross-stitching, rocking back and forth on her chair nice and slow. "Nope."

"No cleaning up no frog poo?"

"Nope."

"No chance we gonna wake up one day and find a million baby frogs in there?"

"Nope," Meemaw jabbed her finger with a needle, swore a bit, and stuck it in her mouth. "Grrhh strr ssdd bbb."

"What?"

Meemaw took her finger out of her mouth and looked at it for a second to make sure it wasn't bleeding none. "I said, girl at the store-"

"What store?"

"The new one in town, the one with all them books and games and learning stuff. Luther likes it."

Pa drew in a breath to let Meemaw know, in no uncertain terms, that he didn't give one red damn what kinda store Luther liked, and that no son of his should like stores fulla books better than football, and that anyone who stayed at home all reading books and stuff on the computer when he could be outside doing chores or running through the woods or learning how to shoot was highly suspect, but Meemaw cut him off.

"I said, girl at the store where I bought them said they were both boys, and there weren't gonna be no frog babies."

"You telling me you got the boy frogs that are homosexual?"

Meemaw shook her head. "No, Pa. I got him frogs so he'd have something to take care of, and maybe keep him company." She looked over at the door to the boy's room. On the other side of it, he was no doubt sitting on his bed, reading a book. "Boy needs something to keep him company." Then she turned back to her cross-stitch, and the set of her shoulders said that there'd be no more discussion. You didn't push Meemaw at a time like that, and Pa knew it.

He just grumbled under his breath that he'd rather of gotten the boy a damn dog instead.

Luther loved the frogs, and thanked both Meemaw and his Pa seven or eight times each; Meemaw for getting 'em for him, Pa for letting him keep 'em.

"S'okay," Pa had muttered. "You just take good care of 'em, you hear?"

"Yessir," Luther said, and took them straightaway up to his room. He came back down half an hour later to announce that he'd set them up on the corner of his rickety old desk near the window, so they could get some sun once in a while, then ran back upstairs. An hour after that, he came down to say that he'd moved 'em to the night stand, 'cause it wasn't near as rickety. A half hour after that, he came down to say he'd decided to name 'em Dale and Cale, after Pa's favorite drivers, and after that he didn't come downstairs no more to talk about them, 'cause Pa had made a good dent on the case of Genny Cream Ale he'd bought himself for Luther's birthday, and he'd threatened to take a strap to the boy's backside if he ran down the damn stairs one more time to talk about the damn frogs.

Luther got the hint. He went back up to his room, shut the door, and, by Meemaw's estimation, spent the next hour trying to figure out how to tell which of the two frogs was Dale, and which one was Cale.

"Your son," Meemaw said, and went back to cross-stitching.

Luther was good as his word when it came to feeding the frogs. He would have walked them, too, and housebroken them as needed, but since they were frogs living in a plastic box, he had to settle for dropping four tiny brown food pellets into their tank, twice a week.

"Looks like turds," Pa grumbled to himself when he saw Luther do it, and wouldn't feed 'em himself until he heard Meemaw clearing her throat in the doorway behind him. Then he picked one pellet up, looked at it for a slow moment, and dropped it through the little hole into the tank. It sank, slowly, while Luther beamed at him and said, "See, Pa, it ain't so bad".

Pa grunted something that was pretty much just a grunt and watched the pellet fall. The two frogs hovered in the water, motionless, watching it slip past. He studied them and decided they were ugly cusses, with warty little faces and fat, soft mouths. Then, all of a sudden, one - Cale or Dale, he couldn't tell which because they looked exactly the goddamn same - gave a little kick, and sprang forward, and gulped that little pellet down.

"See, Pa! Isn't it amazing? He just snapped that right up!" Luther was all smiles and excitement.

"Disgusting, I mean, yeah, amazing," Pa answered him. "You sure they can't get out?"

"They couldn't get the lid off if'n they wanted to, Pa," Luther answered, all serious-like. "Can't reach it from the water line."

"Good," Pa said, and stomped out past Meemaw on his way to the teevee room.

"I think he likes you," Luther told the frogs, and dropped more pellets in the hole.

Come July, Luther got bundled up to go off to some camp or other. Meemaw'd arranged it all. She'd talked to the boy's teachers and gotten him on the list for what she told Pa was a science camp for promising but economically disadvantaged youth. Pa had asked what that meant, and Meemaw told him that it meant for four weeks, Luther was gonna get to play with the sorts of things only rich kids usually got to.

"As long as he doesn't get any ideas," Pa muttered, and gave his blessing.

Luther was overjoyed. After thanking both Meemaw and Pa for agreeing to let him go, and promising to write every day, and swearing to be a good boy who'd make 'em proud, Luther asked his Pa to do something for him.

"Feed the frogs while I'm gone, Pa? Would ya? You ain't gonna half to do it but once or twice a week." And Pa couldn't find it in his heart to say no, so he agreed to feed the damn frogs while Luther was gone.

"Thanks, Pa!" Luther said, and flung his arms around his father. "You're the best."

"Uh-huh," said Luther, and patted his boy on the back. "I guess I am."

Days passed. Pa dropped Luther off at the bus depot, where a school bus full of kids just like the boy was waiting to take them all off to wherever the heck they were going. Luther sat in the back row so he could wave to Pa out the rear window, until the bus finally pulled too far away for them to see each other. Pa got back in his truck after that and headed back home.

He was alone in the house, Meemaw having taken her annual extended trip to go visit her sister in Branson. The quiet was nice, though Pa had to admit he kind of missed the boy running downstairs to tell him the latest fool thing he'd done at school. He sat down on the couch, turned on the teevee, and cracked open a beer.

Three weeks later and maybe three letters from Luther later, he remembered the frogs.

They were floating in their little cube when he found them. Cale was on his back, or maybe Dale was, but neither of 'em were moving. "Aww, crap," Pa said, and flicked his finger against the plastic of the cube to see if either of 'em was still breathing.

Neither of 'em moved.

"Now come on, you damn...damn frogs! Git up! Move around some! Tell me you ain't dead!"

The frogs didn't move. They just drifted, lazy-like, across the top of the water.

Pa cussed a little and grabbed some of the food. He crammed it into the hole so fast half of the little turd-pellets missed and bounced away. But a few made it into the water, and they either stuck on top and drifted with the frogs, or sank like indecisive rocks, slowly to the bottom.

Pa cussed some more, then picked up the little plastic box and shook it. some water sprayed out the top, and the sand and pebbles on the bottom of the case got all swirled around, but the frogs just bashed against the sides and then floated away again. Plus, Pa realized as he shook it, the water inside smelled bad.

Hell, it smelled terrible.

It smelled like dead things were floating in it. Which, he was pretty sure, there were.

Pa cussed one last time, then put the case down on the windowsill. He considered calling Meemaw to ask her advice, but that seemed like a bad idea. She'd give him no end of hell about forgetting his promise to the boy and forgetting to feed the damn frogs, and what he needed right now was solid advice, not some goddamn guilt trip.

His next thought was that he'd just go down to the store where Meemaw had bought them and get replacement frogs. As far as he was concerned, all them looked just the same. And even though Luther swore he could tell Dale from Cale, he was pretty sure the boy wouldn't be able to tell the difference.

The problem being, when he called the shop where Meemaw had gotten them, the young thing on the other end of the line said they didn't carry them anymore. She said they were a seasonal item, and this apparently wasn't the season, and besides there'd been some kind of health scare off in Oregon or Minnesota or some place like that about how some of the frogs had come to the US sick with some kind of disease, and--

Pa hung up halfway through the explanation.

Time, he thought, for plan B. Which was to leave the frogs right where they were. Then when Luther came back and found 'em like that, he'd act all surprised and say, "Well, they were fine the last time I fed them." Which, he thought, was sorta kinda technically the truth.

But either way, Luther would get over it, and then he'd get the kid a proper pet, like a dog, or a, well, a dog.

And satisfied with his decision, he walked out of Luther's room and shut the door behind him.

When Luther came home, he hopped out of Pa's truck before it was fairly stopped moving. He ran right past Meemaw doing her cross-stitch in a rocker in the front room and went straight up the stairs without hardly saying a word. The door opened, the door closed, and Pa braced himself for the explosion. In a way, he was almost looking forward to it. He'd been practicing his "surprised" look for a week, and wanted to get some use out of it afore he forgot how.

Any second now, he told himself. Any second.

A minute passed. Then another one did. And another, and another. It was a full quarter hour before Luther came rattling back down the stairs.

"Thank you, Pa!" Luther said, grabbing Pa in a hug. "Thank you for takin' such good care of Cale and Dale while I was gone!"

"I swear, they were fine when I--" Pa stopped and blinked. "I mean, of course, son. Gotta take responsibility for your responsibility."

"They look great, Pa. Thank you so much!" Luther gave him one last squeeze, then ran back upstairs. "I'll tell you all 'bout camp later," he yelled as he went. "We made a robot!"

Then his door slammed again, with Pa looking up the stairs after him, and Meemaw looking at Pa.

"I saw your face there, boy," she said. "Turn around and look at me."

Slowly, staring down at his shoes, Pa did. Meemaw nodded.

"Thought so. You didn't do no care-taking of them frogs. I'm guessing you thought they was dead, didn't you?"

Pa nodded, miserable-like. "They were dead. I saw 'em. Shook 'em up.

 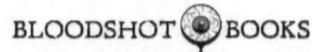

Tried everything to get 'em to move. They just kind of floated there, dead-like."

Meemaw's mouth narrowed in disapproval. "And you decided that you'd lie to your own son about that rather than take responsibility. I despair of the days I spent raising you, son, if you treat your own son that way."

"I tried to replace 'em," Pa said, by way of defending himself. "But the store said they didn't carry them no more, and that some of the frogs had been all sick, and--"

She cut him off. "Well, I'm thinking it's more likely that you just went up there when those little fellers were sleeping and thought they were dead. You never were too too bright." Pa opened his mouth to protest, but Meemaw shushed him. "Don't argue none, 'cause it's true. Now you just go on up there and tell your son how glad you are that his pet frogs are alive and well, and I will make sure that boy never leaves them in your care again."

Pa stared at her for a minute. Meemaw stared back, and as usual, Pa folded. "Yes'm," he said, and started up the stairs.

"And don't you have one of them fits of conscience and say nothing, you hear me!" Her words chased him the rest of the way, and he went into Luther's room.

The boy was sitting next to the window when Pa came in, hunched over and talking to the plastic tank. Inside, the frogs didn't seem like they were paying no attention, swimming in lazy little circles in the cloudy water.

"Son," Pa said.

"Oh, hi, Pa," said Luther, half turned around. "Didn't hear you come in. I was telling Cale and Dale all about camp."

"I thought it was Dale and Cale," Pa said.

"Nope. Cale and Dale. That one there's Cale. You can tell on account of the way he's kind of got that little pattern of spots on his head, right there. Can you see it?"

Pa leaned in and stared at the frog Luther indicated, trying to discern any possible pattern of dots that might be visible. He saw none.

The frog - Cale, if Luther was to be believed - stopped swimming. It just held there in the water, bulgy eyes staring out at Pa. It made Pa uneasy, especially 'cause that stare made him feel like that damn frog wasn't looking at him so much as it was looking into him, or maybe through him.

A frog ought not to do that to a man.

"Luther!" Meemaw's voice came up from the downstairs. "I need you in the kitchen, boy. Finish up what you're doin' and git on down. Those 'taters ain't gonna peel themselves!"

"Yes, Meemaw," Luther answered. "You can stay here if you want, Pa. The frogs like you."

"They what?" Pa asked, but Luther was already gone. Wind socks would have flapped in the breeze at his departure. Pa stared after him for a minute, then turned back to the tank. Both frogs were now floating upside down, eyes closed and mouths open.

"Holy crap!" said Pa and picked the tank up. "Don't be dead, you can't be dead!" He pulled the tank close to his face, staring in at the now-motionless creatures. "You were just fine a minute ago! Don't you dare, you hear me?"

There was a moment of stillness. Then, sudden-like, both frogs flipped over and started swimming. One bumped its snout up against the plastic on the side Pa was staring into and, with infinite deliberation, closed one froggy eye for a half second. It held Pa's gaze a minute longer, then swam away.

"Son of a bitch," Pa said. He put the tank down and backed away.

Over the course of the next week, the tank got noticeably cloudier, to the point where Meemaw suggested that it was high time that someone changed the water. Pa wanted no part of it, but lucky for him, Luther said he'd do it.

"My frogs, Pa," he said, and went off toward the kitchen.

"Why's he going to the kitchen?" Pa asked.

"He's settin' out some water. Got to let it stand to get enough air in it for the frogs to breathe proper," Meemaw replied. "Tomorrow, he'll do the switch. Just don't go drinking out of that pitcher."

"Huh," said Pa. "Imagine that."

Pa couldn't sleep that night. Every time he closed his eyes he'd see that one frog what ought to have been dead give him that slow wink, and that would make him sit straight up, all bug-eyed and afraid.

Finally, he couldn't take it no more, and swung his self out of bed. The snoring told him that Meemaw was still asleep, and Luther had gone to bed hours ago. He snuck downstairs and into the kitchen. The pitcher of water they boy had left out was right where he'd left it, on the counter. Presumably it was sucking down air, though Pa couldn't see it.

Instead, he picked up the pitcher and dumped the water down the drain. Then he set the pitcher back down on the counter and snuck right back on up the stairs to his bedroom. Those frogs weren't getting their water changed tomorrow, no sir. That meant the lid would stay on their little case for another day, and that meant there was no chance they'd get out and do whatever it is that inch-long zombie frogs do.

He had no idea, he reflected, what they might actually do - try and eat him, mebbe - but whatever it was, it was bound to be no good, and he'd stopped it from mebbe happening for one more night.

He closed his eyes and slept. And tiny dead frogs chased him through his dreams.

◉   ◉   ◉

In the morning, Luther didn't say nothing about the empty pitcher. He just filled it back up again. Meemaw gave Pa the stink-eye, and the frogs' water looked a mite worse than it had the day before, but that was the extent of things.

That night, Pa poured the water out again.

In the morning, Luther looked at him funny, but didn't say nothing this time, neither. And so they went back and forth, Luther filling it up and Pa emptying it, for the better part of a week and a half. Meanwhile the water in the little tank got a little fouler every day, 'til you could barely see the frogs swimming in it. Pa was just fine with that, but Luther wasn't, 'cause he thought his frogs might drown in the mess. So he got up the guts to ask Pa if he was maybe sleepwalking and pouring out the water in his sleep, and Pa allowed as how that might be the case (even with Meemaw staring daggers at him while he told the bald-faced lie).

"Then I'll take the pitcher and put it in my room, and lock the door," Luther said. "That way you won't knock it over in your sleep, Pa."

"That's smart thinking, son," Pa said weakly, while he tried to figure how he could get hisself into Luther's room and dump that water without waking the boy up in the middle of the night.

Thing was, he couldn't see how. And so the next morning during breakfast, Luther announced his intention to change the water that day. Pa choked on his coffee and shot damn near half a biscuit out his nose. Meemaw thumped him on the back until he stopped coughing, at which point he allowed that it might be best if Luther did that while Pa was off at work. To give the frogs time to get used to their new home, y'see, before Pa came home.

Luther, whom Pa was beginning to suspect didn't have the good sense God gave a discarded pack of cigarettes, thought this was a good idea. And so Pa went out to the garage and Luther went off to the bathroom, on account of him not wanting to spill nasty old frog water everywhere in the kitchen.

That night, when Pa came home, Luther was waiting for him on the porch. He looked upset.

"What's wrong, son?" Pa asked, as that was the fatherly thing to do.

"It's Cale and Dale, Pa," said Luther. "I was switching their water and I turned around and they disappeared!"

Pa took a step back. "Disappeared? You mean they went poof like on the teevee?"

"I mean they must've got away. I'd used Meemaw's spaghetti spoon and picked 'em up to put 'em in the fresh water while I dumped out the old stuff, and I got rid of the dirty water, and I turned around to pour the clean water in and they were gone! Must've hopped out or something!"

"Mebbe they went down the sink," Pa said, thinking it would a fine thing if they had gone down the sink, or maybe the crapper.

"They might still be in the u-bend, then. Can you look? Please, Pa, can you look?" Luther's eyes got big as saucers, 'til Pa had to look away. He mumbled someone about getting the damn tool kit, and cursed himself for six kinds of fool when Luther ran off to get it. He didn't want to open the sink up, 'cause only bad things would happen if he did. If he was lucky, the frogs would be gone, and then Luther would bawl his eyes out. If he wasn't, the frogs would be in there, those damn dead frogs with their staring eyes and nasty slimy skin and--

"Here you go, Pa!" Luther dropped the toolbox at his feet, making one hell of a racket. Pa picked it up and headed to the bathroom, muttering under his breath as Luther tagged along. He cut the water and unscrewed the u-bend from the sink, and then handed the part to Luther. "Take a look for your frogs, son. If they ain't in there, then I don't know where they are."

And that was the problem, Pa realized. If they weren't in the u-bend, well, mebbe they had gone all the way down the drain.

Then again, mebbe they hadn't. They could have fooled Luther - Lord knew *that* wasn't hard - and hidden somewhere in the bathroom. They could wait there until night, then come out and go looking for him. He'd be in bed asleep and he'd have bad dreams about slimy cold things on his face, and then he'd wake up and see them right there, sitting on him, staring at him, and then they'd--

"They're not in here, Pa. They're gone!" Luther sadly handed the u-bend back to Pa, who gave it a look just to double-check.

"I'm sorry, son," said Pa. "Better go tell Meemaw. She got you them frogs."

"Yessir," said Luther, and shuffled off down the hall. Pa watched him go, then turned back to repair the sink. He did it careful, and he did it slow. And he did it expecting any minute now he'd be feeling little froggy feet on the back of his neck.

Instead, he got Meemaw yelling his name. And that made him straighten up, which meant hitting his head on the underside of the sink, which meant cussing, which Meemaw didn't approve of, so she yelled his name again. This time, he managed to pull himself out, and turn 'round and look at her.

"You're gonna find them frogs," she told him. "No ifs, no ands, no buts."

"Meemaw, they're gone," he said. "I took apart the sink. They weren't nowhere in there. Gotta be halfway to the water treatment plant by now."

"If they are, you'd better start a-running. Cause that boy of yours loved them frogs, loved 'em real good."

Pa sighed. "Meemaw, I gotta tell you, there was something 'bout those frogs that just wasn't right."

"Do tell."

"You know I killed 'em, right? I didn't feed 'em and I killed 'em and they was dead. And then Luther comes home, and suddenly they ain't dead, and so help me God, I caught 'em looking at me. I'm telling you, it ain't right."

Meemaw cocked her head. "And whose fault is that?" Pa opened his mouth to answer, but before he could Meemaw pointed and said, "Is that one of them there?"

"Where?" Pa tried to back away and get up and hunker down all at the same time, which meant he banged his head on the sink again. While he was laying there cussing, Meemaw smiled at him. "Nope, guess I was just seeing things. Happy hunting, son."

For the first time in his life, Pa considered moving out of the house he'd been born in.

He spent the rest of the evening looking for the frogs, Pa did, with a little help from Luther. Luther looked upstairs in his room, while Pa looked pretty much everywhere else. He looked in the kitchen. He looked in the icebox. He looked under beds and in closets and down in the cellar and up in the attic, and he looked in places no self-respecting frog had any business going.

Of the frogs, there was no sign. Luther started out hopeful, but that only lasted a couple of hours. By the end of the night he was sad and dragging, and Pa ordered him off to bed. As for Pa, he kept looking a while longer, but not too much longer. Eventually he gave up and popped open a beer, which he drank a little faster than normal. Then Pa took himself off to bed, set the alarm, and closed his eyes.

In the dark, he thought he heard croaking.

That was stupid, he told himself. Dale and Cale didn't croak. Never had when they were alive, weren't going to start now that they were dead.

He closed his eyes again. Thought about sleeping. Thought about Cale and Dale waiting for him to fall asleep. Waiting for him to be on his back with his mouth open, snoring like he did (according to Meemaw, who made a fuss about such things). Waiting for him to be defenseless. Helpless. Waiting to do something terrible.

He sat up then, and didn't close his eyes again that night.

One night turned into two turned into three, and Pa started looking like a wreck. His eyes got bloodshot and his hands got shaky. He couldn't hardly eat, he couldn't hold down beer, and twice he nearly took his truck into the ditch out where the Masonville Road crossed Route 86. At home, he kept looking for the frogs, even after Luther gave up.

"They gotta be here somewhere," he said. "Gotta be." Luther told him it was OK, and that Cale and Dale were in a better place, but that didn't stop Pa. He was convinced now, convinced the frogs wanted blood for blood and were waiting in the house for the right moment to strike.

Even Meemaw couldn't convince him to stop looking. Pa didn't go so far as to say she was in cahoots with them when she tried, but didn't say she wasn't neither. Eventually, she gave up and went back to her knitting, saying Pa must've gotten concussion on the bottom of that sink, and that only time would fix him up.

Pa heard her grumbling, and he shook his head. He didn't have concussion. He knew the frogs were out there. And he knew they were waiting for him to let his guard down - if he didn't find them first. Even if between himself and Luther, every inch of that house had been searched and no one had said they'd seen the frogs, Pa knew the truth.

It was late at night on a Sunday, a full two weeks after the frogs had vanished. Luther was in bed, reading under the covers with the help of a flashlight. Downstairs, Pa had been crashing around in the kitchen all night, shouting 'bout how Dale and Cale were hiding somewhere in Meemaw's pots. The banging had been going on for a full hour, and Luther expected it to go on for a few hours more. That was life with Pa these days, but that was all right. A fella could get used to most anything, if he put his mind to it.

"Ain't that right, boys?" he said to the frogs perched on the edge of his bed. "Don't you worry none. I ain't gonna let Pa find you again so he can hurt you again. Y'all can just stay here, with me, forever." He held out his hand, and one by one, Dale and Cale hopped up into it.

They sat there for a second, and then slowly, all careful-like, one of them winked.

Writer, game designer and cad, Richard Dansky has contributed to over 40 videogames. The author of 6 novels, including the Wellman Award-nominated VAPORWARE, he has also worked on over 130 tabletop RPG titles and published numerous pieces of short fiction. He lives in North Carolina with his wife, their library, and an indeterminate number of bottles of single malt whisky.

Follow him at http://rdansky.tumblr.com

BLOODSHOT BOOKS

GOOD OL' BUDDY

BY ROB LAMMLE

BUDDY lies on the floor in front of me as I watch TV from my easy chair. He lifts his head, but I barely notice it; his hearing is so acute he probably heard something down the street. However, my assumption is corrected when I hear the muffled sounds of car doors slamming outside. I sit up straight and look out the window to the gravel driveway.

"Shit! It's Heather and John!"

I leap from the chair and grab Buddy by the collar, hoisting him to his feet. He doesn't want to go, but after a minor struggle, relents, and I lead him into the kitchen. I turn the knob on the door leading to the basement and Buddy does his best to keep from going in; he pushes back, but his feet slide on the linoleum floor. I succeed in getting him to head down the stairs, but after only a few steps he stops and turns back to look at me with his sad, puppy dog face.

"Buddyyy," I whine, "you know I don't like to do this. I'll come get you as soon as I can, ok? You know I'd never abandon you, Boy. I'd be all alone without you."

We lived out on a ten-acre farm, surrounded by cornfields and unused cow pastures. The closest kid my age was three miles away, Jimmy Deakins, and he was a spoiled jerk who always made fun of my stuttering problem. Except for my parents and the almost daily visits to Grandma's house just a mile down the road, I spent my youth alone, playing on log piles and lying in the pasture watching the clouds float by. I could have really used a dog to pal around with, but my father refused no matter how much I begged. He always said dogs (or any pet for that matter) were too noisy, ate too much and were too much responsibility for me to handle. There's not much a five-year old can do to argue against that.

Thanks to my virtually solitary upbringing, by the time I was old enough to go to school I was pretty much an introverted outcast. My stuttering got worse when I was nervous, so what would take me thirty seconds to say around my parents would take me five minutes around the other hyperactive strangers in my kindergarten class. They made fun of me as kids do when someone's different.

I barely spoke ten words until second grade when my teacher, Mrs. Sans, realized my problem and started me in speech therapy. Stopping the stuttering really didn't help my social status, though; the brand had been made and I was forever different than the other kids. I think that was why I was so happy to have found Buddy. He and I were both a little different and, even though he was an animal, he seemed to understand that I loved him no matter what - and he reciprocated.

◉   ◉   ◉

Luckily, I always keep my front door locked, a precaution I'd learned years ago shortly after I found Buddy, so Heather and John have to wait outside, knocking, until I can get back to the door. When I finally open it, I can see tears running down Heather's round face.

"Heather? What's wrong?" I beckon the two inside. John immediately runs to my plump easy chair – one of his favorite spots to be at my house. Heather puts her arms around my neck and cries into my shoulder; I respond by putting my arms tightly around her waist and give her a little squeeze.

"Honey, what is it?"

"Oh, it's terrible. Do you remember my friend Amy?"

"Sure."

"Well, last night she was coming home from a date and some drunk crossed the yellow line and hit them head-on."

"Christ. Is she ok?"

"They don't know, yet. She was thrown from the car. All I know is she's still alive, but the doctors aren't sure for how much longer."

"God, Heather, I'm sorry to hear this."

She looks up at me with her red-flushed face; her eyes and cheeks are puffy with sorrow. "Could you watch John for a little while? I need to go down and see her; be with her family."

"Of course. Take your time; I had nothing planned for the day anyway. He can even spend the night if he has to."

"Yay!" John yells, bouncing up and down in my chair, oblivious to the hurt his mother is feeling in an innocent, five-year old sort of way.

Heather looks back at him and smiles, "Well, I don't know if I'll need to stay that long, but we might take you up on the offer anyway." She turns back to me, "I'm not sure I want to be alone tonight."

I hug Heather again and smile. "I'll take care of you."

She buries her face in my shoulder, but doesn't cry. "I know you will."

"Ewwwwww... gross!" John inserts his commentary on the scene. Heather and I both laugh out loud.

"Ok," She pulls away from me, "I'd better get down to the hospital." Heather walks over to her son and puts her hands on his cheeks, surrounding his face. "Now you be good, ok?" She kisses his forehead.

"Yessss, Mom." He rolls his eyes.

She comes back to me. "Thanks again. I'll try not to be too late." When she kisses me, I can taste the saltiness of her tears.

"It's ok, really. We'll have a good time today. You go take care of your friend."

"Thanks. Love you." She opens the door to walk out.

"I love you, too." I respond. And really do mean it.

I watch as Heather climbs into her car, a beat-up old Chevy Cavalier, and close the door only after she's started backing out of the driveway. I then turn my attention to the little munchkin sitting in my chair.

"Hey! What're you doing in my seat?" I ask John, while sweeping him up in my arms and throwing him over my shoulder; his joyous giggles are like music to my ear. I plop down in my chair and set him on my lap. He snuggles in beside me as I cradle him in my arm. We watch baseball for a while, talking about the players and the bad calls, but eventually he succumbs to the lazy Saturday afternoon ritual of a good, hearty nap. I can hear his steady, breathy snore and it doesn't take long before I've joined him in Slumberland.

I'll never forget the day I found Buddy. I was out playing around the woodpile and heard a faint cry; it was sort of a wheezing whine if you will. I followed the noise to its source, a small cavern formed by logs overlapping one another. There in the dark was a mutt that had just given birth to six pups. They were quite newborn, still covered in wet, matted fur; their eyes still sealed shut with mucus. They could only lie there and struggle against the odd feeling of freedom. The mother lay on her side, exhausted from the effort, and was barely able to lift her head when my face appeared above her litter.

All the puppies were the same brown color with long, shaggy hair. Who knows what hodge-podge of breeds they were, but I suppose that doesn't really matter, as long as they're healthy. It especially didn't matter to me as a kid who would have loved to own a dog regardless of its pedigree. However, upon closer inspection, one little guy was different from his brothers and sisters.

Its body was shaped like a dog – hairy, four legs, and long snout – but the similarities stopped there. Its eyes were startling: four, black, featureless globes rested on top of the head. Two of the eyes were in the proper place for a dog, but the other two were further down on the snout. There were no eyelids to be sealed shut; the lenses, shiny and reflective like those of a spider. The little guy's teeth were already huge; his lips couldn't even cover them so they lay exposed, white, brilliant and sharp. His paws were easily the size of his head, a good two inches across – he was going to be a big boy all right. His tail was unlike any other dog's I'd seen, too; it was almost like a lizard's, scaly on top and ringed underneath, but pitch black and cool to the touch.

But the thing that most set Buddy apart from his siblings, were the black tentacles that grew from his sides. At first I thought they might be leeches or some other kind of parasite my fourth grade education hadn't spoken of yet. I considered picking him up and trying to get them off, but I wasn't sure what the mother would do if I reached into her cave in a movement that could be interpreted as a threat to her young ones.

For the next few days, I came to the log pile to check on the progress of the puppies. They were slowly beginning to crawl around, still blind, searching for their mother's milk. However, when the little monstrosity would approach his Mother's belly to feed, he was immediately snuffed off with her snout; she refused to let him near. I felt sorry for the little guy and wondered if he'd make it. In hindsight, perhaps Mother Nature knew better than to let him survive.

The first Saturday after the pups were born, I ran down to the wood pile as usual to check on them, but was sad to find they had disappeared from their hiding space; all except the little oddball who had been left behind to die. He was crawling on feeble legs, straining to find his mother, letting out a faint, barely audible, whimper; his tentacles hung limply from his side in defeat.

I was still convinced the extra appendages were leeches of some kind, so I picked him up and tried to pull them off. The little pup howled with pain as I tried to free him from himself. I realized what I was doing and rolled them over to get a closer look. They were like an octopus' arm, lined with large suckers that grasped at the open air trying to latch on to something. For some reason I touched the underside of a tentacle and soon found my index finger wrapped up. The tiny arm pulsed like it was alive.

I was bound and determined to keep the little guy whether my dad had anything to say about it or not. I took him out from his woodpile cavern and he squealed in pain as the sunrays struck him. I hid him under my shirt as I ran through the pasture to my "secret hideout" by the creek.

The sound of a kid's car stereo driving by wakes me from my baseball-induced nap. I can see that John is not by me anymore and immediately go to look for him. I have a feeling I know where he is – in his closet.

Buddy and I live in a small, two-bedroom house. Obviously, I only need one bedroom for myself, but I have the other setup as a den where I keep my computer, books, CD's, that sort of thing. Back when Heather and I first started dating, John didn't really have much to do at my house. So in an effort to make his visits more enjoyable, I told him he could bring over some toys and store them in the empty walk-in closet in the den. Soon he was bringing something – a toy, a book, magazines, baseball cards, comic books - with him every time they came over. I even brought him a Super Nintendo and a twelve-inch color TV, both rescued from my parents' attic when I visited at Christmas, and set them up in his little cave. I made an agreement with John – whatever was in there was his business; I never went in the closet without his permission. I think it made him feel good to have someplace all his own, plus it built a real foundation of trust between us.

Of course my "secret hideout" was no secret to my parents, but similarly, it was the one place on the farm they let me have to myself. I'd scraped together old pieces of plywood and junk from around the farm, borrowed my dad's tools, and built this little shack down by the creek. I'm not sure it would have passed the building inspector's code, but it was a good enough place for me to go read comic books, listen to cassettes on my old player, and keep stuff I found around the farm.

Over the years, I'd amassed quite a nice collection of beer cans and bottles from the drunken, creek-side parties the high school boys would have; a few old car parts that, frankly, I have no idea how they got there; Indian arrow heads, and my prize possession – a February 1975 issue of Playboy, published the same month I was born. It was worn, ragged, faded, and water-damaged, but none of that mattered because - it had naked women inside. I sat for hours looking at the pictures of Mary Walters: 34/24/36. She was a buxom redhead whose turn-ons were: men who were confident, well spoken, polite, smart and funny - pretty much everything I wasn't except for maybe the polite one. She was beautiful, and to this day, I still prefer redheads.

I rushed into the shade of the plywood roof and took the little puppy from under my shirt. He didn't cry out now that he was out of the sun, in fact, he was back to his docile self. I overturned a cardboard box full of baseball cards and lined it with an old blanket my mother let me have. I laid little Buddy down inside, but when I tried to pull away, his tentacle was still wrapped around my finger, pulsing like it was before. I gripped the tip of the arm and squeezed, pulling at the same time and felt resistance; it didn't hurt, I just couldn't get the suckers to let go. I tried again, this time squeezing at the base of the tentacle by his ribcage, and the little arm calmly unraveled itself. Much to my surprise, I was bleeding from small puncture holes where the arm had been coiled. I felt no pain; in fact, my whole finger was numb from some kind of anesthetic. I panicked a bit, bundling the old blanket around my digit, but the next time I looked, the holes were healed and the bleeding had stopped. I realized then that Buddy had fallen asleep, probably quite exhausted from his liberation from certain death, and now, apparently, a good feeding from my unwilling finger. I covered him with the fold of the blanket and read Ms. Mary Walters' likes and dislikes for the hundredth time while he slept.

Just as I suspected, John's closet door is slightly ajar. I knock before opening, but I still startle him. He quickly throws something behind his back and holds it there nervously, looking up at me like he's been caught red-handed.

"Hey!" I smile and step inside. "Wanna play some Nintendo?"

"Yeah. Um...could you come back in a second?" His face turns an unusual shade of pink.

"Sure. Just say when." I step back outside and close the door behind me. I have to smile as I remember almost getting caught by my Dad during one of my Mary Walters sessions. I'm sure John, at only five, doesn't have access to a Playboy just yet, but it's probably something just as scandalous in his mind; a comic book that he's not supposed to be reading, maybe. Regardless, I give him time to put whatever it is away. All boys have secrets.

Buddy stayed in my clubhouse and I came to visit him every day after school. He was always hungry and, while he was still small, I let him use his tentacles to suck from my leg or my arm. However, one day I almost passed out during his feeding and I realized that I was going to need to wean my little Buddy onto some other form of food. He was getting large enough that he could get out of his box without me around, so I had to rig up a lock on the outside of my hideout door. This gave Buddy free reign to run around the room and capture mice, squirrels, and just about anything else that made the mistake of trespassing through a gap in my amateur construction handiwork.

I can remember sitting in the shack one Saturday afternoon reading comics and watching little Buddy, maybe four months old, track a good-sized raccoon that had gotten inside. The coon was easily twenty-five pounds – a huge thing. When Buddy hunted, he didn't sniff around like a normal dog; he simply let his tentacles move across the ground like an insect with antenna. I'm not sure to this day if he felt vibrations or if he actually "smelled" with his strange appendages; either way he tracked down the intruder with minimal problems and had soon sucked the old bandit dry.

It was the first time I'd seen Buddy eat his prey once he'd drained them.

Using his massive jaws and razor-sharp teeth to cut and break the bones and flesh, he made quick work of the coon. I was a bit disgusted by the sight, but at the same time fascinated to see him bite clean through the hard skull of an animal and into the meaty brain. He had quite a voracious appetite.

"Do you have anything to eat?" John asks me after kicking my butt in Street Fighter on the Super Nintendo.

"Yeah. What do you want?" I ask standing up from one of the beanbags I bought for him.

"Got any cookies?"

"Sure. Oreos ok?"

"Yeah. And milk."

"Coming right up. You wanna play Mario Kart next?"

"Yeah!" John pops the Street Fighter cartridge out of the machine and begins rummaging through the stack of old games made long before he was born.

As I'm walking down the hall towards the kitchen, I hear the phone ringing. Nearest is in my bedroom, so I step inside to answer it. It's my Mom, so I sit on the edge of my bed and chat with her.

After the typical "how you doing?" chit-chat, Mom asks, "Do you know what today is?"

"Um...no." I respond.

"It's the anniversary of poor Andy Bellis' disappearance."

About a year after I'd found Buddy, I was well into fifth grade and things had begun to improve on the social front. I finally had a friend - a pudgy, coke-bottle glasses-wearing kid named Andy Bellis. Andy was sort of an outcast at school, too, because of his bulk and the fact that his family didn't have a lot of money. The main thing that drew us to each other was our love of comic books.

He was a hardcore fanboy – plastic bags and cardboard backings, he knew the difference between mint and fine condition, and could recite almost issue by issue the entire history of Spider-Man. I was a bit more of a casual reader, but was still more versed in the exploits of Batman, Superman, and the Fantastic Four than most kids in our class.

Andy used to invite me over to spend the night on Fridays and we'd stay up late discussing comics, Transformers, He-Man, Star Wars and even the occasional question-and-answer session on girls. We could name every one of the characters in Jabba the Hutt's palace from Klaatu to Salacious

Crumb, but didn't have the first clue as to who or what an "orgasm" was; pretty typical boys, I guess.

The first time I had Andy out to the farm for a stay-over, I was a bit nervous about Buddy. I didn't know if I should introduce him to Andy, or if I should go with my instinct and leave my little dog my little secret. I purposefully avoided the shack until Andy asked to see the infamous February 1975 Playboy I had bragged to him about on many occasions. I tried to change the subject, but he was adamant about getting a glimpse of Mary Walters: 34/24/36.

It was dusk when we arrived at the shack and Mom would be calling us in for dinner soon. As we got closer, I told Andy to wait on the other side of the creek while I ran across the fallen log that served as my bridge and got the magazine for him.

I undid the combination lock and crept through the cracked open door doing my best to keep Buddy inside. We'd begun to play in the pasture at night (he was still sensitive to sunlight) and I was afraid he might think it was time to go and come bursting out into the open. However, all was quiet inside my little shack as Buddy was nowhere to be found. I frantically looked for my dog and soon saw a huge chunk of the back wall had been pried loose and flung across the room, knocking over the beer can collection. Buddy was outside. I crawled through the hole, hoping maybe he was standing right outside, but much to my disappointment he was gone. Buddy liked to play at the log pile where I'd found him, so that was my first destination.

Mom and I talk about Andy, and Dad, and Grandma, and the Women's Auxiliary Club Pancake Breakfast coming up next weekend, and after a good ten minutes, I finally hang up the phone. I continue my trek down the hallway, through the living room and into the kitchen. However, when I get back to John's closet, the door is wide open, the menu screen of Mario Kart is on the TV, but John is nowhere to be found. I set the milk and cookies on my nearby desk and retrace my steps down the hallway.

The bathroom door is closed, so I knock gently, "You in there, John?"

There is no reply. I open the door and the room is empty.

Confused, I go out to the living room, but he's not there. I look outside the window, but he's not running around in the front yard. In the kitchen I look outside and he's not in the backyard either.

When I got to the woodpile, the sun had gone down for the day. The

crickets had already begun to chirp and the junebugs were starting to emerge. I hoped Buddy had cornered a rabbit and would be making his strange wheezing bark while thrusting his tentacles into the pile to grasp at his prey as I had seen him do before. However, Buddy was nowhere to be found. I called for him numerous times, but he never came. My mind was racing as I tried to figure where he might be next.

I ran to our house, my heart about to burst from the effort and the tension, and searched the backyard. Buddy was always curious about the house, but I did my best to corral him into the pasture and the perimeter of my hideout. I stopped by the garage, grabbed a flashlight from the storage closet, and ran to the orchard. The beam crisscrossed the apple trees; I scared an owl, but did not find my dog.

I searched the tool shed. I searched the barn. I searched up and down the lane and into the old cow pasture. As I stood at the end of our driveway leading out onto County Road #258, for some reason – I still don't know exactly why – I suddenly knew where Buddy was. Something in my gut told me he was back at my hideout. As this thought flashed through my mind, another flashed through at the same time – Andy.

When I turn away from the kitchen window without finding John in the backyard, I notice the basement door is slightly ajar.

I arrived at my clubhouse, expecting to find pudgy Andy standing by, possibly with the front of his pants a little soaked from being left alone in the scary, dark woods. Instead, I found his thick pair of glasses and nothing else. I picked them up, folded them shut and held them in my hand, to give back to a frightened little boy when I saw him again. My flashlight beam swept back and forth around the area and there was still no sign of him. "Andy?" I called out in panic, but got no reply. I figured the obvious place for him to go would be my hideout.

I gently pushed the door and stepped inside. There in the beam of my flashlight, was Buddy hunched over Andy, simultaneously using his tentacles to drain the boy of his blood and his teeth to tear into Andy's chest to get at the soft, fleshy intestines. He didn't even flinch when the light hit him, he simply continued his feeding frenzy. For the next ten minutes I watched as my Buddy devoured every last bit of the geeky fifth grader. When he finished, he turned, ran to me and put his paws up on my leg as if he was ready to play now. Tears streamed down my face.

I slowly open the door leading down to the basement. I stand at the top of the wooden stairs, peering into the darkness below.

"John?"

I get no reply.

I flick the bare light switch and many small splotches of light come from the corners of the dank, unfinished, basement. I take five steps down.

"John? Are you down here?"

I still get no reply.

Buddy biting through the skull of the raccoon flashes through my mind's eye.

I rush down the stairs.

There, in a corner of the room, is Buddy, leaning over the body of John; his pulsing tentacles are already wrapped around John's little frame. I can see I'm too late; John is now only a husk of humanity. There's nothing I can do to save him. As I ascend the stairs in a haze, shutting off the light as I exit, I can hear the snap of bone as Buddy begins the second course of his meal. I bow my head and close the door behind me.

I ran.

I ran as hard and as fast as I could, encouraging Buddy to follow me as we made the one-mile trek to Grandma's house. It was well past dinnertime and I was sure Dad would be at my hideout any minute now looking for us.

Grandma's house was easily sixty years old at the time. It was the house that she and my Grandpa raised eight kids in – including my Dad – and she'd be damned if she was going to leave it while she was alive. She shouldn't have been living there, quite frankly. She was eighty-three, could barely see, could barely hear, and needed a wheelchair to get around. She spent a better part of Dad's inheritance installing the chair lift so she could reach the second floor.

In the backyard of this farmhouse was a set of large, double doors leading underground into the fruit cellar. I couldn't tell you how many times I'd used the empty bunker as my commando team's secret base that had to be defended against Nazi SS who were attacking from the apple orchard. But tonight, and for who knows how much longer, this was going to be my Buddy's new home.

I nimbly worked the combination lock – had the numbers memorized since I was in first grade - and swung open one of the doors. Buddy looked at me with his black, spidery eyes, unsure of what I wanted him to do. I tried

NOT YOUR AVERAGE MONSTER

to tell him to go down into the darkness, but he only stared at me confused. Finally, I grabbed his collar and began to lead him down. He resisted, his claws dug into the ground, but I got him inside just the same. I hurriedly closed the door behind him and re-secured the lock. I told him I'd be back tomorrow and not to worry. He responded with one of his breathy whines through the crack in the doors.

By the time I'd returned to our house, dripping with sweat and my heart racing a million miles an hour, Mom was already on the phone with the police. She ran to me, crying; she put her arms around me and hugged. I pushed her away in a panic and asked if she'd seen Andy. Shortly after, my Dad came in with a flashlight and shotgun in his hands; he'd been out looking for us.

I explained how Andy had wanted to see a comic that was stored down in my hideout. He waited outside as I ran in to get it. Well, it took me a little longer than I'd anticipated to find the comic and when I finally emerged from my shack Andy was gone. I found these – I displayed his glasses still in my hand – and that was all. I yelled for him, but he did not respond. I ran down to the creek's bank and he wasn't there. I ran over to the woodpile and he wasn't there, either. I finally ended up at the house, worried I'd get in trouble if I came in without him, so I got Dad's flashlight and continued my search alone. However, after a while I decided I'd better get some grownups involved in the hunt, even if I got grounded for a year.

Andy's parents were devastated; the whole town was devastated really. After the search for Andy's body came up blank, the manhunt for the kidnapper began. Police scoured our farm, (I hid my Playboy in the woodpile before they arrived) and then went on to neighboring farms with a fine-toothed comb. They stopped by Grandma's and noticed the fruit cellar in the backyard, which was a bit scary. But she insisted it was locked at all times and there was no way a boy could have gotten in unless he knew the combination. Heck, it'd been so long since she'd gone in there, she couldn't even remember the combination. When the cops asked if they could break the lock to be sure, the stubborn old mule refused and asked them to be on their way unless they had a warrant. Luckily, they never bothered to get one.

For about a week after consuming Andy, Buddy didn't need to hunt for anything when I let him out at night; he simply wasn't hungry. Actually, those were some of the best nights we ever had together. Instead of waiting for him to get food for twenty or thirty minutes, Buddy and I would play fetch with sticks in the oat field behind Grandma's house. We played tug-o-war with his old blanket, though Buddy had learned he could sweep my feet out from under me with his tentacles so it was never a very long war. And he'd follow me down to the creek to chase frogs and fish. I wanted Buddy

202   BLOODSHOT BOOKS

and me to have this kind of free time more often. Besides, how could I keep the cops going on the kidnapper story if there were no other kidnappings? Eventually they'd realize this was an isolated incident and come back around asking more questions about Andy's disappearance. I soon realized what I had to do.

❂   ❂   ❂

What am I going to do? Heather will be home soon. How can I explain this to her? Should I run? Just pack up the truck and leave? No, I love Heather too much to make her worry about her son like that; I couldn't do that to her.

❂   ❂   ❂

Really, Andy's disappearance was the best thing that could have ever happened to either one of us boys as far as popularity with our schoolmates went. Suddenly, everyone was talking to me, asking me questions, wanting to know what happened; I became, well, not popular, but un-invisible.

Andy, on the other hand, was one of those kids you wouldn't recognize at the ten-year reunion. You could run into a classmate twenty years later, swapping old stories, and he'd tell of the prank he pulled on little Andy Bellis and you would have no recollection of whom he was talking about. Andy was not memorable, nor would he have ever been if he hadn't disappeared so mysteriously in fifth grade. Now, forever, the class of 1993 would remember the name of Andy Bellis.

This newfound social status of mine offered me some good opportunities to get Buddy's food supply. Kids in my class, but especially the kids a few grade levels down, had a morbid curiosity and wanted to see where Andy had disappeared. I'd lead them down to the creek on our bikes and we'd walk by the creek bank. My story of Andy's final hours was always different; I just made it up as I went along. Finally, we'd reach Andy's last known location – my Grandma's backyard. I'd point to the fruit cellar where Andy and I were playing; the tourist and I would creep up into the grass and open the lock. A quick shove down the stairs, a slam of the doors and Buddy and I had an extra thirty minutes to play each night for the next week.

❂   ❂   ❂

I can hear Heather's car door slam. I'm sitting in my easy chair again, trying to figure out what I was going to do when this moment inevitably arrived. I meet her at the door, opening it to a still-puffy, red-faced woman who looks like she's had a rough day. She holds a wrinkled tissue in her hand.

"Hey. How is she?" I ask as Heather comes inside.

"It's not good." Heather and I make our way over to the couch where I put my arm around her and she leans into me for support. "It took over a hundred stitches on her face. They're pretty sure she'll never wake up from the coma. Her parents are trying to decide right now if they should pull the plug."

"Awww, Honey." I pull her tight, "That's awful. Really awful. How are you holding up?"

"Oh..." She wipes her red nose with her tissue, "I just want to lie down and rest."

"Ok." I reply while already clearing the couch of pillows. "C'mon, let's lie down."

Unlike most serial killers – I guess you could call me that, although I didn't actually do the killing – my problem wasn't getting rid of the bodies, mine was getting rid of the bicycles. I'd walk his latest victim's bike down to my hideout and use the tool set Dad had given me to dismantle it into their smallest possible pieces. Everything could be deposited in a coffee can and buried or scattered around town without drawing attention. Everything, that is, except for the bike frames. These required late-night trips down to the town's junkyard for Buddy and me. Although it, ironically, took away from our playing time, at least we were together.

I wasn't kidnapping one child per week – I was smarter than that – but the sheer number of disappearing kids was causing quite a stir in our little town. The police were on a rampage looking for the bastard who was taking them. Parents were telling us kids not to get any rides from people we didn't know, not to accept any candy. McGruff the Crime Dog even made a special appearance in our town to educate us about "stranger danger".

When the police weren't coming up with any leads, every unmarried man over the age of twenty-five was brought in for questioning; the small-town mentality of "There must be something wrong with him if he's not married by now" was their justification. It was a witch-hunt not seen in our town since the McCarthy era.

My kidnappings continued for the next four years, but by then the heat had grown too strong. Eighteen children had disappeared in that time and families had either moved away or had their kids on such short leashes that my opportunities had waned to nothing. Buddy ate rodents until I was sixteen.

It was that year Dad bought me a beater of a pickup truck off Old Man Williams down the road. It was dark green and rusted – mainly rusted –

 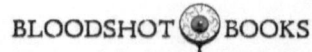

had no muffler, and ran on diesel. I loved it. Now, Buddy and I would ride around at night, his head stuck out the window just like any other dog would, but also his tentacles flapping in the wind, unlike any other dog could.

The truck didn't help my standing on the social ladder. The spoiled jocks that drove their flashy S-10's and used hot rods laughed at my rusty girl, but I didn't mind; I'd grown used to being "uncool". I did try to fix her up a little – put on a new muffler and tried to do some bodywork to repair some of the holes – but it didn't really help her much. My truck was what she was and that was fine by me.

The truck allowed Buddy a much wider hunting ground when we could drive out to secluded woods ten, fifteen miles away. Buddy ate like a king on rabbits and even the occasional deer, helping him grow even larger. I'm not sure why, but Buddy matured much slower than most dogs. Whereas normal dogs have reached their potential in two or three years, Buddy had been with me for six now and he still wasn't full-size. This made me wonder how long he'd live and if the standard "dog years" even applied to him.

Of course, having the truck also upped our hunting radius for Buddy's favorite delicacy. I'd travel to surrounding towns; most were small farming communities like my hometown, but far enough away the parents hadn't worked up into a frenzy about a kidnapper on the loose. It was much easier pickings and, since I was mobile now, I rarely ever took from the same town twice in a year; this kept the pressure off a bit. It wasn't always easy to get little kids into my scary, old truck, but you'd be amazed at what the lure of junk food and a chance to play the latest Super Nintendo game would do to their better judgments.

"Hey, where's John?" Heather asks as I lay behind her on the couch, my free arm draping around her belly.

"He's in his hideout playing Nintendo."

"Was he good?"

"Yeah, he was fine. We played Street Fighter for a while."

"So he kicked your butt, huh?" Heather gives out a little laugh.

"I let him win!" I laugh along with her and squeeze around her mid-section tighter.

Finally, at the age of twenty, I moved out of my parents' house and got my own place in the city. My Mom cried when she helped me pack up my truck. Dad shook my hand and told me he was proud; I could see he was

fighting back tears as well. I told them I was going to stop and say good-bye to Grandma before I left, who was now into her nineties, and drove off down the lane with almost all my worldly belongings in the truck.

Grandma barely knew who I was. The poor lady had gone almost completely senile, but I said good-bye and hugged her before I left out the back. It was late in the afternoon when I went to get Buddy, but because of his aversion to sunlight, had brought a blanket to cover him up as we made the one-hour drive to my new place. By then the sun would be on its way down and it would be easier to bring him inside the small, two-bedroom house I was renting.

It was great living freely with Buddy. At night after work, he and I would sit in the living room and watch television. He had gotten so large that he would lie in front of my chair and I'd prop my feet up on his massive back like a footstool. He had to have been two hundred pounds, if not more.

Sadly, this meant that eating one person wouldn't hold him for a week anymore and stray dogs and cats had become little more than appetizers.

Luckily, we lived in a rough neighborhood and there were plenty of bums, winos, drug addicts, and miscreants around, that Buddy could eat quite well two or three times a week. Like a good owner, I always had Buddy on a leash as he wrapped his tentacles around a drunk passed out next to the Dumpster behind some greasy spoon. I had become quite bored to the sight of intestines as Buddy would finish his meal; sometimes helping him locate parts that had been scattered during his manic feedings.

Buddy's main courses were the throwaways of society; no one really missed them when they were gone. The police might half-heartedly investigate the disappearance of a vagrant who hadn't shown up at his regular barstool for a week, but they never dug too deep. No one cared and that made Buddy's life, and mine, much easier. We were truly happy for the first time.

After two years of solitary "bum hunting", as Buddy and I called it, my years as an inexperienced bachelor had come to a close. I met Heather Gardner, a co-worker at the factory, and we seemed to hit it off. She wasn't Cindy Crawford or anything, but she was attractive. We had a similar background – grew up in a small town, and were ostracized from our peers at an early age thanks to some superficial difference (she'd had a lazy eye that had since been corrected). We were both awkward and strange around each other, but for some reason we were fine with that. I guess as long as we were both uncomfortable it made us both comfortable.

"Ya know... I've never felt this way about anyone before, Heather."

 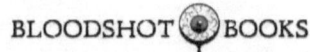

"I know. Me neither. Not even John's father."

"It's like we were together in a past life. The way we seem to know each other so well."

Heather smiles. "I think we're meant to be together, don't you?"

"Yeah. I do."

Heather pauses before asking, "Should we make it official?"

"Get married?"

"Yeah."

"I thought I was supposed to propose."

"Welllll…" Her voice rises as though I should take the hint.

We had developed our relationship slowly, starting out as acquaintances at the break room table, working our way to lunch hours at the coffee shop, and then the occasional dinner and a movie. After four months, I got to meet little John, her then four-year old son.

John had never had a male figure around, but rather than be scared of me, he was fascinated; he watched me do everything. I taught him the rules of the sports we'd watch together in Heather's living room, him sitting on my lap. I steered him towards baseball, the sport I always most enjoyed as a youngster. I was forever destined to play right field with all the rest of the little league losers, but he took to second base like a fish to water.

For his fifth birthday, I bought him his own glove and we played catch in the front yard while Heather sat in the shade of an elm tree with a smile on her face. I could see the glimmer in her eye as she watched her son have a father for the first time. That night was my first time to ever make love to a woman.

Heather and John would make the trip over to my place sometimes and I'd have to lock Buddy downstairs; I had purposefully found a house to rent with a basement for when guests stopped by. He wasn't thrilled to be down there and always stood at the foot of the stairs watching me, whimpering with his strange, wheezy little whine, as I ascended to the house above. I felt bad about having to do it, but I couldn't let anyone see him. They wouldn't understand. I couldn't live without Buddy.

"I have a confession to make." I said.

"What?" Heather asks with whimsy.

"John's not in his hideout playing Nintendo."

"He's not? Where is he?"

"He's in the basement playing with the puppy I bought for him."

Heather sits up with a start. I thought I had done something wrong.

"You bought him a dog?"

"Yeah, but it can stay here with me."

She collapses on top of me, kissing my face and hugging me. "Oh, you're the greatest. John's wanted a dog, but we can't have one at the apartment." We kiss passionately before Heather pulls away. "I want to marry you. I don't care if you're supposed to ask me or I'm supposed to ask you. You're the best thing that's ever happened to me and John and I want to be with you. I want us to be a family."

I look deeply into her eyes, "I do, too." She kisses me again before falling limply with her head on my chest, my arm cradling her. We lay in blissful silence for a few minutes.

She's playing with a button on my shirt when she asks, "What kind is it? The dog, I mean."

"Mutt. You wanna see him?"

She lifts her head, "Yeah."

Heather grows concerned when John doesn't answer her calls as she descends the dark stairs.

"Why are the lights off down here?" She looks back at me to ask.

I don't answer her.

When she's halfway down, I push her the rest of the way, run back into the kitchen and slam the door behind me, making sure it's locked.

It never occurs to me that Buddy wouldn't be hungry after eating John. It's been the most agonizing two days of my life to hear Heather begging me to let her out. She says she broke her ankle when I pushed her and she's dragged herself up the stairs to the door, but it's locked. It's dark, and she has a feeling that something is down there with her; she keeps hearing strange breathing from the dark recesses.

She begs me to let her out. She begs me to tell her where John is. But I can't leave in case Heather should figure some way out of the hole. Perhaps it's a form of justice that I'm forced to stay and listen to her.

I can't be angry with Buddy. It's my fault John found his way into the basement. I should have put a lock on the door. It was my fault I'd left Buddy alone. It was my fault for feeding Buddy the way I did for all those years. Buddy was simply acting the way he had been trained. To him, children were nothing more than food.

Finally, on the second morning after I'd thrown Heather, quite literally, to the wolf, the basement is silent. I stay home from work just in case, but later in the day I can hear Buddy scratching on the door with his six-inch claws, making his whining wheeze sound. He's ready to leave and I cautiously open the door. Buddy comes bounding out, jumping up and down, happier than I'd seen him in years. I walk downstairs to the basement below and find no sign of Heather; Buddy had grown hungry in the night.

I pack up some things – my clothes, my knick-knack memories, and my old Super Nintendo – and pile them into the truck. Buddy and I drive west, not exactly sure where we're going. I just have to put as much distance between myself and that house as I can.

I'll miss Heather and John and the life I could have had. But, I just can't live without my Buddy.

Rob Lammle is a full-time cartographer and part-time writer out of St. Louis. When he's not working, he's watching movies and TV shows, reading books, podcasting about pop culture, and spending time with his family. You can follow his online adventures over at www.spacemonkeyx.com.

This is his first published story, but hopefully not his last...

INSECT

BY MARC LYTH

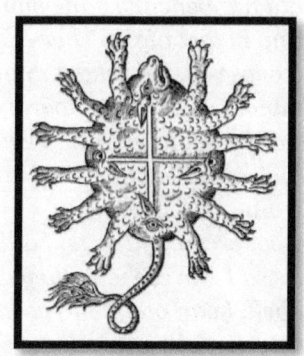

I can't wake up. Light burns my eyes. It feels like I'm dragging myself out of a deep pit. I'm so fucking tired. I need to sleep again. I close my eyes and roll over.

My hand lands in something... squidgy. It's vile. What the hell is it? I tell myself to wake up now, you fool. Don't be such a lazy bastard. The sergeant will put you on latrine duty if you don't make a fucking effort now.

I open my eyes and slowly they adjust to the light. The mess I've stuck my hand in is what's left of a body. Who the... Oh my God it's Tom. What the fuck?

Tom's chest is a gaping mass of holes, his arms are covered in what appear to be defensive wounds and his head has been almost severed by the knife which is still stuck in the middle of what's left of his torso. His blood is all over me.

I can't clear my fucking head. I need to get this stupid brain of mine in gear. Quick. I look around. Private Tom Gillott's isn't the only body here. Why can't I remember what happened? I can count eight bodies in the clearing we stopped to camp in last night. There's someone missing, but I don't want to check these corpses to see who it might be. He might be dead somewhere else for all I know. I can't remember a fucking thing.

I take a deep breath and try not to vomit. I need to do this. The bodies are fresh but there's still a stench of spilled guts and internal organs. The flies are already having a field day.

Three of the bodies are covered by jackets. Laid out all nice and respectful. I move the coats so I can see who they are. It's Sergeant Kelly and privates Tyson and Campbell. I can only tell Tyson's body from his tags and the tattoo on his upper arm. His face is missing, replaced by a mess of burnt tissue.

Now I know who all these bodies are I know that the missing person is Moseley. I should have known. None of the corpses are ginger, although it's difficult to tell with a couple of them because of massive head wounds.

Could Moseley have done all of this? He's a big lad, and he's good in a fight - we all are, it's in the job description - but still, he's one of the nicest lads in the squad. He wouldn't turn on us all like this.

Fuck! Why can't I remember what happened? Last thing I remember we... we were heading back to base camp after that waste of time recon exercise and...

I look round for any usable gear. First thing I find is a molten lump in the remains of the fire that appears to be the radio.

None of us were carrying mobile phones. They made sure of that before we left base camp. This means I can't call for help. I'll have to walk back to base camp. My skin crawls at the thought of the trek in this heat.

Which way were we headed? I think east. There's a stream in the valley over there, if I'm right. My memory seems to have swiss-cheesed itself. Holes everywhere.

I need to do something. I'll head for the stream; follow that to the river, then to the road and from there to base.

I debate on whether to take another gun with me. There's no ammunition so they're only good as blunt instruments. I decide to leave them all behind. I take the knife from Tom's chest just in case I run into whoever or whatever did this.

The small amount of food still in the ration bag is inedible, coated in blood. The map is also buried under a bleeding corpse and unusable.

It looks like there's very little left here that's worth taking. Not that I can trust my memory right now but we were on our way back and we... I should only be a day's trek from base camp.

I hear a noise from the bushes and duck down. I can see a shape moving through the shrubbery, black military army boots visible from my prone position at ground level. I look up and I can see a mop of ginger hair just above the top of the greenery. Moseley nearly failed his basic training on his stealth manoeuvres and it looks like he's back to his old habits. Lucky it's only me here.

"Martin!" I say. "I'm over here."

I'm still not certain if he's responsible for this or not but there's only one easy way to find out. His reaction isn't what I expected.

"Get away from me!" he yells and starts running in the opposite direction.

Now I'm even more confused. I run after him and catch him easily.

"Martin, it's only me," I say as I grab his shoulder. He stops running and turns. His knife is in his hand and aimed straight at my stomach.

Instinct takes over and I step back as I block downwards, grabbing the wrist and twisting it. The wristlock takes hold and his arm stiffens. When I swivel round on my right foot he's flipped perfectly onto the ground. I grab his elbow and bend the arm as I kneel down next to him. I still have one hand gripped round his fist so he's unable to drop the knife. With his elbow bent at ninety degrees, the blade is millimetres away from his throat.

"What the fuck happened Martin? Tell me now."

"Don't kill me!" he begs me.

"I'm not going to kill you." I say, even more confused now. Is he saying this because I've killed someone? I know I look like I have. Or does he think I'm looking for revenge for the others?

With his free hand he picks up a rock and tries to smash it in my face. It's *a bad mistake on his part as it makes me duck, rather than move backwards like he must have hoped I'd do. The knife blade moves downward as I do, piercing his throat and severing the windpipe. He makes a horrible gurgling sound.*

"Fuck! Martin, I'm sorry. I wasn't tryi..."

He stares at me and tries to say something as his blood sprays over me, joining the rest of the bloodstains on my uniform. He clamps a hand over the gaping hole in his neck. This creates enough of a seal on the wound for him to manage to croak out his last words.

"You killed them..."

His hand drops limply to the side and his eyes glaze over. He's dead. I'm now the lone survivor, and apparently the killer of my entire squad.

It all began with an insect the colour of dried blood.

The squad had been marching for six hours, back towards base camp after a recon exercise out in the countryside. Apart from the Sergeant, they were all fresh from basic training and this was their first overseas posting. None of them were used to the heat of this almost equatorial country and they were suffering for it.

Sergeant Kelly yelled "Moseley! Catch up, even Campbell is beating you."

"I only stopped for a piss, Sarge!" Moseley shouted back as he jogged to catch up with the rest of the men, zipping his fly up at the same time. "Cheeky cunt." He murmured under his breath, but with a wide grin on his sunburnt face. This really wasn't a great place to be ginger.

Base camp was another day's trek through tough terrain. They shared it with a Red Cross outpost and various civilian volunteer workers. This was a peaceful country; the natives appreciated the help they gave. It made this posting a good tester for newbies. After three weeks with these new recruits the Sergeant could see already who was going to love their army life.

Lloyd Campbell certainly wasn't going to. How he'd got through basic training Kelly wasn't sure. He was struggling to keep up with the others. He was six foot two and, from what the other guys said about him, had nearly cried when he'd been forced to cut his chin length blonde hair and shave off his straggly goatee.

Ryan, on the other hand, was one of the most dangerous men in a fight that the Sergeant had ever met. He might have looked young enough that he was carded in every pub they ever visited, but he was pure muscle and physically fit to go with it.

Kelly checked his watch. It was nearly time to stop. A quick glance at the sun sinking lower on the horizon confirmed that it would be dark soon. The terrain ahead would be too dangerous in the dark. The clearing they'd just entered seemed like as good a place as any to set up camp for the night.

"Right soldiers. We'll set up camp here. Come on, get moving! You know what to do"

The young soldiers moved with a practiced efficiency, setting up improvised lean-tos round the edges of the clearing. Davids, McMahon and Jackson rapidly built a small fire, McMahon cheating by pulling out a small gold coloured cigarette lighter. The fire wasn't needed for heat in this country, but as a cooking fire for whatever meagre rations they would soon be eating. The nights were cooler than the days but still too hot for most of these guys who'd been brought up on council estates in the north of England.

Kelly watched them with a sense of satisfaction. This was turning into a good little unit with the exception of Lloyd. He'd spotted the lighter McMahon had used for the fire but wasn't too bothered. He'd done the same as a new recruit. He was almost impressed at the forward planning it demonstrated.

"What are we having to eat tonight? We've almost run out of rations." Lloyd Campbell's high pitched nasal whine broke Kelly's train of thought.

"What do you think Campbell?" Kelly yelled. "Look round you, see if you can catch something!"

This was one of Kelly's favoured tactics with new recruits. He knew how many rations they needed for a four day trek like they'd just been on. But if they had enough food and all the right equipment then it wasn't a proper test of a soldier's worth.

That was why he made sure they never had quite enough. It wasn't strictly what the rulebook said but he didn't care. This meant the men were guaranteed to learn more survival techniques and gain practical experience of living off the land.

Nathan Tyson and Kyle Powell were already gathering fruit they had seen in the trees as they passed. Taliesin Davids and Gary "Zed" McMahon, having finished with the fire, were laying snares in the undergrowth.

Kelly felt sorry for Davids. What kind of parents gave their kid a name like Taliesin? It was no wonder the kid was a geek. Still his brains seemed to have come in handy a few times on the expedition they'd just completed and there was no doubting that he was a lot stronger than he looked. He'd taken Campbell down easily in a wrestling match the previous night.

McMahon was a grumpy sort. He missed being at home with his wife and kid but he'd get used to it. Maybe he'd even find advantages to being so far away from his family. Tyson was a great asset to the team. His only fault was the fact that if his nipples were any bigger they'd meet in the middle – hence his nickname, Nips.

A scream broke Sgt Kelly's train of thought again. Again it was Campbell's irritating whiny voice. He looked in the direction of the noise and saw Lloyd dashing out of the bushes and quivering like a little girl.

"What the fuck is wrong with you Campbell?" It was Moseley who'd shouted this, giving voice exactly to Kelly's feelings.

"In there" Lloyd pointed a shaking hand into the bushes he'd just rushed out of. "A huge insect!"

There was a pause as the nine other men in the clearing absorbed what Lloyd had just said, and then they all burst into gales of laughter. Zed put a protective arm round Lloyd's shoulders, "Did a big nasty creepy-crawly attack poor 'ittle Lloydy-Woydy?"

Lloyd glowered and stalked off toward the shelter he'd earmarked for himself. As he slunk off he pulled a notepad and pencil out of his pocket.

"Poor thing," said Powell. "He's going to write a letter of complaint about us."

"Campbell! Stop where you are!" Kelly yelled as Campbell tried to escape into his shelter. "You're a soldier now! What are you doing running away from an insect?"

Kelly stepped into the bush Campbell had exited so quickly. Even he was taken aback for a moment when he saw the insect. It was huge, a good five inches long, about half that width and it was a dark red/brown colour. It looked like some sort of cockroach but fatter and much, much bigger. Its pincers were a couple of centimetres long and it looked like it could inflict a nasty bite if it wanted to.

Still Kelly had a point to prove to the men, and especially to Campbell. He reached down and picked the thing up. It squirmed in his hand as he stepped back out of the bush.

"Is this what you were so scared of Campbell?" He waved it in Campbell's face and felt real pleasure as the private backed away in disgust. "This isn't something to be scared of. This is a light snack if you're so hungry! Here, have a bite!"

He waved the insect once more into Campbell's face, pushing towards the poor young man's girlish lips. Campbell cringed and backed away towards his shelter.

"Soft bastard." Kelly hesitated for a moment, then raised the insect to his own mouth and took a bite, crunching though the carapace and into the soft tissues beneath. He'd eaten bugs before on active duty, but never anything this size. Normally you could just put it in your mouth and swallow without having to worry too much about it.

This was easily the foulest thing he'd ever tasted. It had a bitter acrid flavour with an iron aftertaste of rotting blood. He grimaced and threw the remaining half of the insect on the fire where it sputtered and fizzled as it died. With a real effort he managed to suppress the gag reflex and swallowed the chewed up substance in his mouth.

"See Campbell. That's how you do it." He turned away and looked for his bag. He needed a drink of the water that was in there. If he didn't clear his mouth of the taste of that insect he was going to throw up. He discretely rubbed at his wrist where the damned thing seemed to have stung him.

Private Tyson was the first to start laughing and he led the round of applause that followed Sergeant Kelly to his kitbag. Campbell failed to join in with the applause and completed the interrupted trip to his shelter with a sulk on his face.

The next half an hour in the camp passed without any real incident. None of the snares that had been laid out seemed to have caught anything. Moseley, Davids and Tyson went out on a quick hunting expedition but had no real luck. They were about to give up when Davids made a grisly discovery.

By the side of the path he found the dead body of a large rodent. It had been lying dead for a few days. There was a trail of blood leading behind it. Tal followed the trail into the undergrowth and stopped dead in his tracks. "Uh guys," he said, "I think you should see this."

The other two soldiers followed him into a small copse just off the path. In the clearing were the remnants of the strangest battlefield any of them could ever have hoped to see.

Lying all around were the rotting carcasses of scores of animals, big and small. There were wild dogs and rodents of assorted sizes. They were gathered together in clumps, some with jaws clamped on legs and necks of other creatures, some with stomachs ripped open and other animal's snouts still inserted in the gaping holes.

The stench was close to unbearable.

"What the fuck!" Tyson's exclamation summed up the thoughts of the others in three easy words.

"I think we know why we've not seen any animals round here." Tal said.

"Shit." Moseley nearly gagged at the smell. "I think we're on fruit diet tonight. This is knocking me sick."

"Why would they all do this?" Davids knelt down to examine one of the creatures on the sidelines, some type of large vole. "It looks like this guy was one of the winners in the fight but it bled out and died anyway." He poked it with a twig. "Shit!" he exclaimed "Look at its head."

Moseley leaned over to look at the dead thing on the floor. The flesh on its scalp had split open in a dozen places, the skull clearly visible beneath the discoloured fur. He turned away in disgust. "So what? It got its face cut open in the fight? It's amazing anything walked even this far away from that." He pointed into the mass of bodies.

"No," said Davids, checking a few of the other animals nearby, "This is wrong. These don't look like claw marks"

Nips shook his head. "Martin's right. They've been out in the sun too long. They're claw marks. They've been chewed on and all kinds. Let's just get back to camp."

As the soldiers argued, they failed to see the insects that crawled out from the battlefield. Swarms of the red cockroach type things emerged from under various piles of bodies. These were much smaller than the specimen that the Sergeant had snacked on, an inch long at most. They were camouflaged well against the blood that coated the floor.

They converged on the three men stood at the entrance to the clearing. What would have happened if Tal hadn't kicked the dead vole in frustration can only be guessed at. Instead of moving to the sound of the raised voices, the streams of insects changed direction and followed the motion of the dead rodent, swarming over it in an apparent attempt to feed. As the streams met, they turned on each other, fighting for the morsel beneath.

The noise of the pitched miniature battle attracted the attention of the three men. They stared at the insects ripping each other apart on the dead thing only yards from their feet.

"Well it's official." deadpanned Tal. "I am now officially freaked out." He grinned nervously at his two colleagues. "Let's get back to camp."

The men slowly backed out of the clearing and ran back to the camp as fast as their legs, still exhausted from the day's trek, would carry them. In the clearing the insects continued to kill each other, as blood crazed and lethal as the dead things they'd crawled out of had been.

Back in the camp, Lloyd had recovered from his sulk and was gamely trying to keep up in a fitness test between Privates Gillott, Powell and Hargreaves. They were using a fallen tree for tricep dips, followed by press ups with the feet raised on the log. These were then followed by sit ups and yet more press-ups, but this time clapping the hands on each lift.

McMahon sat by his shelter, shooting the breeze with Private Jackson. They were the two oldest of the new recruits and the only two parents in the group. They swapped baby photos and wagers on who was going to win the fitness test.

Campbell had had enough and collapsed face down in a sodden mess of sweat on the floor. He slowly rolled onto his back and lay staring half at the sky and half at the muscular form of Ryan, still going strong with his press ups beside him.

"You knackered already Lloyd?" Ryan laughed as he pushed himself off the ground and clapped before landing on his outstretched palms again. His baby-face glistened with sweat as he lowered himself to the floor, his short shock of jet black hair plastered to his scalp.

Lloyd just nodded and lay still, trying to gather the energy to sit up and, eventually, to somehow move back to his shelter.

 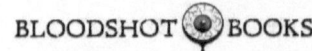

The next one to drop out was Tom Gillott. He wiped the sweat from his brow and joined Zed and Warren on the sidelines. It would mean looking at baby photos for the dozenth time but he was exhausted. "I'll have a fiver on Justin to win" he said.

Kyle glanced over and flipped him the finger as he reached the top point of his sit-up. Tom winked at him and sat down. Almost instantly he had a picture in his hands and Gary was telling what "the Boy" had achieved at school last month.

The sergeant watched the proceedings from his own shelter. He was waiting for the hunting party to return with some decent food. He was feeling remarkably tired. As soon as he'd eaten he was assigning the sentries for the night and going to sleep.

He didn't need to wait long for the hunting party to return. He listened to their cock and bull story about some kind of hell on earth for furry critters and an insect rebellion and asked them in his own creative ways if they thought he was born yesterday.

Kyle and Ryan called it a draw in the contest and watched with amusement. It was always fun to watch the sergeant tearing into one of the others. You had to be careful not to laugh out loud or his wrath could easily turn in your direction. Ryan couldn't help it though and, when the sergeant screamed into Tyson's face a particularly fine insult relating the size of his nipples inversely to the size of his IQ, he snorted with laughter.

"Who was that?" Kelly snapped round to face the onlooking soldiers. When no one answered he grinned widely. "Ok," he said, "if you're going to behave like schoolchildren, I'll treat you like schoolchildren. It's bedtime. And since our friends here have brought us back no more supplies, we'll all have to go without supper. Campbell, Tyson, and Moseley, you're on sentry duty till oh one hundred. Powell, Davids, and Gillott till oh four hundred. Jackson, Hargreaves and McMahon, you're on till dawn when we'll get moving again."

Kelly watched the soldiers scatter to their respective shelters except for the three sentries who took up guard positions at different entrances to the temporary campsite. They had no ammunition in their guns, this was after all a practice exercise in a friendly country but Kelly insisted on running things like a true warzone as much as possible.

Satisfied everything was fine for the night, he retreated to his own shelter. He checked the radio was still working and lay back on the earthen floor of his shelter, his head resting on his rolled up jacket as a pillow and was asleep in moments.

Campbell was on sentry duty closest to the sergeant's shelter. When he was satisfied the whole camp was asleep and he'd heard the sergeant's breathing turn into a relaxed sleeping pattern he reached into the pocket on the left leg of his combat pants and pulled out a can of deodorant which he sprayed liberally under his shirt. The cold spray felt like luxury after the heavy exercise of the day so far. He put the spray back in his pocket and pulled out his notebook and pencil. There was enough light from the fire to allow him to work on his latest poem.

He heard the sergeant make a loud grunting noise followed by a distorted whining scream. All three sentries did, but Campbell was closest so he was the first to look into the shelter. That meant he was the first to die.

Kelly's face had turned an odd shade of puce and he was sitting in the middle of the shelter, staring straight outside.

"Sergeant? Are you O…" was all Campbell managed before Kelly stood up, scattering the wood of the shelter all around, took his rifle in his hands and brought it round up an golf-swing motion, the perfect arc connecting squarely with Campbell's jaw. Campbell flew backwards and landed on his back near the fire. The sergeant followed, diving on top of him before he could move and slamming the rifle butt once more in his face.

As Lloyd stared woozily up at his attacker, Kelly threw the rifle to one side and picked up the pencil which Lloyd had dropped as he landed. The Sergeant laughed, a bestial noise which scared Lloyd almost as much as the knowledge of his impending death. He twisted under the sergeant, turning on his side in an effort to wriggle free. Sergeant Kelly raised the pencil and stabbed it into Lloyd's ear. Then he reached down for the radio which he used as a hammer to drive it deep into the brain.

Lloyd shuddered twice and lay still.

The whole attack had taken only a few seconds. Tyson was the next closest and had watched in disbelief as Campbell was thrown across the camp. He shouted for Moseley to get his arse over there quick and help out, and raced to the fire to try to stop Kelly, swinging his rifle in through the air like a baseball bat.

He was too late to help. Kelly stood after finishing off Campbell and side stepped Nathan's clumsy swing with ease. He then stepped in and smashed the radio into Tyson's forehead.

Nathan's scalp split open like an overripe fruit, blood spilling from the hole as he staggered and fell to his knees. Kelly laughed the bestial laugh again and roundhouse kicked Nathan in the back, causing him to fall over face first into the fire.

Nathan had never experienced anything like it. He tried to stand, to push himself away from the heat and the pain, to allow himself to breathe again, but the sergeant's foot was now planted firmly in the small of his back, stopping him from moving. The skin seared off his face and his hair caught fire, the remnants of the dye he'd used turning the flame an interesting green colour.

In his days in med school before he'd switched careers, he'd read how in extreme situations the brain could switch off the pain receptors. He prayed this would happen to him as he felt his trachea burn and his lungs shut down. The last sensation he was conscious of was his eyeballs popping in the heat, a brief trickle of his aqueous humour trickling down the ruin of his face before he felt nothing more.

"You fucking cunt" screamed Moseley as he raced across the clearing. "Get the fuck off him!"

He ran straight at the sergeant, holding his rifle in both hands. The sergeant aimed a punch but Martin blocked it with his weapon before using the butt of the rifle to break Kelly's nose. As Kelly staggered backwards with blood pouring down his face, Martin hit him again, across the temple this time. Kelly fell onto his hands and knees and Moseley kicked him hard in the ribs. Kelly was flipped onto his back and Martin continued kicking him and stamping on him, all the time screaming and cursing at him.

By this time the whole camp was awake. Powell, McMahon and Jackson dragged the screaming Moseley off the prostrate body of the sergeant. Kyle received an elbow to the face, splitting his lip and he backed off. Jackson and McMahon had it covered in any case.

"I think that's enough now." Jackson yelled as the two of them pinned Martin to the floor.

While Tal and Ryan pulled the body of Private Tyson off the fire, Tom and Kyle knelt down next to the sergeant.

"He's not breathing," Tom said, checking the sergeant for signs of life.

Martin stopped struggling, pinned under the combined weight of Warren and Gary. It was the first time he'd killed another human, and it was his own sergeant, a man he'd been proud to call a colleague and a friend. He needed to be alone for a while, to try to adjust to this new reality. That he was a killer. Even if just in self defence. He tried explaining this to the men pinning him down, but all that came out of his mouth were wracking sobs.

Kyle joined Tom in dealing with the sergeant. He tilted Kelly's head back and clamped the sergeant's nose shut with his thumb and forefinger. "Tom, you know how to do chest compressions?"

Tom nodded and positioned himself over the sergeant's chest. Kyle wiped the blood from around Kelly's chin. Then he made the biggest mistake of his life when he leaned over and started mouth to mouth resuscitation.

The smell is knocking me sick but I search the pockets and bags on all the bodies. There are a few water bottles and Zed has a lighter in his pocket which I take. Campbell has a spray on deodorant in his pockets. The Sergeant would have killed him for bringing that along. I don't need it so I

throw it to one side.

The only other thing of interest is his notebook. In the one section I can read, he seems to have been writing a love poem. I don't know much about poetry but even I know it was bad. I wonder where the pencil he always carries is. When I see it, I decide I don't want it and move on to the next body.

This one is Powell. His real name was Kyle but he was called Justin by most people because he bore an unfortunate resemblance to that little prick Justin Bieber. His lifeless eyes stare blankly from his bloodstained face at me as I check his pockets.

He has a large and very deep stab wound in his left hand side. It looks like the knife would have pierced his lungs and heart, killing him instantly. The blood pooled in his clothes makes the few items in his pockets completely useless.

His cheek twitches suddenly. I struggle not to cry out in shock. With that hole in his side he can't possibly be alive. I look more closely at his face and realise that he didn't actually move. There's something under his skin moving around, a grotesque bulge moving up his face and onto his forehead. The shape vanishes under his hairline.

As I stare in horror one of his eyes changes colour – the white of the eye becomes blood red, slowly at first but once the process starts it quickens rapidly. Now his eyeball starts bulging the same way the skin was just a moment ago. With a quiet pop, which sounds horribly loud in this cloying heat and loneliness, his eyeball splits open and a number of insects start crawling out though the hole.

They're blood red and shaped something like a cockroach but with larger pincers. They're tiny, about half a centimetre long by about two millimetres across the torso.

Kyle's forehead starts squirming again as about half a dozen of the shapes appear from under his hairline. The shapes find a scratch on his head and congregate round it. I imagine I can hear the gnawing sound as the scratch becomes an open wound and more of the insects come crawling out, larger than the others, a good centimetre long at the smallest, the largest is close to an inch long.

I break out of my panicked state and scrabble for the discarded aerosol can. As the insects start swarming across Kyle's face I flick on the lighter I found earlier and spray deodorant across the flame. The jet from the can ignites and I have a small portable flamethrower which I direct into the face of my ex friend.

The insects shrivel and burn as Kyle's face blackens. The heat of the flame causes his other eye to pop and another small swarm of insects rushes out only to be cooked in the flames.

The smell of searing flesh makes me feel horribly hungry. How long is it since I last ate?

I hear a ripping and scuttling noise and turn. While I've been incinerating my best friend's skull, Sergeant Kelly's face has also split open. He has insects crawling out of his ears and nostrils as well as from his head wounds. I turn the flame on him as well but I'm too late to stop some of the insects from scuttling off into the undergrowth.

I try to stamp on as many as I can but they vanish easily into the shrubbery. The can in my hands is feeling way too hot now so I throw it in after them. There's a loud bang as the canister explodes. I know it won't have killed any more of the things but it gives me a sense of satisfaction to imagine that it did.

Slipping the knife into a holster on my belt, I set off towards the valley. I take a last glance at my former comrades. With their burned faces Powell, Tyson and Kelly look like a set of hellish triplets from my darkest nightmares. I ask them all quietly for forgiveness and move towards what I hope is civilisation.

Kyle straightened and spat blood from his mouth. He nodded to Tom who linked his hands and placed them on the sergeant's chest. He leaned forward and pushed down hard, putting his weight firmly on Kelly's sternum. There was a loud cracking noise as the sergeant's ribs, several of which were already cracked from the kicking Martin had given him, broke completely and his breastbone sank through though his torso. A fresh gout of blood spurted from his mouth and nose as his lungs compressed to a fraction of their working size.

Tom toppled forward as the ribcage gave way beneath him. With an effort he managed to straighten up and throw himself back, narrowly avoiding collapsing across the now definitively deceased body beneath him. He stared at Kyle, his face white.

"He had no real chance anyway." Kyle murmured, his face also drained of colour. They stood and turned to face Martin, still being held by Gary and Warren.

Martin continued to sob. Had he been free to move, he would have curled into a foetal ball and stayed there.

The seven men sat in the clearing staring at each other, none of them talking, each trying to process the events of the past two minutes. The only sound to break the silence was Martin's crying.

Eventually Warren voiced all their thoughts.

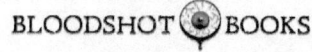

"What are we supposed to do now?"

Tom stood up and gestured to Kyle to help him move the body of the sergeant. "Start by showing some respect to the dead," he said.

The men silently laid the three dead bodies side by side. Kyle and Tal found jackets to use as sheets and covered up the faces of the deceased. Once this was done, Tom signalled the men to gather round. Martin was left lying in his pool of grief by the fire.

Tom sat next to him and stroked his ginger hair. "Come on mate, come back to us."

He eased Martin into a sitting position and hugged him tightly. Martin's sobs slowly subsided with the more gentle human contact. He finally managed to ask for the alone time he craved.

"OK," Tom said. "But stay where we can see you. We don't know what's going on here. We don't know why the sergeant did that to Lloyd and Nathan. Did you see anything?"

Martin shook his head and crawled to the opposite side of the clearing where he sat against a tree.

"Let's just radio for help" Gary said. "They'll send a chopper for us."

"Kelly had the only radio, and it looks like he used it to kill Lloyd." Tom replied. "He always comes out on... came out on these exercises short of equipment. Fuck him."

"I'll run to get help then." Ryan volunteered.

If anyone could do it out of the squad it would have been between Ryan and Kyle. They were by far the fittest in the group. Kyle was looking listless and tired though.

Gillott shook his head. "It's too dark. You'd never make it. We'll have to stay till the morning and you can go for help then."

"What are we going to say though? We've got three men dead and no story that makes sense to explain it!" Gary asked.

"What's the alternative? We all go AWOL and the bodies are found... That looks great for us then doesn't it?" Tom snapped.

Kyle yawned and announced he was going to sleep. Despite the dirty looks from his comrades, he retreated to his shelter while the remaining soldiers discussed the situation. They talked about the sergeant, the good times and the bad with him. They talked about sneaking Nathan into barracks after he passed out drunk on a night out. As they talked only Davids noticed the grunting noise and the strange distorted scream that came from Kyle's tent.

They all noticed when Kyle stood up suddenly, scattering his shelter. His face was a strange colour and he had his hunting knife in his hand. His breath was raspy and almost inhuman. He laughed and ran straight at the group of men, the knife raised.

"What the hell are you doing?" Warren pulled his own knife from its

 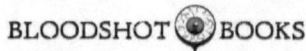

holster and tried to hold his ground as the other soldiers instinctively moved out of the way. This was Jackson's final and greatest mistake.

Kyle was left handed. In a knife fight, the left handed person has an automatic advantage against a right-hander. He's used to his opponent using the opposite arm. Right handed people aren't.

Warren's blocking move missed entirely and Kyle plunged the hunting knife straight through his chin and thrust upward. He felt his jaws pinned together as the knife pierced his tongue and broke through the hard palate at the roof of the mouth. He gurgled on his own blood as Kyle removed the knife and plunged it into his cheek, just below the right eye. This time the blade entered the cranium and pierced the brain. He slumped to the floor as Kyle pulled the knife out and turned to face the others.

Four of the men had spread out and formed a circle around him. Martin had curled into a ball on the other side of the clearing.

"Put the knife down Justin!" Gillott barked at his former friend. "We don't want to hurt you. Just put the..."

Kyle raced at him with the knife. Gillott sidestepped and prepared to block the knife swing but stumbled when it didn't arrive.

Gary had jumped in and rugby-tackled Kyle as he raced forward and now the two of them were struggling on the ground together. Kyle had dropped the knife as he landed and was scrabbling to grab it again as Gary tried to pin him down.

Ryan kicked the knife out his reach and it landed at Davids' feet. He aimed a kick at Kyle's head but Kyle managed to twist and block with both arms. He wrapped his arms round Ryan's legs and twisted again, pulling Ryan forward so he fell on his face and lay there stunned, blood leaking from his nose and scalp where he'd hit the floor.

Fights for life in reality are rarely as graceful and coordinated as fiction and films would suggest. They're messy and vulgar affairs, even the best trained fighters fumble in the heat of the moment. Punches are thrown that miss entirely. It's ugly and brutal, but for the victors, essential.

Gary struggled to hold the squirming little shit but he seemed stronger than ever. Suddenly Kyle grabbed a large rock and twisted round again into a sitting position with Gary now lying prone in his lap. As Tom and Tal leapt forward to try to prevent yet another tragedy, he brought the rock crashing down on Gary's skull and laughed as he heard the satisfying crack.

Tom and Tal, in a scene that would have been funny in any other circumstance, managed to run into each other as they both aimed for Kyle. They hit the floor with a crash of heads.

Kyle turned his attention to Ryan, who was wiping the blood out of his

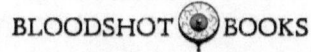

eyes as he tried to get his shit back together. He straddled the prone Hargreaves's muscled chest and raised the rock again. As he started to bring the rock down on Ryan's young face he stopped, a look of surprise in his own eyes, and slumped forward.

Tal stood above him, the knife in his hand. He wasn't the strongest fighter but he was one of the brightest, and his technique was excellent. He'd plunged the knife in the optimal spot between Kyle's ribs and pierced the heart with his first stab.

Hargreaves squirmed. The corpse had landed so the stab wound was almost directly over his face and Kyle's blood was flooding into his mouth and nose. He rolled over and pushed the dead weight off him and spat out the viscous fluid.

"Fuck, I think I swallowed some" Ryan tried to wipe the blood off his face with the edge of his shirt, smearing it across his own wounds in the process. He sat up. "What the fuck is going on? We've got to get out of here."

"We'll never be able to see our way down into that valley in the dark. We've got no choice but to wait till first light" Tom said. He turned to Taliesin who was still staring at the bloody knife in his hands. "Are you ok?" This was Davids' first kill too.

Tal dropped the knife and staggered over to the fire.

"I think it's something to do with those insects," he said, staring into the flickering flames.

"What are you talking about Tal?" Tom asked.

Tal started explaining about the clearing they'd found earlier that day, or was it yesterday? He'd lost track of time. Even in the middle of the night the heat was still sticky and draining.

Ryan yawned. "Look, if we're not heading back now I'm going to catch some sleep."

Tal glared at him and continued with his story. Martin joined in and between them they filled Tom in on every detail of the strange battleground they'd visited earlier.

Tom shook his head. "What's that got to do with all of this?"

"Don't you see?" Tal asked. "Kelly grabs this big insect. Did it sting him? I don't know? But he goes crazy and starts killing everyone.

The animals in the clearing just kept fighting each other even as they were bleeding out. That's not normal. I've never seen anything like it. That's what's happened here, first the Sarge and now Kyle, they just wouldn't stop till they were dead."

"When we saw the insects they were fighting each other? What's that about?" Martin asked.

"I read somewhere that if you lock a hundred spiders in a room together, eventually what you'll have is an empty room with one very well fed spider in it." Tal said. "I think these things are like that, they limit their own population growth."

Martin wasn't convinced. He wanted to be. If there was a good reason he'd had to kill his sergeant, he might be able to live with himself again. "But that doesn't work still, Kyle didn't touch the insect. Why did he go crazy?"

Davids thought for a moment. "I honestly don't know."

They talked more about the possible reasons for the violence of the night but failed to reach any agreement. The one thing that the three of them did agree on was that they should plan the route back to camp for the next day. Tal retrieved the map from his pack and they worked by the light of the fire to plan the trek.

Ryan lay sleeping on the ground behind them, snoring softly, his sweat creating trails in the blood that still coated his face.

The conversation turned once more, inevitably to the events of the night. "Before they went crazy, the sergeant made this strange noise. So did Kyle." Tal said.

"What kind of noise?" Tom asked.

"It was a sort of a grunting noise, and then a weird type of scream."

Behind them, Ryan's eyes blinked open. He grunted and shook his head, a distorted scream emitted from his lungs as he sat up.

"Oh are you awake now Ryan?" Tal didn't even glance behind him. "Yeah, it was just like that. You're not being funn..."

He was unable to finish the sentence because Ryan's knife slammed into the back of his skull, severing the spinal cord at the topmost point. He was dead before he hit the ground. He landed on the map, his blood pooled on the hillside and the valley they would occupy till nature rotted their corpses away.

Martin had seen Ryan sit up and had started to back away. With the fresh outburst of violence he stood and ran off into the countryside, leaving Tom to his fate.

Tom also tried to run but Ryan was far faster than he was. He had no chance. Ryan threw him to the ground and leapt on top of him, raining down blows with the knife indiscriminately into his slim body.

For a full five minutes he continued his frenzied stabbing of the body beneath him. The former wiry frame of Private Gillott was swiftly reduced to a bloody pulpy mess. So savage was the attack that it only took one blow to all but decapitate the bloody corpse.

Eventually Ryan sensed there was no life in the pile of mangled tissues he straddled. He looked round but there was no sign of any more life forms in the area.

With a lack of anything to kill, the creatures controlling him relinquished

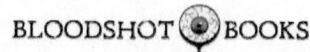

their hold and let him sleep again.

◉ ◉ ◉

I can see the trail where we all arrived here last night so I hope that if I continue in this direction I'll find the safe path down into the valley.

The heat is overpowering. I can feel my skin crawling with it. I cover my head with my hat and march onwards, alone.

After about ten minutes I find a dead rodent by the side of the path. It looks like it's been there for days. There's a trail of blood leading up to it. Out of curiosity I follow the trail.

I enter a clearing. There are dozens of dead animals here, all twisted and mangled together. The stench is overpowering. As well as the dozens of large animals, there are hundreds of dead insects, like cockroaches but red, the colour of fresh blood.

I hear I scuttling noise and three giant insects appear from under different piles of dead animals. I have a sudden flash of memory to last night. The sergeant biting one of these things... It seemed funny then. These are larger though, all of them nearly a foot long.

I stamp on the one closest to me and crush it. The other two race toward me and I back off quickly. The two cockroaches bump into each other and seem to forget that I'm there. They face each other and slowly circle before the smaller of the two lunges at the larger.

Another memory flash... Nathan told the sergeant something.... I'm sure it's important, but this heat is really getting to me. It feels like something just crawled over my spine. I leave the clearing and continue on the track.

After about an hour I find what appears to be the path down into the valley. It's difficult terrain. The slope is covered in loose rock and steep drops. It would be completely impassable in the dark.

Taking more care than usual - I feel like I'm going to pass out – I slowly make my way down the side of the valley. The rocks are hot to the touch and the ground beneath me seems to be trying to make me slip. I lose my balance and drop my bag as I grip onto the cliff face. The bag tumbles into the ravine.

I can't remember the last time I drank or ate but from the empty feeling in my gut it was too long ago. The shimmering heat is almost hallucinogenic. I have to stop to make sure I didn't really see something moving under the skin of my left hand. It's just the heat combined with a lack of food and drink, and the nightmare of what happened with Kyle.

I eventually reach the bottom of the valley. The stream is the greatest thing I've ever seen in my 19 years. I throw myself to the ground and drink straight from it. I never knew water could taste so much like life itself.

There's no sign of the bag. It was dropped upstream from here and I need to head downstream. Refreshed from the drink I start walking. Sure enough, the stream joins another and widens, following that it leads to a river. I know that the river must lead to people. I pick some fruit from the trees nearby and sit to rest.

After one mouthful of the fruit I start retching. All the water I drank seems to come straight back out of me. Once my stomach is empty I continue dry heaving till I can barely stand it. For the first time in years I feel like crying.

Another memory flash... Kyle with a knife...

I can't carry on any longer. The heat is killing me. I'm weak from throwing up and I can't find the energy inside me. It's like those times pushing weights when you know you can do it but your body just refuses to do what it's told. I can't find the strength to move. I lie back and close my eyes to the blazing sun.

I remember years ago, before I was in the army, on a training run with a friend, when I wanted to give up and said I couldn't run any further, my friend said to me "Of course you can, you're Ryan". In hindsight it was a kinda tacky and stupid thing to say, but at the time it spurred me on. I try the same thing now. It's worked a couple of times when I've needed it. Stupid as it is.

Of course you can do this, you're Ryan.

I open my eyes, ignoring the creeping sensation in my skin.

Come on man! You're Ryan... Get a fucking move on!

I sit up. I take a deep breath and with one more "You're Ryan" I stand and walk down the bank of the river.

I don't know how long I'm walking for. Time no longer has a meaning in this heat and humidity. I stagger forward almost blindly. The heat makes my skin crawl. The surface beneath my feet changes into a path without me realising. Sometime later it becomes a dirt road but I don't know when that happened either. I just keep moving forward.

I see a shape in front of me. It's a girl. I try to call out but my throat is too dry. All I manage is a hoarse cough. I'm at the limits of my strength now and my knees barely support me. No amount of "You're Ryan" can make me carry on now. I stumble to the floor as the girl sees me and runs toward me.

As she gets closer I realise that it isn't a girl after all. It's the son of one of the Red Cross workers at the camp. He's tall and skinny with waist length dreadlocks and hips that any woman would be proud of.

"Danny?" I croak.

He catches hold of me as I fall and pulls his mobile phone out of his

pocket. He shouts into the phone before turning his attention to me. He assures me that help is on its way and asks what the fuck has happened and lots of other questions which I can't answer.

He pours water on me from a bottle he carries. It feels heavenly and I grin widely. I point at my mouth and he puts the bottle to my lips.

"Ok, small sips only" he says.

The water tastes even better than the stream. I want to grab the bottle from him and drink it all but Danny pulls it away from me.

The noise of a motor breaks through the sound of his soothing voice and some men and women appear behind him. I think one of them is Dan's mother Louise. She holds something in her hand.

"You've done really well Danny," I hear her say before she turns to me. "Ryan, you'll just feel a little scratch," she says as she takes my arm.

I think I see a look of disgust on her face. I don't look that bad, do I? She sticks a needle in my arm and the world goes black.

Louise looked from Danny to the sleeping body of Private Hargreaves. "Are you ok son?" she asked.

Danny nodded. "Have you ever seen anything like this, mum?" he asked. "It's like there's something crawling under his skin."

Louise shook her head. Ryan was in a bad way. The first thing she'd noticed about him was that he was coated in blood. The second was that he was suffering from complete exhaustion and then she'd spotted the lumps on his skin. The moving lumps. She didn't even want to guess what that was about. They needed to get him to the medical centre.

She signalled to the military drivers to help get him into the back of the Land Rover. Danny climbed in after them and ten minutes later they were in the camp.

"I'll get a stretcher," Louise said as she jumped down from the back of the vehicle. "Keep an eye on him for a minute."

Danny stroked Ryan's face. Ryan had always been good to him and he hated seeing him like this. He hoped and prayed to the gods he didn't even believe in that this would end well.

He heard a noise outside and stood up, looking out of the back of the land rover to see if it was his mother returning. Behind him, Ryan made a grunting noise and sat up with a weird distorted scream.

Danny turned. "Ryan!" was all he managed to say before the young soldier leapt at him and they both tumbled out of the vehicle and hit the floor behind.

Ryan punched Danny in the face several times, dislodging the piercing in Danny's lip. He struggled to crawl away from the crazed attack but Ryan wouldn't stop.

He pushed Danny to the floor and pinned him on his stomach. Reaching down, he ripped out a handful of dreads by the roots and wrapped them round Danny's throat.

Danny strained and bucked under the weight of the young private, but he wasn't strong enough. He felt giddy and lightheaded. The sensation was almost pleasurable. The longer that Ryan gripped the dreads round his throat, the less strength he had. He could feel the blood trickling down his scalp where the dreads had been torn out.

He became aware suddenly that he had an erection. It seemed an inappropriate reaction to the current situation. He felt himself cum as Ryan tightened the cords even further. That and the dreamy feel of approaching sleep were the last things he experienced before he died.

The noise of the struggle had attracted attention and a pair of soldiers now stood with fully loaded guns shouting at Ryan to let the boy go!

Ryan stood and laughed again. He pulled the knife from his pocket and moved toward the soldiers.

"Stop or we'll fire!" one of the soldiers yelled.

Ryan took no notice and raised the knife, running at the men threatening him. Both of the soldiers opened fire at once. One bullet hit Ryan in the shoulder, the other in the head. The back of his head exploded and he flew backwards, landing in a sprawled heap over the corpse of Danny.

Louise ran out from behind the two soldiers and straight to her son's dead body. She pushed the dead private off her son and attempted CPR. She didn't notice the blood red insects crawling out of the shattered remains of Ryan's face. They were camouflaged nicely among the gore and general carnage.

The insects had had more time to breed and grow in Ryan's body than they'd had in anyone else's. And his body had stayed alive longer, giving them more nutrients. These were bigger and there were more of them. The fist Louise noticed was when a dozen of them crawled over her leg and started biting. She screamed and brushed them off.

They scattered into the undergrowth and into the living area of the camp. No one gave them much notice. They were just insects. They stung a few people. Some were squashed. Some were washed downstream in the river. Some fought little battles between themselves but there was room to spread out here and lots of fresh creatures to share.

Later that night, as Louise somehow managed to sleep in her husband's arms, Lisa Harrison was on sentry duty at the entrance to the camp.

She'd heard about the incident with Private Hargreaves and, like everyone else, wondered why he would do such a vile thing. She listened to the night time noises of the camp, the gentle snores and grunts from the closest tents, the muffled conversations. With the odd feeling caused by the events of the day she knew she would need to be on her guard tonight. Nothing felt right any more. She would be ready for anything tonight she told herself.

But when the screaming started, she was already too late.

Marc was born at an early age. This happened sometime in the seventies. He hasn't died yet. His hobbies include breathing and not stepping out in front of buses. He currently exists somewhere in the North-west of England with his cat, Balrog. He's had a few stories published previously and hopes you like this one.

THE KEEPER
BY KYA ALIANA

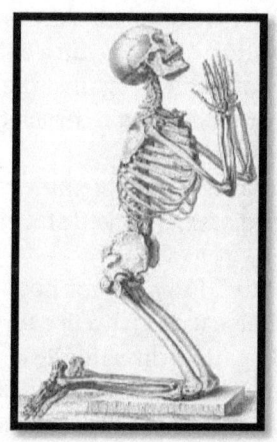

THE musty old-town smell mixes with the stale mist that rolls in off the low tide. It's not a smell easily forgotten and it certainly isn't the first time - nor the last - I'll smell it.

You're never getting out, a voice in my head taunts.

Rain crashes down in blurry sheets. My feet slosh across the flooded street. The warm yellow lights of the coffee house glimmer in the distance.

This is it... my last night as a teenager. Where am I going? I don't want to leave. Being a teenager is the one thing I know how to do. The new decade looms over me and I can already feel myself changing... into what? I haven't the slightest clue. I lose sight of the world around me just before I smack into a wet figure.

"Sorry," I say half-heartedly. My body stiffens and my heavy wool coat hugs my shoulders. The street lamps, dimmed by the pouring rain, cast shadows across his face.

"You look cold," he states.

I feel him eyeing me up and down. I shudder, but not because of the cold.

"I'm fine," I say. My tone is stronger than I expect.

"Please, come inside," he invites. A bell chimes as he heaves open the door. Holding it for me, he adds, "I'll buy you a coffee."

"Thanks," I smile. My boots squeak against the hardwood flood. I search around for a welcome mat or something to brush them off on, but there's nothing.

His tall body hovers over me. A rush of panic and I scoot aside. The barista meets him at the counter and says, "Wicked storm out there, kids! Glad you made it in safely."

Kids. She calls us *kids.* Sure, I'm a kid for now. All that will change at midnight. I won't be able to use it as an excuse for much longer. My twenties are full of the unknown. My path is directionless.

"I'll take a coffee. Black," he orders, reaching down and pulling out his wallet. "And whatever she wants." He looks back at me and offers a smile. In the light, I can see his face for the first time. I decipher what I can. He can't be much older than me... Maybe a few years, tops. His eyes look right past me... Beyond me... Through me... Into me? I'm not sure. Regardless, it creeps me out. Why can't I read him?

"Same," I say boldly without thinking. It's not my usual, but how bad can it be? The man's presence throws everything off; I'm even more unsure of myself than before. I'm changing... 20 rapidly approaches and everything will change. At least that's what *They* say.

The barista chatters in the background about the weather, wondering aloud if it will snow. She places two steaming mugs on the counter. I walk over and cup the mug in my hands. I close my eyes, breathe in the fumes of my caffeine addiction, and smile ever so slightly.

"Careful," the deep voice warns.

I ignore him and press my crusty, chapped lips against the brim of the scalding mug. The first sip is always too hot anyways, but damn it feels so good. My tongue tingles and shards sting my throat. I feel the liquid filling my body. It's bitter, much more than I'm used to, but I kind of like it that way.

I open my eyes to the coffee shop around me. The tall man and I are the only ones in here and I begin to wonder why. Usually this place is packed. Then again, I'm not typically here so late. I look around for something to focus on, but there's nothing. I have no choice but to turn my focus to his brooding face and empty eyes.

"Is it hot?" he asks.

"Yeah. What did you say your name was again?" I ask, shifting my weight awkwardly.

"I didn't," he replies with a sneer. I roll my eyes and shake my head openly, watching his reaction. The corners of his mouth twitch as he hides a smile.

"Sit." He nods over at a table. I think it's supposed to be a request, but it comes out as a sharp demand.

"Join me." I challenge.

"Happily," he obliges with a slight nod.

I'm not quite sure why I invited myself to participate in a power struggle. I walk over and plop down my mug. My long arms awkwardly move as I struggle to take my coat off. He just sits there smiling. Amusement fills his eyes and my cheeks go red hot with blush.

"Gage," he says smoothly, letting the word roll of his tongue.

"Hmm?"

"My name. It's Gage," he repeats curtly, fighting for eye contact. The way his eyes sink into me lights a spark from deep down. I get the feeling we've met before, but I can't remember where.

"Oh," I say, "I'm Deseray, but everybody just calls me Des."

"Very nice to meet you, Deseray," he says, making a point of using my entire name. His slender fingers reach out as he extends his hand across the table. He gently removes my right hand from gripping my mug, and brings it up to his lips. His soft kiss sends gooseflesh down my arms. His smile lights up his face and turns it softer than it seemed before.

I don't know what to think. No one has ever done that... it's something you see in movies, read about in books. Who is he?

"You're timid," he notes. Is that how I'm coming off? I can't detect a hint of emotions behind his words... is he curious, sad, mad, concerned?

I remain quiet and cross my legs back and forth, begging for comfort. I search the coffee station, but the barista is in the back. I cup the mug firmly between my hands again and take another sip.

My last coffee as a teenager, my mind churns.

Get a hold of yourself, Des! It's the end of a decade, not the end of the world.

"What's going on beyond those beautiful eyes of yours?" Gage inquires. I see a tiny spark of excitement in his pale blue eyes, but just as quickly as I notice, it flashes away. I peer up at him from under my long eyelashes, the mascara sticks every time I blink.

"I don't know you," I say slowly.

"I hear conversation helps with that," he retorts.

"Still though," I say with a shrug, "I'm shy."

"I don't know *you* and I'm not shy," he says softly, inching closer.

"Yeah, but that's different." I tilt my head to the side.

"How so?" he asks, propping up and letting a smile beam through. I finally relax as he seems a little more happy-go-lucky. I've captured his attention. I feel the control shift and a sly smile teases my lips.

"Well," I say in an assertive tone, "I'm a girl. And I'm not wearing a black trench coat at dark, standing outside the coffee shop without so much as a cigarette to use for an excuse, watching the rain crash down like some sort of creep."

"Creep? Ouch!" he teases. He dramatically places his hands over his heart and falls backwards, sulking deeper into his chair. I stifle a giggle, but can't hide the smile.

The wind outside roars and I hear the harsh droplets of rain beat against the window.

"You from around here?" I ask.

"Born and raised." I try to read his expression... wishing I could read his thoughts.

"Same," I reply. Having a normal conversation starter seems rather dull. I like him. He's different. I could use a new friend... someone who isn't still wrapped up in all the teenagery drama of high school even if we're in college now. Perhaps this new decade won't be so bad after all.

"What are your plans?" he asks, leaning closer to me over the table.

"For?"

"Getting out, of course."

"They say we're never getting out of this town," I challenge.

"They? Who's they?" He tries to hide it, but I see it behind his eyes.

"You know," I analyze his reaction meticulously.

His eyes shift around the shop and then fall back to me. They linger with mine, making contact for as long as I'll allow. I can't look into them... it's like he's blocked them off. I've always been able to read people so well... but he's different. I have to get to know him.

"You can see them too?" he asks lowly. A rush of endorphins floods over me. Energy rises around me, as if the night itself is coming alive.

I smile to myself. In a way, Gage shatters my confidence. He makes me question what I know about people... how I read them. And in another way, he challenges me and I like it. I've never felt challenged before.

"What do you see? Do you hear anything?" I ask urgently. My heart leaps into my throat and sticks like a gristly piece of steak that's been chewed for far too long to hold any flavor. I can't breathe. I can't think. I'm focused on Gage and only Gage. What's he hiding? An intrigue pulls from deep inside... a *need* to know.

"Can I get you anything else?" the heavy accent punctures my thoughts. I jolt upright, spilling what little coffee I have left all over the floor.

"I'm sorry, hun, I didn't mean to scare you," she says as she begins to clean it up.

"Allow me," Gage says, taking the rag from the barista. They lock eyes and she smiles.

"Th-thank you," she says.

"Of course. Now, why don't you start to close up, it's almost time to lock the doors."

She nods and heads off. How did he do that? She could lose her job for letting a customer clean something up. She knows that.

"I think I better be going now," Gage stands.

"What?" My mind races and screams with protest. We aren't done here. What does he know? No one has ever been able to see *them* before... not like me. No one is like me.

"The coffee shop is closing any minute now. It was great to meet you, Deseray and I sincerely hope we-"

"Do you have plans for tonight?" I press urgently.

"No. Why?"

"Perhaps we should finish our conversation elsewhere."

"If you insist," he says, handing me my coat. My heart races. He's coming with me.

The door swings open and the frigid air takes over the heated room. I don my coat and already have a foot out the door before the barista calls out, "Be careful out there."

"Beautiful night," Gage tries his hand at sarcasm.

We walk down the sidewalk. I take two steps for his one for a while before he notices and slows his pace. The night doesn't seem as cold and bitter with him beside me. I want to bring up The Shadows but I don't know how...

"I don't think it's a coincidence that we met tonight, Deseray."

"Neither do I," I say. My voice wavers in the night. What's happening to me? I feel funny. Different. Nervous. Why do I want him to like me so much? I shouldn't care.

"I've been waiting for someone a lot like you," he says.

"So, I'm not the only that sees The Shadows," I say, wondering if that's what he means.

"There aren't very many like us left."

"Why not?"

"You're very special. It makes me happy that I've found you. Someone who will truly understand."

"I feel the same way," I reply with a smile.

It's silent for a while as we aimlessly wander.

"Where are we going?" he asks eventually.

"I don't know," I say with a shrug.

In the back of my mind, I know we'll need to go our separate ways. The rain is barely mist now, but the rumbling thunder in the distance promises more to come.

"Well then, let's just keep walking," he suggests with a comforting smile. He's slowly coming to life as the night takes over.

The lights flicker down as we walk past the closing shops. I shake my head at the small town, closing before ten at night. That's Ghastly Peak for you.

What are you doing? Turn around. You know you can't do this, the voice hisses and yet I disobey. It can't order me around forever.

"How long?" I ask out of the blue. I really need to get better at this conversation thing.

"What was that?"

"How long have you been able to see them?" I clarify.

"It's not triggered. It's something you're born with, Des."

I breathe out a sigh of relief. I didn't do anything wrong. I'm not alone.

We continue to walk as I think about what to say. It's all so much to take in. We reach the end of Main Street and turn down a back road. No street lamps. I heave a heavy sigh. My breath turns to a cloud of mist, disappearing quickly in front of me. I pull my coat tighter and wish I'd listened to my mother this morning. She said it would snow. The weatherman on Station Five disagreed, but moms always know best.

A raven swoops down in front of me. I grit my teeth and move forward. The wind picks up around me. The closer we get to the coast, the denser the fog gets.

"What was that?" Gage's alert voice sends a wave of panic charging through my body.

"Nothing," I hiss way too quickly. A stinging sensation takes over as the

 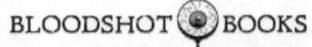

wind pierces through my clothing. "It was nothing."

But I know he saw the raven too.

◉   ◉   ◉

My brand-new, speedy-fast, red sneakers race across the floor. My grubby 5-year-old hands catch me as I trip over my own two feet.

"Slow down," Mommy insists. My feet clomp up the stairs and I pause midway to peek through the railing. The Shadows crawl across the floor. Soon they'll take over the entire house.

The reds and pinks of the setting sun shine brightly through the large and tall window next to the front door. I want to bathe in their rays forever, but night will be here soon. They'll come for me like they always do.

"Mommy!" I call out, but there's no answer.

"You don't need her," Betty says. Betty always comes around sunset. I smile.

"Mommy! Betty's here," I call out, "come meet her."

"Dessy, stop it!" my mother's stern voice echoes down the long hallway. I wait patiently and she comes into view.

"But mommy-"

"Des, for the last time, Betty is not real. You need to stop this."

"Honey, it's perfectly normal for her to have imaginary friends," Dad comforts, walking in from his reading den. I inhale deeply. He smells rich of what mommy calls "too much expensive tobacco". He holds a wooden pipe firmly between his teeth and smiles at me. He gives a short wink and I try to wink back, but really it just feels like squinting my eyes.

"Betty's real. She's the nice one."

My dad smiles at me and nods his head.

"But The Shadows will be here soon," I say with a frown.

"You have nothing to worry about, sweetheart," Daddy says, walking over. He reaches his hand between the rails, ruffles my hair, and pulls me forward, kissing me on my forehead.

"The Shadows..." I start, and then pause, not quite sure how to explain them. I got tired of trying.

"They can't hurt you."

"Remember what the nice doctors said. It's all in your head," Mommy reminds.

Daddy glares at her and mutters something in her ear. I frown because I can't hear him. I hate it when he keeps secrets. Mommy walks away in a quick bustle, mumbling something under her breath.

"Read to me?" I ask, my eyes begging as I peer into my dad's hazel eyes.

"Of course. But you have to sleep quickly. We have a big day ahead of us,"

he says. His heavy feet climb the stairs, pausing half-way to scoop me up in his arms.

"What's tomorrow?" I ask.

"Tomorrow's the picnic, my dear. We're going to the coast. You can even bring your bathing suit and play in the waves," he promises.

"Will you be there?" I ask, clutching his shoulders. I never want to let him go.

"Yes, I'll be there," he answers softly.

"Good. I miss you, Daddy."

"Daddy is very busy with work, Des," he explains, gently setting me down on the bed.

"But I'm going to miss you," I say quietly, looking down at my hands. I know better than this. I shouldn't say anything.

"Miss me?"

"When you're gone."

"At work? Sweetheart, we've talked about this."

"No. Not at work," I say, chewing the dead skin around my fingernails.

My father tenderly pulls my hand away from my mouth and asks, "then where?"

"When you're gone to the place you don't come back from."

"What are you talking about, Des? Who said something to you?" he asks.

"The Shadows say that you don't have long left."

"The Shadows, huh?"

"They say you're going away very soon and there's nothing I can do about it."

He pulls me close against his chest and tells me that it will be okay. I breathe in his tobacco scent again, wanting to remember it forever.

I feel The Shadows surround Gage and me as we continue to wind down the back roads. Gage saunters through the night as if it were made solely for him. The rain turns to an icy sleet and I begin to wish we were closer to shelter.

As we near the coast, my chest tightens. Gage doesn't mind The Shadows. Maybe he's not the same. Maybe it's only visual for him, and not energetic.

"The storm's getting bad," I say.

"The Shadows are here," he states, ignoring my concerns. "What do they say to you?"

Droplets sting my face with a bitter bite, ice when it first hits and then quickly melting its cold juice all over my skin. The wind stings too, but soon enough my face numbs.

"They tell me about the end. They told me about my dad when I was little," I say, pulling deeper inside my coat. I don't want to go here. I don't want to revisit.

Gage stops. He turns and places his hands on my shoulders. "They took your father?"

The ocean roars. We're getting close now. The Shadows gather from every nook and cranny, race from behind every tree. I feel their presence... everything is stronger than before.

"Yeah. I was five. It was a family picnic."

"What happened?" Gage asks, his voice rich with concern.

"He went off. They never found his body." Warm drops flood the corners of my eyes, but the ferocious wind wipes them away.

"I'm sorry," he offers, getting the hint that I don't want to talk about it. The waves crash around me as we turn the final corner. I feel the waves pulling at me. I haven't been back here since...

The parking area is empty. The beach is closed, but that doesn't faze Gage one bit. Shadows pour from all corners of the darkness. They're tall, ever-changing figures, masked by the night. I catch a glimpse of the looming lighthouse to my left and a sinking feeling weighs my heart down. I swallow hard against my cold throat. The icy rain flirts with the thunderous waves.

"Maybe we should turn back," I say. But the ice is getting bigger. Soon it will hail. I know just as well as any sane person that we won't have time to make it back to town before the storm gets too rough.

"It's going to be okay," Gage says. He wraps his arms around my waist and pulls me close. His warmth fills me and for a fleeting second, I truly believe his words. "You must have a lot of questions," he says.

"Why are you here?"

"Because you asked me. You wanted me with you. You wanted answers." Silence.

"Am I your first?" he asks.

"First?"

"Who can see them?"

"Yes," I confess.

"They're gathering now," he says, turning to me and staring deeply into my eyes. It's dark and I can barely make out his dominating figure but his eyes are crystal clear.

"I know," I whisper, unable to gather my wits. I take in a shaky breath and nod. He takes my hand and I smile. He'll help me. But... Gage is different. Gage is blocked... I don't have control anymore, I can't read him, so what makes me think I can trust him?

"Why are they all here?" he asks me, like I know.

"How would--"

"Listen to them," he urges in a voice not unlike my father's. It brings me back. It gives me strength. He feeds my confidence.

I take in a deep breath of the salty aroma. Gage's presence fills me with a newfound spark of energy.

Turn around, Dessy. There's nothing for you here, the shadows heckle. I feel them absorb me, pulling me away from the lighthouse and back to my house.

"I really should be going," I step away. We're farther down the beach than I thought we were. I feel an urgent rush bubbling from inside as lightning strikes behind me.

"It's getting bad out. We need shelter, Des. The lighthouse," Gage says, his grip on my hand tightens. Our fingers are intertwined, there's no breaking free.

"No," I say, my voice wavers and shows my fear. I curse myself for being transparent. I gave him control again. "The lighthouse has been deserted for years," I say.

"It will be fine. It's shelter."

"I can't!" I protest. My oppressed emotions begin to surface.

"They scare you," he says, as if he's having an epiphany. His voice carries me back to a time I've spent years trying to forget.

"No," I insist, but the memory pulls at me.

I have no choice. There's a bond like no other; one I can never break. One I can never get away from. Gage has captivated me, intrigued me with knowledge, and now I am his.

My numb fingers tap against my wet jeans and I shake my head.

"You don't have to let them scare you. You don't have to be afraid."

"Dessy! Get back here," Daddy's deep voice demands.

I freeze dead in my tracks. My speedy-quick sneakers screech to a halt and skid against the pebbles below me.

"Where were you going?" Daddy asks, kneeling down beside me.

"To the lighthouse," I reply simply.

"You must never go there," he demands, his eyes boring into mine. I nod softly. He's never spoken like that to me.

"I won't," I promise, my baby voice wavering.

"You scared me. You can't just run away like that," he scolds. Even when he's stern, there's a warmth to his voice like no other.

"I'm sorry," I say, feeling him lift me off my feet. I like it when he carries me.

"What do The Shadows say?" he asks. I love Daddy. Daddy understands

The Shadows. He never tells me, but I think they talk to him too sometimes.

"They say that I need to enjoy today."

"Well, I agree with them," Daddy says, patting me on the shoulder before setting me down. I take his hand as we approach the blanket and umbrella. Mommy sits beneath, reading her book.

"When will you leave?" I ask.

"Soon," he says. I look into his eyes again. He's strong. He doesn't cry like I do. But there's something behind them. Something that I've never seen before.

"What's wrong?" I ask immediately. I've stopped walking and I'm waiting for him to answer.

"One day, they'll come for you too."

"Daddy, Mommy says the shadows aren't real."

"Sometimes mommies and daddies get scared too easily," he explains, "We just want everything to be okay."

"I get scared too," I say, struggling to speak over the rumble of the waves.

Daddy kneels down next to me.

"I love you so very much," he says, placing a hand on my shoulder.

"I love you too," I say.

This is it, *the shadows hiss.* This is your final moment.

"Run along to mommy now, and take good care of her," he orders. I nod softly. He wipes my runny nose on his sleeve and it's then I realize I'm crying.

"Go on. Remember to be brave," he says. I hesitate, swinging my foot back and forth, kicking the sand. His eyes linger on me before he turns his back to me.

"Daddy!" I scream, but he doesn't look back. "Daddy!"

I watch my daddy slowly slip away to the lighthouse, The Shadows consume him.

That night in my bedroom, The Shadows sit with me, constraining me. I hear my mother around me, but all I feel are the shadows where her arms should be. Mommy's crying and she can't find the words to explain what happened. Eventually she lets me go and rolls over. Her tears have stopped. The Shadows flood my room. They watch us like ravens, looming over my bed. Mommy can't cry anymore. She just curls up, into a tiny ball, knees to her chest, her breathing finally steady. I can't talk about The Shadows anymore.

Mommy doesn't understand.

Mist rolls in, engulfing us in my cloud of hazy memories.

"You didn't," I gasp, jolting back to reality.

"I saw everything," Gage admits, pulling me in for a hug. I sink into his arms and let my pent up emotions free for the first time since that night. "It's okay," he comforts, "it's all okay."

"I don't understand," I say, pulling away to look into his eyes.

"You and I share something very special, Deseray. Our paths are not just intertwined, but have joined. This is the start of something written in the stars. We're connected by The Shadows, and that connection will only deepen. It's by that connection you were able to let me in, to let me see."

"No," I say, suddenly feeling violated. I push him away and he stumbles backwards, catching himself before falling down. I clutch my hands at my sides. That was *my* memory. How dare—

"Des, we need to go to the lighthouse! It's getting worse out here. Please, can't we talk when we're inside? I'll explain everything. Your father would want-"

"Just stop!" I hiss, holding out my hand. I need to get a grip.

"I need you to be safe," Gage commands.

My heart pounds. My ears are hot. My body is cold. He sounds possessive. What does he care if I'm safe or not? Why would care about me? This was a mistake. I should've never come out with him.

Turn back, Dessy, The Shadows beg.

"Fine," I say and I push past Gage, trudging over to the lighthouse. I face the brutal wind, but I'll make it.

The lighthouse's ominous presence looms over the beach. As we move closer, it appears to grow. The Shadows flood around it, crashing against the worn exterior.

"Aren't you coming?" Gage asks.

"No," I say boldly.

"Why not?" he sounds like a disappointed child. Not at all the angry response I'm expecting.

"I can't," I say, turning around. I feel the lighthouse screaming at me to come inside. I'm on the brink of taking my chances with the storm. As if in protest, thunder claps and lightning crackles mere feet away.

"Remember to be brave." Gage strikes an inner chord by using my father's last words.

I love the numbing cold wind outside. I hold my breath, wishing I didn't have to feel anything. Wishing I could forget the memories.

Gage grabs my hand and with a sudden jerk, he pulls me toward him. His eyes piece into mine. Their pale blue only reminiscent of what once was there earlier in the evening. With a short pang in my wrist, I jolt back to reality.

"I am brave," I say powerfully.

"Good. After you," he says, pulling the door wide open. He pushes me

 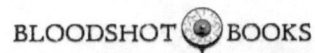

inside before I can change my mind.

The liquid in my ears pounds out a steady staccato rhythm. I look around the dark tower, making out glimpses of shadowy objects.

"Here," Gage says. The sharp switch of a match. I gasp and catch a whiff of a smell that's been absent for far too long. My father's tobacco. It fills my lungs and tears of bittersweet memories surge forward. But with my next breath, it vanishes as if it were nothing more than a distant dream.

The winding stairs circle to my right. How high does it go? What's at the top?

"Bigger than it looks," Gage's voice echoes in the cobweb-filled stairwell. I follow Gage up the stairs. My fingers trail along the dusty wall, leaving behind a streak of new where the old consumes.

"What would you like to see?" Gage's daunting voice suddenly raises the hairs on my arms. A flash of light overpowers my vision and I see a fleeting shimmer of a man with my father's soft eyes.

"What?" I ask, jolting back to the stairwell all too quickly. I look down and realize I'm easily twenty feet high already.

"Did you say something?" Gage inquires.

"No," I say, doing my best to sound decisive.

The Shadows follow behind me, methodically covering the stairs as soon as the light wavers away. The squeak of the lantern sets my nerves on edge. My eyes widen as the squeaking abruptly halts. I bump into Gage's back before realizing that he's stopped climbing. He turns to me and holds the lantern high to his face. His eyes flood my mind, erasing all consciousness, and I fall helpless to his enigmatic energy.

A soft red light surrounds me, enveloping the world around me into a bitter, surreal focus. Feet dangle in front of me, kicking violently. My eyes follow the legs and I see two trembling hands grasping at the rope around his neck. The hard grunts in perfect rhythm with the kicks. His entrancing hazel eyes nearly unrecognizable as the red, bloodshot eyeballs threaten to pop from the darkened sockets. His eyes are full of sheer terror. His purple face is swollen and pudgy. Sweat pours from his forehead, dripping onto the floor. His choking falls silent and his body falls limp, drooping and slowly swaying from side to side.

"Dessy," Gage's sing-song voice teases, snapping me back to reality with the harsh sting of a rubber band.

I drop to my knees. I want to break down. I want to give up. I stare up at

Gage's dead eyes; they mock.

"What was that?" I demand to know, hoisting myself up.

"I'm the keeper of secrets." A wicked smile plays at his lips.

"I want to go back." I clutch my stomach.

"My Shadows aren't going to let you go now. We've come too far." *His* Shadows?

"I'm going to be sick," I manage, stumbling up the stairs. I can't fall behind. Fear surges through my veins. I feel the shadows sting and try to pull me down. They grip my ankles, locking me in place, paralyzing me for a mere second.

The Shadows crawl out from all corners of the darkness. I run in a desperate hope to catch up with Gage. I trip up the stairs, but am quick to my feet. I can't fall behind...

"Run, run, run, as fast as you can," Gage's playful voice chimes through the lighthouse. My foot crushes the rotten wood and falls through the stair. My weight crashes down....

C - R - A - C - K

My wrist buckles. A yelp of pain escapes. There's no time to get up. The Shadows fill me with an excruciating pain matched by no other. The happiness flees from my soul and the will to live slowly slips away. An ear-piercing scream fills the tall lighthouse and I soon realize it's my own. Searing pain relentlessly jabs my entire body over and over again. I grit my teeth and clutch the stair above me to pull myself up. Free. But only because The Shadows love the chase. My feet stumble over each other as I strive to catch up with Gage and escape the deadly grasp of The Shadows.

"You can't catch me..." Gage's voice trails off.

I reach the top and look around. My wrist throbs in sync with my heart. The room is bare, but the vibrant Shadow energy is stronger than ever. The lantern shines in the corner and I jerk my head toward him.

"Deseray," he breathes out softly, as if it's a poem in and of itself.

I'm debilitated by the powerful scent of my father's sweet tobacco. I cry out, falling to my knees; images of his mangled and purple face refuse to exit my mind.

"I've waited a long time for this," Gage's venomous voice spits. His footsteps near me, rattling against the old rotten wooden floor.

"Please," I say like a soft dog-like whimper.

His low growl reverberates through my body. "I like it when you beg."

I feel my flesh creep as if it wants to slowly slink away. *Remember to be brave,* my father's voice booms in my mind.

 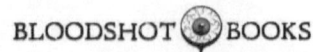

"Look at me," Gage demands.

I don't want to look, but I feel compelled. His pale, elongated fingers caress my cheek as I look up at him. "Good," he praises. His fierce eyes light up in their black sockets and that bone-chilling smile appears.

"I want to show you something." He opens his coat to reveal tiny little pockets. Some of them glow... reds... blues... a purple. Some are pitch black.

"Oh yes, I have lots of goodies to offer."

He runs his hands to the side as if to demonstrate his full inventory. He pulls a tiny vial from one of the radiant blue pockets, the light follows it. He opens the other side of his coat and again streams his hand from top to bottom. This time, it's full of dangling shrunken heads, spinning slightly as they're hooked by the gray straws of their withered hair.

"What are you doing?" I ask.

The heads glint at me, shriveled and worthless. I look away, forcing the bile back down my throat.

"It's not often I get to show off my..." he pauses to flaunt a sinister smile, "collection. Your father's essence is in here somewhere," he says, feeling all his pockets.

"My-my," I blubber over my words.

"Your... your..." he mocks. His eyes glower.

His eyes pierce mine and I can't look away no matter how hard I try.

"You're so young and innocent, so sweet and savory. But you were far too young when I first discovered you." He shakes his head, clicking his tongue. "I've been waiting for you to ripen. And now..."

"Leave me alone!" I demand, pushing him away. He smacks the wall with a hard thud. He smiles and shakes it off.

"I'm not cruel," he says, looking at me. His eyes soften just a bit as he inches closer. "Just because I'm soulless doesn't mean I'm evil."

My chest constricts my heart, locking it in place.

"At least My Shadows warned you about your father. Surely you're grateful for such things?" I bite my lip. As if he did some great favor by sending his Shadows to warn me. Anger swells inside.

"Oh, but Dessy, you were so little... You deserved a bit of warning."

His eyes penetrate my innermost thoughts. I feel his own Shadow slink into my body. My flesh creeps like little bugs are crawling under my skin.

"I'm The Keeper. I keep the Shadows... the Souls... the Essence."

I'm silent.

"They do exactly as I say... hurt who I say... kill who I say... I hold their essence. I am their Keeper. And soon, I will be your Keeper too. Are you ready?"

"Never," I spit.

"Very well. Let's talk until you are. You didn't know your father very well, did you?"

"I knew him well enough," I grunt. I go to take a swing at Gage. I have to escape. I have to get out of here. He dodges and shakes his head.

"Hold her," he says calmly, and The Shadows swarm, paralyzing me.

"Your father could see The Shadows too, did you know that?"

I struggle to get free, but The Shadows are too strong.

"Your father actually thought he could take me out. He wanted to protect you. You're so strong, Dessy. Well, at least I thought you were. You would think as the supposed Chosen One you would be a little more charismatic."

I grit my teeth and ask, "Chosen One?"

"Oh yes. You're to free The Shadows. But if you ask me, you were always destined to become one. I loved killing your father. He put up a fight for a good long while. Much better than what you're doing. Honestly, Des, he would be so disappointed." Gage shakes his head slowly.

I ball my fists, allowing the energy of The Shadows to consume me. I beg them to let me use the energy. Something from deep within shoots out and casts a bright light around me, knocking the shadows back.

"Impressive," Gage compliments with a smile. "But not good enough. You should be excited, Des. A fresh start to a new decade. Happy Birthday, by the way. Oh! Your present!" he exclaims.

He pulls one of the tiny heads from his pocket. Its mouth is stitched shut with giant black string. Its eyes are sewed shut. The tuft of blonde hair is pulled back into the finest ponytail he uses to dangle the head in front of me. The skin is stretched and old, deep leathery wrinkles consume the eye lines. Bony cheeks prominently stand out.

Gage drips a single drop of the illuminating blue potion on the top of the head. My father's mangled remains contort to a twisted knot. His mouth moves and a deep moan fills the air. His eyelids twitch but stand no chance against the stitches.

"Deseray..." the muffled voice of my father resounds in my ears.

"No!" I scream, knocking Gage to the ground... with my raging anger, with my energy gathered from the shadows, I'm not quite sure which.

"Ooh, look at you, all empowered," Gage teases.

I won't let him get to me. I feel the electric energy buzzing in palms and when I look I see light filling them. What's happening to me? I force the energy from my palms. I watch Gage twitch as the lightning energy zaps him. His body convulses and twists. I smile to myself. I love watching him writhe in pain... but it feels so wrong.

I stand there, captivated by his body trapped in the lightning. My palms still buzz with energy. I can see the light stronger than ever. I deliver more shock and watch as his body pulses in pain. His lips are withered and dry. His face is old and worn. I'm sucking the life from him.

I hear a sharp pop and bolts of lights fill the room... reds... purples... blues... it's the essence. It's all breaking free. As the essence breaks, The Shadows fly off... escaping his clutches once and for all.

Kill him, quickly! The Shadows beg. They're free now. Their bond was broken long ago and now I'm just... torturing.

"Deseray... you've freed them. Now let me go," he begs. His eyes are no longer empty... they hold a soul... his soul... My heart tears. I can't do this. The crackle of the lightening stops and the buzzing returns to my fists.

He slowly climbs to his feet, his body shaky.

"Look at what you've done," he says. My heart lurches and tears surface as I see the burn marks across his face.

"I may have lost my collection tonight, but I will not lose you," he vows. He takes in a deep breath and I feel my soul start to go with it. I lose my breath and my body freezes. I beg for the energy to return to me, but it doesn't listen. I had my chance. I was too weak. My body feels cold, empty... my eyes will soon be blank like his. I can't go on... I don't want to. He's taken everything from me.

"Daddy," I say, running toward him. I fall into his arms and hold him close.

"I am so proud of you, my sweet Deseray," he says, kissing me on the forehead.

"Why can I see you?" I ask after a minute.

"You're different now, Des. You're The Keeper. You were too strong for Gage."

"But."

"Shh, it's okay," he promises, "You can protect those who see the shadows. You're better than Gage. You will set things right. You're the chosen one."

"Daddy..." but I can't find the words to continue. I close my eyes but am unable to stop the tears. I know what's coming. I don't know how, but I just know. My arms tighten around him and I feel him slowly slip away.

I awake the next night, just in time to catch the bright green flash as the sun slips beneath the waves. My father has found peace. He's entered the next world.

I meander into town. I feel the flesh sacks hurry past me, eager to get back to the warmth of their houses. I see one of my shadows trailing behind and I smile. He once told me his name was Gage. That was eons ago. Now, I am his keeper. One day I will send him to find peace... but not tonight.

Kya wrote her first novel at thirteen and didn't stop there. Now, nine novels later at twenty years old, she's turned her reading and writing addiction into a career she loves. She self-published five books in her teen years, and is now branching out and exploring more traditional publication opportunities. She is a full time writer living with her husband in the beautiful Virginia area. Writing is her greatest passion in life; she's found her calling in the horror world. Ever since she read her first Stephen King novel, she's been hooked.

Always eager to learn, Kya Aliana will be the first to spark up a conversation with a fellow author. She always strives to improve with each story as she steadily masters the several dark layers of horror.

She has dedicated this story to Taylor Grant.

TEETH
BY MARK CARROLL

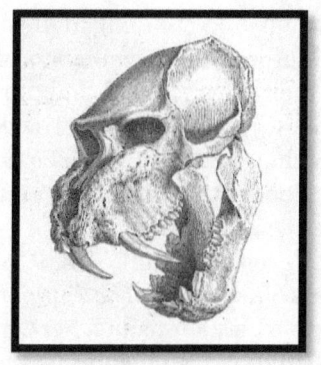

P.J. woke from the nightmare about her Alec; she'd heard something wrong. Naturally, that meant checking on the stuffed spiders under her bed; stuffed, because the monster that used to live there didn't know the difference. She sniffled, remembering the night she and Alec had driven it from under her bed and into the closet.

How brave he'd been, all fury and claws and teeth, covered in blood - his and the other's. She remembered what he'd whispered to her as he grew cold in her arms. The monster in the closet hissed at her from its perch atop the clothes rack, but the red ribbon and the sachet Gramma taught her to make still dangled from the closet doorknob, and that was all it could do. She gritted her teeth and got to work.

She dug her flashlight out from beneath her pillow and swept the room with the circle of light. She heard the strange sound again. The flashlight flickered, so she turned it off, biting her lower lip like Mother told her not to. Everything was fine in her cold little room, so the sound must have come from outside.

P.J. shivered. She remembered huddling in the downstairs bathroom, in the tub with Daddy and Mother, while the Big Storm blew through the County. It blasted down their street, a thousand thousand angry animals scratching at the walls, the windows, the roof. The door was closed, but the bathroom's little window showed them the strobe flashes of lightning. Thunder shook the walls, louder than the rain and wind and the witches Gramma said rose above all such storms.

The storm passed, and even without the TV, P.J. kept herself amused. She had her books: art books, *Nancy Drew*, *The Hunger Games*, history books, and old books Gramma gave her; her paints; her camera that used to be Daddy's before he got a better one; and binoculars to watch for interesting things. She kept the last two close by, just in case. P.J. figured a strange sound somewhere was a 'just in case.' She picked up the binoculars and crept along the floor to her window to look out.

Junk was everywhere – leaves and limbs and paper and siding and trashcans. Lots of the houses were dark because their families had moved away after the Big Storm. P.J. figured maybe six families stayed on her street, scattered around, windows still taped and backed with plywood; that left a lot of sad, empty, broken houses. She couldn't see much more with the dim light of an early morning, but something kept tickling her eyes, making her blink and tear up. She rubbed, yawned, and slid down from the window, ready to go back to sleep. Movement caught her eye and held it.

There was something in the mirror that wasn't there. P.J. stopped, not daring to let her own reflection show up in the silvered glass. The mirror was one Gramma insisted Mother give to her. They'd fought about it, and she remembered all of the shouting and words she didn't understand, at least not then. In the end, Gramma got her way and P.J. had her mirror, which she kept polished and clean.

The thing in the mirror kept moving, so she focused in on it. Her head turned this way and that, trying to make it out, and she found the right angle.

"Uh oh," she said, under her breath. There was a boojum.

She was just ten, but Daddy called her 'precocious,' Mother called her 'precious,' and Gramma called once a week to dream about strange things to her. P.J. giggled, covering her mouth so the boojum couldn't catch the sound and eat it. She kept watching.

The boojum was a little twisted thing, a ragdoll-sized shadow, all a-swirl with thin little straps that cracked like whips, or Daddy's belt when he'd sneak up on her and make the leather pop to make her shriek and chase him around the house. There were little white things all along the straps, and the leather belts that pulled the boojum around like a centipede's legs made it look much bigger than it really was. P.J. knew that boojums and beasties did that sometimes to make themselves look bigger, like birds puffing themselves up or lizards showing their necks all red.

It crept out of the upstairs window of the Quinlans' house, and started walking down the side, the wiggling straps snapping to tree branches and the fallen power pole to steady its way. The Quinlans were a family that still lived on their street. P.J. played with their son sometimes.

She frowned, then remembered the binoculars in her hand. P.J. brought them to her eyes and looked at the boojum, now much-expanded in her vision, and sucked in a breath. Up close, P.J. glimpsed ugly wrinkles and spindly fingers, squinty eyes above a long, witchy nose. Its teeth were crooked and wrong, too big for its mouth; P.J. saw why. The wriggling, snatchy straps had teeth in them, stuck in the oily, filthy leather, each atop a darker stain. P.J. could guess what those were, too.

She watched it creep down, then across the street to one of the sad houses, slipping into the shadows. Just like Nancy Drew, P.J. snuck over to her desk and got out a notepad, flipping to a clean page, noting which house it was. She got a picture, with the camera, too. Evidence. There wasn't anything she could do until Mother or Daddy got her up, so she went back to bed, snuggled a pillow, and dreamed about silver coins falling from the moon.

"Daddy, what does the Tooth Fairy look like?" she asked.

Daddy put a serious expression on, which meant he was getting ready to kid with her. Mother rolled her eyes while she was taking down tape from a window, and stuck her tongue out at P.J. She giggled, since a good mood meant that Daddy and Mother would be more likely to answer her questions and think nothing more of it.

"Well, Pea," he said, scratching his stubble. "The Tooth Fairy's supposed to be really tiny, and she's got wings to fly around. Sort of like Tinkerbell, I guess."

"What does she do with the teeth?" P.J. pressed, eating her cereal, watching them.

Daddy looked at Mother with a raised eyebrow, like Spock on TV.

"Got an opinion, hon?" he asked, teasing. "I think the Tooth Fairy takes them to Tooth Knox, but..."

Mother yanked a particularly sticky piece of tape down, and hmphed.

"Don't turn this into a game, Franklin," she said, wadding the tape up and throwing it into a cardboard box. "Fairies are serious business. Nobody knows where the Tooth Fairy takes the teeth, or what she does with them."

Daddy rolled his eyes in perfect imitation of her, then winked at P.J. and Mother; Mother laughed as she left the room, box in hand.

"Well, Sweet Pea, it sounds like it's a mystery," he said, mock seriously. "Tell you what – soon as the library opens up, I'll walk with you down there and you can look it up, okay?"

"Okay!" P.J. declared. She knew she could find out about the boojum in the back rooms of the library.

"Think you can ride your bike back?" he asked. "I've got to help around the house."

"Uh huh."

"It's a done deal, then. Finish your cereal, kid, then we'll head out," Daddy said.

Her bowl went into the trash bag, since the water was off and it was plastic anyway. She wiped her hands off after using the big bottle of Purell and started for the garage. She'd almost made it before Mother caught up with her.

"Why were you asking about the Tooth Fairy, honey?" she asked, sitting on the stairs next to the living room. "You're a little old for that, aren't you?"

P.J. sighed. This always happened when Mother thought anything strange might be going on. It had something to do with Gramma; they didn't get along. P.J. thought Gramma was neat.

She had no choice but to answer, truthfully. It was one of Those Things.

"I saw a boojum coming out of the Quinlans' this morning," she said. "I thought it might be the Tooth Fairy, but I didn't know for sure, so I asked you and Daddy."

Mother paled, the tired circles under her eyes darkening. Rubber-gloved fingers went to her forehead above her left eyebrow, rubbing.

"Pea, we've talked about this, honey," she murmured, trying to loosen the knot P.J. knew was under her fingers. "There's no such thing as boojums. No.

Such. Thing. Okay?"

"But mother..."

"No, Petra Jane," Mother said, louder. "We are not having this discussion again. We had it when you said there was a boojum under your bed, then when there was another one in your closet..."

"Mom, it was the same one...!"

"No, it wasn't, because it's not real!" she snapped. "I don't care what Gramma told you. There are no such things as boojums. Do you understand?"

"But...!"

"Enough! Not one more word about this, do you understand?" Mother said, voice sharp.

P.J. sniffed, ducked her head, and nodded. Mother was more than cross, well into angry, and if she pushed it any more, she wouldn't be able to go to the library to speak to Miss Thomasina. Dismissed, she shuffled to the garage to get her bike.

"Hey, kid," said Daddy. "You going to be okay? I overheard."

"Uh huh," P.J. said, very, very softly. "I'll be okay, Dad."

He ruffled her hair, face brightening with a smile.

"It's the storm. It's got everyone rattled, even your old man," he teased. "I think getting you out and about will do you both a world of good."

Daddy started out of the garage, and the clouds started to lift from P.J. He was always the peacemaker, and sometimes P.J. thought he used to be a cowboy or sheriff in the old days, before he was Daddy. *The Dad with No Name*, roaming the Old West, making people stop fighting with kind words and a smile instead of a gun. Of course, he had a gun, but that was because he was a policeman in the City.

As they walked, P.J. watched the streets, especially the shadows. There were other kinds of boojums that came out after something bad happened - boojums for accidents - sometimes crowds of them for car wrecks, boojums for fires, and boojums for floods. Gray men and hollow men and women with crow's eyes all out to do something bad to nice people. The thought made her shiver, her heart felt heavy and slow. She remembered Alec, her fuzzy buddy, her cat, legs planted, back arched, eyes aglow in the moonlight as he hissed and spat at the boojum from under her bed.

He'd been so brave. He was just a cat, but she was his human, too. When the boojum wanted to drag her off to the other side of the darkness, he fought like his bigger forebears, all claws and fangs and fury. Alec gave her time to drive the boojum into the closet where P.J. could trap it. She'd been crying when she carried his still, cooling body to the street.

When Mother found him the next morning, she thought he'd been hit by a car. It hurt to think of. P.J. missed him, and she hated lying. Grownups didn't understand the battles little kids fought until they were very old and wise like

Gramma.

Daddy had helped make a little wooden box for Alec, and the three of them had buried him in the backyard, in the spot where he liked to sun himself. Mother had said Words in the Old Tongue, which she never did. But she had, and for a little while, she and Gramma didn't fight. It didn't last, which made P.J. sadder still.

"Penny?" Daddy asked. He'd stopped. "For your thoughts."

P.J. squinted her eyes, sniffed, and wiped at the tears. Daddy caught it all in the reflection off the library's window, and wrapped a heavy, warm arm around her.

"We all loved him, and he loved us," he said, softly. "But he loved you best. He was a good boy, a brave cat. Petra, I'm so sorry."

For a while, they sat there on the curb, with the junk and the fallen branches, the leaves and the glass, eyes raining in the afternoon sun.

That made her smile. In his way, even as a grownup, he believed her. He didn't ask what had really happened to Alec, not because he didn't want to know, but because he trusted the secrets children kept. P.J. thought Mother knew what happened, but she didn't want to. Mother came from the City, so that was understandable.

The City was a Bad Place. When they drew in class, P.J. made beautiful maps, and whenever she drew maps of the County, where the City was always had the legend 'Here There Be Monsters.' That was a true thing, and the children nodded solemnly when the grownups weren't looking.

"Looks like we're here, kid," Daddy said, smiling again. It had been a good cry, and they both felt better. "You know the rules-"

"Uh huh. Back before dark, come back right away after I'm done, and if I'm late, call. I know, Dad."

"Love you, kid," Father said, kissing the top of her head. "Be good, and watch out for those boojums, huh?"

The interior of the library was cool and dim, even with the big battery-powered lights the workers had strung up since the power went out. P.J. smiled to herself, and waved at the kids and teenagers reading, at the librarians, getting vague replies back. She went among the stacks, headed for the back rooms.

Nobody but staff was supposed to go into the back rooms of the library. They were left over after the original building burned down. The grownups called the back rooms the vaults, because that was where the very old and valuable things were kept safe. After the fire, the county people had left them in place instead of demolishing them, saying it was historical. That suited P.J. fine, because the back rooms were where she knew she could find Miss Thomasina.

"Hello?" she called, once she'd slipped past the door hidden behind the stacks. "Miss Thomasina?"

The room scented of dust, of old paper, the tang of newsprint, and the smell of all of the cats that had moved in. Lithe shapes glided through the shadows, eyes glittering in the gloom, watching her. A few growled and purred and muttered, but most remained a silent Parliament.

P.J. stepped to a circle of light nearly in the center of the room and waited.

"Hello, dear," Miss Thomasina said.

Miss Thomasina was old-young today, a woman with hair that might be silver, might be white, or even calico. Looking at her, one couldn't have placed her age; she seemed anywhere between forty and seventy. As P.J. watched, she saw more of Miss Thomasina, the old person clothes, the folded hands, the bright eyes, the sharp teeth.

"I seek secret knowledge, the knowledge of the moon, the knowledge of the sun, I come seeking the wisdom of your Parliament," P.J. said. Gramma had taught her the words. "I come to beg a boon of the children of Bastet, of Sekhmet, for yours is the knowledge of shadows and whispers."

Miss Thomasina nodded formally. Around her, the cats lay, or sat. None moved, all eyes upon P.J.

"You speak well and true, for a human," Miss Thomasina said. "You speak the words that most humans have forgotten save in dreams, and your Alec is known to this Parliament. We would hear your boon, Petra Jane Connor, human of Alec."

"There's a boojum," she said. "I saw it, and I think it hurt the Quinlans. I want t make it stop before it hurts anyone else."

"What does our Parliament care of humans that become prey?" Miss Thomasina asked, contemptuously. "But the Parliament knows your secret heart, Petra, we know what you truly desire. It is a thing we have knowledge of."

P.J. blinked, caught off-guard.

"I don't understand," she said. "I need to know how to stop the boojum, that's all."

The smile widened, and Miss Thomasina stretched, pacing around P.J.'s circle of light, strutting with the surety of knowing what P.J. did not.

"We know your secret, dreaming heart. We smell your true desire in your tears," she fairly purred. "You wish to bring Alec Five Lives back to you, to guard you at night, to pet during days. We know how to do this, and should like to share it."

Each word was a blow, and P.J.'s heart thudded in her chest, tears rising unbidden to her eyes. Gramma had told her the nature of cats. Cats liked to play with their food. P.J. swallowed the pain and tears. She found her voice. She wasn't the prey here.

"That is a true thing you speak," she said, and the Parliament of Cats smiled as one. "But it is not my boon. My boon is the secret knowledge of defeating the boojum."

"For Alec Five Lives' sake, we will grant this boon, child of man," Miss Thomasina whispered, the sound of the Parliaments' bodies moving, their claws scratching. The voice of the Parliament smiled. "But the cost will be blood and innocence. Alec Five Lives will never return to you."

The voice of the Parliament spoke again, and spoke truly.

P.J. stopped a block from home, looking into the darkened windows of the sad house, and was sure the boojum could see her. That was good. She had a few hours of daylight left to start putting things together, to think about what the Parliament had said to her.

Boojums couldn't be hurt by regular people most of the time. That hadn't been a surprise, because of what Gramma had told her about the boojum in the closet. They couldn't be really hurt because they weren't really real, only a little real, but they could be locked away and bound. Every boojum was different, so what had worked on the under the bed (now closet) boojum wouldn't work on the tooth fairy boojum.

P.J. hadn't wanted to speak to the cats, but Gramma only had a few teeth left, and she didn't want Gramma to lose them. The idea made her smile after a moment's reflection. Any boojum that tried to mess with her Gramma would end up bottled, jarred, or sent back to the Wherever with its butt on fire.

The cats had told her what to do, and she didn't like it one bit. She'd have to get her slingshot and shoot a bird. After that, before the moon rose, she'd have to go to the back yard to do the ugly part of the business. She stuck her tongue out at the boojum's sad house, and made a face at it, what she thought of as her mean witch face. The Parliament of Cats had told her that the boojum would need to be challenged and made to think she wasn't afraid of it. They had also advised she grow better claws in case the business didn't work, but that wasn't happening.

She pedaled, feeling the boojum's eyes on her, making her neck hair rise. She looked over her shoulder and spat, hard, a real loogie that splatted against the curb. It made her feel mean, but after what the cats had said and done, feeling mean was good. She could hear the leather straps it whipped around creak and snap angrily against the windows and walls of the sad house. It couldn't come out during the daytime, as she'd suspected, which was good. That made it mad, and making the boojum mad was even better.

Mad boojums were stupid. They could also be much more dangerous, but P.J. thought she had this one's number. It was a Sneaky Pete, which was what the pirate in her favorite books called things that skulked and slunk and that he had no patience for. She didn't have the pirate's ship, or his jolly crew, or a cutlass, but she had the business, and that would have to be good enough. She looped around at the end of the block, headed for the Quinlans'. She'd have to see what the boojum had done before getting down to the real business.

The block over from hers was empty, families fled before the Big Storm to more hospitable climes or to the City. That made it easy for her to ride low and do some Sneaky Pete-ing herself, leaving her bike leaning against the splintered fence while she crept through a gap in the boards. The back door wasn't locked.

There was a smell inside the dark house. Something wet and foul, thick with iron, rotten. P.J. gagged, pulling her shirt up to cut the stink. She moved slowly, fighting the urge to run back out. Every shadow, every creak of the battered old house might be a warning, a boojum, or just itself, and there was no way to tell them apart.

P.J. stopped cold at the threshold of the living room. Mr. Quinlan was still on the couch, would always be on the couch, at least until the police came. She had enough time to see what the boojum had done, written in his wide-wider open mouth, his empty gums, the ruin of his eyes, then she ran, yanking her shirt down before breakfast came out in a sour flood, splashing on the kitchen linoleum. She didn't stop until she was outside the fence, breathing hard to get the stink out of her lungs.

P.J. mounted her bike and pedaled away, down the empty street and down a few long, lonely blocks, trying to hold it together; it's what Daddy would do, she thought.

He was in the front yard, hauling out bags of leaves and sticks to the curb when she wheeled into the driveway. Mother smiled at her from the big window in the living room, which meant the moods of the morning had passed. She wanted to tell them what she'd seen, but it was her fight now; the boojum would come after her next.

"Hey, squirt," Daddy said, wiping his brow with one gloved hand. "You have fun at the library?"

P.J. shrugged, feeling worn out from talking to the cats and being mad and what she'd seen.

"I guess so," she said. "Is it okay if I go take a nap before dinner, Dad? I'm pooped."

He laughed.

"Sure, kid. Sack out for a while when mom and I are doing all the hard work," he teased.

P.J. stuck her tongue out at him and did her best imitation of a flounce as she headed inside, aiming straight for the stairs. Keeping it together.

"Petra, are you all right?" Mother called. "You look flushed. Your father said you cried on the way to the library."

P.J. dropped her backpack, and diverted to the kitchen. She knew how Mother would react if she didn't. Mother was feeling guilty about yelling that morning.

"Uh huh," she said. "It still hurts, you know? It's been so long, but it still hurts."

Mother came over, saying nothing, and wrapped P.J. in her arms. She held her daughter close, stroking her hair, playing the dark strands out between her fingers as if she intended to weave the night into cloth.

"I'm sorry, honey," Mother whispered. "I know he meant a lot to you, means a lot to you. He's still here, and you know cats have nine lives..."

That brought forth the hurt that P.J. held since the Parliament had spoken, and the tears came, hot and stinging.

"He's not coming back, mom," she sobbed, voice ragged.

Mother stroked her hair, and kissed the top of her head when it was all done, looking sad and awful.

"Sweetie, why don't you go read or take a nap until we're ready to eat," she said. "I'll call you when it's ready, all right?"

P.J. nodded and went upstairs. She didn't sleep, or read. Instead, washed her mouth out, checked the sachet, checked her mirror, and got some things out for the business. The little trowel had come from Mother trying to get her interested in gardening. When P.J. grew the kinds of plants and herbs Gramma suggested, she'd been furious and decided that gardening wasn't what P.J. really wanted to do. The knife had come from Gramma, passed over by hand with an admonition to not let Mother know she had it. The slingshot she'd bought with saved allowance money, just in case. Tonight was 'in case', she thought.

Dinner was quiet, punctuated with small talk and the rasp of plasticware on the disposable dishes. Daddy had cooked beer can chicken on the grill, with all of the trimmings, one of her favorites. Mother made sure that everyone got enough, and took over cleaning up. When P.J. rose, Mother reached out and touched her hand.

"Petra," she said. "What are you up to?"

"Nothing," P.J. muttered, feeling guilty enough already. "I was gonna go out back is all..."

"Petra," Mother repeated. "You have that look. I heard you rummaging in your drawers upstairs. The ones you think we don't know about. Where you keep your special things. Honey, please... tell me."

P.J. squirmed. She didn't want to lie, but Mother would keep her inside if she told the truth, which meant that the boojum would be free to do its nastiness. They'd wake up with no teeth in their heads, or worse.

"I don't want to say," she admitted, voice small and quiet. "You'll get mad."

"Is it about what you said this morning?"

The blush came to P.J.'s face, furious red, hot, making her skin prickle. She nodded.

 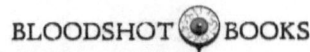

"I see," Mother said, sitting down next to her.

P.J.'s eyes widened, and the blush retreated, replaced by ashes. She nodded again. "It was a boojum, mom," she said. "I swear it was. I saw it in the mirror. It's bad."

Mother looked at her for a long, considering moment. P.J. felt the tears coming again and bit her lower lip. She'd be sent to her room, and the business wouldn't happen. Then the boojum would come. She didn't even have Alec to help her this time.

"Go," Mother said, kissing the top of her head. "Do what you need to do, honey. I'll keep Daddy in our room tonight. We love you so much, you know that, right?"

When P.J. ran up the stairs, it felt like flying.

The sick feeling had come back as the rubber of the slingshot snapped. The grackle screeched, its wing broken, tumbling to earth. This was the business, she told herself. Gramma told her there was always a price, and that the price was too high, so the business had to be done carefully. It was scary and bad, but P.J. knew it was what Father called 'necessary evil.' If she didn't do it, who would?

The bird fluttered weakly, pecking at her hands when she picked it up. That hurt, and she'd need to wash the pecks out after everything was done. Her blood trickled out of the wounds, mixing with the black feathers of the big bird. The blood was part of the business, too. She walked to the spot where Alec was buried, where she'd been digging, and set the grackle in the big, shallow salad bowl.

She swallowed, pressing her lips together, trying hard not to think about this part, about how easy it was to slip the little knife Gramma gave her into the grackle's breast, to snap its ribcage and still its heart, to release the blood into the little pile of herbs and dirt from Alec's grave. She held it there until the bird stopped struggling, and kept going. Necessary evil, necessary evil, she thought.

When it was done, the moon hadn't come out. She mixed and ground and pressed everything together. She managed to keep from crying until she pried open the box Alec was in, until she smelled him. Then the tears became part of the business too. Cats told the truth after all.

Black cat bone and van van oil. A bundle of feathers from a black bird killed under the dark of the moon. Goofer dust from the sachet. It was bigger than it was when it hung on her closet door, and uglier. The scents of lemongrass and citronella mixed with richer, darker ones, earth and blood. She'd made it just like the cats had told her. The business. She spoke the words then. The most important words of all.

"I love you, mister Alec," she said, lowering the little box into the grave. "I'm sorry, I'm sorry. I love you."

NOT YOUR AVERAGE MONSTER

The moon came out then, casting butter-silver light across her face.

She left the window open, after she'd taken her mirror down and positioned it just so. Her door was locked, Mother and Daddy were in their room. Moonlight slid across her floor, and P.J. sat with the mojo in her hands, shaking, letting the fear wash over her and out of her, making her sweat. The boojum could smell it, and that was fine. It masked the smell of what she had, the business.

When it came, it was fast, leather straps whipping and creaking and snapping. It stank, worse than she'd thought. It heaved itself through her open window, its apple-granny wrinkled face looking for her. She'd challenged it, and its kind were proud. She'd made it mad, and that made it stupid. The stench of it made her want to heave, and her stomach quailed.

In P.J.'s hands, the mojo moved. Feathers rustled, and she held it out to the moon, letting the light fall across it. The boojum heard the noise, and hissed, jabbering at her. It whipcracked its leather straps at her, the teeth embedded in them screeching like a fork dragged across a fine china bowl. She screamed back at it, fear and challenge. It went for her, yattering, throwing itself across the room in a single spasmodic movement.

She stepped back, quick, sliding sideways across her bed. Hand under her pillow, fingers closed around the slingshot, its wood still speckled with grackle blood. The boojum scented it and yowled again. It grinned, pausing to put more stolen teeth into its black gums, snapping to set them.

P.J. aimed the slingshot and fired off, missing, something delicate breaking behind the boojum. Her heart hammered in her chest, *boomboomboom*, making her shake. But the sound made the boojum turn even as its straps and apple-granny claws dug into her bedspread. She found the first piece of string she'd tied to her mirror and pulled hard.

Stuck.

She bit her lower lip, and the boojum smelled the blood. The longest of the straps whipcracked over her bed and lashed at her shoulder, shredding her shirt, biting into the skin beneath. Its yammering rose to a triumphant shriek, and more straps stabbed into the bed, lifting it halfway over in a single spasmodic movement. P.J. scrambled away, careening off her bedroom door, jerking the twine again; this time, the mirror flipped. Her hand fell on the second part of the business, and she smiled just a little. She was past the boojum, its wrinkled face and raisin-colored eyes tipped just over the edge of the bed, looking for her. She reached over and turned the big mirror, letting it catch her reflection in the shadows.

She yanked the knob on the closet door, pulling it open. When the boojum dived for her in the silver mirror, it had to pass over the closet's threshold.

P.J. wanted to close her eyes, but she knew that if she did, the mojo wouldn't work its business. She saw the whole thing. She wouldn't let herself smile when the closet boojum closed its zipper teeth and empty clothes arms over the tooth fairy. She wasn't that mean.

When it was done, the closet boojum went back to perching on the hanger rod, just a shadow among the clothes. She pushed the door closed with the broom handle, and hung the mojo on the knob. A single tooth lay on the floor. P.J. picked it up, and put it with her special things. She hung the mirror back up, tired by the end of it all.

P.J. climbed into bed, pulling the remains of the covers up, surveying the battleground, letting the shivers begin. For a moment, the moonlight and shadows and cloth looked like a black and white cat, but when she touched them, there was nothing at all.

Mark has had a lifelong love of horror that started at the age of 6, when his father took him to see Alien in the theater; he hasn't been the same since. He began writing horror fiction at the age of 12, and parlayed that into creating roleplaying games throughout high school and college. He's since returned to writing horror, and has no plans to stop any time soon.

Mark lives in the wonderful city of Austin, Texas, with his wife Jennifer and four cats... all of whom are far too intelligent for their humans' good

BLOODSHOT BOOKS

MEKOOMWESO'S REVENANTS

BY ESTHER M. LEIPER-ESTABROOKS

NOT YOUR AVERAGE MONSTER

IT is disquieting, sinister in retrospect, the letter that brought me to my sister Melissa's house in New Hampshire. Yet shouldn't Raymond, her husband, have warned me if he held suspicions at the time of her miscarriage? I thought he was considering the benefit to me as a recent widow, for whom a change would be wise; then again, maybe not!

Even in Virginia, it was chilly on the late-winter day when I read "Dear Sarah," in Raymond's firm script. "Dr. James suggests a warmer climate for Melissa, but I believe her spirit also needs fostering. To our sorrow she miscarried, and feels a great weariness, thus I'm taking her away to Atlanta and my family, hoping to cheer her with new faces and vistas. Would you enjoy being a caretaker here in New Hampshire for a while? We don't want the home left empty and will pay your expenses and more. This good deed will, I trust, prove a pleasant change for you, plus a boon for Melissa who's feeling very low.

"She has not touched her paints since the loss of the baby and refuses to; indeed, grows wild if I mention them. Her favorite hobby gone in a blink! Frankly, Sarah, I don't understand, for I know what her talent meant. On the practical side while this request is short notice, yet the wood supply is sufficient till spring and the house is at your convenience, should you wish a change. Indeed, Melissa would be happier knowing the place neither empty nor exposed to strangers."

Certainly I was intrigued by the invitation. Since my husband John's recent passing, I'd felt directionless. The recession scotched my teaching job, though John had left me enough to get by. Still, in coming north, perhaps I could gain some perspective and look toward the future. At least I'd liked the North Country town of Peterson, based on my one previous visit.

Yes, last autumn I'd enjoyed spending a week at Melissa's white frame home with blue shutters, a place removed from neighbors, and with a backyard that swept from lawn to a wild tangle of growth merging into mountain slope. I could understand how she needed respite from her miscarriage, while I could use a change from the locale of my widowhood. There was also the lure of Indian legends, for the Abenaki tribe had once lived in New Hampshire—mostly gone now, or intermingled with white folks. Having once been a full-time teacher, I tried to absorb all I could to awaken my students' interest, plus to satisfy my own love of lore and legends.

Now as I unpacked, my thoughts swept back to the week last summer we'd shared. Melissa was overjoyed with her prospect of a baby, and we renewed our closeness. Her lawyer husband Raymond, though friendly, was preoccupied with a case, so we two had a week of being close again, giddy and

BLOODSHOT ● BOOKS

girlish. Indeed, my sister bloomed: brown hair gleaming, and eyes dancing, as she tugged me from my car on arrival. Her house proved comfortable and artistic, though much of our time we spent outside in sunny weather.

Not yet clumsy with pregnancy, Melissa was excited by her extended garden which kept her busy, so she insisted I must see it first. I expected practical rows of tomatoes, beans, and so forth, but was mistaken. We were raised as city girls, and I'd stayed one, so was unprepared for the sheer space behind her home. Past a band of lawn and colorful border of flowers, wild acres swept up to granite crags and a far skyline. Sumac and alders struggled past glacial boulders where blackberry vines tangled against scraggly pines. For me, the land seemed like wilderness. But Mel's creativity shone through it. Sensing an animal hidden in every granite shape, by cunning use of paint she had transformed various boulders into outlandish creatures—just as if a Fairy Queen—and a fey one at that—had waved her wand. A grinning frog, nearly four feet high, squatted amidst briars. Behind that, a bobcat-shape crouched while a wolf drank from a rain-water pool. The trompe l'oeil was so vivid I almost felt frog skin and animal fur. Indeed the vivid forms seemed poised ready to move; a silly fancy!

But my practical self was worried; *Why such an outlay of time and effort! Shouldn't Melissa concentrate on coming motherhood?* Aloud I asked, "What does Raymond think?"

"He doesn't see the stones as I do, *alive*," she replied. "He suggested I find some temp job for now or at least offer art lessons." She tittered, "How unnecessary! We've money enough, and why marry a lawyer if not to have a nice life? Of course I'll be tied down with the baby, so I plan to accomplish as much as possible now."

"Your child will inherit quite a kingdom," I remarked, gazing up the slope toward a far, craggy peak, and Melissa giggled, quite pleased with this ambiguous statement.

Next, on that serene morning, she took me to her basement work room filled with paint cans and gardening tools. I perched on a straw bale while she showed off gallons of acrylics, brushes of all sorts and sizes, and tucked in one corner a computer with photos on the screen; these depicted briar-hugged rocks as they appeared before, then after, their bizarre transformations.

"Yes, I'm obsessed," Melissa declared cheerfully, though I detected an undertone of defiance. She pushed back a lock of hair. "When I stare long enough, each boulder reveals its inner shape to me, and the way to transform it. I sense the mass and bulk somehow; just where its shadows are cast, plus the mood of the enduring land; night and morning, late and early."

"You're a little pagan," I'd laughed fondly. But I felt uneasy.

Now, in the present, I soberly folded Raymond's letter; read many times since I journeyed up to this alien North Country in mud season, and became a solitary guest in their home. Had I been wise? Could I count this as an odd vacation; time to get in touch with myself, so if the locale didn't suit—or they wished to return sooner than planned—I could simply move out?

But how silly to worry about the possibility of leaving when I'd barely arrived! Indeed, I had immediate, practical chores to deal with. For a start, I must daily bring in more wood for the cast iron stove, so there would always be a handy supply; and should shop as much as possible at the local "Mom and Pop;" for good will and to meet neighbors, plus write to Melissa with more candor than I chose to say by phone. Party lines were long outdated, yet small town folks had a mysteriously efficient grapevine and of course I was gossiped about as a newcomer.

I couldn't pinpoint rudeness, but the villagers proved reserved. I was an outsider, and their clannish attitude, I speculated, had started Melissa on her own solitary hobby of decorating stones. By no stretch could I imagine her playing weekly Bingo or view Raymond serving as a volunteer fireman. Yet the fire station was the most popular clubhouse for town men, while most women belonged to the Rebeccas, the female equivalent of the Oddfellows club, and lived for Bingo night.

Though I'd settled at the beginning of March, there were still several months of cold-time to cope with, so mentally I prepared for blizzards and loneliness. Yet snow, oddly, did not come. Instead the landscape was locked in by frigid fog banks and occasional vague flurries that whirled about, but refused to settle. Frost penetrated ever deeper, while the air smelled iron-tanged. The local weekly reminded readers of "sure" weather signs grandfolks swore by, concerning height of wasps' nests, behavior of crows, and so forth. Still, oldsters I observed gathered at the country store seemed uneasy, plus hushed when I came near, as if discussing matters not revealed to an outsider.

Indeed, frozen fog persisted onward from my arrival like a vast gray hand pressing on the landscape and my soul. Sometimes it parted to reveal nearer hills, yet always returned by nightfall. The temperature hovered in the teens, with roads heavily salted against glare ice. Rumors flew in the local Mom and Pop store, not told to me, but apparent in hushed whispers that ceased if I drew near.

Secrecy was disquieting, but reality could be worse. Indeed, there was a dreadful early AM auto accident just days after I arrived, occasioned—police determined—by a vast, newly-gaping pothole caused by frost heaves. Specifically, two brothers were killed and a third boy injured, when their pickup hit the hole, then swerved into a stone wall just outside the village where the speed limit opened up. The dispatched ambulance had wailed like a banshee, bringing me awake past midnight.

If lonely, I kept busy writing letters to southern friends, trying to keep an eye on stocks my husband left me, and reading books I felt I ought to. For company I adopted a white stray tomcat who moved through the house like a silver ghost; dipped into North Country history, and very soon visited the elementary school. Having been a teacher till hard times cut my job, I knew principals always needed subs, especially in flu season. What better way to learn the nature of a place than through children? I must have made a good impression on the principal, for I was called in to take an art teacher's place within a few days of my application.

Along with instructions, I was shown a pleasant room with a large supply closet at its rear which led to a second door and another room beyond. The morning passed smoothly. My skills were fresh, I was a novelty to the kids, and—unlike Melissa—enjoyed a paying job. However, during lunch break while searching out construction paper, I overheard voices in the farther classroom, and my sister's name riveted my attention.

"Melissa was so eager, letting the kids roam around touching the rocks, plus allowed them to climb all over. But Jamey says he's afraid of the frog since it winked at him."

"He's only five."

"*I've* felt something," the unknown voice continued. "Laugh if you like, but our house has a slant view with just a bit of that garden, if you call it one, but the stones beyond seem to watch with strange staring eyes. Why, Terry says something came right at them causing the accident," the low voice continued, 'Yes, a solid ton of stone. He claimed the police got it all wrong. Those boys didn't hit the wall from the pothole. Instead, something blocked the road—a form immense and wicked—forcing them to swerve. Must have been an illusion, for nothing was *there!*"

The second voice snickered. "I suppose the kids hadn't shared a few six packs and maybe smoked something funny?"

The first voice changed the subject. "It's good that woman and her husband left, but now I'm told her sister's here! Flatlanders act so superior, wanting to mess around and meddle. Leave nature to nature, I say."

I put my hand to my mouth, biting my thumb nervously as I eased backward into my classroom. Melissa and her painted rocks disturbed the locals; that seemed plain. And what could a boy—the only survivor to tell the tale—possibly see that could resemble a ton of stone and block the road? *Had* drink or illusion caused such tragedy?

It occurred to me I should research Abenaki culture, so on my lunch break I consulted my laptop. What were their burial customs? Had Melissa disturbed sacred ground? The stony tangle did not seem suited for graves.

However, I did learn this tribe's bodies were wrapped in a birch bark shroud called *buskanigan*, and the remains were preferably interred in sandy soil. At the ceremony the living solemnly chanted, "Now our aged man is going to sing a dead song." But what if the man deceased were young?

For a moment I was amused. If the dead proved buried amidst rocks and brambles in back of Melissa's home, instead of in more yielding sand, no wonder they wanted out! But then I was ashamed of my reaction. Death was never amusing, and *were* their spirits still sentient? Why, perhaps whites had deliberately slaughtered them by offering infamous *smallpox blankets*, passing on a paleface disease under a guise of kindness! If that were true, surely their hatred was justified. In that case, perhaps they hadn't even been buried—just left to rot in a barren area of rocks no one claimed!

Suddenly I found it singularly odd that for two months, in spite of scarce snow-cover, I'd never once ventured into the back yard or beyond. Of course the tangle was rough and unappealing at this time of year, and with that as an ongoing excuse, I saved my first excursion for a gusty late-April day. Clouds scudded above, scrubbing the air, and I hoped to clear myself of wintry thoughts. The rocks, now freed of snow, certainly seemed garish to my eye. Mel *was* a little pagan—but what could be malignant about a hobby of painting stones? Unless, of course, my darker speculations were true!

Close up, I realized how much more Melissa had accomplished since my first visit, and my complacence ebbed. The new beasts emerging from granite were unfamiliar; strange amorphous shapes seeming more out of necromancy than the grinning frog, bobcat, and wolf she first showed off to me. What was she thinking; and—before the baby's tragic loss—had she planned on painting ever more ambiguous, nightmarish forms? Hobby or compulsion? I blinked. For a moment immense shapes appeared to shimmer and shift; an unsettling illusion which persisted until I rubbed my eyes

Later that day I set lawn furniture at the house's front, though space facing the road was skimpy. I also relocated my bedroom to face the road, ignoring intermittent racket of trucks as they swept through town, gathering speed for Cotter's grade, or, from the other direction laboriously groaning up the steep incline. I could hardly admit to myself, a sensible woman, I too felt a strange aura out back--some malign presence!

But I was not truly frightened until one mid-May evening. A full moon shone over the mountains as I spotted my cat Snowflake in a flashed glimpse of white, strayed far up in the stone garden. This seemed odd, for to my knowledge he didn't venture there. Had he heard something? Grasping a flashlight, I stepped out. If the moon shed harsh light in slanting rays, it also left large blots of inky shadow. Toward the back of Melissa's domain, the boulders were larger; ten and fifteen feet high—gross, glacial erratics, dropped like turds from the last ice age. The air seemed vibrant with unseen wings or presences, possibly bats out of hibernation? I shuddered. Evidently lightning had pursued some creature into this strange realm.

As I walked farther, fascinated despite unease, my sense of time and vision became distorted. The moon seemed first nearer then farther, and one moment I seemed to have progressed but a few steps, while at the next, glancing backward, I could not spot the reassuring backdoor light.

I stumbled on, flashlight barely touching darkness, seeming to enter a shifting nightmare. Indeed, ghastly shapes flowed past that, to my disordered thinking, appeared as giant stones! Yet I also sensed animal shapes—and above all vague forms like travesties of men. Had some primitive force made revenants out of long-passed Abenaki sachems? *Indian zombies; dead Red?*

My reading had mentioned the foul-tempered and fear-inducing spirit of Mekoomweso who became so heavy when enraged that he sank through stone! Was his spirit commanding the undead and disrupting nature? Surely superstition! If only my husband were alive to talk to and reassure me! But now wind rushed past my ears and a noisome stench invaded my nostrils. Shuddering, I stumbled backward and, while turning, saw a flash of white other than the moon, and there loomed my cat, puffed huge in fear. I scooped him up, ignoring his raking claws. He hissed in terror as, in front of us, a huge boulder wrenched loose from its socket, and I screamed, diving sideways, cutting a long jagged gash on my arm as I fell. But at least neither cat nor I were crushed.

Clawing free, Snowflake fled. Now my flashlight didn't work though its battery had seemed strong. Thoroughly shaken, I stumbled downhill and homeward, imagining treacherous ground heaving beneath my feet. Gasping with effort, at last I reached the back door. What I had experienced seemed to go far beyond the speculations of small-town, superstitious teachers. Had I truly seen rock move against flesh? I shuddered again recalling the recent car accident, the two dead youths, and what the third lived to describe. I was now convinced that a malevolent and atavistic force of Red Man's magic had crushed their car.

Yes, from that night on I believed the glacial stones were stirred to vengeful sentience by a reawakened ancient force. Had the spirit of Mekoomweso urged long-graved minions to fury because pale-skins had claimed tribal lands and, by means of horrid smallpox blankets, had killed them all, with the horrid deed now swept aside or sugared over?

Come daybreak, filled with both curiosity plus nervous superstition, yet I felt a justified loathing, I descended to Melissa's workroom and carefully searched for the photos she had left on her computer. They were gone! I recalled the words of her husband's letter; that she preferred her possessions not exposed to strangers. Yet I wasn't a stranger, and she herself had showed them to me. But now they were missing, and perhaps her husband had erased them. Quite likely he didn't realize I'd seen them.

Still, I possess a good memory, and mind's eye replayed those strange scenes. Since then it seemed many rocks had shifted, and not just ones Melissa had painted. Surely New Hampshire wasn't earthquake-prone! I fought a queasy feeling warning me that—with no intention to do so—my sister had indeed loosed some nightmare power. In a surge of fury, revenants of a destroyed tribe had somehow reached from the grave to claim her expected child, perhaps even her sanity, and the lives of two boys, wrongly blamed for their car wreck—with the third shaken so badly, it was whispered, he seemed deranged.

What might happen next, and why had I escaped? Abruptly I recalled the St. Christopher medal pinned inside my jacket lapel. My husband John placed it there when he gave me the garment for my birthday, as he retold the tale of the travelers' patron saint. Did the charm protect me, allowing me time to escape? I chose to think so.

When I climbed up from the basement I was emotionally exhausted, but with a shaky hand I texted Raymond explaining why I could no longer live in his house, and asking if he had been candid about Sarah's health. His reply came soon enough, but even before I received it, I'd packed, planning never to return. My brother-in-law responded:

Dear Sarah,

We have great expectations again, and my girl's come slowly back to her sunny self. But what you tell me is indeed horrid, and I'll erase your message and this response. I'd not have Melissa upset again, as I'm sure you understand. Having said that, here is what I know.

She was five months along when she climbed on the back of the rock she calls the Unicorn. It's only waist level with easy access, but somehow she slipped. She thinks she hit her head and was knocked unconscious. Later she declared, "Something pushed me!" But what? Ghostly hands? Then Melissa sobbed out that our baby was gone!

"Gone?" I asked my wife exactly what she meant.

"Sarah," she screamed at me. "Taken! Taken!"

I got her to a doctor immediately. He was a soothing family consultant, but no gynecologist, who opined there was no fetus to lose; that Melissa had *experienced a hysterical pregnancy. Yet I myself had felt the child kicking or thought I had! Is there a logical explanation—or are you correct that revenants; the land's permanent occupants, still seek revenge?*

Melissa appears to believe the doctor's reassurance that she had too active an imagination and needed more company, plus now must follow a firm schedule of rest and meals. We don't talk of what happened. But I've done some sleuthing and ordered aerial maps of Peterson, plus searched many legends of Coos County.

In colonial times, my acreage was the site of an Abenaki encampment until the white man's smallpox plague wiped out multitudes, leaving even friendly redskins vowing revenge. So, are time-lost spirits raised from the dead? That, since evil was done to them, they repay it? What horror followed over centuries of beheading, scalping, plus scorching of flesh I care not—dare not—imagine! But it does seem now, from the grave, the head sachem has found a way to avenge his people!"

Pausing in my reading, I pondered. My brother-in-law had come to my conclusion. When Melissa, unaware of history, began her rock painting, a vengeful force re-surfaced, and who knows when (or if) that force can be satisfied? Yet fire is a traditional purge, and if paint covering the rocks blistered away to char, perhaps the wakened evil would ooze back into soil, leaving the living in peace.

So it seemed the buck was passed to me. My sister had inadvertently reawakened evil, but could I somehow negate it? What could I accomplish, and how? With quivers like hideous cobwebs touching my spine, and neck hairs astir, I set my brother-in-law's letter down while my mind raced.

The garage held a container slosh-full of gasoline ready for the lawn mower, and Melissa had left paint cans behind. These would have a use now far from what manufacturers anticipated. I myself would spill the flammable paint, set alight the depraved rock garden, and hopefully banish those spirits that betrayed her, an innocent.

Precautions? Oh yes! My car is packed and parked far from here, while dusk is the hour of supper in the village, a time no one is apt to see me. God willing, later tonight, Snowflake--safe in his carrier--and I shall leave forever.

Already it is late afternoon and I dare not wait. My St. Christopher medal is securely sewn into my clothing; Indeed, I finger it through cloth as I write. This letter will be posted when the deed is done, and I urge—once read—you destroy these words.

Twilight crept near. Holding terror in check, I picked my way through briars and soon as amidst the horrid stones. Wind blew briskly from the southwest to drive the fire I lit away from the village and into the winter-withered, dry tangle that swept up the mountain. By the time an alarm is called, (*if* so) and engines arrive, I pray the curse will be destroyed, the old revenant and his spirit-comrades dissipated or pinned once more in unmarked graves. I understood their fury, and could even hope they'd rest. Certainly personal fear wouldn't stop me.

I have scattered the dry straw bale that Melissa left unused, and soaked the bits with gasoline. Luckily no one lives close enough to observe my actions with clarity if they do happen to look. Just at sundown I will light the conflagration, flitting as a dark shadow among shadows and then— pray God—can flee to safety. Twilight is a time suspended between light and dark, hope and fear, and I must not falter!

Now it is time. Striking a match, I smell its sulfur tang and toss it outward, hearing the swift crackle of fire, then flit away; a moth *not* drawn to flame. A whoosh flares behind me. Though a full box of safety matches rests potent in my hand, just one proved enough, and I dropped the box and watched it roar up; flames licking outward—yes, let the everything burn!

With snow melted away now, vine-tangled landscape is dry. My heart too is dry. I flee, feeling ravening heat spreading behind me. Fleeing, I exult as the conflagration spreads, roaring like a thousand beasts. I glance back only once to see brambles flare and hear the rising sap of scrub pines exploding. Writhing shapes loom silhouetted against smoke as I whisper comfort to distant Melissa, though I realize she cannot hear and perhaps would refuse to comprehend my action if she could. Before I turn away, something wails, a spirit-sound, high-pitched and eerie, in hatred and despair even as a spectral hand of smoke reaches for me, only to be dissipated by wind.

I run away, panting. I know my car is ahead, I wrench open the door, start the motor, rev it, and grip the steering wheel like Death follows me—*as well may be!* Snowflake is safe in his carrier, but cowering, terrified. Still, I allow myself a groan of relief to see the road stretch away.

Yes, I am still fearful of boulders bounding from their sockets, seeking to crush metal like I might step on an ant. But for the moments, in the fury of the conflagration, it seems nothing can reach me.

As I flee Melissa's home my heart judders in my chest, I have a lifetime to lament the boys who died and the baby Melissa lost. How many others have perished; red or white, whom I will never know about? My hand leaves the steering wheel for an instant to finger my medal.

Will it protect me forever if those lost souls sense what I have done? I am not vengeful. May the Abenaki tribe rest despite us; too-arrogant and interloping palefaces. Native tribes did not ask us to come over the water, but we did.

If you doubt my tale, at least look up the story of the white man's *gift* of germ-ridden blankets. Lord above, forgive all our human trespasses! But is the curse really purged, and will brittle bones be found when brambles are consumed and embers turn to gritty ash?

I cannot stay, but where can I begin again? No story ends when the last word is set on paper. The horror of what was, of what I did, or what a priest might have done better, clings to me, and will forever. Must I always quail at lighting a simple match? Will I see Melissa once more; can we hug and move forward—or is too much lost and changed? And what, now, may dark nightmares bring?

Esther's fantasy and horror has recently appeared in ANTHOLOGY YEAR THREE: DISTANT DYING EMBER, CANOPIC JARS: TALES OF MUMMIES AND MUMMIFICATION, plus BUGS: TALES THAT CREEP AND CRAWL.

She presented her lecture IT'S ABOUT TIME to the New York Poetry Forum, NYC, Manhattan, on Saturday, October 10, 2015: "A World Poetry Day Celebration". THE POCKET ROCKET, her second fantasy book for children, will be out from Peony Press for Christmas 2015.

Esther writes a monthly online column for the e-mag EXTRA INNINGS from the University of Wisconsin, edited by Marshall Cook; prior to which she wrote poetry columns for WRITERS' JOURNAL for thirty years, along with illustrations. Esther has won and judged many poetry contests, and served as POET IN THE SCHOOLS for Putnam County, Tennessee.

She currently is appointed "Northern New Hampshire's Poet Laureate for The White Mountains Region".

WHAT ROUGH BEAST?

BY BILLIE SUE MOSIMAN

BLOODSHOT ◉ BOOKS

MONTGOMERY'S ankle twisted when she stepped down from the tractor. The ground was too far away and a gopher hole was waiting for her misstep. She fell onto her side into dry grass, letting out a faint protest. *Now what?* She wondered.

She had only half the field mowed and meant to stop for the day. Evening approached and the far sun was dying. Off in the glistening, icy air the Rockies rising behind her land were white with snow halfway up the crags. Soon the snow would swirl here and lock her indoors most every day with the wood stove.

But the fields needed mowing and now her ankle screamed like raging fire. She'd probably pulled a tendon. She didn't think it was broken, but she couldn't be sure of anything.

She glanced toward the cabin. Inside was her poor sister, Bonnie, and a nephew and niece, John and Teralouise. Bonnie had come to her for help when there was no help, when it was too late. Her mental illness was beyond Montgomery's scope of knowledge. Bonnie was off her meds and refused to go back on them. What could anyone do? It was 1949 and they wanted to give her shock treatment and keep her incarcerated, but Montgomery wouldn't allow it. "No," she told the doctor, "definitely no, I'm taking her home with me."

"She won't get better," he'd said.

"Well, she can't get worse the way she will if you shock her."

"You're wrong about that," he said, turning away. "She can get a lot worse."

Pain shot through her leg and she called for help. Could they see she'd fallen? She stared at the cabin door, willing it to open. To her surprise Johnny did open the door and stood there with a hand to his brow, looking her way. She yelled for help. He seemed to hesitate, but then came loping across the field to her. With his assistance she was able to rise to her good foot, lean on the boy, and hop to the cabin. Once inside, she asked Bonnie to get a cold pack. Bonnie sat at the wooden kitchen table staring ahead as if no one had spoken to her.

"Bonnie!"

This shook her loose from her thoughts and she looked at Montgomery. "What is it?" she asked.

"I've turned my ankle. I need a cold compress."

Bonnie slowly rose and moved as if through molasses to the sink. She pumped the hand pump and wet a cloth, squeezed it damp, and brought it over to the chair where Montgomery sat, a grimace on her face. "No good,"

Bonnie said.

"That's right, this is not good for us. I have too many things to do before the snow comes."

"No good cabin," Bonnie said, going back to the table to sit.

"What's wrong with the cabin?" Montgomery had bought it and the land from an old gold miner. It was perfectly sound, though for the four of them the one open room was crowded.

"Demons in the walls," Bonnie said, looking down at the table.

"Oh my god, let's not get on that again, Bonnie, you scare the kids."

Bonnie shrugged and lifting her right arm pointed to the front wall of the cabin. "There," she said. "And there and there and there." She pointed to each of the four walls in turn.

Montgomery looked over at the children and shook her head to let them know this wasn't true. It was their Mama talking crazy again. Johnny looked away from her and Teralouise stared out of big wide eyes, her body stiff. Montgomery hated how Bonnie scared them. It took her hours at night to settle them into sleep afterwards.

That evening the ankle swelled until it was thick and red. Bonnie couldn't be persuaded to make dinner so Johnny took over and fried up hard-rind bacon and heated beans from the day before. After dinner, night was full upon them and Johnny lit the kerosene lanterns. Bonnie hadn't moved, even to eat. He took away her untouched plate.

"Undress, wash up, and get in bed," Montgomery directed the children. Soundlessly they did as they were told. When Bonnie brought them here they'd been wordless, like mice in a small cage. As much as Montgomery hugged them and spoke to them softly, read to them from a book of children's tales, and spent time looking into their eyes, they still didn't open up.

That night, lying beside Bonnie in the bed, firelight from the woodstove dancing over the ceiling, Montgomery's hand was suddenly grabbed by her sister, nails digging in. "What?" she whispered, turning to look in the dark.

"Demons," Bonnie whispered, too terrified to point them out.

Montgomery looked but saw nothing, of course. Her sister was mad and nothing she said could be taken seriously.

Bonnie stiffened, then began to writhe, letting go of her sister's hand. Her scream rose from deep within her chest and shattered the night. The two children sat up in their bed, hollering too.

Montgomery sat up, feeling the quilt pull at her ankle, and that shot pain up her leg, but she had to stop this madness. "Bonnie! Stop it! There's nothing gonna harm you."

Just as she said that the quilt was ripped by invisible hands from the bed and thrown onto the floor. Bonnie's body spasmed with her abdomen rising up into the air and then her entire form rose, clearing the mattress. That's when Montgomery screamed.

❀   ❀   ❀

Montgomery took the damp cloth from Johnny and patted Bonnie's face with it. She was limp now, sprawled on the bed as if she were a ragdoll thrown down. "Cover her feet," Montgomery told Johnny. As he did so, his mother didn't move. It was as if she were catatonic now, the experience thrusting her so deep into her mind she had been lost. She would neither speak nor move.

"I don't know what to do," Montgomery said, then wished she hadn't as her confession appeared to unhinge the children. Both Johnny and his little sister Teralouise ran around the small confines of the cabin wailing in grief.

She struggled from the bed, putting her bad foot down on the cold floor carefully. "No, no," she said softly. "Oh no, I didn't mean it. Your mama's gonna be fine, really. She just needs some sleep."

She knew it was a lie, but the children were terrified. She'd had them light the lanterns to dispel the darkness and that had helped. There were no demons present. Yet some force had attacked Bonnie and lifted her from the bed.

Therefore, the truth was that Montgomery really didn't know what to do. She couldn't let the children know that. Today she'd send them outdoors and try to resolve this. She wasn't religious and owned no Bible. She didn't even know who the pastor was in town thirty miles away. But she'd heard of possession and she now thought that was what plagued her sister. A demon, yes, though she couldn't see it. Something caused Bonnie to rise stiffly from the bed. She hadn't hallucinated that.

She had both Johnny and Teralouise in her arms, shushing them, covering their little faces with kisses. They both trembled and cried. She held them until they calmed, then told them to dress and go outdoors. They could stack the firewood. But they mustn't come inside unless she called them, did they understand?

Once they were gone, Montgomery hobbled to the bed and took hold of Bonnie's wrist. "Where is it? Did you bring it here, Bonnie? Has it been your companion for a while?"

Bonnie stared at the ceiling unblinking and didn't respond. Montgomery felt anger like a rod straighten her back and she let go of her sister's hand. "Come out and face me! I won't be such as easy target, will I? Come out, you cowardly bastard and tell me what you want."

The air grew electric and Montgomery's hair stood on end along her arms and the nape of her neck. She felt a presence. She shouted for it again to show itself.

A crackling rent the air, the sound like great logs burning. Montgomery

 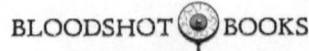

held steady, her legs planted wide despite her turned ankle, her shoulders thrown back. "You go after the weak and the broken. Come after me and see what happens! I banish you back to Hell from whence you crawled!"

Her taunt was successful for the roof timbers shuddered, the air now sparkled with light and from the midst of it came what looked to be an angel, one with wings, but with a countenance so severe Montgomery had to look away. She was startled beyond comprehension and her mind felt addled. She had expected a horrible monster and here it was a majestic being of light and horror. The visage on the face alone was enough to shrivel a woman's soul.

Her voice broke, trembling in a lower register as she said, "What are you? What do you want?"

"I've come for your sister and... eventually you."

"Because we're godless heathens? God protects us nevertheless."

The angel laughed like thunder, shaking the cabin, and Montgomery cowered, hunching her shoulders. She inched near the bed and took hold of her sister's hand. "You leave her alone. Her husband was killed on the railroad, leaving her penniless. She has two beautiful children who need her. Now let her go, she's suffered enough."

"You think suffering is my plan? That it's anyone's plan? Life is suffering, woman. You haven't learned that? Humanity is meant to suffer, suffer and die alone. I don't care about her suffering or yours. I don't care about children or the elderly or the crippled and despondent. She called for me and I've come. She wants to go and I'll take her. There's nothing to stop me."

He spoke truth. He pulled Bonnie's body from her grasp even as she tried to throw herself over her, and lifting her into the air, her eyes blinked finally, a single tear falling. She looked at Montgomery as if she were sorry, and then in a flash they were gone, the great beast of light and the frail human woman.

Montgomery fell to her knees at the bed and wept. She hadn't been strong enough; she hadn't been persistent and full of resolve. She'd lost her sister and it was all her fault, all her fault.

Lying again, Montgomery told the children their mother had left by the back, taking the old black mare to town where she could get treatment. They gave her quizzical looks, but what could they do? Their mother had disappeared.

After days, her ankle improved so she could stand on it and she returned to the fields for the mowing. If the grasses were allowed to stay tall and dry they presented danger from lightning strikes that would set the fields and then the cabin on fire. It was early November before she got the mowing done and she arranged for a school in town to take the children. They were too sad and alone on the ranch. They needed other children for companionship. It would cost her half her wheat crop next year, but at least Johnny and Teralouise would be safe and she'd pay anything for that.

She found herself obsessing over the disappearance of Bonnie and the creature she'd seen who had come to take her away.

She thought to see the pastor in town, then decided not to. How would he explain a demon that was an angel, a deathly, earth-and-man-hating angel? How could a heavenly angel bring death and destruction? She assumed he was a Fallen one, not one of God's emissaries, but a rogue in league with the Son of Morning, Lucifer.

How beautiful he'd been until she looked upon his face. Then all of Hell and every hatred ever felt looked back at her and she knew he was not what she thought he was.

Each night she prayed, and having never prayed before, she felt a fraud, yet still she did it. She was now convinced the world was not nearly as simple as it appeared and that dark things walked among men listening to thoughts, and sometimes acting on them. She could understand Bonnie wishing to die. She'd loved Michael, her young husband, and his violent passing had left her empty. She, like a lot of women, couldn't bear to live without her love.

"I won't let you have me," Montgomery whispered as she straightened the cabin and swept the floors. "I'm not like Bonnie."

Time passed as it will do and the years tumbled one upon the other. Johnny and Teralouise grew up and left the state, never saying goodbye to their Aunt Montgomery. Well, she had abandoned them in a way, hadn't she? She expected nothing from them.

Montgomery's hair grayed and the chores were harder to do. A man came in the summer of 1959 offering his labor in exchange for room in the barn. This man, Gary Burtolson, became first Montgomery's helpmate, then her lover, and finally her husband. She never told him about the angel and her sister's disappearance. They didn't talk much, but they spent hours together in bed, exploring one another's bodies. They built love like building a stellar lasso to hold back the earth from spiraling out of orbit. Love heaped upon love made them strong, resilient. It created a wall against whatever the world could throw at the couple.

In the third year of their marriage, when Gary was adding an addition to the cabin, he fell from the roof and hit his head on a stone. He died instantly. When Montgomery found him she knew she was about to lose her mind. She couldn't stop sobbing. She covered him and went to town for the coroner. She wept the entire trip and back again, a big black hearse following her up the mountain to the cabin.

That night she still wept, her heart feeling as if it had truly broken into pieces, and she would surely die from it by morning. She lay on her side in the

 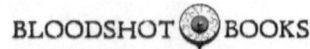

empty bed, mourning, when light sparked all around the room and the huge, monster angel was back.

Not having seen him in years, she looked him in the face and thought she was blinded. She turned away, shutting her eyes, and his voice filled the cabin.

"I told you I'd take you too," he said.

"I've done nothing wrong."

"Neither did your sister. She just asked for an end to it."

"I...I..."

"Now you've asked for the same and I'm here to take you. To the end."

She didn't know if that was what she wanted or not. She might as well, she thought, since Gary was gone, she was old, and the place she loved so long was falling apart. What did she have now to live for?

"Will I see Bonnie? Will I be reunited with Gary?"

Silence spun out like a web and she sat up then stood from the bed to face her fate. "I said, will I see Bonnie and Gary?"

The angel spread his wings and bowed down low to look in her face. "In the end? Where you asked to go? Right to the end? Do you think anyone will be waiting?"

She trembled now and began again to weep. "I'll be... alone?"

"You won't *be* at all," he said, sweeping her into his arms and winking her into the invisible paradise of nothingness.

Johnny returned to the cabin, summoned by authorities when his Aunt Montgomery disappeared from the homestead. He found her husband had died in an accident just before she vanished. Just as his mother had also vanished when his own father died and they'd come to stay in the mountain house. He didn't understand a thing about it. But here he was and he'd inherited the place, so he might as well get started trying to fix it up. The field needed mowing, the fences repaired, the roof still leaked, and the new addition wasn't finished. He hoped Cynthia would like it here once he got it in shape. They could live here nicely if he put in some of the modern conveniences.

He strode into the one big open room and looked around remembering the little bed shared with his sister near the wall and the larger bed here were he stood, the one his mother and aunt slept in. He'd never really blamed Aunt Montgomery for putting them in the town school. It had been for the best.

He sneezed at the accumulated dust and began to turn for the door where sunlight fell across the bare floorboards when there was a feeling of electricity in the air and from the corner of his eye he thought he'd detected sparks of light swirling just to the left and behind him.

He turned, but nothing was there.

He shook off the premonition and walked outdoors. He and Cynthia would love it here, and he'd grow wheat and corn, he'd raise goats, and they would have a family. They'd live a simple life the way they always wanted.

His sister Teralouise had told him not to come back, to sell the old place, but she was superstitious, always had been, and he ignored her warning. "There's no ghosts," he told her. "There's no demons. Mother was just ill."

He couldn't see an end to life. He was young, handsome, and in love. The world went on forever in his mind, forever and ever, nothing to hinder it, no suffering to stall it, and with this abundant land at his fingertips, Johnny began the chores so he could hurry and bring his Cynthia to her new home. Her new life. Johnny, like his Aunt Montgomery, was unafraid. The cabin, if haunted, wouldn't deter a modern man.

He didn't believe in the supernatural. He was fearless because there were no beasts or demons who could stop the future. Not one. Still... if he was wrong and there was something... *Something Odd...* he'd handle that too when it appeared. He had no other choice, did he?

He whistled as he worked, he dreamed of Cynthia, and the home they'd make here, and all the while the ageless Rockies looked down on him without pity, for he was nothing more than a man.

Billie Sue MOSIMAN is the Edgar and Stoker nominated author of sixteen novels and more than two hundred short stories that were in various anthologies and magazines over the years. She is most well-known for her suspense novels, the latest of which is THE GREY MATTER, nominated for a Kindle Book Award.

She will be publishing an anthology with stories by women in February 2016 titled FRIGHT MARE- Women Write Horror.

PIETY
BY JOHN BRUNI

JUDAH Crenshaw used to be the most pious man he knew. He went to church every day, sometimes more than once. He gave more to the collection plate than any other parishioner, and he sang hymns louder even than the preacher. Not a day passed without his fervent prayers.

All of this changed when he saw Reverend Jordan torn to pieces by a savage beast unlike any he'd ever seen before.

It happened late one cool and crisp night as autumn crept up on the world. Judah's wife busied herself with cleaning dishes while his two sons knelt before their bed in the other room, whispering their prayers. The farm fell silent as it usually did at this hour. Only the crickets sang from the fields under the velvet, star-bedazzled blanket of night.

Judah sat by the fireplace, packing his pipe. It was the only vice he allowed himself, and anyway, he felt certain the Bible said nothing about smoking. Still, it bothered him, so instead of striking a match, he decided to visit the reverend and find out the good Lord's take on tobacco.

He made his excuses to Rachael—who graciously understood her husband's ways—and went out to the barn to saddle his horse.

The stirrups creaked as he stepped into them, hauling himself up into position. A tiny little throb of pain spoke up in his back, barely noticeable but there. At the age of forty, he figured this to be the beginning of his descent into decrepitude. Soon his sons would bear the brunt of the work around here, and that suited him fine.

The horse thumped its way down the dirt path, and Judah felt swallowed by the night. The illumination from his house faded behind him, and now he saw only with the aid of stark moonlight. The whirring sound of the crickets grew louder, punctuated by an occasional owl hoot.

It reminded him of home. He hailed originally from the backwoods of Pennsylvania, where he'd misspent his youth helping his pa brew moonshine, and though he never firmly believed in it, he took part in his ma's bastardized powwow ways.

Out west, in the rich fields of Nebraska, very little reminded him of the peaceful, almost lazy ways of home. Only the night made him feel like a child again, when darkness shrouded the fields, and he could close his eyes and pretend to be in his native woods.

Before long he reached town, where the sounds of drunken debauchery dispelled his reverie. Civilization tended to do that to a man. Had he never gone to Philadelphia, he would never have become enchanted with the ways of the Christian church. He'd still be an ignorant yokel, sinning with his old man and practicing empty and meaningless magic with his mother.

He never would have met Rachael, either. He never would have found true happiness.

He rode past the rows of saloons, ignoring the raucous, tinkling music from within. Harder to ignore were the sounds of revelry. Laughs, cries, shouts, declarations. The rhythmic stomping of dancing boots.

All of the stores were closed. The only other building that showed a sign of life was the sheriff's office. A candle burned in the window, and someone made a loud, metallic rattling sound. A disgruntled prisoner, perhaps?

Judah turned a blind eye to it all, and as he reached the end of town, where only the church resided, its white steeple in sharp contrast against the sackcloth sky, the noise of late night city living passed away. In fact, he could hear nothing but the deafening ring of absolute silence. Though the church had a huge yard out back, no crickets could be heard.

The horse slowed. Judah hadn't given any commands, so he nudged the animal forward. It stopped, a small whine in the back of its throat.

"Come on, Sue," he whispered. "Get going." He dug his heels in a bit, and the horse continued. Its head shook back and forth in a skittering way. Though it was night, Judah figured Sue had wind of a snake.

He tethered his horse to the hitching rail and made his way up the steps into the church. Inside, a few candles burned, but he found no one around, not even the reverend. Thinking Jordan was in the rectory, Judah walked down the aisle, pausing to take a quick knee before a statue of the crucified Christ, and made his way around back.

Before he reached the rectory, he felt kind of funny. His arm hairs stood up uncomfortably, and the back of his neck tingled. He hadn't felt this way since childhood, when his pa's still was about to be raided by the local deputies.

And then he sensed an odd animal smell, almost like a bear's, yet muskier.

He heard a loud *thunk* as something fell over in the rectory. Someone wearing heavy boots clopped along the hardwood floor. He wanted to call out the reverend's name, but his throat seemed suddenly small. He couldn't even squeak as he moved toward Jordan's private chambers.

The smell in here was worse. It mixed with the deep, gassy smell of shit and something else. Something . . . coppery, like when Rachael was on her menses.

A light breeze pushed his hair back as he realized that the window had been broken. No, that wasn't quite right. The window had been torn clean out of the wall. The sill stuck out in all directions, a splintered mess.

And then Judah saw the reverend—what remained of him—and the hulking beast hovering over him.

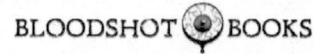

BLOODSHOT BOOKS

At first his eyes refused to process this unholy thing before him, but after a moment, he started categorizing it in terms his mind could comprehend. A diadem of horns—akin to a buck deer's antlers—topped its bear's head. The rest of its seven-foot-tall frame was a shaggy pelt not unlike a buffalo's. It had no feet but hooves, exactly like a goat's.

But its face and hands were pure human, and evil shone from its almond eyes and razor-toothed grin. Its taloned claws—opposable thumbs and all—rooted around in the reverend's body, or so it seemed at first. Judah peered past the mess of blood and sundered flesh to see that Jordan's legs had been broken and twisted away, giving the beast easy access to the reverend's most private of parts.

The beast had dug its hands into Jordan's groin—deep—and now it uprooted his genitals in one awful scoop. It brought the handful of obscene flesh to its mouth and bit into it, yanking its head back like a dog working a bone, and chewing its prize with the sloppy, slobbery chaos of a hungry animal.

In that moment, as Judah watched this horror, he knew that there was no God. No all-powerful being would ever consent to the existence of such a monster.

It lowered the final piece of Jordan's genitals into its mouth like a delectable morsel and chewed, blood slipping down its hairy chin. Its eyes closed in ecstasy as it smacked and slurped until it swallowed. Then, it looked directly at Judah and grinned, showing off teeth that belonged to a mountain lion.

Fear flushed through Judah's system, and his consciousness fled him. The next thing he knew, he woke in his own bed, body slicked and sticking to the sheets. Relief flooded his thoughts as he realized that the horrors of last night couldn't have been real. The beast had been a fevered nightmare, perhaps brought on by a bad piece of food at supper.

But then he found Rachael in the kitchen, preparing breakfast. As he sat down to a plate full of eggs, toast and bacon, she asked how he felt.

"A bit shaky," he said. He thought he might mention the nightmare, but perhaps the subject matter would be too strong for the fairer sex.

"You came home an absolute mess," she said. "I don't know what you got into, but you were terrified out of your mind. All you wanted to do was hide in bed. You trembled so much I thought you'd break the bed. What happened last night?"

Judah didn't tell her anything. He had to have dreamed the whole thing. Monsters didn't exist, and if they did, God would protect him from them. So not wishing to seem like a fool to his own wife, he remained reticent on the matter.

Yet when he went outside to begin the usual chores, he found his horse

 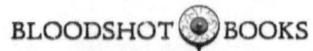

outside the barn, breathing heavily with its flanks practically whipped away. Had he done this to the poor animal in an attempt to flee . . . something?

Then he heard the news. A neighbor stopping by for some water and a quick jaw told him that something had gotten to the reverend. "Must've been an animal. Tore him to pieces, it did. Ugly sight. Even the undertaker puked."

Judah felt something move uncomfortably in his guts, and breathing became difficult, as if he wore an ever-tightening girdle. He flashed back to last night, to the beast reveling in the reverend's severed works. He felt that horrible fear again and fought the urge to look around just to make sure the beast hadn't snuck up on him.

That night, his fear became more real. As he closed up the barn, ready for dinner, he smelled the unmistakable musk of the monster, and he felt like he was back in Jordan's rectory. His heart flailed against the inside of his chest as he whipped around, deathly afraid that he would see the monster a split second before it did to him what it had done to the reverend.

Nothing. No movements. No sound. The musk faded, but he took his pitchfork with him back to the house. Once more, he barricaded the door, and when he went to bed, he kept the pitchfork close at hand.

When he did this a third night in a row, Rachael said, "What's gotten into you?"

Judah fumbled with words, trying to express confusion at her question. It was a futile attempt, and she made sure to let him know with her next breath. Finally, he said, "I can't explain it. Something... happened. I—"

"You don't say your prayers anymore," she said. "Whatever happened's been eating you pretty bad."

He blanched at her choice of words. An image of the beast eating Reverend Jordan came to mind, and he shook his head, trying to banish the gristly scene.

"You've got to tell me what's wrong," she said. "I'm your wife, Judah."

She looked so concerned, but he knew she'd never believe the truth. As for himself, he didn't *want* to believe, but it stuck in his thoughts like a piece of corn between his teeth.

But the truth had to come out of him. It was all he could think about, even as he toiled at work on the farm. It poisoned him, and if he didn't talk about it, it would wither him into a man old beyond his years.

"I saw what happened to Reverend Jordan," he said.

"How—?"

"I went to see him that night, remember? And . . . and I saw the thing that et him. It was... " He trailed off because something didn't seem right. Though it was a calm night, he could hear nothing. No crickets, no birds, not even the grunting sound of pigs in the pen out back. His neck tingled, and he sniffed the air for any kind of musk.

"Judah," Rachael said. "What—?"

His eyes darted to the window, and for a split second he saw the face of the beast leering at him through the glass. It grinned, eyes twinkling, and then vanished from the pane.

Judah grabbed up the pitchfork and rushed to the window. The whole thing had happened so quickly he wondered if he'd imagined it. He didn't know what he feared more, catching a retreating glimpse of the monster, thereby confirming his fears, or nothing at all.

"What's wrong?" Rachael asked.

Swallowing, he forced his hands to stop trembling. "They're saying a bear mauled him. Well, it weren't no animal that done it." He then described the monster as he stared out the window, looking for any sign of it.

Rachael couldn't look at him when she asked, "Did you stop by the Lady Gaye that night?"

This remark hurt him, and then he realized it shouldn't have. Sin couldn't exist if God didn't. "You know I've never had a drop to drink."

"You came home in a state that night. You don't even remember it. Maybe—"

"It wasn't drink, Rachael."

Silence. Then: "Why do you keep looking out that window?"

"I'm afraid that creature might've followed me home."

She didn't look at him quite the same since then. His demeanor thereafter didn't help, either. As soon as the sky started to darken in the east every day, he barricaded the house and refused to let their kids outside. He stood vigil at the windows with a newly purchased rifle. Before, he wanted nothing to do with guns. Now he stayed up late in his chair, his rifle across his lap, a finger in the trigger guard.

All of this had a bad effect on Jeb and Jubal Crenshaw. The former, older by three years, hated his old man for this new tyranny. He wanted to see his friends after supper and maybe do a little hell-catting. At fourteen, he'd just begun developing an interest in things in which his parents would disapprove. The nightly lockdown inspired anger and sulking in him. However, the latter bought into Judah's paranoia. It got so bad he spent his evenings hiding in the bed he shared with his brother.

Rachael couldn't tell which of the two had it off worse. As for herself, she couldn't bear to sleep next to her own husband. He screamed a lot while dreaming and shivered so hard the bed shook. At times, he would flail out and accidentally strike her.

She wanted to give him the benefit of the doubt, but in this present state, he was dangerous, not just physically but emotionally. Who knew how badly he'd already stunted Jubal's growth?

One morning, while the boys were already at their chores, Rachael sat at the table next to Judah and said, "I want to leave, and I want to take our kids with me."

He gazed at her through heavy-lidded, sleep-deprived eyes. More veins than iris looked out of their puffy cocoons at her, the whites covered in a red, cobwebby film. He said nothing.

"Darn it, I don't want to go, but you're making this impossible. Have you even seen that... whatever it is since that night?"

He ignored her and turned his attention to the window. Even though the sun shone down on every inch of the farm, he still felt concerned whenever the kids were outside.

"You're not going to fight me on this?" When he said nothing a third time, she uncharacteristically cursed. "I want to protect them. From you. But if you just talk to me, maybe we can figure this out."

He jerked, as if someone had startled him from behind. "From me? Why? I'm trying to keep them alive."

"From a figment of your imagination. I've never seen that thing, Judah. And I think you see it, but only in your nightmares. Sometimes you scare me."

He stared dumbly at her. It hurt that she thought for a second that he would do anything to hurt his family, and he wanted to burst out at her. But then he thought that this might work out for the best. By taking the kids away from here, she'd be saving them from the thing that killed Reverend Jordan. He swallowed hard, forcing his indignation back into his guts, where it festered like an infected boil.

"To hell with you, Judah. I don't know why you're doing all of this, but I'm not going anywhere. From your silence, I have no choice but to think you want us to go. Maybe now that you don't live up to your religious beliefs, you want to play around a bit. Maybe go to a few saloons. Maybe even find a new woman. But I refuse to let you do this. You won't get out of this easy."

No. She couldn't stay. She and the kids had to leave, even if he had to make them. Yet he didn't know if he could. He'd never raised a hand to her in all their years together. What if she called his bluff? Would he really have to hit her?

"Get over yourself." His voice was hoarse and dirty, and it hurt his heart to utter these words. But he knew her very life depended on it. "Don't you get it? You're not wanted here. You want the kids? Take 'em. Get out of here, you no good cunt."

The last sentence came out awkwardly, as he was not used to cursing. But as he watched her face wilt at the words, he knew he'd gotten the job done.

He let his eyes glaze over, and he did not acknowledge her for the rest of the morning, not as she packed her bags, not as she wept in the kitchen, not even when she tried to say goodbye. It took all of his power to not break down in that moment. His heart yearned to break through his chest, to take back his awful words, but he refused to let himself give in.

Finally, the door closed. He stood and rushed to the window, where he watched her and the boys on the wagon, headed for town and the stage that would take them to her folks in Kansas. The sun still hung in the middle of the sky, so he knew they would be safe.

As he watched the backs of the heads of his children, he wished he could have said goodbye to them. He wished they would at least turn around to give him one last glimpse of their faces, something to hold with his memory as he tried to go to sleep at the conclusion of each day.

They did not comply with his wish.

That night, just before the sun slipped from the sky, Judah went to the barn to lock up. He stepped inside to make sure all of his animals were present when he nearly keeled over from the powerful odor of beast. It normally smelled bad in here, but now it overwhelmed him, causing his eyes to water and his chest to hitch. Then, just as the stench became the most unbearable, he remembered what it signified. His blood juddered to a halt in his veins, and he gasped, desperately trying to breathe. He didn't have his rifle because such monsters could not walk in daylight. Now he had no means of defending himself.

He turned to run, but his feet tangled up against each other, and he fell to the straw-covered floor. He did not hesitate to push back up to his feet and sprint for the safety of his house, to his rifle. As he went, he could have sworn he saw a pair of eyes glittering out at him from the darkness of a stall.

Judah spent the entire night going from window to window, clutching his gun at the ready. He routinely sniffed the air for the telltale musk of the monster. At every sound, even those as quiet as the house settling, he jumped like a frightened child, but he kept up his vigil until dawn. Even then, he waited for sunlight to bathe his entire property before he ventured out to the barn.

Outside, he could smell the musk, but it was so faint the beast couldn't still be around. Inside, he discovered all of his animals slaughtered, their bodies split and torn, their blood painting the walls and straw, now drying to a rusty shade. Had it been this way last night, and he'd been too scared to see it? He didn't remember hearing the animals, and wouldn't the presence of the beast have driven them mad with fear?

Then, he realized it had eaten none of them. At least, not entirely. While all the females had just been torn asunder, all the males had lost what made them male. All that remained were ragged holes surrounded by teeth marks.

There was no way he could clean up this unholy mess, so he got some kerosene and razed the barn. He watched from his porch as the fire billowed up, licking at the light blue sky like fingers reaching for Heaven.

He thought back to his youth, to the powwow he'd practiced with his mother. Had she ever heard of an animal like this? Was there something in her books that could explain this monstrosity? He wished he'd kept his copy of *The Long Lost Friend*. Maybe then he could do a little research of his own.

His sister Ruth had taken over for his mother after she passed away. Judah considered telegraphing Ruth, but he knew he'd never get an answer soon enough. Even so, any telegraph agent entering those woods would be shot for a federal officer by Old Man Crenshaw, who still moonshined in those parts.

No, Judah was on his own. If only he could gain mastery over his fear. Then, perhaps, he could shoot the beast and find out if bullets could vanquish it.

He considered going to town for help, but he dismissed the idea. Who would believe him? Besides, he thought about all that open land with no shelter and shuddered, even if he would be making the trek in daylight. Home it would have to be.

Instead of doing chores, he did necessary tasks. He made sure he had enough water in the house. Since he didn't have any more animals, he stopped by the smokehouse to load up on jerky beef. Lastly, he tore down his fence and used the wood to cover up all the windows of his house and to reinforce the door. He made an extra crossbeam to use as a barricade.

At the end of his labors, he sealed himself off in his house, even though the sun still lingered at six o'clock, and sat down to eat. When he'd staved off his hunger, he cleaned the rifle.

Later, as Judah tried to relax by the fire, he heard someone knock on his door. Annoyed—after all, it had taken him a long time to bar the entryway— he went over to the front of his house and said, "Who goes?"

No one answered him.

He regretted not adding a peephole so he could see who was out there. Then again, it would only have weakened the door to the creature. Besides, would the monster politely knock like a neighbor? He decided to open up and see who it was.

Just before he touched the knob, the knock came again. It sounded kind of forcible, so he drew back. "Who goes?" he asked again. Once more he received no answer.

"God damn you! Speak up!"

The knock came a third time, harder than before, and this time it didn't stop. With each hammering blow, the door juddered wildly in its frame. Judah backed away, holding the rifle close to his chest, shocked that the wood didn't splinter.

Bracing himself, he aimed the gun at the door and waited, resisting the desperate urge to run. But he knew he couldn't run. By barricading himself in, he'd given himself no way out.

The door stopped convulsing, and everything became quiet again. Only the monotonous tick of Rachel's grandfather clock filled Judah's ears as he continued to stare at the barred entryway. "Hello?"

Laughter. Deep, rich laughter came through the door, reverberating in his chest like a loud song, but there was nothing delightful about the sound. Judah's mouth dried up, and the back of his neck flushed and tingled. Now he felt the urge to put the gun in his mouth and pull the trigger, ending this madness in the most merciful way he knew.

"Little pig, little pig, let me in."

God! It could talk! He felt like screaming, but he knew he'd never find the breath for it; he couldn't even find any with which to *breathe*.

Finally, the fear built up so much he couldn't hold it in any longer. "Go away!" he howled. "Please! Go away!" He dropped the gun and cowered in a ball on the floor. He no longer cared about survival. He just wanted this to be over.

He barely noticed that the monster no longer tried to gain entrance, nor did it speak again.

It was dawn before he gained the courage to open the door. Only a lingering whiff of the beast's stench remained, as well as scuffed hoof marks on the porch.

His hands couldn't stop shaking, so he hunted down a bottle of grain alcohol Rachael used for disinfectant. After a few belts, he felt calmer, and he wondered why such a wonderful feeling should be railed against by men of God.

Judah spent the next couple of days locked up, eating poorly, and sipping at that bottle. Nothing happened, but he kept up his seclusion, not even going outside to defecate. On the third day, however, the stink got to him. He was also out of alcohol, and he wanted to eat something—anything—other than jerky beef.

At noon he took up his rifle and headed outside with the intent of shooting some veal. He cautiously wandered outside, even though the world shone with brightness. There were few shadows, but he watched them regardless, just in case.

After an hour, though, he let his guard down and started feeling human for the first time since he'd went down to visit Reverend Jordan, which seemed like a lifetime ago. He took in the fresh air and could practically taste the rich, fecund scent of corn. His belly rumbled, but he restrained himself from raiding the crop too soon.

Motes of dandelion fluff dotted the air around him, and he playfully blew a cirrus scrim of them away. As he did, he saw movement from the corner of his eye.

There. From the line of corn stalks. A woman stepped out, throwing her

 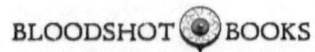

gorgeous head of dark hair back from her face.

Rachael? It was either her or a heretofore unknown twin sister. What was she doing here? Did she come back for him? He felt a longing twinge in his heart. Oh, how he'd missed her. He missed her presence at the dinner table, her thoughtful discourse at prayer time, the way she felt next to him at night.

Her eyes met with his, and the twinge migrated lower in his body. Soon, the front of his pants felt pinched and tight, and he moved forward, eager for his wife's embrace.

"Oh Rachael," he said. "I've missed you so. I'm glad you came back to me."

She stepped forward, a smile spreading across her face like the buttery light of the rising sun. "Judah. I had to see you. I missed you, too." She held out both hands to him.

Even as he folded her arms around him, he felt like something was off. Rachael didn't quite sound herself, but he didn't think too much about it. The building heat of his loins took precedence, and he shuddered when their bodies pressed together, and his rigidness prodded her just below the waist.

"My. You *have* missed me." Her hand wandered down to the bulge under his belt and caressed him, rubbing gently.

Heat exuded from Judah's body, and it practically evaporated off the top of his skull. He moaned as she unbuttoned his trousers and unlimbered his manhood.

Rachael primed his pump, gently squeezing, and Judah could feel his climax burning within him. Too soon. He leaned forward and kissed her, touching her face with his field-scarred hands.

Odd. Her cheek felt like his after a couple of days without shaving. His impending orgasm threatened to distract him from this quandary, but there was something too strange about her.

Something shifted in her face just as she dipped her head down toward his sex, mouth open and ready. Excited as he was about Rachael's intentions—she'd never done anything like *this* before—he almost dismissed it as a trick of shadow. Then, he noticed for a split second that it looked like she had deer's horns on her head.

Just like the beast.

The image of Rachel melted and flickered away, and Judah watched as the beast raised up his penis toward its razor sharp teeth. He screamed, going soft immediately, tearing himself from the monster's grip. He stumbled away and rolled backwards, almost striking his head on the base of a tree.

The smell of nature vanished as if someone turned off a switch, and his nostrils filled up with the beast's musk. He flailed around in the dirt, seeking his rifle and finding nothing. Now the beast loomed over him, grinning down at him, licking the palm it had used to stroke Judah's sex.

Where could the rifle be? He cast his eyes wildly, hoping it was close enough to reach, and then he saw it at the monster's feet. Casually, the abomination stooped and picked up the gun. It examined the weapon briefly before snapping the barrel in two like it was a twig.

Just like he had at the church, Judah fled, and when he came back to himself later—locked away in his house—he had no memory of it. All he knew was the beast had nearly killed him, just as it had killed the reverend.

And it had done so in broad daylight.

Now he had no refuge in the sun. He had no weapon. And considering its strength, the beast could easily get inside to him. He had no hope. He felt certain that he would die within the hour.

Why hadn't it killed him before? Was it toying with him? What did it want from him? Could it be just the taste of his flesh?

Something thumped on the porch. Again. A third and fourth time, each sound growing louder. He imagined those heavy hooves clopping closer, and his heart picked up its pace. The dark reek of the monster permeated even through the thick reinforced door. A loud rending noise battered at his ears, and the door—along with a goodly portion of the frame and wall—disappeared.

The beast's monstrous bulk stood in the threshold, a silhouette against the blazing sun behind it, and it took its first step into Judah's house. The creature opened its mouth, showing off its slavering chops, and reached a hoary hand toward its victim.

And in that moment, as fear practically tore Judah's heart out, searing every nerve in his body, epiphany struck, and he knew the only thing that could save him. Mustering all of his strength, he shouted one word: "Wait!"

The beast paused, and its thickly furred eyelids fluttered.

Laughing, no longer master of his own body, Judah rushed to his mantle, where he kept his Bible, and threw the book into the fireplace. As it had not been lit, the tome thumped down in the ash and sent up a cloud around it.

"I renounce Jesus Christ!" Judah shouted. He spat onto the dusty cover. "I was deceived, and I regret every moment of my worship of a false god. I feel like a fool!"

The beast smiled. Instead of finishing off its prey, it leaned back, its stout arms crossed, and waited.

"I should have seen the sign," Judah whispered. "As soon as I saw you, as soon as your existence disproved God's, I should have known. I should have started worshipping you right away."

The beast chuckled. "Go on."

"You are clearly a powerful being, the most powerful I've ever seen. You have abilities. You must be a god. And now, if you'll spare my life, I'll spend the rest of my days dedicated to worshipping you."

The beast's arms came untangled and swung at its sides as it straightened its body. "You know what I require of you, Judah Crenshaw."

Judah thought back to Reverend Jordan and to his slaughtered animals. A part of him thought he was mad for even considering this, but when he reflected on the matter, it would be a small sacrifice, especially since it had almost gotten him killed earlier.

He rushed to the kitchen and retrieved a butcher knife. When he returned, he undid his trousers and let them slide down his legs. He took hold of the head of his penis, stretching out the entire organ, and placed the blade against the shaft.

"No. It must be erect."

When Judah looked up, he saw Rachael again. Completely naked. Before the kids had been born, which meant no loose skin. No stretch marks. Just young, taut womanflesh.

Judah grew bigger in his hand as he watched this specter of his wife fondle herself, and just as he came closer to climax, he knew what the beast wanted.

Just before he cut himself, the beast said, in Rachel's sweet voice, "Don't forget the balls."

Judah pressed down with all his might and sliced. Fiery pain burned along his flesh as the blade bit into him halfway through the shaft. Blood exploded from the wound, and he felt his final orgasm rocket through his body, shooting thick crimson spurts onto the floor.

And even though it hurt him like nothing else on earth ever had, he forced himself to pull back and slice again, desperately hoping he could get the whole thing this time. He got the rest of the shaft and hit no resistance as he reached the sac. His testicles unraveled, and his manhood held on only by a strip of scrotum.

Judah couldn't bear to use the knife again, so he gripped a handful of his genitals and tore it away from his body. Blood audibly pattered down on the hardwood floor as he stumbled forward, holding his gristly prize aloft.

The beast had banished the image of Rachael, and now it reached out to Judah's gore-slicked hand. Daintily, it plucked the jumble of meat like picking a piece of lint off a shirt and lifted it up to its mouth, where it popped it in like a piece of candy. It chewed, absorbing all the sexual energy he could from this charged piece of flesh, and its own member stood up, tumescent and large like a man's forearm.

Judah collapsed, still feeling the dying pulse of his orgasm as blood pumped from the ragged hole between his legs. "May I . . . live?" He barely managed to get this gasp out.

"You may, my servant. There's just one more thing."

Gently, the beast turned Judah's trembling body onto his back and knelt down between his legs. Throbbing pain, combined with the animalistic stench from the beast, smashed whatever remained of his sanity as he howled with laughter. Part of him knew the beast's intention, and that part had made peace with it.

He spread his legs wider to accommodate the monster's girth. The hole, where once his genitals had been, stretched—not unpleasantly—as the beast thrust into him. Judah could feel his guts compress to make room, and he clutched the beast's hairy back, screaming its praises, worshipping it as loudly as his cracked and ruined voice would allow.

And that was the last thing he remembered for a quite some time.

Days later, he awoke in his own bed, but not once did he wonder if it had all been a nightmare. He felt the closed, knotted flesh between his legs and knew this wonderful dream had been true.

How would he tell Rachael and the boys? *Could* he? No matter. They were gone, abandoned him what seemed like years ago. All that remained of his life was the slight bulge in his belly.

He smiled warmly down at it and thought he felt something move inside of him.

John Bruni is the author of TALES OF QUESTIONABLE TASTE and POOR BASTARDS AND RICH FUCKS from StrangeHouse, as well as STRIP from Riot Forge. His short work has appeared in many places, including anthologies from Comet Press (VILE THINGS), Pill Hill (A HACKED UP HOLIDAY MASSACRE) and the GG Allin tribute BLOOD FOR YOU. He was the editor and publisher of TABARD INN and is currently in charge of Strange Story Saturdays for StrangeHouse. He lives in Elmhurst, IL, where no one eats anyone's genitals (or so he's told).

THE SERPENT'S ARMY

- A VALDUCAN STORY -

BY SETH SKORKOWSKY

JUNE 1, 1981

TRAVELERS shuffled past in varying shades of anxiety, their bags clutched to their sides or rolling behind them on leashes. A nearby crowd anxiously watched the white letters flip and click across the schedule board like helpless gamblers before the roulette wheel, praying for no delays. The stink of sweat, tension, stale smoke, and a hundred flavors of perfume filled the airport like an oily fog.

I stubbed my cigarette out in the ashtray and checked my watch. The number of travelers trickling out from the Customs area had begun to wane. A lean woman with short, boyish hair strode out, scolding a somber-looking teen in clipped French. I only hoped that meant they were processing Max and Alex's flight.

A blue-uniformed security officer wandered lazily by and stopped near a bank of payphones behind me. That all-too-familiar paranoia tickled up the back of my neck. Have I been standing here too long?

No. I pushed that away. People stand in airports all the time. Fifty-five minutes is nothing.

Still, the guard's presence made me nervous. Dämoren rested inside my briefcase, and airports get real testy about bringing loaded guns inside. The fact she was a century-old revolver would make little difference. But I sure as hell wasn't going to leave her in the car. I drew a fresh cigarette, and glanced back as I pulled out my lighter.

The guard was strolling away.

With a relieved grin, I lit my smoke and looked up in time to see Max Schmidt exiting the door ahead. His dark suit and slicked-back hair made him look like some high-fashion Secret Service agent, sans tie or sunglasses. He held a suitcase in one hand, a long black case in the other. Even locked up, trusting a baggage handler with his holy sword, Lukrasus, had to have been hell for him. Valducan knights normally wouldn't take a commercial flight, opting for more... creative means of bypassing Customs. But time was of the essence if we were going to get this lamia before it struck again.

I raised a hand for him to see me, but the Austrian was already coming my direction, gliding through the crowd with that dancer's grace of his.

"What's the point of taking a Concorde if you just have to wait around after you arrive?" I asked.

Max snorted and shook his head. "So you can get into the line faster." He set his suitcase down and we shared a one-armed hug. "How are you, Clay?"

"Can't complain."

"That," Schmidt said eyeing Dämoren's case, "is the most hideous thing

I've ever seen."

I grinned down at the black and white cowhide briefcase. "This your first time to Texas?"

"It is."

"Well, here this is considered quite fashionable."

"God, I hope not."

I laughed and looked past Max's shoulder. "Where's Alex?"

"He had to stay behind."

I froze halfway through a drag. "He didn't come?"

Max shook his head. "He was asked to assist with some of the Order's affairs."

"Hmm," I grumbled. "Well, his loss. Between the gunslinger and the sword dancer, ain't nothing can stop us." I ignored Max's tightening lips. He never liked his nickname, but I'm the only knight he lets get away with calling him that. "Come on, let's get out of here and get a drink."

I led him down the escalator and into the exhaust stink and rumbling engines of the parking garage. "So how was the funeral?" I asked.

"It was a good service." He loaded his bag into the trunk. "I wish you had been there."

"Mistress Meadows and me never really saw eye to eye. Besides," I said, sliding into the car, "someone has to keep hunting. Demons don't just take time off when one of us dies."

Max slipped into the passenger seat and looked at me, blue eyes smiling. "With that sentiment, I think maybe you and she were more alike than you know."

Choosing not to respond, I started the engine and pulled out into the rat maze of roads. Pink and red clouds streaked the sky, heralding sunset. "I really wish you could have gotten here earlier. Rest up before tonight."

"Rest?" Max chuckled. "You're getting old, Clay. Your report said we're dealing with a lamia."

"Yeah. Six months ago, police picked up a real shit bag. Biker named Mudrat."

Max's brow rose at the name, but he said nothing.

"Snagged him on a warrant for stabbing a man. But this guy was fucked up high when they got him, like angel dust or something. Took four officers to drag him down and he still managed to break one of their arms. He had two puncture wounds in his shoulder, still bleeding when they got him. About an inch apart. Got a picture of 'em when they booked him. Whole time he's talking crazy shit like how he's the chosen one of the angel's army and all that." I fished a couple quarters out of the console, and paid the tollbooth lady.

"Anyway," I continued, pulling onto the highway. "Next day, Mudrat gets in with one of the guards, bangs him up really bad, ends up getting himself killed. No loss. But during the autopsy, they discover two things. First, there weren't any drugs in his system save a little dope. Second, the puncture wounds had completely healed within fifteen hours. Coroner thought it was weird, and sent the finding off to some others to get opinions. One found its way to a guy I know in Houston who called me."

"Could just be insanity," Max said in his usual devil's advocate tone. "The twin punctures could be vampire or any of a half-dozen other breeds. Why do you think it a lamia?"

I shook my head. "I didn't at first. Just came to check it out. But then things started adding up."

"Such as?"

"Mudrat belonged to a gang calling themselves The Coyotes. About six months ago, they started changing their theme from coyotes to snakes. Recently started calling themselves the Serpent's Army. Now I've met enough bikers in my day to know that they get real cranky at even the thought of changing their name. Gangs fracture for that sort of thing. But no one left. Seemed unanimous, which, trust me, is weird. Lot of coyote tattoos to cover up. Next thing I found was a girl named Stephanie Muller went missing. Her brother reported that she'd recently started hanging out at a bar called The Kickstand. Last time anyone saw her was February fourth." I looked over at Max, his face lit in the glow of the setting sun. "There was a new moon that night."

His lips tightened. "So you think a lamia has enthralled an entire gang?"

I nodded. "Lamia love new moons, and if they're feeding people to it, that's when they'd do it. And in case you didn't know..."

"Tonight is new moon," Max finished.

"Bingo."

Max let out a long breath. "Anyone enthralled will protect the fiend to the death. How big is this motorcycle gang?"

"Maybe twenty." I grinned at his sudden frown. "Don't tell me that's got you worried?"

"Ten to one," he said. "Not good odds."

"You're forgetting about Miss Snakey."

"Not at all. After I've eliminated it and half of its men, that still leaves ten for you."

Brows raised, I turned to meet his serious blue eyes.

A self-satisfied grin pulled at the corner of his mouth and he looked back to the road. "Not good odds at all."

I opened my mouth, searching for a witty response, but all I could muster was, "Fuck you."

"So." Max coughed and wiped away the smile. "What's the plan?"

 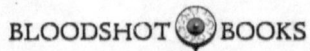

"Well, if The Serpent's Army is going to offer a victim to their master tonight, we need to keep an eye on 'em. See if they go to it or if it comes to them. Once we see her, take her out before she kills anyone, and if they are under her spell it should, hopefully, put an end to it."

Max nodded. "And they gather at this Kickstand?"

"That's right."

"So when you said we should get a drink...?"

"You got it. Though," I eyed Max's trim suit, "you might want to change first."

It was dark by the time we reached The Kickstand, a little one-story job half an hour outside Fort Worth. A few cars and pickups sat in the gravel lot. A wall of motorcycles stood before the front, the red and blue neon from the sign gleaming off their chrome.

Inside was dim, smoky, stank of beer and overfilled grease-traps. Zeppelin blared from a rainbow-strobing jukebox near the bar. Several rough-looking guys were clustered near the pool tables. Patches decorated their denim and leather vests in random, yet uniform order between them. Some appeared military, mementos from 'Nam, others were skulls and snakes. Tattoos and bracelets adorned their sleeveless, leathery arms. Several women were draped over their shoulders, laughing. Most looked to be professional fender lizards, but a few looked like tourists, gussied up for a night on the wild side with just the sort of men their daddies would shit themselves if they saw them with their little girls.

Max came in behind me. He'd changed into a T-shirt and jeans, but still managed to wear them in an almost formal manner. Curious eyes followed us to the bar, seeming to say, 'You boys walked into the wrong place.'

The girl behind the counter was a skinny brunette whose tank-top plunged so low I couldn't help but stare at the V between her tits. We ordered our beers and found a table near one corner, beneath a black and nicotine-yellowed POW flag.

After a couple minutes of idle chat, our attention mostly focused on the gang by the tables, Max finished his beer and asked, "What do you think?"

"Well," I said, lighting a fresh cigarette, "guy with the walrus moustache looks to be Chuck Schaeffer, leader of this little cadre. Everyone's orbiting him." I glanced to a Burt Reynolds wannabe leaning over the table for a shot. "Guy on the stick has a piece. Keeps peeking out when he bends down. One behind him, fatty with a ponytail, has one, too."

Max nodded. "As does the man with curly blond hair, but that's not what I was asking."

Pretending to scratch my ear, I stole a look at the blond. Damn, it. Max was right.

"What is our plan?" Max asked.

"You notice their manner? Hollow eyes, gleam of sweat, the tense undercurrent?"

He nodded.

"Seen that look before. Addicts in need of a fix."

"They keep checking their watches," Max said. "They're waiting."

"And more keep showing up to wait with them."

I sucked a drag and let it out. "If it's here, it's in the back or maybe there's a basement. Doubtful, though. Too loud for a lamia, and a snake-woman is not too likely to come slithering in here with all these people. They're probably going to go to it once all the junkies are assembled, or maybe after close it'll make an appearance. Just wanted to let us see what we're dealing with first."

Max ran a slender hand along his jaw and surveyed the room. "I think I've seen enough."

Sweat rolled down my neck and onto my already clinging shirt. The car windows were cracked only a little, so no one could see us inside. A hundred yards up the road, The Kickstand's lights burned bright against the country dark. More cars and bikes had arrived, then as the hours rolled by, many of the cars left, but the bikes remained.

My fingers idly traced along Dämoren's leather holster resting in my lap, following the lines along the ten-inch blade mounted beneath her barrel. That electric tingle of fear before a hunt always abated at her touch. The holy revolver soothed me, assured me that together nothing could stand in our way.

Beside me, Max dabbed his brow with a dark handkerchief, his other hand resting on the broadsword between his legs. His thumb circled the octagonal pommel. Maybe Lukrasus did the same sweet assurances for him. I licked my lips, urging them to ask, but couldn't. A Valducan knight shouldn't ask such things because they wouldn't want to be asked it themselves. Each relationship was personal. A holy weapon was a knight's spouse, parent, and child all rolled into one, an angel forged in steel. Dämoren had been a sword once. Then she was broken and rebuilt into a pistol, rising back like a demon-killing phoenix.

Max checked his watch and shook his head. "Too dark. Do you know what time it is?"

"Eleven-thirty by my guess," I said, watching a couple shuffle their way

 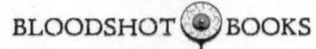

back to a pickup. "Bar closes at midnight, so it won't be long now."

Max's grip tightened on his sword, but he said nothing.

The minutes crawled by, then after all but three cars had left, The Serpent's Army filed out of the bar, several women among them, and began saddling up.

I straightened in my seat. "Looks like we're going to it."

Engines roared and thrummed. Chuck Schaefer rolled out first on a big pair of ape-hangers and gunned his engine. The rest followed suit, throwing up a cloud of dust as they rode out of the gravel lot and headed north.

"I count eighteen motorcycles," Max said.

"Let's just hope that's all of 'em." I waited until the last rider had left, then started the car.

Cool air whooshed through the open windows as we raced down the dark highway. The line of red taillights wormed around the bends ahead, their speed increasing.

"Don't get too close," Max warned. "But don't lose them."

I lit a cigarette and blew smoke out the open window. "Just who the hell do you think you're talking to? Don't worry."

Six miles later, the red lights flared in succession as they slowed and turned off the road. Dropping to a normal speed, I continued toward them. The bikers were filing in through an open sliding gate of some salvage yard, hidden behind a tall metal fence. Orange firelight flickered inside. We drove past, catching a brief glimpse of some junked cars, then continued on.

Half a mile later, I turned back around and pulled off the road about two hundred yards from the gate. "You ready?"

"Let's meet your lamia," Max said, then opened the door.

I stepped out and strapped on the gun belt. Over the sound of cicadas and frogs, engines roared in the distance. "Keep an eye out for any lights up the road," I said, tying the end of Dämoren's holster around my thigh with a leather thong. "There might be stragglers."

"And just who the hell do you think you're talking to?" he asked with a dry smile.

"Yeah, yeah." I drew Dämoren and checked her cylinder. Seven rounds. "Let's go."

Max pulled Lukrasus from her sheath and together we hurried along the tree-line toward the yard. Rock 'n roll blared as we drew closer. I guessed by the now closed gate that no one else was expected. The high sheet metal fence wrapped around the front of the property and continued through the trees. I nodded to Max and we followed it around, keeping low.

Near the back, the top of a train boxcar loomed above the wall. There weren't any tracks nearby, which led me to wonder how in the hell they got it in there.

"How's this?" I asked.

Max scanned around, set his foot against the fence, and pushed. He nodded, and without a word walked in a crouch straight up the side as casually as if it were lying flat on the ground. He peeked over the top and whispered, "They're gathering in the middle. Some kind of stage."

I lifted my hand. "Can you pull me up?"

Frowning, Max reached down and took hold of my wrist. He pulled, but only succeeded in sliding toward me. Evidently, Lukrasus' gift, which allows Max to choose which direction gravity pulls from could only work for him. It was worth a shot, though.

He released his hold and motioned to the boxcar. "If I laid on top, you could jump and grab my hand."

Even if I could make that jump, there was no way I could without banging my knees and boot toes against that sheet metal like a gong. Besides, I had no desire to show Max just how ungraceful I really was. "No good." I looked further down the fence line. "You go on up and lay low. I'll find another way in. On my signal we can hit that demon bitch from two fronts."

Max's brows drew close together. He opened his mouth to say something, when cheering erupted from inside the yard.

"Go on," I said. "We're almost out of time."

He nodded, then crawled spider-like, sword in hand, up the wall and onto the rail car.

Dämoren out front, I quickly crept around to the back side of the property. Another cheer broke out, followed by a woman's piercing scream. Short, terrified, it repeated over and over like an alarm or a skipping record. Ahead, a vertical wedge of light flickered through the fence wall, glowing like a flare in the moonless night.

I moved closer. A sapling had grown up, pushing two of the panels apart, maybe five inches at the widest. Peering between them, I could see the bikers gathered before a raised platform, their faces lit in orange firelight. Not one, but a pair of lamia stood on the stage, their backs to me. Their naked torsos were those of slender women, their creamy, flawless skin darkening as it met the scales of the giant snake tails that began at their waists. One was in a diamond pattern of green and gold. The other was an oily black, matching her long hair. This was worse than I'd thought.

Four men pressed a pair of women toward the platform. One, a blonde, was still shrieking her broken record screams. The lamia swayed back and forth hypnotically as the women neared. A bony rattle sang from the diamond one's tail, giving me a moment's shiver. The black lamia opened her mouth, wider than any human. The shrieking blonde fainted into the men's arms.

I raised Dämoren. One well-placed shot could take out the rattler and end this sicko sacrifice.

A gun barrel jammed into my ribs. "Drop it, asshole."

The instant of fear squashed away as my muscles tightened, ready to spin, knock the gun aside and cut the throat of whichever idiot was stupid enough to press a gun into me.

"Do it," a second voice ordered.

Damn it. From the corner of my eye I could see Burt Reynolds beside me. I couldn't see the second guy.

"Now," Burt said, shoving the pistol harder.

I nodded, removing my finger from Dämoren's trigger. Left hand open, I slowly lowered and set the holy revolver on the ground. They were going to have to shoot me before I'd drop her.

Burt took a step back, gun leveled. "Turn around."

I did, fighting the urge to search the darkness for Max.

The other guy, a man with greasy long hair, held a Mac10 Ingram, his hand clasped around a giant silencer. I sighed in the relief I hadn't succumbed to the urge to bitch-slap Burt for his rookie mistake. Greasy could have cut us both in half with one trigger squeeze.

Burt holstered his .45 and picked up Dämoren. I nearly kicked him for touching her, but Greasy's machine gun made me refrain.

Greasy motioned with the barrel. "Walk." And the two men led me around to a door at the far side.

"Look what we found," Burt declared as he shoved me through. My eyes watered at the sudden stink of smoke and diesel fumes. Fires burned within several perforated steel drums. The crowd turned and parted.

Chuck Schaefer stood at the foot of the stage, eyes wide with some inhuman fury. Blood dribbled from a pair of holes in his breast. Almost everyone had the same wounds, the same lustful rage.

"What is this?" Chuck roared.

"Found him out back," Greasy said.

Burt held up Dämoren.

The black-haired lamia's yellow eyes locked on the holy gun. "Bring him here."

Burt pushed me again, leading me past junked cars and piles of scrap. The two lamia rose up, ignoring the two unconscious women before them.

"Oppressor!" the diamond one hissed, then opened her mouth, revealing twin fangs. "I'll eat this one." Her jaw unhinged, opening wider, ready to eat me whole. That damned rattle started up.

White spittle clung to the corners of the bikers' mouths as they circled around me like wolves. Their huge pupils only verified that the demons' drugged venom had them enslaved. I didn't dare look at the rusting train car.

"I remember you." Chuck's head cocked as he leaned closer. "You were at the bar. Had a kraut buddy."

I only looked up at the demon bitches, glaring at me with hungry hate. *Max, you'd better do something.*

"Where's your friend?" Chuck demanded.

I met his whiteless eyes. "Fuck you."

The biker's fist came up so fast I didn't see it. It slammed into my jaw, sending me stumbling back into the crowd.

The distinct three-clack cock of Dämoren's hammer sounded at my ear.

"Answer him," Burt Reynolds snarled, gun leveled at my head.

"Let him go!"

All heads, including mine, turned to see Max standing atop the train car thirty feet away, broadsword down at his side.

"There's the German," a guy with a green bandanna sneered, pointing as if no one else had noticed.

Max's eyes narrowed on him. Growing up in a refugee camp after the war, Max really hates being called that. Light gleamed off Lukrasus' blade as he lifted it up.

The black-scaled lamia recoiled and hissed at seeing the sword. "Kill them!"

Guns raised in Max's direction, but before they could fire he shot off the top of the railcar like a missile, slicing bandanna guy's head off as he flew past. Max landed feet-first along the side of a stack of cars then sprung again before the guns could move on him. Twisting mid-air, he clipped the arm off a man with a pistol and skewered another before the blood spray had hit a screaming redhead square in the face. He leaped skyward, flipping and twirling.

Dämoren's hammer snapped forward with a crystalline click as Burt pulled the trigger. Nothing happened.

I grinned. Dumb fuck. Dämoren wouldn't shoot me. Before Burt could wrap his brain around that, I grabbed his wrist, yanked Dämoren from his hand, and slashed her blade right through Chuck Schaeffer's throat. Burt screamed in rage but I cocked Dämoren and shot him in the eye, unleashing a plume of gun smoke.

Shots erupted around me. Bikers were scrambling to hit Max as he flew through their ranks like a dancing Angel of Death. Changing the direction of his gravity at will, he moved in graceful random arcs, impossible to predict.

The green and gold lamia turned to retreat.

Not so fast. I cocked Dämoren and fired. The blessed slug took her right between the shoulders. Silvery blue demon fire ignited from the killing wound as she pitched forward, rattler tail lashing and balling.

I was about to take out the other one, when I saw Greasy level his machinegun at Max. I knocked the gun aside as he pulled the trigger,

 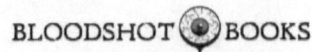

peppering a dozen shots into a station wagon. Then I slammed the revolver's blade down into his skull.

I grabbed the fallen machine gun in my off hand and took down three more shooters with a pair of short bursts, emptying the mag.

Max slashed a biker's gut, then somersaulted past me and over the stage. The black-tailed lamia was already across the yard, slithering over the fence. The metal tanged as he landed against the side, straddling her, blade down between his feet and through her spine.

Silver-blue fire burst from her eyes and mouth. He wrenched the blade free and she fell. The remaining half-dozen of the Serpent's Army staggered, their masters slain and souls now freed. They crumpled, unconscious, to the ground.

Max strolled back across the field of dead and unconscious, his face sweating. Burning blood flickered along his blade. "Great plan."

I holstered Dämoren. "Had to improvise." I nodded to the two demons, now blanketed in ghostly fire. Half an hour and any trace of them would be gone. "Worked well enough."

He shook his head. "Honestly, Clay, your definition of success terrifies me."

I shrugged and pulled the Ingram's strap over my shoulder. "We won. At the end of the day, that's all that matters."

Max eyed the machine gun. "Plan to keep that?"

"Hell yeah." I grinned. "Makes me feel like McQ."

His brow rose in a puzzled stare.

Not a John Wayne fan, then. "Come on, you uncultured bastard. I could use a drink, and this time, you're buying."

NOT YOUR AVERAGE MONSTER

Raised in the swamps and pine forests of East Texas, Seth Skorkowsky gravitated to the darker sides of fantasy, preferring horror and pulp heroes over knights in shining armor.

His debut novel, DÄMOREN, was released in 2014 by Ragnarok Publications. Seth's second Valducan Series novel, HOUNACIER, was published in 2015.

When not writing, Seth enjoys tabletop role-playing games, cheesy movies, and traveling the world with his wife.

You can find him at www.skorkowsky.com

WHERE THE SUN DON'T SHINE

BY PETE KAHLE

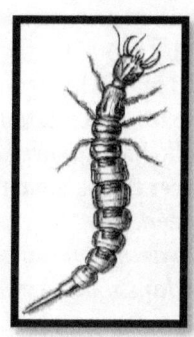

SATURDAY MORNING - Gordy Melbourne woke in agony on the couch in his living room with no idea where he was or why his gut hurt so much. With a drawn-out groan, he pulled himself to a seated position, immediately realizing that he was completely naked and covered from head to groin in what appeared to be dried vomit.

"Jesus Friggin' Christ, what did they get me into now?" he moaned under his breath.

By *they*, he meant his best friends Hector Nieves, Ross McGraw and Seth Mahler - partners in crime since they had all met each other back in 1989 in the same freshman homeroom at Winthrop Crane High School in Stonechurch, MA. Hard to believe that had been over twenty-five years ago since they still acted like foolish teen hooligans whenever they were given the chance to let loose. Gordy was supposedly the responsible one, the one to rein them in when their ideas put them in danger of bodily harm, but from the evidence surrounding him, he had failed miserably this time around.

He leaned forward and rubbed his face vigorously. A flurry of brownish-green puke flakes fell to the stained carpet in a cascade from his whiskered cheeks. Gordy looked around the room, taking in the disaster in all its glory. A trail of mud, gravel and dried leaves led from the front door into the kitchen, before a more recent path meandered into the living room to a spot next to the coffee table. There he had apparently stripped naked, left his filthy clothes in a pile and crawled over to the couch where he had passed out and upchucked on himself in his sleep.

I'm lucky I didn't choke to death on my own vomit, he thought. *I wouldn't have been found for days while I rotted and became a permanent part of the couch.*

Gordy shuddered and began to examine himself. Dried vomit and mud were caked like paint in his chest hair leading all the way down to his matted pubes. His arms and legs were covered with bruises and scratches. The nail on his left forefinger appeared to have been ripped off halfway to the cuticle. The sharp pain on his right flank turned out to be a yard-long abrasion from below his hip to his armpit. There were also a couple of large dime-sized puncture wounds there that wept a cloudy sticky liquid as if he had been stabbed by someone and dragged on the pavement. The holes throbbed in time with his heart.

Have I been in a fight? What the hell is going on?

He stood up and almost immediately fell to his knees with a short shriek. His ass and legs burned as if something had torn away a few layers of skin down to the muscle. Sobbing for a moment, Gordy reached far back between his legs and felt raw meat with shreds of torn flesh and hair stuck to the skin with dried blood.

Raw hamburger, he thought. *Something ground my ass into Grade A chopped sirloin*. He gingerly moved his fingers forward and was relieved to find that, although bloodied and tender, all of his vital male equipment was still intact.

Holding his breath, he whimpered and staggered to his feet. He leaned against the wall for support, leaving a trail of muddy, bloody streaks on the way to the bathroom down the hall.

The harsh fluorescent light revealed a monstrosity in the mirror. He wasn't a handsome man by any stretch of the imagination. At 38, he was the typical American white male. Thinning brown hair, muddy brown eyes, thirty to forty extra pounds that had settled in his gut and ass and the stereotypical goatee that many overweight men of his generation thought would give them back their jawline.

Now, however, he looked even worse than he had imagined, like a ghoul risen from its foul, sodden grave. The sclera of his right eye was suffused with blood from burst capillaries and, below it, his cheek looked like an over-ripe plum, swollen with juices and ready to burst. Gordy touched it lightly and nearly blacked out from the pain.

My cheek is broken, he thought, wondering if he had a concussion or worse. Hematoma. Aneurysm. Brain damage. *Whatever it is, I should call 9-1-1*, he thought, then instantly forgot the notion when he opened the shower door and stepped under the steaming spray.

He watched, mesmerized by the blood and mud swirling in red and brown spirals down the drain. It reminded him of something but, in his current state, he couldn't retrieve the thought and it slid away into the recesses of his mind.

His ears began ringing, his vision blurred and he had to grab the metal bar on the wall to avoid falling down. Voices chattered and gibbered over and over in his head...

...thedevilsassholethedevilsassho
lethedevilsassholethedevilsassh
olethedevilsassholethedevilsass
holethedevilsassholethedevilsas
sholethedevilsassholethedevilsa
ssholethedevilsassholethedevils
assholethedevilsassholethedev...

...twisting his brain into knots. A flood of vomit spewed from his throat covering himself and the glass shower door as he let go of the bar and fell to his knees in a daze.

He sat there on the shower floor sobbing as the spray beat down on his head until he was able to climb to his feet. The puke washed off rather easily, but the dried blood was another matter entirely. It had scabbed and caked all over his lower back and ass crack. He didn't even want to consider what could have caused such an injury or where it might have happened. For all he knew, he had been gang-raped by a family of inbred hillbillies Deliverance-style out in the woods.

Squeal like a pig, boy! C'mon, squeal! Yew shore got a purty mouth!

Unable to scrub away the dried blood as hard as he would have liked, he simply let the water dissolve the clumps as best as possible, and let the heat of the spray soothe his pain as he tried to remember what the hell had happened to him over the past few days.

SATURDAY AFTERNOON - He was feeling slightly more human after the shower and two Percocets that he had left over from when he had his wisdom teeth pulled last year. On second thought, he took four. He wasn't ready to venture out of his apartment, though - didn't want to leave his house at all – not even to see a doctor. The pain was still present, but not so bad that he couldn't think things through.

After his shower, Gordy changed into fresh boxers and a threadbare shirt that said *Jesus Hates the Yankees!* He collapsed once again on the couch (after flipping the cushions over so he didn't sit on the stains) and turned on the television when he realized that he didn't even know what day it was.

"Saturday?" he muttered when he saw the date listed on the channel guide. "What the...?"

As far as Gordy could tell, he had lost nearly four days of memories. His last recollection, foggy though it may have been, was from Tuesday morning when he had woken up at the crack of dawn to go meet the guys and head out... *somewhere*. And that was the problem. His memories simply ended there when he left the apartment complex in his beat-up Honda Civic.

In retrospect, he probably shouldn't have taken that many Percocets. His pain had been numbed, especially in his nether regions, but his concentration was shot to hell now. It was only after zoning out and watching twenty minutes of a documentary on the mating habits of African hyenas that he came to his senses and realized that the phone was still in his grip and he had yet to make any calls to see how the other guys were doing. Perhaps they could shed some light on his injuries and what they had been up to in the interim.

He called Ross first. Like Gordy, Ross was "between relationships" and he had much more free time than the others. Unlike Gordy, however, Ross did not have a job, nor did he live on his own.

He lived in his parents' house in the basement.

Of course, Ross would argue with anyone who described his living situation that way. According to him, it was much more than that. His room in the basement was technically called a mother-in-law apartment due to the fact that it had a separate entrance around back and he could come and go as he wanted (as long as he was quiet). But there were a number of other factors that complicated his claim.

For instance, he only had a half bathroom in what was actually a cramped converted closet, so he had to take showers upstairs. The washer and dryer for the entire family was just off of his living room, and although he did have a refrigerator, it was filled with beer, ice cream and microwave burritos. His place smelled of beans and drier sheets. Accordingly, he ended up eating most meals with his mom, dad, and sixteen year-old twin sisters upstairs.

And then there was the fact that he didn't have his own phone line downstairs.

One of the twins answered on the first ring.

"Hi Katie. Put Ross on the phone."

"I'm sorry. Who is this?" she answered in a saccharine tone.

"Gimme a break for once, Katie. You know it's me – Gordy. Can you please get him to come the phone? It's very important."

"This isn't Katie." Gordy could hear the sneer linger in the silence that followed. The twins didn't particularly like him that much.

"Kirstie... sorry," he sighed and corrected himself. "Can you get him? It's really urgent."

"I go by Kit now... and, just so you know, Katie wants to be called Kat."

Jesus Christ. Give me a break...

"Ok, Kat – I mean Kit – I'll remember that from now on. Can you please get him? Seriously. It's kinda important."

Kit paused, apparently enjoying the act of stringing him along for a few seconds, before relenting. "He's not here."

"What? Do you know where he is?"

"I dunno, Gordooooo," she dragged out his nickname in disdain. "You were with him last, weren't you? I haven't seen him since you dipshits left on your trip last week. I thought you weren't coming back until tomorrow, anyway."

"Wait... what trip?"

"Don't play stupid, Gordo. You know what trip. The one you all were planning so you could get back to nature and do some primitive "male bonding". That's what we heard you say when you thought we weren't listening. I thought it was your idea in the first place."

< BLINK!>

Gordy gasped as a light flashed behind his eyes and a sudden rush of vertigo overwhelmed him. His guts clenched and he became lightheaded as a torrent of mental images overwhelmed him, flooding his senses. His eyes rolled back and he fell back, slumping over the stained arm of the couch, telephone falling from his grasp to the floor.

TUESDAY AFTERNOON - *Gray clouds obscured the sun. A steady drizzle of rain leaked from the sky as the four men hiked up the beaten dirt path. They all wore large backpacks filled with the essentials for a few nights away from civilization – including a significant amount of alcohol - but it was obvious that none of them had been camping in quite a while.*

"Gordo – where the fuck are we?" bitched Hector as he stumbled on a small tree limb in his path. "Do you even know where this lake is? This was a completely stupid idea - camping at this time of year."

"Almost there," he responded. "You'll like it. I swear."

"We'd better," grumbled Hector again. "My shoes are ruined now."

"No one told you to wear your Jordans, man. We all knew it would be wet. Don't you have any boots?"

Hector just muttered unintelligibly in response.

No snow had fallen yet this year, but the perpetual gloom and the smell of rotting, wet leaves hung in the air. The trees had only a few orange and yellow stragglers left clinging to the branches. The last time he had been up to the lake was over two years ago when his parents were still alive. Winter was only weeks away and Gordy realized that this was probably not his best idea, but he wasn't about to turn back now. The guys would never let him live it down. He resolved to persevere and keep marching onward.

A dog or coyote yipped in the distance and Hector let out a whimper, eliciting taunts from the rest that he sounded like a little girl. Seth lagged behind as usual, staying out of the conversation and surreptitiously sucking on a lit cigarette like it was his mother's tit. Ross was the only one who seemed unbothered by the weather, probably because he was already well on his way to getting shitfaced, taking a swig every few minutes from a scarred pewter flask. Big surprise there, huh? What was actually astonishing was that he hadn't already sparked up a joint. He was probably saving that for after their arrival.

Ross wasn't the only one who had started drinking. For most of the hike, Gordy had been nursing a PBR tallboy in one hand while gripping a sturdy branch he had appropriated as his walking stick. He already regretted coming along on the trip, but he could never admit that to the guys. He had been the one who had planned it and talked it up over their misgivings. And now, of course, he was sick. The possibility that he would catch a bug had never even crossed his mind, but here he was, wheezing and coughing like an asthmatic schoolboy.

The first hour of the hike hadn't been too bad. The incline had been gradual and the path was easy to follow, but once they took the trail that led up the mountain to the lake and the elevation increased, his friends began to whine and complain. Especially Hector. Up ahead, the mountain rose sharply on a sheer grade to a cliff face at least fifty feet tall. The trail hugged the face before disappearing around the bend. Worst of all, debris littered the forest floor. Branches, tree limbs, and in some cases even entire trees, had fallen across their route, roots thrust out of the ground as if a moody giant had torn them free. Part of the dirt path even appeared to have been washed away. As they continued up the incline, evidence increased that something had scarred the land in the recent past.

"I guess there actually was an earthquake," grunted Seth.

"Huh?" Ross said, looking back. "What the hell are you talking about? I didn't feel anything."

"Not today, dipshit."

Gordy intervened, "Wait... was that the one on the news a couple of months ago? I think I heard about it."

"Yeah. That's the one. It wasn't very big, but supposedly the epicenter was right around here."

Gordy looked around. "Probably why all these trees are uprooted, huh?"

"Ya think?" Seth rolled his eyes and took another drag on his cancer stick. Ross and Hector snorted at his comment. Gordy held back a retort and continued up the mountain. After a few more minutes, though, Gordy was finally on the verge of calling it quits. He was just about to suggest that they turn back and head down the mountain when nature intervened and the light rain transformed into a torrential downpour.

"Are you kidding me?" yelled Hector at the sky. "Are you seriously kidding me? Just what we fucking needed!"

Yelling in frustration, they were soaked to the bone within seconds. The drumming of the rain on the land around them was deafening. Ross hollered, pointing out a mammoth, twisted maple tree half a football field

*away that had planted roots in the cracks at the base of the cliff face. Seeing
no other shelter remotely close to its size, the four men raced to the meager
cover beneath its sagging branches.*

"Damn it, Gordy," cursed Hector.

"Oh, give me a break. Like I had anything to do with this."

*"You could've checked the weather report," muttered Seth as he pressed
against the mossy trunk of the tree, vainly covering his eyes to avoid some of
the more powerful squalls.*

*Gordy was about to retort again when Ross blurted out, "Guys, there's
a cave here!"*

*On the cliff face behind the tree, one of the cracks in which the roots
were growing was large enough for a full-grown man to squeeze through.
Even with his bulky backpack, Ross, who was not a small man, could
obviously wriggle through the gap.*

"That won't fit all of us," argued Gordy. "It looks dangerous."

*"Screw that. If you're not going in, I will," Hector said, rushing
forward. He ripped away the foliage that had camouflaged the entrance
and leaned in, illuminating the interior with the flashlight app on his phone.
Lightning flashed and a crash of thunder sounded close behind them. He
laughed and took off his backpack. "It gets a lot wider after a few feet. Big
enough for all of us! I'm going in."*

*"Wait..." Before Gordy could protest, Hector wriggled past the narrow
opening into the wider passage beyond. Ross and Seth ducked in after him.
Gordy let out a string of profanity and, seconds later, followed his friends
into the crevasse.*

Gordy was shitting fire into a hole in his back yard when he came out of
his fog. A guttural howl escaped him as what felt like a torrent of molten lead
laced with shards of glass streamed in a brown arc from his ravaged colon. He
was leaning forward on his knees, straddled over a foot-deep hollow that,
based on the grass and mud caked beneath his fingernails, he had recently
excavated with his bare hands. Each spasm of his guts released another
steaming discharge into the hole, so painful that he nearly blacked out in
agony again. He couldn't even think.

Finally, after he had apparently emptied the entire contents of his body
cavity, Gordy fell forward sobbing and curled into a ball. He lay there in the
afternoon sun and moaned for a few minutes before crawling to his feet and
looking himself over. He was naked from the waist down. Red and brown
streaks ran down his thighs. A few feet away, the remnants of his boxers lay

torn to shreds, stained with blood and fecal matter in a ball at the foot of his porch.

"What the fuck is going on?" he blubbered. Something was seriously wrong with him. First, he had lost four days of memories and now this? Who knew what he had done in the lost four days? Gordy did even want to think of what could have happened while he was blacked out. Maybe he had a concussion. Some type of head injury had to be causing these blackouts. The alternative was not something he even wanted to consider.

And then there was the river of shit that was pouring out of him. He didn't know if it was a disease or some sort of bizarre intestinal infection, but he knew that he had to see a doctor as soon as possible. That was an unmistakable fact. It just wasn't normal to crap like a fire hose, especially with what felt like enough force to perforate his intestines. He didn't even want to consider why he was doing it in a hole in his back yard.

Gordy normally hated doctors – in fact, he couldn't remember the last time he had gone in for a physical – but this time there was no other alternative. He would have to suck it up and seek some help, but first he needed to get clean. Again. He pulled himself slowly to his feet and staggered toward the hose attached to the spigot on the side of his house.

Thankfully, he lived in a relatively wooded area. The Tumasovs, his closest neighbors, couldn't have seen him doing his business unless they walked through a few yards of brambles that separated their two properties. They were an old antisocial Russian couple with at least ten quasi-feral cats and dogs that used his and other yards in the neighborhood as their own personal toilet. He had waved to them a few times when he first moved in, but when it became obvious that they didn't want to be friendly, he gave up and left them alone.

He hoped they had at least had their windows closed because he had been screaming pretty loudly and, based upon the pain in his throat and the hoarse quality of his voice, it had been going on for quite some time. Perhaps he was lucky and they weren't home.

Each step he took induced another wave of burning agony in his nether regions, but he eventually made it to the faucet and gingerly turned it on. He gasped as the water hit him. It was so cold, but the initial shock gave way to relief as the icy flow numbed his raw wounds. Closing his eyes, Gordy let the open hose run freely over his bloody hindquarters, rinsing away the stains and the chunks. The pain was still there, but at least it had subsided to the point where he could think again.

Blearily, he examined his hands. His fingers were raw and swollen, his nails torn and bloody. Dirt stained his pores. Dozens of fresh cuts and abrasions scarred his palms and knuckles. It looked like he had been digging with his bare hands for hours, and when he looked around the yard he realized that might be closer to the truth than seemed possible.

In addition to the open hole where he had been recently occupied, there were at least five – no, make that six – similarly-sized mounds of torn-up grass and earth. Odds were that he had also made a *deposit* in those holes as well. That settled it – he needed to get to a doctor ASAP. Whatever was going on was much more than an intestinal bug or food poisoning. Neither caused people to black out or go into a fugue state, did they? It needed to be taken care of immediately, but before he could do that, however, Gordy had to change his clothes... *yet again.*

He climbed the back steps and reentered the house, hobbling like an arthritic old man. Remarkably, other than the fact that the screen was wide open and his cell phone had been left unattended in the middle of the kitchen floor, there was no sign that anything else had happened inside the house since his blackout.

He finished cleaning up in the shower, and pulled on a t-shirt and the baggiest pair of sweatpants he owned. His stomach gurgled and he felt pressure in his lower abdomen. *Goddamn, I'm bloated. Feels like I swallowed a bowling ball*, he thought. *Please let this be over soon. I don't think my ass can take this anymore.* He was deciding whether to go to the ER, or to see if his primary physician had any open appointment soon, when a series of thoughts occurred to him. *How did I get home? Why can't I remember driving? Is my car even in the driveway?* Heading to look out the window facing the street, Gordy racked his brain for any hint of what had happened since they had hidden in the cave – if that was even an actual memory rather than the remnants of a nightmare.

Thankfully, his fears were unfounded. His beat-up Honda Civic was parked out front, half on the driveway and half on the piebald turf that he pretended was a front lawn. It was undeniable that it was a dreadful parking job, but otherwise the vehicle had emerged unscathed.

A barrage of barks and growls filled the air. He turned around, wincing at the agony in his ass, and realized that the animal sounds were coming from his back yard. The growls became louder. Peppered with wailing and intermittent yips, the baying was coming through the window over the kitchen sink. Gordy limped over and peered out. One of the neighbors' dog was in his yard, going psycho barking at something on the ground. Right around where he had left his droppings.

"What fresh hell is this?"

A BESTIARY OF HORRORS

TUESDAY EVENING - *Ross started drinking first. In other words, as they all had known, he had been drinking the whole while, but now that they were stranded for the duration of the storm – and it looked like it would be a continuous downpour all night – he made the executive decision to salvage the day and make sure everyone got utterly shitfaced like him. Ross loved to drink, but he preferred that others drank with him. It was easier to deny that he had an alcohol dependency that way.*

Gordy initially took it easy with the alcohol intake. He had the thought in his head that the rain would stop soon and he could get them to the cabin where they would start a fire, dry off, and get thoroughly obliterated in front of a campfire. Soon, however, he realized that they would probably be sleeping in the cave and it quickly became apparent that he would never live this down, so he might as well have some fun.

They had all brought some beer, but without a stream in which to refrigerate the cans, it was piss warm, so they started on the hard stuff right away. Gordy and Hector had each brought a couple bottles of cheap rum, Seth had his usual bottle of scotch, and Ross had filled his Camelbak canteen with Kool-Aid and a generous amount of grain alcohol.

Things got stupid rather quickly after that.

After several hours of drinking and praying for the storm to subside, the guys grew restless. The four of them huddled in various stages of undress, waiting for their clothes to dry. Even though there was still at least an hour of daylight remaining before sunset, the rain clouds outside obscured the sun and the illumination inside the cave was little more than a dim glow from the entrance, muted and gray. Gordy did have a couple of flashlights, but he only used them sparingly in order to conserve the batteries on the chance they would be here through the night, namely when they were searching their backpacks for alcohol. During those brief moments of light, they saw that the cave became funnel-shaped, narrower towards the back wall where a small waist-high opening led into darkness.

The howling wind blowing across the cave entrance produced a continuous haunting sigh that hissed off the walls like the final gasps of dying men. A mutual chill traveled up their spines at the sound. Conversation had ceased earlier. Listening to the rain, they had come to the obvious conclusion that they would be staying the night. Hector had already unrolled his sleeping bag and passed out. Gordy had changed out his wet clothes and now sulked next to him in his pajamas until they dried off. Seth sat near the entrance, smoking another cigarette and watching the rain pound the earth mere feet away, while Ross paced around in a nervous circle like a dog waiting by the door to go outside.

"I'm bored, guys." he said, slurring his words. "This seriously sucks."

"I said I was sorry, dude. I should've known better," Gordy replied. "Next time we'll go to Foxwoods and play the slots."

"Foxwoods?" I'd rather go to a Pats game and tailgate. We could watch them stomp the other team"

"And be home sleeping in our own beds," interjected Seth.

"Anything would be better", he said. "Hey Gordo, let me borrow that flashlight for a bit."

"What for?"

"Just want to walk around the cave a bit and see if we missed anything."

"Fine," Gordy said, handing over the SureFire. "Don't use it for too long. It's expensive and we may need it later."

He nodded and flicked on the beam, immediately blinding Gordy, who cursed as he covered his face and stumbled back into the wall. Ross ignored his friend's pain and walked away, waving the light in a back-and-forth pattern along the walls and floor.

Other than the debris of the past few months – branches, stones and leaves mainly – nothing seemed to stick out and spark his interest, until the flashlight beam washed over the hole on the far wall. He looked in the opening with the light and immediately realized that the small tunnel curved down into a narrow chimney. Aiming the beam down the shaft, he realized something immediately.

"Holy crap, this is deep," he exclaimed. "I can't even see a bottom." To prove his observation, he picked a baseball-sized stone from the floor and dropped it down the hole. Nearly ten seconds later, the sound of it hitting bottom echoed up to them.

Seth looked up sharply and walked over with a curious look on his face.

"Try that again," he said.

Ross repeated his action and Seth counted the seconds.

"Nine," he reported.

"Wow... that must be like a football field."

"Try five of them. It would have to travel a few hundred yards to take that long to hit bottom."

Ross shook his head in bewilderment. "How do you even remember that? We took Physics over a decade ago."

"You might still know it too if you didn't spend your high school years stoned off your ass," blurted Gordy from the other side of the cave.

Seth laughed as Ross grumbled under his breath. He seemed about to respond with a when he cocked his head and frowned. "Do you hear that?" he said as he stuck his head back in the hole.

"Hear what?" Gordy said. "All I hear is the rain."

"Ross, give it a rest," Seth added with a sigh.

"Shhh, shut up! Just shut up! Stop talking and listen!"

Seth and Gordy exchanged worried glances. They had been friends with Ross for a long time. He had a severe inferiority complex and they were well aware that he had a short fuse when he felt he was being mocked, especially when he was drunk. Sometimes it was fun to needle him until he did something that he would regret the next morning, but now was not the time for him to have a meltdown. Neither of them would put it past him to rush out into the night and get lost in the storm where he would probably get struck by a falling limb from a tree or maybe die of hypothermia. That was definitely something they did not want to deal with at that moment.

So they held their tongues and shut up... and, surprisingly, they heard the noise, too.

A slick, rustling sound came directly from the hole in the wall. Hearing it painted a picture in Gordy's mind of someone crumpling a large amount of cellophane at the bottom of a well. Crackling and echoing up the twisting stone chimney, the noise sounded like a chorus of whispers that moved with an organic ebb and flow.

Ross, grinning at the looks on their faces, proclaimed, "I told you I heard something!"

Seth walked back into the cave to take a look. "It's gotta be an echo. Some trick of the acoustics warping the sounds of the storm."

"Maybe an underground stream?" suggested Gordy.

Ross shook his head. "Nah, it seems like something's moving down there. Up and down the sides of the hole."

"Shine the flashlight at it."

"No shit, Sherlock. I've already tried that, but it's too friggin' deep. The light can't reach that far down."

"Let me try looking," interrupted Seth. Ross handed him the flashlight and he looked down the shaft, carefully aiming for the center of the darkness. Nothing. Shadows and stone walls extending down. That was all.

"Sounds like a giant bowl of Rice Krispies down there, but I still can't see shit," he admitted. "It's black as hell down there."

An updraft of warm air hit him in the face and he pulled his head out coughing as he tried not to vomit. The smell of rot and methane filled the chamber, so thick they could taste it on their tongues. Hector woke screaming. "Aaauuggh! What is that? It smells like the Devil's asshole!" He ducked back into his sleeping bag and covered his head. The others covered their faces with their sleeves and alternated between holding their breath and trying not to fall down laughing as he spewed forth a barrage of muffled Spanish profanity.

Seth began shouting in a fake Speedy Gonzalez accent, "Andale! Andale! Es el Culo del Diablo!"

Normally Gordy would have sighed in disapproval when Seth or Ross blurted out an ignorant comment like that, but now he couldn't even catch his breath. He was already feeling a bit sick from the amount of rum he had drank and the stench was more than he could handle. Sinking to his knees, he attempted to filter it out by breathing through the fabric of his sweatshirt.

Behind them, Ross was on a mission. He ran to his backpack and pulled out a long thin object wrapped in plastic. He peeled the wrapper off, revealing a bundle of long, thin, brightly-colored cardboard tubes – roman candles left over from the 4th of July. He had planned to light them one night at the cabin, but now seemed more appropriate.

"This'll light things up," he laughed as he separated. "I'm gonna shoot this down where the sun don't shine – right down the Devil's Asshole." Pulling out his lighter, he walked to the opening and stuck his head in once more to check if anything had changed.

The smell of decay was even stronger and the beam from the flashlight still could not penetrate the stygian depths of the shaft. "This is gonna be awesome," he muttered to himself. He flicked the lighter and held the flame to the wick.

Back behind him, both Seth and Gordy were watching. Hector was still huddled in his sleeping bag. Seth was somewhat confused. Gordy, on the other hand, felt nervous when Ross pulled out the fireworks, but he couldn't think clearly.

"Ross --" he said. "What are you --?"

The wick sparked and ignited. Ross pointed it down the hole and prepared for the pyrotechnics to begin. All at once, the pieces all clicked together and Gordy knew what was wrong.

Methane.

Fire.

"Stooooopppppp!" Gordy screamed, but it was far too late. The gas ignited and a plume of fire exploded into the main cave.

Something was making the dog lose its mind. It straddled the edge of the shit pit in the center of the yard and howled so loud that it seemed its throat would rupture. Gordy recognized it as the one he considered the alpha male of the Timusovs' pack of untamed mutts. He didn't know its name, but since one of its favorite activities during the winter was to scour Gordy's yard for frozen poopsicles for a midday snack, he liked to think of it as the Unholy Ravenous Turdmonster.

The Turdmonster was an extremely large dog. Scratch that - it was freaking humongous. There was obviously some St. Bernard blood in its

bloodline, or perhaps a Bull Mastiff, or some breed that regularly gets mistaken for a horse or a baby mammoth. Gordy also thought that there might be some poodle in its lineage since its hair, though matted, overgrown and filthy, was on the curly side. If it weighed anything less than two hundred pounds, Gordy would eat his hat.

Though it could have intimidated anyone who was unfamiliar with it, Turdmonster had never bothered Gordy or scared him. Before today, he had only heard his canine neighbor bark a few times, and those instances were in response to other dogs yapping down the street. To be honest, Gordy's back yard would have been much more unsanitary if it hadn't been regularly looking for some snacks. Whenever Gordy came out during one of its frozen feces foraging missions, it just gave him a look that said *Okay, okay, hold your horses, buddy. I'm outta here*, and then he slunk into the woods between the yards. The unspoken agreement between them had always been that neither one of them would deny the other passage through the back yard. It was an amicable truce.

As its booming barks echoed through his and the neighbors' yards, Gordy went to look out the screen door to see what was causing the canine meltdown. The Turdmonster was thoroughly enraged by something in the hole where Gordy had had his unfortunate accident earlier. Quietly, he stepped out onto his back deck, careful to avoid the boards that creaked, and leaned against the wooden railing to get a closer look.

Now that he was closer, he heard a whisper of something in the air in the few moments between the barks and growls. *Bubble wrap*, he thought. *Sounds like someone is popping bubble wrap. A shitload of it.* The weird noise was coming directly from the makeshift toilet. He wanted to go investigate, but, with the Turdmonster in a mindless frenzy less than ten yards away, he realized that the idea was ill-advised.

Seconds later, the opportunity presented itself. Turdmonster leaned forward sniffing and whining at what he saw in the hollow. The big dog appeared confused and frightened. A hole filled with shit wasn't something it found every day, but it seemed to sense that something was off kilter. The bubble wrap noise seemed to increase in pitch and a flash of movement lashed at Turdmonster's muzzle. He reared backwards with a sharp yelp of pain. The dog scrambled frantically away from the hole and turned tail, yipping in panic as it ran away, blood leaking from a deep circular wound that had been ripped from its nose by whatever had attacked it.

What the hell just happened here? Gordy thought to himself. He looked around but the Turdmonster was long gone, having run off into the trees.

Did something attack the dog? What the hell is in that hole? He would rather not see the contents, considering where they had come from, but he had to see what had scared the dog away.

Taking the wooden stairs gingerly, Gordy stepped down to his lawn and walked to the edge of the hole, wincing with every movement. He still heard the popping bubble wrap sounds and they were growing louder as he came closer. Reaching the hole, he peered in and immediately staggered back, nauseated by what he saw.

He had expected to see the remnants of a soup of blood and feces soaking into the earth. Not pleasant at all, but instead the pit revealed a mass of worms writhing and churning in the stew. *No, not worms* - worms didn't have scarlet pincers and mandibles and dozens of small, thorny, chitinous limbs. Worms weren't translucent and their innards weren't visible - at least Gordy didn't think so. He could see clumps of the most recent meal they had eaten (and he was pretty certain he knew what had been on the menu) passing through their abdomens.

Again, Gordy felt sick to his stomach and more than a little afraid. Did he really crap those things out, and were any still inside him? He steeled himself and peeked over the edge again to get a second look. This time, he forced himself to take note of the details, regardless of how disgusting they were. If more of these worms/grubs/larva were actually still inside him, he would need to be able to describe them to the doctor. They could be some type of exotic parasite that he had picked up in the woods. Who knew what diseases he could have now?

The larva swam in the pool of waste, rolling over each other in a slimy tangle. Their constant motion and chittering mandibles were the source of the bubble wrap sounds. Gordy realized now that he couldn't delay any longer. He had to go to the ER immediately, and he needed to bring a sample of the larva so they could quickly identify what they were. To do that, he needed some tools.

A not-so-quick trip to the kitchen later, he was back at the hole with New England Patriots souvenir cup (that Hector had left in his sink last week), and a plastic ladle (which he would toss in the trash as soon as he was finished with it).

"Ugh, this is vile," he muttered as he skimmed a couple of the smaller larva from the surface of the pool into the cup. Each were about an inch long and they began wriggling furiously as soon as they were pulled away from the warm comfort of the pit. Violently, even. As if they were calling for help...

Gordy secured the lid of the cup and turned to walk back into the house and call for a ride to the ER when something jabbed his left ankle. All strength in that leg and fell to his knees. A sensation of burning acid spread past his knee into his thigh. He looked back to see what had attacked him. One of the larva was attached to his leg, but this one was much larger than the ones in the cup. By a factor of ten, at least, perhaps as much as twenty times larger. It was the size of his forearm with serrated pincers larger than his thumb buried in the meat of his left calf. The larva squeezed the pincers again, cutting deeper into the meat. Through the jelly-like flesh, Gordy could see a gland beneath each of the pincers pumping the acidic venom into his muscle.

With each squeeze, the burning crimson liquid seared inside him, cauterizing his pain receptors and gradually numbing his lower leg, but Gordy was too shocked to care. The sight of the giant gelatinous larva had triggered a critical synapse in his brain, opening the floodgates, and he remembered the missing days.

He remembered every horrible second.

The explosion was instantaneous. A blinding white radiance filled the cave, followed milliseconds later by an equally powerful swell of scorching heat that had the three of them diving for the cave floor to escape it. And then, as soon as it happened, it was over.

The cave smelled like burning hair and ozone. A high-pitched ringing muffled their screams. Hector whimpered in panic from inside his sleeping bag; Seth and Gordy were sprawled on the cave floor, amazed that they were still alive; and Ross leaned against the wall, moaning in pain. Even in the dim light of the cave, it was apparent that he had taken the brunt of the explosion in the face. His hair and eyebrows were singed and the skin on his face was bright red as if he had been sunbathing without any sunblock for hours.

"Asshole!" screamed Seth, losing his usual cool composure, "You stupid, braindead burnout asshole! What the fuck were you thinking, Ross? Have you killed every single brain cell in your skull?"

"Dude," muttered Ross. "I'm sorry. I made a mistake."

"It was a mistake that could have gotten us all killed, man," said Gordy. "You gotta tone it down with the 'crazy and unpredictable' act. It's old."

"Man, I said I was sorry! We wouldn't have been here if you had…"

"Gimme a break, Ross. That's beside the point. My mistake has no connection to your decision to shoot a roman candle off at all."

Hector sat up suddenly and cocked his ear. "Guys, is it me or is that weird noise getting a lot louder?"

"What?"

"That noise," he said, pointing toward the opposite wall with the hole where the fire. He was right. In the minute since Ross' adventures with gunpowder, the sounds echoing from the hole had steadily increased in volume until it could easily be heard from every area of the cave. Needing a

distraction to calm his nerves, Seth walked over to the gap in the wall and stuck his head in to look down the shaft.

Seconds later, he was engulfed by a crawling, slithering mass of pincers and claws.

The plastic ladle was not an optimal weapon at all. Gordy whacked the giant larva over the head three or four times, but it just bounced off the rubbery flesh like a spoon bouncing off of a Jell-O mold. The greasy foot-long grub let out a few clicks and hisses, but it wouldn't release its grip. By then, his left leg had the worst case of pins and needles he had ever experienced, rendering it thoroughly numb and useless.

He reversed the ladle and tried to pry the thing off him by inserting the handle between the pincers and levering it out of his leg, but the handle was too flimsy. It snapped in half and all that remained of the handle was a jagged six-inch stump.

"Goddamnit!" Cursing, Gordy desperately stabbed it over and over until he finally cut through the rubbery skin and it popped like an old blister. A cloudy foul-smelling sludge slopped from the wound onto the ground as the larva froze in death and slid off his leg. Scooting backwards a few feet, he began to sob in great heaving gasps.

Everything from the past few days was now fresh in his mind as if it had just happened within the hour. The wounds on his ankle matched the two swollen holes in his armpit, only smaller and closer together. He rolled over onto his stomach and began to drag himself around the side of his house toward the garage. He still had to get to a hospital, but before he could think of that, he had to take care of this and other nests. These creatures could not be allowed to live.

A tide of twisting mouths and slime poured from the breach in the cave wall, swarming over Seth and flowing into the cave. The sounds resembling bubbles popping and thousands of claws scraping against the stone deafened them. The wormy mass was so heavy that the ones on the bottom were crushed; their vile innards coated the cave floor with a slick layer of viscous sludge.

Ross was the next to be overwhelmed. Holding his burnt face in his hands, he never had time to recognize the threat coming for him. The worms flowed up his legs and torso, biting and stinging their way into his nose and mouth. He fell to the floor choking on them and soon was lost from sight.

 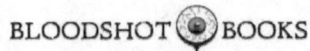

Gordy was closest to the entrance. He screamed at Hector, exhorting him to get out of the cave. Hector was in a panic, trying to pull his way out of his sleeping bag, screaming for help when the zipper became stuck.

"Gordy! I can't get out," he begged. "Please!"

Without thinking, Gordy ran forward and yanked on the zipper tab. It was thoroughly jammed; a folded bit of nylon was caught between the slider and the teeth. There was no time to work it loose.

"Fuck the zipper," he yelled. "Rip it open. Pull yourself out!"

Hector's eyes widened. Looking back into the recesses of the cave, he wailed, "GORDY!"

Gordy turned around. The crawling sea of grubs was nearly to them, but the monstrosity beyond them was what caught his eye. A massive specimen was pulling itself out of the shaft through the hole in the wall. The grubs flowing across the floor ranged in size from half an inch to three inches long. This one was the size of a full-grown man.

Anyone who had watched as many Animal Planet documentaries as Gordy had could identify it as the Queen.

Pushing the last of her bulk out of the gap, she flopped to the floor, crushing hundreds of her spawn as she landed. A flurry of wet squelches sounded as each of her two dozen legs emerged from muculent cavities in her sides, unfolding to gain purchase on the slippery floor. She rose up and faced the two remaining friends across the cave, snapping her blood-red clapperclaws together like a chef sharpening her knives. Scarlet venom leaked from the tips. Though Gordy couldn't see any eyes along her flanks, it was dreadfully apparent that she was looking directly at him. She began to drag her immense bulk in his direction.

With a hoarse desperate cry, he dropped Hector's sleeping bag, turned toward the narrow entrance of the cave, and ran blindly for his life. Behind him, Hector's screams of terror were quickly muffled as the worms reached him and filled his mouth.

Gordy pulled himself up on his good leg and dragged himself around the corner of his house by leaning against the vinyl siding for support. His other leg was completely useless from the paralyzing venom that the grub had injected, but he still managed to shuffle along with his three good limbs.

I let my friends get slaughtered by those things. It's my fault we were even in that goddamned cave. The horror of what had happened repeated itself in his mind over and over again. He saw his friends' dying faces again and was overwhelmed with nearly crippling guilt. Even if their actions may have slightly contributed to the situation, ultimately Gordy knew that he was at fault.

He turned the corner and, as he had expected, found the garage wide open. At the back, covered by an oil-stained tarpaulin, his old riding mower sat in the corner. He hadn't used it in nearly two years, ever since he had begun paying an entrepreneurial neighborhood teen to mow it twice a month. He crossed his fingers that it would start. Otherwise, he was out of options.

Ten minutes later, after an effort so draining that he had vomited on the garage floor, he sat on the mower and managed to start the ignition on only the third try. At his feet, on the mower deck, sat a 5 gallon jug of gasoline. It was only about half full, but he didn't have anything else that was flammable, so that would have to be enough for the job he was about to do.

Driving with his left hand, Gordy held a propane grill lighter in his right ready to ignite the gasoline and fry those vermin. He exited the garage, leg limply splayed out to the side, and turned the corner into his back yard where the churning holes remained. The sound of the mower drowned out the noise coming from the original hole, but he could still see the frothing, churning soup of grubs ahead of him. He drove the mower to the open hole and poured a few splashes onto the surface. Immediately, the grubs began writhing and jumping out of the gory sludge. One flick of the lighter and the hole was filled with dancing flames. Gordy smiled to himself as the grubs sizzled and popped. He continued around his yard, soaking the five other mounds where he had left a deposit with gasoline. Once all six holes were burning, he sat there to make certain that the contents were thoroughly burnt to cinders.

As he watched the six plumes of black smoke rise in the sky, he felt some discomfort and nausea as the burning shit stench filled the air and blew back in his face. Disgusted, he retched on the opposite side so violently that his upper abdomen spasmed and he doubled over the steering wheel as more violent convulsions rippled through him. He fell off the mower holding his gut as another sharp pain hit him. It felt as if someone was stabbing him... from the inside.

Gordy rolled onto his back screaming. He pulled up his t-shirt and confirmed what he had feared. A large bulge in his abdomen had pushed his navel inside out, and a two inch long pincer covered in blood and gore was slowing digging its way out of the umbilical cavity.

Freedom was less than ten feet away when the Queen caught Gordy and slammed him to the cave floor. He wailed as she climbed his back and pinned him beneath her mass clamping her pincers on his right flank. The jagged barbs pierced the flesh directly beneath his armpit and the paralytic

venom pumped into his body. Within a minute, he was unable to move more than with the slightest of tremors.

Circulation and breathing slowed as he was dragged back into the dark cave. He was still conscious but his perception was altered to the point where sounds echoed and everything he saw faded in and out in a slow-motion strobe effect.

Thankfully he was numb, feeling no pain and only the slightest of pressure.

Once the Queen had pulled him back into the main cavern, she left him on his side on a layer of bodies of her crushed and scorched spawn. He could see now that she had been injured by the roman candle. A foot-long burn mark like molten glass scarred her upper flank and a pungent ooze leaked from the wound.

Hours passed.

Thousands upon thousands of her children crawled along the floor and flowed up the wall in the dim glow of the flashlight that still cast its beam from where it had fallen. A few even walked along the ceiling, sometimes dropping to the floor and bursting with a wet impact. Many of them climbed his frozen body as if he were only an outcropping of stone around which they needed to maneuver. Across his arms, legs, mouth and eyes, he felt their sharp feet scratch along his skin. None of them, however, attempted to crawl inside his mouth or other orifices, nor did they feed upon him.

His friends were not so lucky.

Little remained of Seth. He had been consumed down to his bloody bones. Even his clothes had been eaten, except for his wristwatch, the eyelets of his boots and his beloved Captain America belt buckle that he wore when he could be certain that no one of the opposite sex was likely to see him.

From his vantage point, Gordy could only see the upper half of Ross, but what he saw would have made him scream in terror if he was able to make a sound. The grubs had crawled inside his body like the carcass of a wild animal left to decompose on an African veldt. Gases had bloated his face and torso to twice their size and the constant motion of the creatures feeding on his interior caused his skin to ripple like the ocean tide. Hector seemed to have suffered the same fate as Ross, but since he was still stuck inside the sleeping bag, all Gordy could see was the seething flow of grubs entering his body through the eye sockets.

More time passed. Despite his paralysis, Gordy became quite hungry and desperately thirsty. The Queen had been out of sight since he had been tossed aside, but he could hear her massive bulk slide around the cave from time to time.

Suddenly, the grubs began flowing in his direction and surrounding him. A subsonic humming vibrated the cave and tingled the surface of his skin. *The cave seemed to get warmer and a smell like horse piss tainted the air.*

Something was obviously different about her as she slithered into Gordy's view. She seemed larger and her skin was awash with a pinkish mucus. She circled him three times in an ever-tightening spiral. As she rolled by on the final pass, the heat radiating off her body was palpable.

It was at that point that he saw the ovipositor.

Gordy knew what that horrible thing was the second he saw it (Yet another benefit of watching too many Animal Planet documentaries). He understood that an ovipositor is an egg-laying organ generally located on the tail end of an insect's abdomen. In this case, it was a foot long with a fleshy sheath surrounding a black segmented organ that protruded from the butt end of the Queen.

All signs pointed to the unequivocal fact that the Queen was going to stick a Humongous Monster Insect Dick inside of him and plant a few hundred thousand eggs. Technically "dick" was not the correct term since she was a female, but for all intents and purposes, it performed the same basic function as a penis did. It penetrated.

Gordy gibbered and screamed in his mind as the reality of what was going to happen crystallized in his mind. Covered in warm, glutinous, reproductive mucus, the Queen slid on top of his frozen body like a nightmare lover. As she rolled him over, some of the mucus filled his mouth and nose. For a few long seconds, he couldn't breathe. His sight began to blur, his ears began to ring, and he was momentarily thankful that this mouthful of bug sludge was going to kill him before the Queen could consummate their union. Unfortunately, however, his involuntary survival instinct was in full effect. His gag reflex was triggered and he vomited out the sludge just as the Queen spread his legs and struck.

The pain of the impalement was so great that he immediately passed out.

Another pincer tore through the flesh of his belly and a grub equal in size to the one he had already stabbed to death emerged through the wound wrapped in the shredded remnants of Gordy's intestines.

This was it.

This was the end

This was how he would finally die.

After all he had survived in the cave, with the ghosts of his friends haunting him, now he was going to perish wallowing in a pool of his own blood and shit in his own back yard. Somehow it didn't seem fair at all.

Another grub poked its head through the bloody gash and he felt more of them – dozens more - writhing inside him.

◉   ◉   ◉

FRIDAY, JUST BEFORE DAWN – Gordy woke to the smell of his friends' rotting bodies. It was darker inside the cave, with only the fading light of the flashlight, which had been kicked to the opposite wall and now cast a meager glow on the surrounding rocks. Silence hung over the stone chamber like a bloody shroud. Shadowy mounds littered the floor around him, unrecognizable in the blackness. A vile, feculent taste filled his mouth; he spat several times and gingerly lifted his head off the floor. Gummy residue on his cheeks stuck his skin to the stone until he peeled it away.

Gordy tried to move his arms and legs and cried out, shattering the stillness. He tried again and slowly managed to pull himself to his knees, biting his lip to keep from screaming out. Running his hands up and down his body, he noted that he only wore tattered remnants of his pajamas. Other than that, his entire body felt as if it were throbbing in time with his heart. Every spot was tender. He must look like one giant bruise.

Gradually, as his eyes adjusted to the low light, flashes of memory came back in fractured shadowy images... the storm...the explosion... the Queen... the death of his friends... NO! The rest was lost to him in a blur of remembered pain and terror. He knew now what the mounds most likely were and he began to sob again. He cried for a number of minutes, then realized something astonishing. He was alone.

The cave was silent, except for his own voice, and he realized that the Queen and her brood must have left, returning to their lair down the shaft in the wall.

Only one thing was on his mind. He staggered over and grabbed the failing flashlight. Nearly dead, it had enough of a light to find his backpack lying in a dried pool of grub slime. In the outer pocket, amazingly, he found his car keys. Gordy did not look back. He hobbled out the entrance, forgetting everything in his fugue state. All he wanted to do was escape.

◉   ◉   ◉

After Gordy fell sideways off the riding mower, it lurched left and the gas can toppled off. It landed upside down next to him, soaking the grass and ground around him with the last few pints of gasoline. Rolling for a few more feet, it stopped when a wheel fell into one of the burning holes and sat there with the blades spinning through the flaming worm shit stew. Sparks and burning crap sprayed through the air.

Gordy saw none of this. He was too busy screaming, blinded by the pure agony of his abdomen being torn open. He was on his way out to a much better place. There was no way he could come back from these injuries, and he only hoped it would be quick. The grubs writhed in the open wound, covered in blood, shit, and a number of other body fluids. Arcs of arterial blood spouted past them onto the ground. The reek of gasoline filled the air. Gordy tried to grab the larger of the two grubs, but it just wriggled through his fingers and started crawling out of his gut-hole. It slithered up his chest toward his mouth, aiming to burrow back into him from the opposite end. Gordy shrieked and prayed to die before it reached him.

Ten feet away, the mower's front wheel sank lower in the fiery trench, pulling the spinning blade deeper into the blazing waste and changing the trajectory of the splatter. Left and right, burning clumps landed around Gordy from head to toe. One especially large flaming shit patty fell smack dab in the center of the gasoline-soaked grass and instantly ignited the entire area. The flames jumped to Gordy just as the grub reared back, and engulfed him and the grubs in a cleansing inferno. As he died, his screams sounded a lot like laughter.

Sergei Tumasov stood on his back porch drinking his evening tea and staring through the wall of smoke hanging in the air above the trees. A host of flashing red and blue lights lit the evening sky. He finished the last sip, grumbled, and went inside his house.

"What is it?" asked his wife Sofia. "Did you see anything?"

"That boy has finally gotten into trouble, Sofi," he answered. "I knew he was a problem waiting to happen. There are firemen, at least five or six policemen and an ambulance."

"Stop it," she admonished him. "You say that about all of our neighbors. How are we to make friends if you think that all of them are criminals?"

"I was right about him. I'll bet he blew up a meth lab"

"You have been watching that show about that science teacher too much. Not everyone makes drugs in their basement. Maybe there's a medical emergency."

"You are too trusting, dear. Most Americans are selfish assholes."

Sofia laughed, "Should I remind you that we are now citizens? Do I fit that category now?" she said, giving him a warning glance.

"Of course not, my *kroshka*," he said, using her pet name to hopefully mollify her. He looked around absentmindedly. "Where are the boys?"

"In the den. All of them. I think Yuri got into a fight. He has a cut on his nose and he smelled horrible when he came home. I cleaned him up a bit and put some salve on it, but we may need to take him to the vet to check it out."

"Hmmm... I'll check on him and see how he looks." He left her in the kitchen and walked down to the basement. A flurry of barks greeted him when he entered. Their *boys*, ten dogs they had rescued over the past few years, were as happy as always to see him. Mischa, the terrier mix, greeted him by racing in circles around his feet and peeing a bit in excitement. The others, varying in size and age, were content to mill around and nuzzle his hands. All except for one.

Yuri, the largest dog by far, was lying on his chosen pile of blankets in the corner looking miserable. Immediately, Sergei was concerned. Yuri had been with them the longest – over six years - and, though he wouldn't have admitted it out loud, the giant mutt was his favorite, even if he had the disgusting habit of eating his own week-old turds.

Sergei kneeled down next to Yuri and patted him on the flank.

"You've got yourself into a mess. Huh, boy?" he soothed the dog. "What was it? A skunk? A raccoon? You need to be careful, my boy."

The big beast flopped his tail against the blanket and whimpered in distress. He gagged, shook his head and tried to blow air out of his nostrils.

"Are you okay, boy?" Sergei was becoming concerned. Nothing usually bothered Yuri. One time he had even been struck a glancing blow by a car and Yuri had just walked away with a bruise. The car's door panel, on the other hand, had a dent the size of Yuri's head in it.

Yuri began whining frantically. He stood up, walked a few steps and began retching in the middle of the concrete floor.

"That's it, boy. We're taking you to the doctor," said Sergei. He walked to the stairwell and yelled up, "Sofi! Call the vet. I have to take Yuri in immediately!"

He turned back just in time to see his dog vomit up a softball-sized lump of pinkish pudding and collapse to the floor. Sergei ran to Yuri to gather him up in his arms, but once he saw what had come of Yuri's throat, he stopped and stared.

The object seemed to be a shredded piece of one of Yuri's internal organs. It smelled like death, and it was crawling with hundreds of grubs. Their pincers were the color of blood.

NOT YOUR AVERAGE MONSTER

Pete Kahle is the author of **The Specimen: A Novel of Horror**, *winner of The Kindle Book Review's 2014 Kindle Book Award in Horror/Suspense. Next up is a stand-alone tale titled* **Blood Mother: A Novel of Terror**, *due out in the late spring of 2016. He is also the owner and editor of Bloodshot Books.*

In 2014, he organized and edited **Widowmakers: A Benefit Anthology of Dark Fiction** *to help out a fellow author in a time of need. Doing so gave him the editing bug and he decided to try to run a small press of his own.*

Hopefully, he will continue to feed your nightmares for a long time coming.

BLOODSHOT BOOKS

ALSO FROM
BLOODSHOT BOOKS

The Specimen (The Riders Saga, Book 1)
Available in paperback or Kindle on Amazon.com

ISBN – 1495230007

ON THE HORIZON FROM
BLOODSHOT BOOKS

Spring 2016

Not Your Average Monster 2 – A Menagerie of Monstrosities

Blood Mother: A Novel of Terror – Pete Kahle

2017*

The Abomination (The Riders Saga, Book 2) – Pete Kahle

2018*

The Horsemen (The Riders Saga, Book 3) – Pete Kahle

* other titles to be added when confirmed

BLOODSHOT BOOKS

READ UNTIL YOU BLEED